Slave Graves

By Thomas Hollyday

Dedicated to Elliott Coleman
Poet and Author of "Mockingbirds at Fort McHenry"

The author wishes to thank C. Michael Curtis, of the Atlantic Monthly, for his kindness and encouragement, and Cynthia Vann, an excellent editor and steadfast friend. Gratitude is extended to David Simmons, archeologist at Old Sturbridge Village, for reading a draft of the book and making sure the archeological procedures described in the book are true to that science. Special mention should also be made of the insights gained from Frank Fuller's Engineering of Pile Installations, T.D. Stewart's Essentials of Forensic Anthropology, and the old diaries reprinted in George Francis Dow's Slave Ships and Slaving. Quotations are made from "Amazing Grace," Trad., and "We Gotta Get Out of This Place," words and music by Barry Mann and Cynthia Weil, pub. By Screen Gems EMI, Best Selling Record by The Animals, 1965. Finally, thanks are given to the energetic staffs of Old Sturbridge Village Research Library and the Boston Atheneum for their hard work in finding books and otherwise aiding in the research. Last but not least, thanks to my fiction workshop friends for their suggestions on some of the chapters and to my family for their patience.

Chapter 1

"This Goddamned place."

He increased speed, his new BMW roaring down the dirt road heading deep into backcountry Maryland. Sweat streaked down his forehead even though the air conditioner whined at full force. Gravel and dust kicked up by the wheels created a dark following cloud which the car could not escape in the morning heat.

His name was Frank Light and he was the chairman of his university's department of archaeology, the youngest professor ever appointed to the position. At the moment, instead of managing his department, he was going out into the field on a quick reconnaissance, something his graduate students usually did. Frank had no choice. A location needed to be tested immediately and the president of the university had specifically asked him to do the job.

A potential shipwreck site had been discovered in a marsh on the Nanticoke River. Workmen digging the foundations for a bridge had uncovered timbers of the wreck. The marsh was near River Sunday on the Eastern Shore, a region east of the Chesapeake Bay. One of the bulldozer operators had immediately reported the site to the Maryland construction permit authority as the law required. The state regulations were very definite, much to the chagrin of the bridge contractor. Construction had to be stopped regardless of expense until the site was professionally evaluated for historic importance.

The president had told him this job was a favor for a special friend of the university board of trustees, the famous real estate financier Jake Terment. Apparently, if the bridge wasn't built, Terment's whole project and millions of his dollars were in jeopardy. Last night, Frank complained about the special assignment to his girlfriend, Mello, and she had just grinned.

"You've got to realize something when you're chairman, Frank," she had said. "Universities are a business like everything else. You give something to people and they give something back to you."

Mello taught a couple of business courses. He had listened to her and knew doing an evaluation survey for this Terment celebrity might be good for the school and good for him. All he had to do was go down there and look the place over to make sure there wasn't anything significant that was going to be covered up by the new construction.

Mello had kissed him and reminded him that he used to do surveys like this all the time. "Go down there, get the job done, and come on back. Even if you found a galleon, it wouldn't be important enough to hold up a Terment project," she had said.

"Discovering a Spanish gold galleon in the Chesapeake Bay, that would be quite a find," he had grinned.

She had not thought that was funny. "Sometimes, Frank, I don't think you're ready for the big leagues at all, no matter what I try to teach you."

However, this was still a bad time for him to be away from his office. Corrected proofs on his new textbook on archaeology were overdue to his editor. Also, tonight the field school students had planned their annual end of term festivities in his honor. Even with his new responsibilities as chairman, he still liked working with the younger scholars and had looked forward to the party. He'd never missed one of these celebrations. A part of him would always be an idealistic student no matter how he changed with the responsibilities of his career. He smiled as he drove. Mello could never understand this side of him.

"Grow up, Frank, " she had said, kidding him about wanting to go to the party with the kids.

He arrived in River Sunday just before noon. The other archaeologists he met at the national conferences talked about the beautiful climates that they visited around the world. He never had that kind of luck. Like this trip, he thought. He always got to these construction site problems when the locations were having a stretch of abnormal weather, wet from rain, cold from snow, hot from sun. Just one time he would enjoy a project that had decent weather. Then he reminded himself, "Be satisfied. You're smart enough to play the game. Like Mello is always saying, take the jobs no one else wants, smile a lot, and keep your mouth shut. You can wait. There will be plenty of time later to work in the pretty places."

Frank saw the steeples of the churches reaching high over the orderly colonial houses along the narrow streets. As he drove he noticed that the town had grown around a natural harbor coming in from the Chesapeake Bay. Soon he spotted his destination, the Chesapeake Hotel. He drove the BMW under a large banner stretched across the street. The banner, decorated with red and white, orange and black Maryland flags, proclaimed "River Sunday Heritage Day, August 7." Six days from today, he thought. He found the entrance to the hotel parking and pulled into the ramp.

A few minutes later he walked out of the garage into the sunlight, carrying his suitcase. The August sun was brutally hot on his skin. He could smell the hot tar from the overheated street. Moving in the humidity was like pushing his body against a great rubber band. He breathed hard, straining against the heat as though it would finally overcome him and slap him backwards. He climbed the large wooden steps up to the wide porch of the hotel.

"Boom!"

The noise arced and rumbled above the clatter of the street. He instinctively fell on the planked floor of the porch, pushing his body flat, making his hands grasp for protection from the pine planks. Then he stopped, looked up and remembered where he was. Whatever this noise was, it was not war. Incoming mortars in Vietnam were a long time ago in his life. A black doorman, in a red uniform, standing over him, reached down a hand. "I did that when I first came home from Nam," the porter grinned. Two tourist women looked on, amused.

Frank took the man's hand and stood. Momentarily embarrassed, he composed himself by looking out from the porch at the view of the River Sunday harbor. He could see a great number of pleasure boats, sail and power, anchored or sailing out to the Chesapeake Bay in the distance. In the middle of the harbor a huge pile of what appeared to Frank to be large building stones rose fifty feet above the water. They were stacked haphazardly, as if a giant had thrown them there in disgust. A navigation beacon blinked on top of the rocks. Anchored nearby and surrounded by small fishing boats, was a very large and modern white yacht far grander than any other craft in the harbor.

He turned and nodded at the doorman, gave him a thumbs up and walked into the lobby. His eyes adjusted to the darkness after the blinding sunlight outside. In the center of the room, next to a large sign advertising a private Terment Company luncheon, he recognized Jake Terment, from seeing him on television. Terment was a tanned fifty year old man, a few years older than Frank. Frank thought he looked a little taller than he appeared on television. The man stood like a patrician, like a god. Around Terment was a crowd of more than a hundred people, mostly white but with a few blacks and Hispanics. Some were pushing to get closer to his side and shake his hand. The activity reminded Frank of fund raiser meetings back at the university where he had been like those people, trying to promote archeology to wealthy middle aged alumni in rumpled business suits.

Terment looked up from his conversation and saw Frank. He started toward Frank, with the confident smile of a man who had complete control of his environment and all the people in it. The crowd parted, some of the people still following him. The room became very quiet as Terment's attention focused on Frank. In an adjoining room Frank could hear the luncheon preparations, dishes being placed on tables with voices of waitresses providing a pleasant background rhythm.

"You must be Doctor Frank Light, " Jake Terment spoke in a drawl. "I'm afraid I expected an old man with a white beard," he smiled, glancing at Frank's stylish suit. "I think I recognize a man like myself. "

The voices began to hum again and Frank was swept into a crush of people, shaking hands, being introduced. He stood beside Jake, "meeting his friends in River Sunday," as he told Frank. The conversation revolved more on golf stories than construction.

4

Frank was all this time mostly impassive to the excitement around him, still allowing the intense hotel air conditioning to renew him. After a few minutes, chilled into sensitivity, he was able to speak.

" The president said to leave everything, my other work, said to get to your problem right away."

Jake laughed. "I'm sure my company is going to be asked to contribute heavily to your university. Anyway, you get this shipwreck business straightened out. We've got a lot of houses to build. "

He looked around at his admiring crowd. "Was hoping to get one good golf match while I was down here."

His eyes probed Frank.   Frank stared back, wondering what he would say about his own poor golf handicap if asked to play by Jake Terment. Then he recovered and said, "I hope my archeological work can be of some service to you."

"Great. A hard worker. You're all right, Frank Light, " Jake said with another smile.   He watched Frank's face brighten at his compliment.

"I'll do what I can," said Frank.

"Your boss said we would get along.   Said not to worry about anything."

"I'd like to see the shipwreck."

"Do you think you can get us back on track, say in a couple of days?"

"Well, if we don't find anything important in our test pits, then we ought to be done pretty quick."

"Two days is good," said Jake. "We can be building again for sure by Heritage Day. Come on. " He shook his head. "Spyder's been reminding me. Got to give a speech to the faithful."

At that moment a grinning heavyset bald man, with long arms, appeared next to Jake.

"Spyder," Jake said, "This is Doctor Light, the man we asked to come here to help us out. Get him a place at one of the lunch tables. We want to take care of this man. He's one of us."

Frank shook Spyder's hand. The hand was cold, colder even than the air of the room.   Spyder continued the same fixed grin without speaking. He beckoned quickly with his finger for Frank to follow him. They went inside the large better lighted meeting room. A long speaker's table with only two chairs was up on a small platform at the side of the room. Behind the table was a white projection screen, contrasting with the faded yellow walls. Out in the center of the room was a slide projector aimed at the screen. Frank noticed the decorations at the windows. His historian's eye identified them as inexpensive copies of Eighteenth Century festoon curtains. The microphone cackled intermittently adding to the noisy confusion. He smelled the food, a chicken dish laced heavily with pepper.

Spyder pointed to a table at the side of the room. Frank sat down and Spyder, still without saying a word, left him. Frank watched him move away. Spyder walked with a distinctive movement, bent forward slightly with his long arms at his side, almost as though he might pounce to all fours at any moment.

Frank spoke casually with the others at his table as he ate. One of the women repeated several times his occupation, 'archaeologist' as though she were practicing a foreign language.

"Boom," the noise he had heard on the street came crashing over the building. He looked around, alarmed the windows might break or the curtains fall down. The others around him continued to eat. No one was concerned.

"First time you heard our Cannon Club? " asked a man with a bow tie sitting next to Frank. "They keep you alert, don't they?"

"Cannon Club?" asked Frank.

"It's one of our little River Sunday traditions," the man went on, watching Frank.

"Cannon?" said Frank.

"Maryland Confederate Artillery. After the Surrender, the volunteers brought home the tube of their Napoleon 12 pounder. About the turn of the century, then they went and got the old gun out of hiding, fixed her up, started shooting her off again once a year."

"You a member?"

"Why, I'd like to be," he blushed, almost, Frank thought, as if he were ashamed he wasn't a member. "Unfortunately, my family came here and set up long after the Civil War. We're still not even considered natives, much less eligible for the Cannon Club."

Terment was sitting at the speaker's table. In front of the man next to Terment was a rectangular sign that simply stated " mayor" printed by hand in large letters. Terment had no sign in front of him. The mayor, a balding and somewhat overweight man, was dressed in a poorly fitting blue and white cotton suit. He stood, tapped his water glass and as the room quieted, began to speak, his words buzzing like the occasional summer flies worrying the sticky table tops.

"On behalf of all of us in River Sunday I want to welcome all you Terment Company investors. Don't worry about the cannon you've been hearing. It hasn't fired at any people since 1865."

Some of the audience laughed amid the noise of dishes being cleared. The mayor continued. "You're all here to learn about the greatest condominium and estate home development ever planned in the Chesapeake region. I'm right in saying that when it is finished nothing will compare with it anywhere along the tidewater coast from Florida to Maine." He paused. "Today, Jake Terment, the man whose vision has made this possible, one of our nation's greatest real estate developers, has come here today from New York to tell us about it." He looked at Jake. "Jake, as you all know, grew up right here in River Sunday. That makes him one of us." The mayor paused again, then said, "Only he's got a lot more money."

A few laughed at this remark as the mayor went on, "I remember as a child going up to visit at Peachblossom Manor, the Terment family plantation home, Registered Landmark, out on Allingham Island. I remember seeing Jake sittin' in the lap of his father Richard Terment. His father would tell how he was named after his great uncle Admiral Richard Terment who was killed running his outnumbered ironclad into a whole fleet of Yankee gunboats. The Admiral's dying order to his sailors was to bring him home to Maryland so he could be buried at Peachblossom. At his request, they put two loaded Navy Colt revolvers in the coffin so the Admiral could keep on shooting Yankees in Hell." The mayor put his hands over his ears. " Jake's aunts would be sitting there listenin,' and I remember, they would cover their ears and say to little Jake that the Admiral had been a religious man and that he was certainly in Heaven and not in Hell where those people were."

The mayor then rubbed his hands nervously, immediately realizing from the creaking chairs and coughing from the audience that his story about Yankees in Hell was the wrong story to tell.

7

This was a different group, made up of many outsiders, and not his usual River Sunday audience.

Frank leaned over to the pharmacist. "I wonder if those Navy Colt handguns have been dug up yet."

The man turned to him and scowled. Frank put his hands up in defense. "I'm just thinking like an archaeologist. I didn't mean any offense to the traditions here. We dig up things like that to study them." The pharmacist, his face still angry, turned back to listen to the speaker.

The mayor finished quickly. " So, Jake, you 're the man of the hour. Tell us all about it."

Jake stood up behind his chair and quieted the applause. The mayor arranged the microphone. It squawked two times before Jake's voice flowed out on the silent and expectant crowd.

"Thank you for such a pleasant introduction. My father would thank you too if he were alive today. Let me start out by answering some questions that I have been asked since I arrived today on my yacht." He looked at the mayor. "First of all it is not true that when we were kids my friend, the mayor here, gave me this little scar over my eye."

The crowd laughed. Jake continued, "It was Billy, who's your chief of police." Towards the back of the room, the chief of police scraped back his chair and stood up, giving a short bow and waving to several friends in the audience. There was more laughing.

"Any of you newspaper people here today, don't report on my old friend, Billy. He'll be up for police brutality. Seriously, let me say a few words about the development out on the island and especially the progress on the new bridge. Yes," he raised his voice to emphasize the words and said them slowly, "we will finish the bridge on time. We will complete the foundations for the new bridge this summer and build the bridge this winter. The houses can start on schedule next summer."

Jake turned his head and looked directly at Spyder. Then he repeated, "I want to make sure that my partners in New York get the message. We will finish on time." There was heavy applause.

Frank studied Spyder's face but there was no change from the steady grin. Jake went on. "First of all, the butterflies and their trees." Jake paused and looked down at his feet for a moment. "I guess you all know that my wife, Serena, is a movie star." There was an outburst of cheers, whistles, stamping of feet.

Jake looked at the moderator and smiled. Then he turned to the crowd and quieted them with a movement of his hands. "Serena advised me to go easy on the butterflies. You all know her interest in animals. I think she spends as much time on animal rights as she does on her acting. Anyway, my company spent a lot of time and money trying to find a way to solve the butterfly problem. We're real sorry about the Monarch butterflies having to find different trees to land on during their future migrations. We all know, however, that folks buying houses out on the island are not going to like to see all those bugs on their lawns every fall." He paused. "These houses will sell to wealthy people, people like yourselves, winners who have fought to accomplish their success. The fact is that the courts in Maryland are on our side, that we have been told that we can cut down the trees used by the butterflies, that the courts say we can go ahead and build our houses. We made the decision that we want to develop the island to benefit the owners and the people of River Sunday, not the insects." Jake's words brought out more laughter mixed with applause.

"I have heard, from time to time, that my old friend Jefferson over there at his Third Baptist Church tells stories about the marsh where we are building the bridge. He likes to say we can't put the bridge there because that area was a burying ground for African Americans back in the early days of River Sunday. He says it was a slave graveyard."

Jake stopped and looked around the crowd. Then he looked at the moderator.

"Is Jefferson here today? " The mayor shook his head. "No? Jefferson never did know a good business deal," said Jake, smiling as the crowd laughed. "Well, it's all very fine for him to worry about his mythical graveyard. What he doesn't seem to understand is that there are black families as well as white families who want to live on the island in the new houses. I'd like to say to him, 'It's a new world, Jefferson.'"

The crowd applauded politely.

"The Terment family has always owned the farm where that marsh is located. I'm sure no one was buried there." Jake continued. "I will say, however, that a few old wheat schooners, maybe a hundred or so years old, are deserted and rotting up along the Nanticoke River towards the bridge. Mercy, we all played on them enough when we were kids. Seemed to me somebody even set one of them on fire one time. Got the whole River Sunday Fire Department out. You remember that?" Jake looked at the mayor, who grinned nervously.

"Well, as luck would have it, we seem to have another one of those old hulks sunk right in the middle of our construction. I'm not against history but I sure wish one of my workers had not got so excited and called in the government. "

He laughed, "I'm having trouble finding out the worker's name. Anybody know?" There was a chuckle though the audience. He laughed, "If he'd just applied a little bit more power to the hydraulics of that bulldozer blade, there wouldn't have been any wreck left to study and this would never have been a problem."

"Jake's right. Hell, push the wreck back under and get on with it, " muttered the pharmacist to Frank.

Jake looked out over the crowd until his eyes found Frank. "Stand up, Frank. Folks, this is Doctor Frank Light. He's an archaeologist, the best in the country. I borrowed him from his university up north. He's here to identify the wreck, find out all about it so the Maryland authorities will be satisfied, and then, most important, get us back working on the bridge. Right, Frank?"

Frank nodded and sat down.

"I'm sure you'll make him feel real welcome here in River Sunday."

As the applause went around the room, Frank nervously scratched the back of his neck.

Jake looked behind him at the white screen. Spyder turned switches on the wall and the room was night black. Then he started the slide projector and a spurt of white light cut across the blackness. Greens and blues, not bright but pastels of these hues, flowed over the screen. A color map of Allingham Island and the River Sunday region appeared. Some people in the audience gasped at the giant picture.

"I just wanted to take a few minutes to remind all of you what we are planning. Yes, I agree with you people who are overwhelmed by this. This is a beautiful island," said Jake. "We're going to make it more beautiful."   Jake then proceeded to point out the features of the map. At the bottom of the map, to the south, was the town of River Sunday, with its large harbor.   To the west, the left of the map, was Chesapeake Bay. To the north, was the expanse of the Wilderness Swamp, and to the east, the highway going north and south. Further east was the farmland of the eastern counties of the Eastern Shore.

Allingham Island was directly north of River Sunday. The Nanticoke River ran in from the Chesapeake Bay to the east of the island. It passed a headland called Stokes Point where tourists visited the remains of an old War of 1812 fortification. The Nanticoke cut off most of the island from the mainland, continued north almost parallel with the highway and finally went inland. A few miles north of River Sunday a road went west from the highway to Allingham Island. This road crossed the Nanticoke at the old bridge. At the top of the island a waterway called North Creek cut from the Bay through the Wilderness to meet the Nanticoke and finished cutting off the mainland from the island.

Jake pointed to where he was building the new bridge, alongside the old one. The colorful glare from the screen illuminated the faces in the front tables, the ghostly pale faces uplifted to Jake.   "You know," said Jake, looking out over the crowd, " River Sunday is named for all the churches we have here. Well, I got to thinking one day when I was flying across the country. I got to thinking that maybe the Lord had brought me home to construct this new bridge, to build these new houses out on Allingham."

Frank smiled at Jake's use of the divine, but it went over well with the crowd.   When the enthusiastic applause quieted, Jake again pointed to the screen. "On the west side of Allingham Island you can see this little rectangle we put on the map. That's Peachblossom Manor, my family's old home, with its view out to the Chesapeake Bay. I expect to keep Peachblossom in the family, with a few hundred acres as a homefarm. Terment Company owns all the land on both sides of the bridge site except for a small section on the north owned by my neighbor, Birdey Pond. The new bridge, as you can see, is being built on the south side of the old bridge. We'll build our first houses on the south of the island where it faces the Nanticoke. We have selected the name of Terment Town. That's to honor my father who always dreamed of building these houses."

Jake let the applause build, then motioned for it to stop. "We're going to have a reception, a chance for you to see the bridge under construction. I want to invite you to the site day after tomorrow. Come up in the early afternoon for a look see and some refreshment courtesy of Terment Company." He waited a moment while the crowd quieted. Then he said, "We have a special surprise. Serena is flying in from her movie set to say hello to you fine folks."

"We're with you, Jake," a voice shouted from the darkness, and more applause burst out as Jake returned to his seat.

Frank retrieved his suitcase and joined Jake and Spyder. Jake was shaking hands with people leaving the room. In a few moments Frank walked out of the room beside Jake. A tawny cat with black spots on its face was sleeping on the red and white lobby rug.

"That's the cat that was swimming up at the bridge," said Spyder.

Jake looked at Spyder and said absently, "I never saw a cat swim before."

Spyder nodded and walked toward the cat, his grin unabated. He kicked the animal with his highly polished alligator shoe. The cat landed on its feet and crawled underneath a lobby sofa, where it watched, alert, hissing deeply, almost growling.

"Spyder knows I don't like cats, Frank. They bring bad luck, " said Jake.

Outside in the oppressive sunlight, they stepped down off the wide porch in front of the hotel, where the dark green rocking chairs overlooked the harbor and the tourist filled Strand Street. Strangely, in the heat, he heard a distant band playing the lively melody of a winter song, "Oh, Christmas Tree." When he asked, Jake informed him that the music was the state song "Maryland, My Maryland."

"When I was a kid," he said, "first thing they taught you in school was the words to that song. It was one of the first songs written for the South."

Coming toward them were ten or more people dressed as giant butterflies, the orange and black wings bobbing to the music, costumes weaving down the street, contrasting with the orderly colonial restoration storefronts. The costumes intrigued Frank, especially the colors. His eyes roved over their construction, the eight foot height of the wings, The costumes allowed the person inside to show his or her head about halfway up the furry black body of the apparatus, while the wings stretched fully extended about four feet to each side.

When he saw the butterflies, Jake stopped, his face suddenly stern. He waited with Spyder at his side and Frank behind as one of the butterflies stopped directly in front of them. A tall white haired woman was inside the costume.

"Hello, Birdey,"said Jake.

"We'll keep on, Jake," she informed him in a shrill voice. " We have another wildlife expert coming in, this time from Africa. We'll stop you from building that bridge."

"Suit yourself," he replied and moved around her. The woman remained, slowly moving her wings. Jake walked down the street until he reached a green stationwagon with the words Terment Company in white letters on the doors.

"You can get your car later, Frank. I want to show you the construction. "

"Those butterflies," Frank said, " remind me of the monks in Vietnam. The same orange colors. "

Jake smiled, " This is a chance for some people to get their causes in my face. Don't you pay any attention to it."

They were in the car moving up the street. Frank looked out at the harbor. Jake motioned towards the pile of rocks and the great yacht. "Later I'll take you out to my boat for a drink. "

"Sounds nice," said Frank.

"I had my captain anchor her near the monument."

"That's what you call the pile of stones?"

"It's a memorial to June 7, 1864."

"What happened then?"

"The Maryland State Convention voted to free the local slaves."

"Something else I guess you all learned when you were kids," Frank joked. "Who built it?"

"My family," said Jake. Frank realized how serious Jake had become by the tone of his words.

"I'm afraid I've never heard about it before, " said Frank.

Jake's face showed a slight disappointment. "I'm surprised. It's famous. The slave memorial. Brings a lot of tourists to River Sunday."

"Nature, slaves, war, and religion. A real southern story," Frank could not help grinning. Jake did not hear. He continued looking at the monument with pride. Then, as though suddenly awoken from a dream, Jake turned his head to stare ahead of the car.

"Spyder," he said, "Let's move it. I want to get the doctor started."

Chapter 2

Water mirages and waves of heat danced on the blacktop as they drove towards the site. Then the road narrowed leaving less room for an oncoming car to pass. Adding to the danger were treacherous roadside ditches with edges steep enough to turn an entrapped car or tractor on its side. Frank saw water in the ditches, the water half hidden with high grass, but deep and dark.

Frank observed Spyder from where he sat in the back seat. The older man was across from him at an angle. His continuous grin bothered Frank, bringing back memories of constantly smiling Vietnamese during the war, men who appeared friendly yet who turned out in many cases to be his enemy. Spyder was subservient to Jake and acted like a perfect butler, yet his clothes were fashionable, tailored with the same cut as Jake's expensive suit. There was also the repetition of Jake's promise during the speech, that the bridge would be built on time, a comment that Jake had seemed to direct to Spyder.

"One call and I can get some of your company men down here," Spyder reminded Jake. Frank surmised that they feared potential trouble from the white haired bird woman, that she was still in their thoughts.

"No," Jake answered Spyder. "Not yet anyway. We won't get along with local people if we bring in outsiders. Besides, we don't want to do anything that might draw more attention to her butterflies. Bringing in our people might just get her more support."

"What are 'company men?'" asked Frank.

"Sometimes we need special guards for our construction equipment," explained Jake. "Company men are the security forces that we bring to sites. " After that, neither Spyder nor Jake said any more about the woman he had called Birdey.

Spyder began to slow the car. He started to turn left at a small white gate nestled in a huge honeysuckle hedge. Jake raised his hand. "No, go straight. We'll give our expert a little tour over the bridge before we go to the site."

Spyder drove ahead and within a few moments they were close to the river and the bridge. "Here we are at the Nanticoke River, Frank," said Jake, excitement in his voice, shifting slightly forward to see better out of the front window. Frank looked ahead also and saw with a little nervousness that the old bridge was constructed as a single lane, only wide enough for one car, built obviously for the old days of horses and carriages. He had a sudden vision of an overloaded farm truck coming fast from the opposite direction, tomato boxes toppling from its sides, and of Spyder driving the three of them into the truck without a change in his grin.

The car halted as the light turned red.

"You can see why this bridge has to be replaced," said Jake.

"People around here are probably afraid they're going to get killed on it," said Frank.

Jake wasn't amused. "No, nothing like that. It's safe enough. I was thinking more of the inconvenience. We need a wide fast bridge with no stoplights, a bridge people can cross quickly. People who spend big money for houses want convenience."

On the right a three story house sat well back from the road across a long lawn, its estate grounds decorated with small hedged gardens and multiple bird feeders attached to trees and hanging on wires or set on poles. Large trees obscured the house, but Frank could see some ancient roof lines, brick sections and multipaned windows.

Jake grimaced when he saw Frank looking at the house. "That's where that butterfly lady lives."

"Birdey?"

"Birdey Pond. You could see what an old bitch she is. She hounded my father before me, too, always looking out for the butterflies as if they were more important than people."

"I like butterflies," ventured Frank.

The two men looked at him instantly and sternly. "I'm counting on you to understand these things, Frank. Don't let me down," said Jake, with a quick smile.

The light finally changed. At the same time a second stoplight on the other side of the bridge went to red to stop traffic if there had been any coming from the island side. Then the car was on the bridge, its tires bouncing through the broken macadam surface to the iron grate supports. The bridge joined a jetty or point of land with a similar surge of hard ground from the island side. Each point went into the river about forty feet. The bridge had been built out on these points. Its span crossed open water for several hundred yards.

"That's the island?" asked Frank, pointing to land extending beyond a row of trees on the other side of the bridge.

"Yes," said Jake, slowly, his words affectionate in tone. "That's the beginning of Allingham Island. I 'll show my house up there sometime."

The car bottomed with a jolt as it hit a pothole.

Jake grabbed the dashboard. "Town won't maintain the bridge anymore," he said. "The structure was quite an engineering feat when my family built it a hundred years ago." He shook his head.

Across the bridge, Frank could see large areas of cleared land. On this land the access road had been almost completed. Two small cranes and several dump trucks were parked. A green steel barge with great streaks of brown rust and the word TERMENT on its side in large white letters, was anchored to Frank's left, beside the bridge. On its deck were various large engines and generators, concrete mixers, pumps and hoses.

Also on the barge and rising up over the river, like a great sword, was a third construction crane, a very large green unit with a massive pile driver attachment. The system of pulleys on the equipment raised and dropped the tremendous weight of the hammer to drive the pilings deep into the river bed. Beneath the crane, in the water at the side of the barge, was an unfinished cofferdam, steel pilings arranged in a circle to keep out the river water.

"We build the bridge piers on these cofferdams," said Jake. "Pile drivers sink the cofferdams and then we pump out the water and fill them with concrete. You come back next spring you'll see great new white piers going high into the air, looking real nice against the green of the trees along the river. "

He paused. " Unfortunately, everything is on hold while we wait for your research to be finished." Jake bounced in his seat as the car continued on the rough road. They were passing through the old draw machinery section with its rusted ironwork.

"For years now," Jake explained, "Every time a yacht with a tall mast comes up this river, its skipper has stop and to go all the way into River Sunday to get a man to raise the bridge. Even then no one is sure whether she's going to go up or not."

Frank noticed how the concrete railings of the old bridge were cracked from age. Looking down at the road, he saw in places that the river water below the bridge showed through surface holes in the road. He wondered if the car he was in would be the first car to break through the road and fall into the water. Jake talked on, unconcerned.

"When the town found out my company was going to develop the island and build a new bridge, the county commissioners in the River Sunday Courthouse stopped the allocation of funds to keep the old bridge fixed. They just let it rust. Of course, I don't complain because it's just my tenant farmers going up to their farms on the island. Safe enough for them. They run a few trucks and cars across the old bridge every day." He chuckled. " Some of them go drinking in River Sunday at night and I might even hear from Billy about a car smacking into the railing one night or another. "

He confided in Frank, his voice low, "I can remember one day when we kids fixed the stoplight on the bridge to stay red. We held up traffic all day until they come out and reset the light. We sat back in the grass in that same old marsh where you are going to work, Frank. Horns were honking, people yelling, and it was a lot of fun." He got serious. "When my father found out about it, I got whipped good with his shaving belt."

The station wagon stopped bouncing when it reached the other side of the bridge. Off to the right Frank could see a ruined church.

"The Nanticoke Chapel of Ease," said Jake. "Years ago lightning struck the building's roof," he continued, looking quickly at the church. Frank's educated eye studied the old building. He could see where the fire had reduced the structure to jagged up thrust walls and piles of neglected brick and stone rubble. A path outlined by years of young explorers trickled through the front arch. There was an inner void open to the sky that was filled with wild vines. The lush growth maintained an appearance of natural sanctity, yet in the midst of this green he saw remnants of abandoned campfires with piles of beer cans and broken wine bottles scattered on the ruined brick floor.

Jake noticed Frank's interest in the ruined building. "The kids still come out here with their girlfriends," he said. " I've taken my share of girls there too. It's a local tradition. "

Frank smiled, thinking of the irony of those charcoal pyres, left by generations of River Sunday teens, memorializing more the fiery rites of first sex than the scorching words of some long dead preacher.

Spyder pulled off the road and turned the car around until it pointed towards the river again. The car air conditioning protected them from the intense heat outside, as they sat looking out at the construction.

"We got pretty far along with the access road on this side," said Jake, proudly. Frank saw how the area for the new bridge had been ripped out of the land. Beside the old bridge, the ramp for the access road raised up, its massive structure of poured concrete and soil fill dwarfing the old structure. It was leveled to a certain incline, ending at a point near the edge of the river where the barge and the pile driver were positioned with the first of the cofferdams. This new road was poised to connect with the future bridge spans when Jake's bridge project was completed.

Frank got out of the car and stood in the heat. He saw piles of brush stacked at the edges of the construction, the piles of broken saplings and brush and vines testament to the tremendous power of the machines. He noticed too the dead plants, bloated fish, and stained water. Along the shoreline a slick of diesel oil moved out into the river. The oil washed back and forth in the weak tide lap against the few remaining cattails and marsh grasses. Above the purr of the station wagon engine, he heard the clank of a loose cable slapping against the steel sides of the barge as it moved in a slight breeze. The steel resounded like a cry of a person, a child. As Frank looked again at the pile driver and the laddered shaft of the great crane, Jake, restless with excitement, called Frank to get back inside the car. Spyder drove back to the bridge. The car chattered slowly back across to the mainland.

This time, Spyder turned in at the small gate in the honeysuckle. The entry road was more a path for farm tractors than automobiles. There was a cornfield growing high on the left and on the right Frank were tall cattails. He realized this was the beginning of the marsh which would eventually reach the riverbank. Flowering vines and corn plants brushed and scraped against the station wagon as Spyder drove hard towards a small farmhouse a few hundred feet ahead.

Now, as the vegetation thinned, Frank saw more. To the right, past the thinning number of cattails, was a large yellow bulldozer, deserted, its engine quiet. It was parked at the edge of a several acre section of rough and desolate brown soil.

"That's the site?" asked Frank.

"Yes, that's it."

Frank caught a glimpse through the brush and vines of two people near the riverbank, several hundred yards in the distance, leaning over a small machine. In the center of the clearing were a few broken timbers.

"That must be where that tractor ran into the frame of the old ship yesterday."

Jake chuckled. "That's the spot. "

The car stopped in front of the farmhouse. The house was once white with red trim but now the paint hung off the boards. Great trees surrounded it, giving shade in the bright sunlight and making the house still a viable refuge to find cooler air. Jake got out and stood, looking around and checking his watch.

"It's a hot time of day. I guess the archaeologist from the State has taken off for a few hours. She was here this morning before I left for the luncheon."

Frank started to mention the two figures he had glimpsed but Jake had already walked ahead towards the farmhouse.

"Not much of a house," said Jake, pushing on one of the porch pillars. "One of my great aunts took up with a retired Yankee general after the Confederate War. Neither one of them lived to a very old age."

Frank smiled and shook his head. "The Terments were very considerate building monuments to former slaves and giving houses to former enemies."

Jake didn't hear him. "I expect they wore each other out. She was a lot younger than he was. Then, for years the family had tenant farmers in here, one after the other, none of them making it very long. There's still a telephone inside and running water. Nobody lives here now. It's a firetrap. I'll never be able to rent it out any more."

Jake looked back at the site. "When I was a child my father used to talk about filling this marsh in with topsoil and planting more corn. "

Frank stood next to Jake. Even in the shade of the huge trees the heat was overpowering. He had lived in hot weather like this before. He remembered getting out of the back door of the big cargo plane when he arrived in Saigon in blinding heat, walking down the ramp with the huge tail of the aircraft high above him. In Saigon, there was no pleasant greeting by a celebrity, no comfortable lunch, no air conditioned ride in a station wagon. He had felt an initial terror and an urge to run for cover.

Frank saw boxwood, large and overgrown, rambling across the yard and bumping into waist high grass, and treelike shrubs. Among the boxwood were a variety of disorganized perennials and wildflowers blooming in a few clear spots where the sun could get through to them. In this wilderness, touching Frank's carefully shined shoes, were a mass of violets mixed with English ivy, their spring blooms long gone.

He stepped up on the sagging porch which flanked the house on two sides and saw rows and rows of corn plants in the surrounding fields, with a single crow, cawing loudly for companionship, flying slowly across the green mass. Towards the river, beyond the boxwood were glimpses of the light blue of the summer heat on the Nanticoke River surface, a hazy wetness, a dim glint in the sun, with quick wavelet flashes against the darkness of the far shoreline pine trees.

Jake followed him and they walked to the end of the creaking porch, where Frank saw rusty steel tractor implements buried in more overgrown grass, the rotary blades shining bright from recent use by the farm contractor's team in the fields. The porch itself had been screened at one time but now the screen hung like great brown curtains of rust. Around the yard were remnants of wire animal fences of various types, the links of the fences totally overwhelmed by the powerful tangle of green honeysuckle.

In one of the sheds Frank recognized a four wheel drive utility truck like the one he had driven during his months in Vietnam. The truck still had the white star of the United States Army on its door. Behind the cab, he could see a hoist, like a small crane, its metal structure rising from the bed of the truck.

"That truck is mine now," said Jake. "Last tenant left me without paying his rent. He had that truck in good shape. Runs good but the gears are too low for use anywhere but out here on the farm."

He stopped and looked at Frank. "There was one thing when I was reading your resume that I didn't understand. Sometime I'll ask you about it."

Frank nodded, wondering what Jake had found in his background that he did not like. Then in front of another shed Frank saw two cars almost hidden in the tall grass. One was a simple black sedan with a State of Maryland seal on its door. The other was a Cadillac coupe , an older model but well polished, glinting even in the shade where it was parked. Jake saw the cars too.

"They must belong to the government archeology people. They're making more money in these State jobs now, Frank. Maybe you ought to go to work for the state and get yourself a Cadillac."

"I like my BMW."

They heard a small gasoline engine start up.

"Pump engine," said Frank. Scared by the engine noise, a red winged blackbird flew up from one of the mounds of honeysuckle. "That's probably them, scared up that bird."

"Hello," a woman's voice came from across the yard, behind the boxwood. Frank turned and walked with Jake back toward the front of the porch.

"Maggie Davis," Frank called out, recognizing the woman coming forward.

"Doctor Light. My boss said you would be coming in today." Maggie was a plain looking woman, tanned, dressed in a dirty tee shirt, shorts, her feet bare, her blonde hair casually tied up in a bunch with a piece of white surveyors twine.

" I guess you two have worked together before. Maggie's with the State," said Jake.

"Maggie was one of my field school students ten years ago."

"Best teacher I ever had. We all thought so," said Maggie, grinning.

"Good. You two can solve my problem better if you've worked together before."

"You've survived that little controversy in Southern Maryland," said Frank to Maggie. " I see you still have your state job."

"Yes," she said, catching her breath.

"Controversy?" said Jake, staring at Maggie.

"Maggie's such a good archeologist it gets her in trouble sometimes," winked Frank.

"What kind of trouble?" asked Jake, with a glance at Spyder. Spyder nodded and walked away.

"I wanted a dig to continue; the State of Maryland ordered it closed up," she said.

"She made the mistake of saying it should stay open and that upset some people who wanted it closed."

"Well," said Jake, "I hope you want this one closed, Maggie. We don't need any more delays."

Her face took on a half smile. Frank recognized that look. He had seen it before when he had corrected her term paper and she had not agreed with the correction. In those days he would have sat down ready for a long argument from her.

"How is this reconnaissance going, Maggie?" asked Frank.

"Since I got here this morning, I've been working on laying out the project. You'll recognize the scheme. It's your system. "

"Any results?"

"Nothing yet. Lots of surface water. "

"We hear the pump."

"Yes. There are two strange things I've discovered already from my first probes."

"What?" asked Frank.

"First of all the wooden artifact they hit with the bulldozer is in pretty good shape. I would have expected the water in this marsh to have completely rotted it. "

"I told you folks that this wreck was not very old," said Jake.

"Could be the water here in this part of Maryland doesn't have as much salt. That might be responsible for preserving it. What else, Maggie?"

"It's the soil. I'm finding soil strata that shouldn't be here. It might have been brought in from several hundred feet away where I found a borrow pit. It's like someone wanted to fill the place in, cover it over."

"Silting?"

"There's evidence of some silting by high tides, field runoff from rains, but not this soil type. This was definitely re deposited, carried in by humans."

"You know anything about this, Jake?"

"No." He paused, then said, "Nothing. My father wanted to fill it in but he never did. It would have cost a fortune to hire all those men, carry in all that topsoil."

"Another thing," said Maggie.

"What?"

"I did a quick walkover survey of the area. I've never seen so many arrowheads and primitive stone tool artifacts. They must have been dug up by the tractors plowing each year. Hundreds of them. Early woodland, I'd say."

A man walked out from behind the boxwood, coming from the same direction as Maggie. "You must be the expert archaeologist," he said. He appeared to be several years older than Jake, a small black man with a pointed nose and a mustache and gray and white hair showing under his straw hat. He walked towards the porch. He was dressed in shorts and a tee shirt which had printed on it the words Baptist Youth Group. On his feet were knee socks and muck stained high tops. "I heard you talking about Maggie. I told them up at the State that I thought she would be a good pick to come down here, do this work," said the man in a strong voice.

"I didn't know you were interested in shipwrecks too, Jefferson," said Jake without a smile.

"Always interested in things that have to do with people I care about in River Sunday, Jake. You ought to know that by now."

"I haven't seen you since my father's funeral."

"You didn't see me there, Jake."

"I didn't?"

"No, I didn't go. Me and most of the other black people in River Sunday."

"He did a lot for you, Jefferson."

"I would expect you to say that, Jake."

"I'm glad he doesn't have to hear you talk like that."

"I said it to his face long before he died. Mister Terment never listened to anything he didn't want to hear."

The pump continued beating in the distance.

"What are you doing here on my farm?" demanded Jake.

"I 'm a volunteer."

"We don't need any volunteers."

" Sorry, Jake. The state archeology people thought it was a good idea. You see, Jake, they agreed with me that there ought to be someone else here from the local community just in case there were any questions of local black history to resolve. The Governor's Office thought that was a good idea too."

"I see," said Jake. "Maybe I ought to say hello to the Governor now I'm visiting Maryland." He paused, "Funny how you always turn up, Jefferson."

"I thought about the same thing myself. I asked myself a simple question. Why is Jake Terment here? These little houses on Allingham Island are not his kind of deal. No slums to make big profits." The Pastor dropped his voice. "Tell me Jake, when are your green coated tough guys coming in to River Sunday? I've heard how your guys handle anybody who complains about being moved out. I guess that doesn't get into your television coverage though, does it? It's probably bad for the image."

Jake changed the subject. "There's jobs up here in this development." He hesitated. "You know, Jefferson, people call me Mister Terment these days."

The Pastor smiled. "I could call you Termite like we did when we were kids."

Jake quickly turned his attention to Frank. "I don't think anybody would have buried anyone in a marsh. You try to tell that to a person like Jefferson and it's like talking to a stone." He went on, "I'm sure we can let you know if we find anything, can't we, Frank?"

"I think I'll see for myself," said the Pastor.

"We can all work together," said Frank, sensing the two men might be ready to start an actual fight. "It's only for a short time."

Jake said, "Frank, now I don't want a lot of folks coming in here and nosing around. There's a lot of expensive equipment in here, the barge, the bulldozer. Maybe I can't keep Jefferson out of this place. I guess we'll see on that. I want you to keep alert though. Let me know if anybody bothers you."

"A few folks around here don't like you, you know, Jake," said the Pastor.

Jake ignored him. "You look out for a fellow named Soldado," he said to Frank.

"You stole Soldado's house," said the Pastor.

"That's what he says. I don't want him on my land. That goes for the old lady over across the road, too."

The pump stopped.

"I'll have to clean out that carburetor. It's not taking fuel," said Maggie.

In the quiet they heard the sound of wood cracking, like an old rotten limb being pulled from a large tree, a limb with just enough timber left in its center to make a strong noise as it snapped. They heard cursing, a sure sign that a human was involved, that this was not a natural thing.

"Somebody's at the site," said Maggie.

Maggie and the Pastor ran, Jake and Frank behind them, the hundred yards through the tall grass. Frank passed the green mounds of vines where honeysuckle swamped old fences, then moving along a tiny winding path which opened into the cleared area of the now destroyed marsh. There he saw the grinning Spyder, standing among the carefully measured rows of white twine and survey stakes. Spyder was looking at the large piece of rotten wood in his hands. At his feet was the fresh hole from which it had been taken, the hole quickly filling with brown marsh water. The Pastor and Maggie stopped in front of him, speechless.

Spyder held up the wood, the still strong center of the wood jutting out from the rottenness around it. He had picked up one of the artifacts. Frank, as soon as he figured out what had happened, left Jake behind and walked slowly, almost tiptoeing, towards the man. He was afraid that even a tiny noise might startle Spyder, making him destroy the wood artifact more quickly. As Frank got closer to him, Spyder did begin to laugh. The shaking of his body made the wood crumble faster in his hand. A neat cone shaped pile of wood dust grew on the earth in front of him, near his alligator shoes. Spyder dropped the remaining part of the timber and reached down to dust his shoes.

Jake ignored how bewildered Frank, Maggie and the Pastor appeared at Spyder's wantonness. He talked as if nothing had happened. "I've got to get back to my yacht in River Sunday and, Frank, I know you want to get your car and get settled. Why don't you come back and get your room set at the hotel?"

"Maggie, are you staying out here at the job?" asked Frank, finding his voice.

She nodded. "There's plenty of room in the farmhouse. I don't mind at all. I've got some food and the Pastor is bringing some from his church tomorrow. Remember, in school, you taught us to live at the site."

"Maggie's right," Frank, remembering one of his lectures from years ago, and turning to Jake. "We need all the time we can get with the site itself. I've got everything I need in my suitcase. I'll stay here at the wreck so you can let the hotel room go. Right now I want to get to work."

Jake looked at him as though he were unwilling to leave Frank alone with the Pastor and the State employee.

"You want a job done in two days," insisted Frank. "It's going to mean some late evening work. "

"Ok," Jake agreed. "I'm sure you know what to do out here. Look, mosquitoes start to get to you out here you let me or Spyder know and we'll get you a room. Matter of fact you could stay out on the yacht. There's plenty of room. You too, Maggie."

"Like I said, it's better if we stay here and get in a few more hours."

"Well," Jake said, "God knows it isn't much fun digging in marshes. I'll be out again tomorrow to see how you're doing. "

Jake motioned to Spyder and the two of them returned to the station wagon.   As Jake and Spyder started their car, Frank looked at the others and scratched his neck.

"Termite? That's what you called him?"

"Termites work on you without you realizing until it's too late," said the Pastor. "It fits Jake, believe me. Just remember that old wreck is made of wood."

"By the way. My name is Frank Light."

"Pastor Jefferson Allingham." They shook hands. Then Frank said, "We got work to do. I'll change to work clothes and we can see those soil samples, Maggie."

Maggie and the Pastor stared at him. There was a touch of apprehension in their faces and Frank knew that they were wary of him. Their faces showed hesitation, acceptance of the third member of their team but an acceptance given with reserve. They were not sure of him, not sure he was going to do a good job.

Frank smiled. "Look, guys, you two remind me of when I first got in country in Nam in the old days. The other guys wanted to see what I would do when the first mortars came in, a kind of test to see if I was all right, safe to be around."

"We haven't got any mortars here to try you out," said the Pastor, solemnly.

Maggie said, "I remember how you used to be, Frank. That's good for a start."

Chapter 3

The Terment Company stationwagon clattered over the ruts and was gone, dust drifting across the corn field. Frank picked up his suitcase and hefted it up the steps into the old house.

"Give me a minute, " he called to the others.

They turned and headed back to the site. Frank carefully folded his suit and his expensive shoes and put them inside his case. Then he dressed in his work shorts, a cotton shirt and his slouch hat. He had worn that hat to many sites and it had brought him luck.

Outside again, he listened for a moment to the wildlife moving around where he stood, both inside the dense cornfield and also among the hedges of fragrant vines. Birds fluttered, chirped for accent, then shrilled their songs. Gnats worried the bare flesh of his neck and legs. He smelled the aroma of the wetlands, the smell almost a stink coming up from the newly exposed and bacteria rich earth of the excavation. In the heat, he felt his body oppressed by the same forces as those in a great steam engine cylinder, the heat and humid vapor thrusting against him. He wiped the sweat from his forehead. His fingers touched a tiny mole there. His mother had told him long ago that he had that mole for wisdom. He grinned. He wondered what kind of wisdom he would need before this job was over. He started toward the site.

From the pattern of the dried and bent marsh grasses, he could see that an occasional high tide washed over this wetland. Still, that would not be much water and he was surprised that the ground was so wet. The soil on the marsh surface was crusted from the sun but his feet broke through into several inches of sticky muck. It was wet enough to cling aggressively to his work shoes. He wondered where the water came from if not from the river tides.

The bulldozer operator had done his work well. The site area was stripped bare of living reeds, with the only green coming from some older trees surviving around the edges of the marsh and some near the river, loblolly pines and oaks, the pines covered with rough bark on tall and slender trunks. The land was hot and smelly with only the surrounding edges still gracious terrain for its wildlife, especially its small animals. Their night tracks where they came out to inspect this disaster, could be seen among the tread marks of the bulldozer, like the five fingered hands of tiny soldiers searching through crisscrossed chevrons of military tanks. Crushed and dying grasses were everywhere. However, in the still untouched hedges where much of the wildlife still lived, masses of green richness were heavily overgrown and bent under many years of untrimmed growth of wild honeysuckle. Ever present and treacherous wasps and hornets, their stings made ferocious from the stifling sunlight, buzzed on guard among the fragile blossoms of honeysuckle sugar.

"Muskrats," said the Pastor as he watched Frank approach. "Their tracks look like hands."

Ahead, more dead grass extended to the riverbank where there was a small drop leading down less than a foot to the normal high tide or high water mark. The shore was ringed with bits of driftwood, dried seaweed, rotting fish and dead crabs among growths of still living high grass. The tide was low so several more feet of the bank were exposed. A large mudflat extended into the river. It was covered with reeds which, closer to the river, took over from the field grass and mixed with more cattails. On the up thrust parts of these plants, a bird or two darted and competed with various hovering bugs for perches. To Frank's right, towards the old bridge, were several fallen gnarled trees, reaching far out into the river and horribly bent from storms.

"This is going to be as uncomfortable a site as I have ever worked on, " Frank said.   He looked back at the gate to the main road, rethinking Jake's invitation to live out on a comfortable yacht. Then he shrugged in resignation and reviewed the site again.   He could see areas along the edge of the cleared area where Jake's workmen had stockpiled large timbers and pilings, in preparation for the construction of the piers. Beside the stockpiles at the ends of the bulldozer swipes were   tangled brush mixed with torn chicken wire fence and brambles, all twisted in the great rolls of wreckage that were the signatures of those machines.

"Those bulldozers cut up the land quick, don't they?" observed Frank.

"We hope they haven't cleared too much of what we have to study," said Maggie.

"Looks like they took out mostly brush, not much topsoil." Frank grinned. "Just brush full of angry wasps ."

"Don't worry about snakes, " said the Pastor. "They're long gone. The bulldozers scared them away. You see any I'll take care of them. Snakes and me we get along fine."

Frank smiled. "Maggie, we got a great volunteer here. Pastor, if I see any snakes, I'll certainly call you."

Across the river Frank could see the high crane and piled river. "That thing is pretty big, isn't it?"

"Makes a lot of noise. I heard it this morning when I got here. Then the workers shut it down and went back to River Sunday until we get done."

The machine was about a thousand feet away, immense against the tree line. Its steel latticework was profiled against the curves of the old trees. The rusty barge sides brushed harshly against the reeds. The machine lurked, its hammer ready to drive more pilings into the river.

"Big equipment," said Maggie.

"A lot of money," said Frank. He looked back at the pump. "We have to run that all the time I guess."

"Soon as we go down a foot or so the water fills the test pits. "

"That's strange," he said, sniffing the air.

"The place stinks, "said Maggie.

"No. There's another smell. Like burning tobacco from a pipe."

"Nobody smokes."

The Pastor smiled at Frank. "Tobacco smoke?" he asked.

"I smell it."

"I don't," said the Pastor, his face serious.

"Me either,, " said Maggie..

The Pastor looked at Frank. "When I was a boy," he said, "My father told me that if I ever smelled tobacco smoke, and there wasn't nobody smoking, then it was a sure sign that evil was nearby. There was a local legend, come down from the Nanticokes that used to have their villages around here, that the smell of burning tobacco was the way the good spirits kept the evil ones away."

"Do you think the spirits are after me? " asked Frank, smiling.

The Pastor, his face thoughtful, said, "They might be after any one of us."

"I don't smell it anymore, " said Frank.

"If you guys are through with your ghost stories, let's look at the wreck, " said Maggie.

The three of them squatted around the remnants of the wreck. On all sides were stretched the tense white surveyor strings, their clean straight lines out of place in the construction disorganization of the site. Besides the wooden stem piece that Spyder had destroyed, there were several other timbers that had been ripped by the bulldozer from the ground. Some were of substantial size. Most had fresh marks on them where the bulldozer blade had cut into the old wood as it pushed them upward out of the soil.

"Cant frame construction," said Frank, as he gently touched the heavy timbers. "The old ship carpenters built them this way for a long time. It solved the problem of strength when the bow rounded to the stem and the frames could no longer be at right angles to the keel."

He pointed to some round pieces of wood that stuck halfway out of the timbers. "The way they connected them was by these wooden pegs. That's a sign this wreck might be old. The problem for us is that in ship construction the carpenters often used the older methods in newer boats. Especially in a rural area like the Eastern Shore. So it's hard to date her this way ."

"It's a start," said Maggie.

"Oak . I'm pretty sure of that. Whether it's American oak or English oak I 'd have to have an expert take a look. It might tell us where she was built. Then again the American merchants shipped a lot of oak to England. "

He looked closely at a part of one of the frames. "I think this timber was burned at one time."

"That fits with what I found in one of my probes," said Maggie.

"Sometimes the carpenters charred the wood so it would bend around the frames. However, this looks more like destructive burning. These timbers are likely from the lower hull below the waterline. That might mean the part above the waterline burned away before she sank. Then the river water put out the fire in the lower section. Let's see. " Frank put some numbers in the ground at his feet. "So if the hull was twenty five feet from keel to deck, and she drew fifteen feet, all we may have is the lower fifteen feet. If she was sitting on the bottom when she burned, say at low tide, then the waterline might have been high and dry, well above the water surface, and we may have less than fifteen feet of her."

He sat back on his heels and reconnoitered the site, his eyes moving along the white surveying lines, thinking of promising excavation areas. He tapped some of the up thrust stakes lightly with his archaeologist's trowel as he looked. He scratched his neck and adjusted his hat.

"OK," he said. " What do we know and what do we think we know ?"

"There's at least the bow section of a ship here and no reason to think that the rest of her isn't here," said Maggie.

"Can we assume that it's all here running out toward the riverbank and down a few feet under the surface?"

Maggie nodded. "I think that's right. I think we should set up the dig on that orientation."

Frank continued, "If this ship is early, if she dates to the Eighteenth Century or even before then, this would be a significant find. There haven't been many of these early commerce traders found in the Chesapeake Bay. It would be a wonderful find."

He looked at them. "Remember that Jake said it was just an old wheat schooner, beached up here in the marsh, left to rot. Let's not get too excited yet. According to him, she sank and disappeared, maybe less than a hundred years ago. He's probably right because it's his land. He would likely have heard any stories or legends of any shipwreck being here any earlier. I mean, his family settled this farm, didn't they, back in the colonial period?"

"Yes, but he wants us out of here too. I wouldn't rely on him being too truthful," said Maggie.

"Did you find any written records?"

"I did a quick search, at the library here in River Sunday and in Baltimore. There's nothing that I could find concerning any wrecks on this part of the river. There's mention of a tobacco dock here in the early days but the loading place was moved to the Terment family plantation on the other side of Allingham Island. The loading areas were changed often in these rivers because of the silting. The rivers became too shallow to navigate."

Frank drew with his finger in the earth. "Whatever her date, early or late, her bowsprit or any bow timbers will be out here beyond the stem that the bulldozer unearthed. "

He put in the lines. " Here. The stem and the bowsprit. " He looked toward the river. "We have to figure out how long she was. Maggie, what was the size of hull you used for your grid?"

"I estimated eighty feet, figured a line perpendicular to the riverbank and set my datum mark, my center measure, at forty feet from here toward the river."

"That's a good approach. At eighty feet she could have been either a large local schooner, built in the last century, or a three masted colonial trader."

Maggie continued, "Then I set up the rest of my measurements from that datum point. I thought it made the most sense to do all my measurements to the points where I guessed parts of the ship might be buried. I used a benchmark from the bridge construction for my elevations and marked the stakes."

"OK."

"I set up pit locations for excavation just like in your book, Doctor Light. Just like we did in the summer school. I like your system for a job like this. We can move from part to part of the ship if we begin to get some clues or find anything. I started two probes and then I had to worry about the surface water. When you folks drove up, the Pastor and I were getting the pump going."

"Wait a minute." She stood up and walked over to the edge of the cleared section and picked up a large notebook which was resting against a clump of marsh grass. As she walked back toward him, Frank smiled at the light bounce to her step.

"You always found things faster than any of the other students, Maggie. I figured you worked smarter than the others with a little luck thrown in." He noticed the small gold Christian cross jouncing on the front of her tee shirt.

"Still got the cross. Maybe that was it. The source of your luck."

"Maybe," she said, her blue eyes cheerful in the sunlight. "I used to think it was. Some days I still do. You found more than any of us and you didn't wear any cross. You just had that old hat." She sat down cross legged in front of him and the Pastor, her bare legs spotted with dried dirt.

"Here's the plan I drew up." In front of them she spread a diagram of the site itself. It was a drawing of a twenty by eighty foot rectangle surrounded on its four sides by the farm property. On the top was the entrance lane and the large cornfield. To the right was the farm house with its outbuildings and the old box gardens. On the bottom of the diagram was the riverbank and the Nanticoke River. To the left was the large hedgerow, the county road and the entrance to the old bridge. In the center, within the rectangle, she had sketched the deck plan of an early trading ship. The ship lines converged on the point in the diagram where the actual bow frames had been found.   She had drawn the ship's hull parallel to a line constructed direct from those bow artifacts. The line ran back to the riverbank, almost perpendicular to the river, and with the proposed stern of the wreck about thirty yards from the water.

"What's the small x mark to the right between the bow section and the farmhouse?" Frank asked.

"I thought that would be a good spot for the sifting screen and the excavated soil pile."

"OK by me. That will probably become a pretty good sized hill before we're through."

She had drawn a grid precisely over the hull. The hull itself was an oval with three large black dots for the suggested mast locations. Placed on the grid were a series of proposed test pit locations measured out from the datum point marked in the center of the outline. These suggested pits corresponded to Maggie's stakes in the actual site.

"I'll run you through it," she said. "There are twenty six test pits in my plan. They are located three across at different sections running down the hull and I have placed them ten feet apart going across and ten feet apart going lengthwise. There is a letter code identifying each one, so the first is A and the last is Z. The letter codes start A at near the top of the grid at the bow area and end up Z near the bottom of the grid at the stern area. I surmised three mast locations and labeled their test pits H for the foremast, N for the mainmast and T for the mizzenmast. So, " she said, " you start at the port side of the bow with a test pit marked A, then go to the right ten feet. That is test pit B, the original discovery location, right where Mr. Spyder destroyed that piece of stem wood. Go ten feet to the right of that and that is test pit C. You can see how the letters run down the wreck, for example, the crew area begins near test pits D to F, the cargo area runs G to I and down the ship to S to V."

"The whole center of the ship," said the Pastor.

"Yes," she answered, " and the Captain's quarters in the stern near the river would be S across to U and back down to test pit Z. "

She pointed out to the site, "Each stake out here corresponds to the center of the test pit location on the grid."

"Looks like a good search pattern," said Frank. " The ship's beam could be anywhere from twenty to thirty feet at her widest points of sheer and chines. You've set the centers of the pits at ten feet. The pits themselves will be staked in their corners and could go out further to allow for collapse of the old hull sides outward. You're assuming that there will be artifact scatter outward from the hull."

She nodded.

"Which pit do we search first?" asked the Pastor.

Maggie looked at Frank hesitatingly.

"Come on, Maggie. You call it. You've studied the site," said Frank.

"OK. We only have a short time. "

"Jake Terment is talking two days," said Frank.

Maggie looked at him. "Do you really think we can do a good job in two days?"

"We can try, " said Frank.

The Pastor raised his hand. " Let me understand , " he said." We search this site for two days. Then you decide whether they can pour concrete on it and destroy it forever?"

"That's about it, " said Frank. "If we decide that they should hold up the construction any further we better have some good arguments. There's usually a lot of jobs and money at stake. People have to be convinced that there's something here worth all the fuss."

"Terment Company made a deal with my office and the other state officials when this artifact was discovered. They agreed that to leave the decision to an independent consultant, that's you, Doctor Light. Doctor Light does his reconnaissance, tests a few pits, makes a decision what's here or isn't here and makes a recommendation. What Jake Terment wants is a recommendation from Doctor Light that there is nothing here worth saving. Then he'll get a construction permit to continue building the bridge."

"What happens if we find anything that you recommend is significant?" asked the Pastor.

"The law is clear. Historic artifacts are to be preserved. Jake has to stop immediately until the situation is cleared up, the artifacts researched or moved to another site. It would definitely be a major and expensive delay for him and his backers."

"Suppose there are graves here but we don't find them?" asked the Pastor.

"I don't know about that, " said Frank.

"There was never any agreement to hold the site for the discovery of graves. It's the shipwreck that is holding up the bridge, that's all," said Maggie. "The agreement between Jake Terment's company and my office is pretty definite."

"That's because I couldn't get any proof of the graveyard. I'm a clergyman, not a historian. I couldn't find anything in the few records that remain from those days. Most of the records in the River Sunday courthouse were burned by vandals during the Civil War. There's only one man in the parish that talks these days about this burying place. He's very old. His story is too emotional. He keeps talking about Adam and Eve, always quoting verse, too much about the Bible. People like you, Doctor Light, you want facts."

" You have to understand that my job here is to look for a ship, not to look for graves of dead slaves."

"I understand that, " said the Pastor. "There's not any room for an old man who confuses his Bible with his stories."

"Doctor Light?" interrupted Maggie.

"I'm not your teacher anymore so you might as well call me Frank."

"OK," she smiled. "Frank, let's prioritize. We'll start by working back from the discovery area in the bow."

"Could there be gold here, a treasure?" asked the Pastor.

"I wish," smiled Maggie. " Unfortunately, the ones that have gold usually get salvaged right after they sink. Especially if they go down in shallow water like this one. There's a lot of things to look for. Every wreck is different. What you want to find is something to date her by. Something in the soil strata of the wreck that can tie us to the time that she entered that strata. It's highly unlikely we'll find a date stamped right on the ship itself. What we do is date it from things which lie in the soil near it, if we can prove that those things arrived at that spot at the same time. Beside the dating of the artifacts we try find things about the wreck itself, construction, timber, that kind of thing. We want to find out about the people on board, the food they ate, the clothes they wore, the items they had with them."

"Maggie. You said you had already started two pits."

" I dug first at pit A, the location of the port bow area."

Maggie folded her diagram and put it back into the notebook. They walked a few feet toward the bow timbers and came to a two foot square sided hole in the ground. It was almost a foot deep, with some water in the bottom.

"These pits get expanded in size if we find anything," Frank explained to the Pastor. They got down on their knees, heads over the pit.

"Here's what I wanted to show you," Maggie said. "On the side or balk of the pit you can see the different colors of the soil strata. The first strata is made up of silt. That soil comes from the local fields around the site. When it rains here, the silt runs out from the fields into the marsh on its way to the river. I found silt throughout the excavation area. I figure that took a long time to build up. The next strata is what I think was a fill. It's not anywhere but in the ship area. I did some quick shovel probes nearby and found the natural soil profile. There was no fill. That's when I went out and found the borrow pit. I found a topsoil like the fill, in an area that looked like it was dug out a long time ago. It was a big hole in the ground , a gully, with trees growing down inside it that are at least two hundred years old. Then, down along the shoreline, there are pilings, some of them very old ones, that have been set into the bank to keep the soil fill from washing out into the river. Some of that embankment is falling in, rotting away, and the marsh soil is falling into the river."

Frank ran his fingers lightly over the strata marks. "It's certainly interesting. "

"What you're looking at, Frank, that darker soil, was pulled up near the bow timbers, disturbed from below by the bulldozer."

"Let me have your brush," he said. He worked intently at a spot, brushing the soil carefully away.

"I 've got something here. Have you got some tweezers?"
She handed him the tool.

"Here, I have it." He held up a sliver of rusting metal.

"Same type of thing we found in the other pit," said the Pastor.

"Part of a spike or bolt used to hold the ship together. If we could find one in good shape we might be able to tell something from the type of spike. If it was handmade, that would indicate the ship was older."

Maggie sketched the find in her notebook. Frank put the sliver of rust into a small plastic bag that Maggie handed to him. Then they labeled the bag with a marker on a tag giving the exact location measured with reference to Maggie's pit stakes.

"Come on over to the other probe. I want to show you something else," she said.

"This other one is pit Z," she said. "It's in the stern section."

They walked back over the site, stepping carefully over the white twine. As they walked they passed by the soil pile on their left towards the house. Near it was Maggie's sifting frame, of wood with hardware cloth and a hose for wet screening. Already she had completed the sifting of a large pile of soil from the two small test pits.

"I've had that sifting rig with me for a long time. I built it the year after I worked with you. You probably recognize it. It's like the one we had in field school."

Frank nodded. Walking was difficult. There was mire everywhere. Maggie sank to her ankles each time she stepped, slipping through the thin hard crust that the sun formed over the wetness. The Pastor's high tops were totally covered with the soft muck. Frank stopped and removed his heavy boots after a few steps. Soon his own bare feet were clods of earth.

Beside the other pit, neatly arrayed in a white plastic tray were several of the rusty splinters, each with a carefully written label tied to it.

"I'm using your coding system, Frank."

Frank smiled. "With the coding system, Pastor, and with our drawings, notes and photographs we itemize exactly where everything was found and how it looked when we found it. Many times we find that we want to go back to the records of a find with new information and new insight. It's important to see what was there originally. Records are very important. We are dealing sometimes with such little clues that we have to put all the traces together to come up with any information. The records are very important because we can work with them at home, back at the university, or wherever. We can study them, come up with ideas that we would never have time to develop out here on the site. You see, archeology is inherently destructive. Once we've finished with an area, by definition it is destroyed. Our notes are all that is left of it."

"Would you like me to keep some of these finds back at my church?"

"I think they'll be safe here." Frank said, looking at Maggie for her agreement.

She nodded. " I'm keeping everything in the farmhouse or in my car. Safe, especially if it rains. It's clean there. Besides, we ought to be able to get at the material if we need to look up something."

"Well, if you two change your mind and need a place to keep things, you let me know."

Maggie nodded. Her attention was on the small pit in front of them. They squatted by it.

"Here's what I wanted you to see," she said. She pointed with her trowel to dark surfaces on the side of the probe pit. Moving her trowel downward, she explained.

"Here is the silting layer and the darker fill that we had in the other pit. Here is the base layer of the dark clay. Then there is this thin layer of black carbon at the top of the dark clay. I think it shows there was a fire here. It makes me think there was possibly some kind of fire damage to the wreck. This fits with what you saw on that frame section, too."

"A more recent wreck could have run in here at a real high tide, maybe during a storm, then be left here for years, just rotting. Some kids could have come along and set it on fire for fun, " said Frank, remembering Jake's speech.

"That's possible, but it doesn't fit with the wreck being below the fill area, The fill alone seems to date the wreck a good two hundred years ago."

She went on. "I think this area was a cove of water, fed by a stream from back over the fields, and that the action of the stream filled and silted the cove. That stream is probably still there underground and gives us all this ground water. I think this wreck caught the silt as it came off the fields, stopped it like a dam or barricade, stopped it from going out further into the river, maybe speeded up the filling in process. Then the pilings were installed at the river's edge to stop the soil flow even more effectively. There's something more going on here too. "

"What?" asked Frank.

"In the last few years the Nanticoke River has risen here. You can see from the shorelines. That's what is destroying the bank, weakening the pilings. This site might get washed out in time. Then the wreck would be opened up anyway."

"We see global warming everywhere," mused Frank.

She nodded. "The silting of two hundred years is being reversed. Unless the bank is rebuilt, the higher tides from the rising water will wash out the soil and uncover whatever is buried here for all to see. Even if those pilings are reinforced they may continue to collapse. Nothing can stop the rising water."

"The graves too," said the Pastor. "The water will open them up. I mean, if they are here" he quickly added.

There was a piece of orange and black paper caught on one of the stakes.

"You lost one of your journal pages," said the Pastor.

"It looks like a butterfly," said Frank.

Maggie reached down and picked it up, "Clever. Another one of these butterfly things," she said, holding it for them to see.

The Pastor smiled. "You see them everywhere in town, Frank. Mrs. Pond will try anything to keep Jake from taking down those nesting trees out on his island."

"I've seen some of her work already," grinned Frank.

Maggie began to read it out loud.

RED ALERT   RED ALERT
WE NEED YOUR HELP

HELP US STOP THE NEW BRIDGE TO ALLINGHAM ISLAND

HELP US STOP THE CONSTRUCTION
HELP US SAVE OUR FUTURE
THE BRIDGE WILL BE THE BEGINNING OF THE END
OF OUR HERITAGE
OF OUR ENVIRONMENT, OF OUR LIFE.
RED ALERT RED ALERT .

"It's just signed "BUTTERFLIES," she said.

"How did it get here?" said Frank, looking out at the road.

"Maybe she came over when we were up at the porch," said Maggie.

"At least her coming here brought in a breeze," said Frank, smiling, his hand up in the cooler air..

"A breeze is strange coming this time of day, " observed Maggie. "There're no clouds."

"Maybe that guy brought it," said Frank pointing out at the river.

The leaves of the trees and bushes around the edges of the site area rustled slightly . Out on the river they could see a small section of ripples move across the surface and disappear into the shore reeds. Then, through the leaves of the riverbank trees, they saw a white work boat approaching.   It was almost forty feet long, low to the water, narrow with a cuddy cabin in the bow. A long white wooden awning extended part of the length of the craft suspended on iron plumbing pipes built into the side of the boat. In the center was a rectangular engine box, its top resting partly open to cool the engine running under it in the bright afternoon heat. A rusting exhaust pipe extended up through a hole in the awning,   For all its fast lines the craft moved slowly, its engine barely turning revolutions, with each chug a small puff of gray smoke coming from the stack. The craft inched toward a mooring on a crooked tree limb snag staggering from the shallow water about fifty feet from shore.

A lanky muscular man, old and deeply tanned with a white beard, in canvas colored shorts and bare chested,   stood at the side of the boat, steering with a vertical shaft device attached to pulleys and cables along the gunwales of the boat to the open tiller in the stern.   The man reached down inside the boat, threw a switch and the engine idled. Then he went to the stern and, watching carefully the drift of the boat, anticipated his best spot and threw out his anchor. He moved to the bow and when the boat glided to the tree limb, he expertly tied a loop of his mooring line. The man snugged the anchor line and shut down the engine. He opened a can of beer and, observing them on the shoreline, stood silently, drinking.

"You're going to meet Soldado." said the Pastor.

Frank turned from watching the visitor and moved back toward the bow end of the shipwreck.

"I'm going to start working on the starboard side at location I. That is where the side of the ship starts to straighten out on an eighty foot ship . If we can find her width, her beam, we'll estimate her potential length. "

"Pastor, help me get this pump working," said Maggie.

Soldado came ashore a half hour later. He was a towering man, of advanced age. His full white hair and muscular body proclaimed robust health. He walked up to the Pastor and nodded a greeting. Then he looked around at Frank and Maggie.

"So you two are Jake's experts." There was a slight accent to his words, perhaps Spanish, perhaps French, Frank could not be sure.

Frank held out his hand, "I'm Frank Light and this is Maggie Davis."

"Jake Terment, he send you here?" asked Soldado as he shook hands with Frank.

"He asked me to come in and look at the site, yes," said Frank.

Soldado looked at him, holding his head slightly at an angle to the left side so that his eyes were tilted and the tip of his beard folded slightly.

"You look honest." He continued, his voice having a slight Hispanic accent. "Let me tell you something for your own good."

"What's that?" said Frank.

"That Jake, he's up to something."

"Speaking of Jake, he was just here, "said the Pastor.

"I can smell him. The New York perfume he and that runt Spyder put on themselves."

"He told Frank to keep you off the property," said the Pastor.

Soldado glanced at Frank. "I want no trouble with you, Doctor. I'll leave."

"No, " said Frank. "Whether you leave or stay is none of my business. I'm just here to look for parts of an old shipwreck. Nothing else."

"Maybe you are all right," said the Pastor, smiling at Frank.

Soldado said, "There's wrecks beached up on the river. You might learn something looking them over. "

"We'd like to see them, " said Frank.

"I'll come by tomorrow midday. Take you out on my boat." He started to walk away, then stopped. "Maybe I can help you in some other ways." He paused as if he were going to speak again, then walked back to his boat.

The Pastor was already beginning to dig. "Maggie, tell me something," asked Frank, as he prepared his digging gear.

"What's that?"

"What really happened on that site in Southern Maryland?"

"It wasn't the problem everyone thought it was. I was never upset. I simply made a decision and stood by it."

"I read it was a site of a Confederate spy ring. Their artifacts were discovered right in the middle of the parking lot of a new shopping center. "

"The artifacts needed attention, needed to be preserved, needed study. I stood up for the history, that's all. I said the local businessman had to stop his paving machine until I finished."

She went on, "Then the Maryland state legislator from that area called my department and I was moved from the job. The paving machine started up an hour after I left."

"I heard you were kept at a desk in Baltimore."

"There have not been many field assignments since that one, that's true."

"We miss your work in the journals."

"I got this assignment only because the Pastor requested me personally. "

" Look, " Frank said, "Jake Terment just wants to build his bridge. He has a right to do that."

"I guess what I'd like to understand is what you're going to do here. This may be a good site, something we can all be excited about."

"You think I'll just let Jake Terment concrete it over?"

"Will you? Maybe your school needs one of those big Terment Company contributions."

"Don't worry. I'll do my job."

"That's what I was hoping you'd say." She paused, "There's something I haven't told you."

"OK."

"There's not going to be any help from my office on this one."

"No backup, no analysis, no conservation lab?"

"Right. My boss told me before I came down here. She said, 'Don't bother to send over for any remote sensing equipment. You're on your own. It's in all use on other jobs.'"

"I'm afraid," said Frank, "That I can't get anything from the university here in time."

"The problem is that our department is small, " said Maggie." My boss is a political appointee and unfortunately, knows more about how to get votes for the Governor."

"The work will just take a little longer, that's all," said Frank.

"You and I both realize the work will take a whole lot longer without the instruments. As a result, we'll probably overlook a good portion of the history here, " said Maggie.

She stared at Frank, and he felt the pressure of that stare. "Let's see what we find before we get too excited," said Frank.

Maggie walked away without another word.

Chapter 4

A slight cracking noise woke Frank. His habit, learned during the war, was still there. He could wake up with the slightest noise. He looked at his watch. Three in the morning. The night was black. In patches of sky through the overhanging trees, he could see some of the late night summer constellations. Only a bit of starlight filtered through the leafy overhang of branches and into the side of the porch where he had put an old mattress from the house. Maggie's light on the second floor was off. She was still asleep. Strangely, there was no insect noise. Something had interrupted their night talk. As his eyes adjusted to the starlight, he could see shapes of bushes and shrubs. Then he heard the noise again. He recognized the sound. Dry twigs snapping. He saw light flicker off the leaves of a large tree far by the riverbank. He could not see the ground beneath the tree because the great boxwoods were in the way.

He remembered the paper they had found yesterday. He decided to investigate quickly, to see if he could catch someone tampering with the excavation. He stepped off the porch into the darkness, making no noise. He was dressed only in his thin underwear shorts. The dew felt cool under his bare feet as he moved carefully towards the site, toes feeling the way, slugging against the blades of the tall grass. As he drew close to the box bushes, he smelled burning wood. He saw a few sparks of light traveling into the night and coming from the riverbank at the far end of the site. He dropped to his knees and crawled, gradually pushing his head through the tall grass until he saw the campfire. It was a tiny blaze, flickering, crackling. The fire was fueled with twigs and small branches, with only enough energy to send weak shadows. A man stepped from the dark behind the fire. Even in the darkness and the distance of more than a hundred yards, he could recognize Soldado's tall figure.

The old man faced the site and raised his hands in an arc from his thighs until his fingers touched over his head. He was silent, wordless. The firelight flickered across his body, naked except for a short cape drawn over his shoulders. A strange metal shield designed in the shape of an orange jaguar's face hung by a gold chain across his groin. For a few moments he moved slowly towards the wreck. Then he stopped and stared directly at the spot where Frank was hidden in the tall grass. Sweat suddenly ran down Frank's face. Frank did not move, trembling slightly with the fear of the unknown, an anxiety he had not felt since long ago nights in Vietnam. Frank could see Soldado's face, the intensity, and he could see brilliant colors on the man's chest and face. There were streaks of shining paint, wide swaths of brilliant yellow, black and white, changing in the shimmering light from moment to moment as the small fire sparked.

Then the old man looked away. Frank could not tell from the man's movements whether he had been detected. Soldado held two small wires, one in each hand. He brought these wires down to a level with his waist and slightly in front of his body. He moved ahead. With the fire directly behind him, he cast a long shadow out in front. He was black against the fire and Frank could not see the details of his face anymore.

Soldado held the wires in his hands pointed forward, his multicolored body glistening at the edges where the firelight reflected from it, his feet finding their way without error among the tiny stretched white surveyor twines that Maggie had so carefully measured over the wreck. The tempo of his walk followed a rhythm that Frank easily sensed, the footprints in the earth like soft animal paw prints brushing a taut drum skin, yet without noise. Frank recognized the costume, ancient Mayan. His mind sensed the primitive unsung music, like a beat he might have studied that derived from Africa or early America, even Asia. He thought of Soldado as an improbable yet very much in the flesh witch doctor, like an ancient native making his prayer or magic with fire and nakedness and shadows.

After a few steps the rods trembled in Soldado's hands and crossed each other. Soldado stopped and with the toe of his right foot drew a mark of crossed lines on the muddy soil. Soldado then continued moving forward. In a few minutes the rods moved again. He repeated the marking with his foot at another spot. Soldado reached a far point in the site area, turned and raised his hands again to the sky , the rods pointed directly over his head. He remained this way for a few moments, very still, the firelight illuminating the front of his body, luminescent with the multicolored paint, terrifying in the power he seemed to exude.

Soldado dropped his arms and returned to the fire. He sat down cross legged, his back to Frank. He stayed in this position for another half hour, swaying from side to side. Then Soldado stood up and pushed some earth into the small flames with the side of his foot. The fire sparked and died and the night was dark again. The weak starlight was unable to penetrate the blackness of the overhanging great trees around the site.

Frank felt an insect crawling under his stomach as he lay flat on the ground. He twisted his back silently. He did not want to scratch for the bug, did not want to alert Soldado. Eventually the insect found its way back into the earth and the irritation ceased.

Frank listened. In a few moments he heard Soldado wading through the shallow river water towards his boat moored out in the darkness. The footsteps in the water made a wet sound like fish jumping. Finally he heard creaking wooden floorboards in Soldado's boat. There began the slow throb of a workboat engine, and Frank heard the craft rippling the river water as it eased into the channel. The night quiet returned. He stood up and began to walk slowly back to the porch. His exhausted mind tossed with images of orange and black butterflies dancing with yellow witchdoctors as he drifted off to the few hours of sleep he had left before the summer heat began again.

At six AM the noise of Maggie and Pastor working at the site woke him up. Frank pulled on his shorts and walked over. The Pastor had brought some food, prepared by the people at his church. While he sipped a cup of coffee Frank glanced out at the river. Soldado's boat was nowhere in sight.

"Soldado woke me up out here last night," he said, "The old guy was out by the site, singing and walking around naked carrying dousing rods."

The Pastor grinned. "He calls his ritual the song of a thousand men. I 'm acquainted with folks who tell me he has talked to their dead family members. Myself, I've seen him sit up all night saying his Mexican words," said the Pastor. "Nobody around here can understand what he's saying."

"His body was painted and he had a cape over his shoulders."

"His mother made up that Mexican costume for him. He says it's from the Yucatan. You're right. He's close to naked in that rig. Soldado makes a little money finding water. When a person wants to dig a new well, they get Soldado to come up to their farm and locate the best spot for the well. 'Course he don't get painted up for that. "

"I've never seen dousing rods," said Maggie.

" Some of our archaeologist colleagues swear by them," said Frank.

"How do they work?" asked the Pastor.

"The dousing rods are supposed to vibrate if they are near water or metal."

"Why?"

"Some people think they work like our electronic finding devices, forming some kind of relationship with metal or magnetism in the ground below the surface. Nobody knows for sure."

Maggie inspected the cross marks left by Soldado. She pounded a white stake into the center of each mark. Then she precisely plotted these locations on her site plan.

"He marked two of my probe areas. Location H and Location Q."

"H is the foremast area, isn't it?" asked Frank. "Q, that's in front of the mizzenmast, the big cargo area. Interesting. If the dousing works, something metal has probably been identified in those spots. We'll see."

Frank turned to the Pastor. "Pastor, can you dig with us today?"

"Sure."

"If Maggie concurs, you can start test pit M halfway down the port side of the wreck, about twenty feet off the left of the main mast location. I'd like to explore as much as I can about the shape of the hull. If she's an early wreck, she'll be in a fish shape, what they used to call codfish and mackerel, wide beam at the bow and narrow at the stern like a fish. That test pit should tell us something if we are lucky. Maggie and I can teach you what you need to know about excavating procedures."

"It's all right with me," said Maggie.

"Maggie, why don't you try Soldado's location T? That's near the captain's quarters which could have many artifacts. I'll work on Grid I off to the right of the foremast to see if there is more information there about the shape of the bow. We're looking for a round apple cheek curve to determine if she was built in this fish shape."

Frank and Maggie showed the Pastor some of the simpler digging techniques. Frank was working his digging tools into the soft earth of the Pastor's spot when Maggie laughed. He looked up at her.

"What?" he said.

"You're using the same old trowel you had years ago."

"I guess it is." Frank looked at it. "I never thought about it. It doesn't seem to wear out as much as the other ones."

"This job will finish it off. I think the stink of the marsh is worse this morning," Maggie said.

"Yes," said the Pastor. "It gets that way sometimes. "

"Like rotten soil in your garden," said Maggie. "Strange how so many beautiful flowers grow in stink."

The sun heated the site quickly as they worked. Its glare was everywhere and glinted off the bits of silica in the soil and the white oyster shells that appeared everywhere as they dug. The pump hammered away, keeping barely ahead of the constantly seeping water.

"It's like the earth itself is alive," said Frank.

"Oyster shells are from the ancient Native American feasts around here, remains of their eating," explained Maggie.

Down about a foot into Frank's pit, he reached a conglomerate, a stone hard chunk of rusted and chemically fused material, mostly soil but with some rusty items showing in the soil. It was a large oblong object that stretched out from the shipwreck, a few feet from what might have been the side of the ship , extending also beyond the white twine lines that Maggie had designed. The conglomerate was heavy. Frank could not move it.

"Come look at this," he called.

Maggie and the Pastor squatted beside him.

"I want to get this out of the ground. Let's get some photographs first."

Maggie went up to her car behind the farmhouse and got her camera and tripod. She also returned with a black and white scale and a small arrow for referencing the direction north in the photographs. She photographed the object from directly above. Then, for a few minutes they worked along the sides of the artifact, digging out the space around it, expanding the excavation. Knowing time was short they used shovels instead of trowels to hollow out beneath it so they could judge its circumference and length. They were able to determine that it ran out from the line of the marker twine about another ten feet and that it was about thirty inches in circumference.   Frank moved his hand over the artifact.

"Unfortunately, conglomerates take forever to study," he said. "You can't just hack them open. You have to chip at them carefully."

"Sometimes all you end up uncovering is a pocket of air with all the original artifact disintegrated but the shape still impressed in the conglomerate," said Maggie.

"We can make plaster molds to see what the original object was. It's very tedious. Usually on these projects we have remote sensing electronics to look into the ground before we dig to see if anything is there and how it is oriented."

"Yes, that's when we have the equipment," said Maggie not smiling. "How do we get it out?"

"There's that truck up in the shed."

"You're right. She's got a hoist," said the Pastor. He smiled. "I've driven those M37 trucks. Plenty of power. "

"We got truck driving in common, Pastor" grinned Frank. "I'll get the truck."

There was a smell of oil and canvas as he opened the door of the truck. He put the windows down in the hot air and pushed the old canvas top back. The engine started fast and ran well as Jake had said it would. Engine heat soon panted in hot gusts at Frank's bare feet, seething up at him through the steel floor with its ragged holes from some forgotten battle.

In a few minutes Frank had the truck backing towards the site. The grass at the edge of the site parted in front of the back end of the old military vehicle. The engine rumbled as the large rubber cleated tires tortured the earth, inching back toward the test pit. Maggie stood beside the artifact, her arms signaling to Frank. Finally, Frank positioned the large arm of the bomb hoist directly over the object.

"Well done, soldier," smiled the Pastor.

Frank grinned and signaled the Pastor the thumbs up sign. He reached into the bed of the truck and pulled out a yellow lifting strap.

"Let's see if we can get this strap under the object."

"Put it under the center," said Maggie. The Pastor placed several two by four timbers along the conglomerate to spread the tension of the strap. Frank passed the strap under the artifact. The Pastor reached for the strap on the other side and brought it up to the top. Then Frank slipped one end of the strap through a loop in the other end and snugged it up into the air. The Pastor had loosened the hoist chain and pulled it toward the loop that Frank held. Frank hooked the loop and they were ready to hoist.

"How much do you think we can lift with that hoist?"

"The winch on this truck was designed to lift heavy bombs for aircraft. It should have the power we need to get the conglomerate out. " Frank went back to the cab of the truck and climbed in. He increased the speed of the old Dodge engine.

"Ready," he yelled, over the unmuffled engine noise.

"Pull away," called Maggie.

He eased in the winch and the cable tightened. When the cable was fully taut, Frank locked the winch and climbed out to look at the job. "Looks all right, " he said. "You folks stand to the side in case the strap lets go You'll get hurt if it breaks and whips at you." He started the winch again and the truck pulled down on its rear axle. The engine strained . The front end of the heavy truck began to lift upward, its big wheels rising inch by inch into the air.

Suddenly, the conglomerate let go with a ripping noise, dirt and brown water flying into the air. The front of the truck crashed back on its axle. Frank eased the engine and the crane lifted the object effortlessly, higher into the sunlight.

"Good enough," said the Pastor, signaling Frank to start slowing the gears.

"Wait. Stop the winch," yelled Maggie, stepping towards the object.

"What is it, Maggie?" hollered Frank as he immediately halted the winch.

Maggie squatted down and looked up at the underside of the object as it hung about four feet off the ground. "There's something dropping out of it."

"What?"

Maggie tried to get her cupped hands under the object to catch a small stream of soil that was falling.

"It's coming out of a small fissure in the conglomerate."

They crowded around her as she held her hands out. The soil caught in her hands and glinted yellow in the sunlight.

"It looks like gold dust."

Frank bent close. "It is gold," said Frank, in a restrained technical manner, as he tried to get a better look.

"Gold dust" said the Pastor, excited. Maggie moved her hands cupping the gold back and forth in celebration. A piece of black material broke free from the artifact and fell into the bottom of the pit. The Pastor reached down and picked it up.

"It looks like the remains of a pouch, probably someone's moneybag," said Maggie, calming down.

"Hardened leather, petrified almost, " said Frank. " There's some of the dust still caught in the mouth of the pouch."

"Maybe there's more gold inside the pouch," said the Pastor.

"If there is, it is not much." Frank felt the pouch. "Not enough weight for there to be much. What do you think, Maggie?"

"You're right. There's not much gold." They both knew that the real importance of this pouch was in helping date the wreck. If the use of this were as someone's money pouch, that would date the ship at an earlier century. There was a time when people did not have currency and they used gold dust to buy things. The trick would be to tell how this pouch was used.

"Gold or not, let's get this conglomerate off the hoist before something breaks. " Frank climbed back into the truck. He shifted the transmission and eased out the clutch. The truck crawled forward in low range, the object swinging slightly in the air. The Pastor walked on one side of the artifact and Maggie walked on the other, both of them with their hands on the large cluster. They tried to keep it from moving too much and straining or breaking the strap. They walked along in the tracks of the truck wheels as the old military vehicle ground towards the boxwood and high grass at the edge of the site.

Frank finally stopped the truck. "We need blocks under the conglomerate to keep it off the ground. " The Pastor found two short pieces of construction wood nearby and set them on the ground for the artifact to rest on.

"You got your blocks," he said.

Frank then eased the winch and the object dropped slowly towards the wood. When it was on top of the timbers, they removed the cable and put the strap back in the truck. The three stood around the artifact.

"We should try to find some time to chip some of that hardened clay off the thing. It may show something then. If not, we'll have to wait into we can get it into a chemical bath."

"Let it sit for awhile," said Frank. "The wet soil can dry on its surface. I think in this case it will be easier to inspect if we can take the muck off in chunks." He sat on the ground in front of the artifact.

"You folks have to work right hard in this archaeology business," said the Pastor, joining him on the ground.

Frank smiled at Maggie. "It's a lot better than some things I have had to do in my life, " he said.

"Yeah, I guess so," said the Pastor.

"You in Nam too, Pastor?"

The Pastor nodded, " Army Chaplain."

A butterfly flew softly in front of them and for a moment rested on the conglomerate. "Tell me about them," said Frank, pointing at the orange and black insect.

"The Monarch butterfly migrates directly through a spot on Allingham Island," answered the Pastor. " I guess they been doing this for centuries. Jake Terment's father never bothered them, but Jake himself used to kill them. I remember when he was a little boy that he'd see how many he could kill. In their migration, big clouds of them landed on a few old trees near the big house. Jake would go out there and swat as many as he could all day long. Then he would bring buckets of the dead butterflies into the house to show his father. I never saw the old man kill one of them himself."

"Matter of fact," the Pastor went on, "Not long before he died, Mister Terment began to get pretty close to the environmental folks around here. People like Mrs. Pond. They used to have meetings up there in the big room at Peachblossom Manor. The whole group of them took field trips out in the Wilderness Swamp."

"Jake was away making money during this time, building up the Terment Company in different areas of the United States, building skyscrapers, developments, planned cities. He made his money by finding slums he could buy up cheap, then evicting the residents, taking down the houses. He was always big on bulldozers. Then he'd resell the land as prime industrial property. "

"I thought there were laws against that," said Maggie.

The Pastor smiled. "I guess laws presuppose the will to enforce them. You don't see much law being enforced in places where they want the land for the big companies." He continued,. "The old man retired from his real estate business and all his other business. He never did much outside of River Sunday and some small projects here on the Eastern Shore. Jake's father, Mister Terment, he was a big man in a small town. Funny thing though. Jake's father was tough and most of the time, pretty smart. His son was wasn't so much smart as he was tough and lucky. Jake would do anything to anyone long as he made money. Always was that way.

'That's why most of us were surprised when we found he had come back and was intending to put all this money into the island.

We always figured he would concentrate on big projects far away from here." The Pastor winked at Frank and Maggie. "There is a rumor Jake was short on money and the bankers up in New York made him come down here and do this project, put up his own property, so to speak. What I hear from the servants who work up at Peachblossom, they overheard his phone calls to New York. He didn't want to do it. He didn't want anything to do with working on this bridge. Makes sense. I always thought once he got out of this place, he wasn't ever coming back here. Those New York bankers, they're pretty smart.

"Jake almost didn't have any property to put up. Way things were going with all his father's interest in wildlife, folks thought that Mrs. Pond and the birdwatchers were going to get the old Peachblossom farm and any of the old man's properties on the island. People assumed the Terment land was going to be preserved for a park, for animals, and especially for the butterflies.

"It didn't turn out that way. Right after his daddy's funeral, Jake and his lawyer produced a will that stated Jake owned the property as the only heir. Of course Mrs. Pond and all her people went to court but they could get nowhere. She did not have a will that said any different. It was her word against Jake's word. All that she could do was argue that the old man promised her and the others the land for the animals. That did not cut any water with the judge. "

"So there have been bad feelings ever since, " said Frank.

"You got that right. Every chance she gets, Mrs. Pond and her people take on Jake and his people. Jake just wears them down . He has the law on his side every time. He is great for showing up with the police. That's the way he always does. You watch him how he operates. Just quietly stands there with a whole lot of his police friends like Billy beside him. "

There was a loud popping sound. The artifact split open at that moment and pieces of the conglomerate split like the pieces of eggshell breaking loose when a bird is hatched. It broke in half lengthwise and parts lay on the ground. Revealed was a rusty metallic tube about nine feet in length and about eight inches high with ridges around its circumference at different lengths of the tube.

"It's a cannon tube," said Maggie. "The sun must have heated what's left of the old metal, expanded it to break up the aggregate."

"It's a very early cannon," said Frank, hastening to look.

"Probably Eighteenth Century, " said Maggie.

"How can you tell?" asked the Pastor, enjoying the excitement of the two archeologists, as they peered at the old weapon.

"You look at the raised areas on the tube, Pastor." Frank leaned over the gun, sighting along its barrel. "This was how the gunner would aim it. The design of these old guns changed over the centuries. Cannon historians can tell from the ridges around the barrel about when and where the gun was made. Sometimes there's a maker's mark but I don't see one on this gun. Even if we knew when it was made, that still does not tell us all we want to know. Sometimes they were recycled in later ships, captured and used, or simply bought from gun warehouses in London to outfit merchant ships. "

"It's iron," said Maggie. "Strange it hasn't rusted more. These were not the best cannons. The best were bronze. Iron tubes were used on merchant ships, where they would be fired only occasionally and not for war as would be the case on a military ship."

"However, even iron cannons are usually salvaged," said Frank, thoughtfully.

"Why?" asked the Pastor.

"Anything valuable in shallow water is likely to be salvaged. Think like the people who were here when this ship was wrecked. Why would they leave something valuable?"

He continued. "There's something else. A schooner carrying wheat to Baltimore doesn't need a cannon."

She nodded. "This might rule out Terment's idea of the wreck being a wheat schooner." She touched the metal. "If this was an old wreck, why wasn't the cannon brought up?"

"Sometimes these old wrecks were left alone because of disease. People were terrified of plague," suggested Frank. "One good guess might be that this ship was burned because of plague on board. Ships were burned in those days to control disease."

Maggie looked at him. "Plague. Yes. That might explain people's fear. Their leaving the cannon. Maybe the reason the ship was covered over with earth too."

"I must admit, this is a little more than I thought I would find at this construction site," Frank said.

The Pastor chuckled.

"What?" asked Frank.

"I was just thinking how this old cannon, we fix it up, might give them Confederate boys a run for their money one of these Heritage Days coming," he smiled.

Chapter 5

Jake arrived at about nine o'clock, carrying a golf club.

"What's that?" he asked, pointing with the club at the broken conglomerate.

"That is what is left of an Eighteenth century iron cannon, a pretty good sized one, " explained Frank.

"I guess you're going to tell me it was from the shipwreck."

"It was in the wreck location. I can't be sure it was part of the ship but it's likely. Maggie and I are surprised to find a quality artifact like that. We don't understand why this was not salvaged before."

Jake looked at the cannon for a few minutes and then turned to Frank.

"You make too much out of this, Frank, " Jake said. "If you were a native, you'd realize that gun was probably used as somebody's anchor mooring. Sailors on the Chesapeake used everything they could for ballast and for anchors. Maybe it was ballast on the ship that was in here. Lots of old iron and lead got carried around in the boats to keep them from capsizing. I can't tell you how many times the farmers around here turn up pieces of iron in their fields."

"Did you ever hear of anyone turning up a cannon this size with their John Deere?" asked Maggie.   Jake didn't answer her.

"You're probably right, Jake," said Frank, amicably. He could see the image of Mellow waving her finger, advising him not to aggravate Jake on the first day.

"It concerns me, though," said Frank, knowing that Maggie and the Pastor were still checking him out, studying even the subtle voice intonations in his talk with Jake. "We may never know why this gun tube was near the shipwreck. That's what is intriguing, and at the same time maddening, about these archaeological surveys. Even with all the precision our work entails there is still uncertainty and mysteries remain."

"Well, let me know when you find something useful."

"We might have something for you by tomorrow night, " said Frank.

"Can't you get it done by tonight?" Jake looked at Frank, tapping the golf club. There was a lack of the warmth towards Frank that he had shown the day before.   "You're still working for me, Frank. That the way you see it?"

"I have never seen it any different," said Frank, surprised by Jake's sudden serious tone. He scratched his neck for a moment, knowing he was getting himself in trouble.
If he didn't say the right thing he'd lose respect from not only Jake but Maggie and the Pastor.

Jake continued, "Anytime you need to remember why you are here working in the middle of my marsh, near my bulldozer, on my project, you just take a good look at that crane out there on the Nanticoke. There's a lot of money tied up in a machine that isn't doing me any good right now."

"Jake, we're doing the job. Everything is being done as quickly and in as organized a manner as possible," said Frank. He continued, thoughtfully, more authority now in his voice. "There is a way you can help to speed up the process,"

"How?"

"Keep Spyder off the site." This was a demand from Frank, no longer casual. "Everything that he wrecks by accident is something that we have to do over, something that will hold us up in finding out any answers here."

"Sure," Jake laughed, swinging his club at a clump of crabgrass. "You hear that, Spyder? You keep your hands in your pockets."

Spyder grinned, walking behind them.

Frank showed Maggie's site diagram to Jake, pointing out with care each theoretical section of the wreck and carefully explaining what they hoped to find. Jake asked questions from time to time and appeared interested.

"Jake, most of what we need to find out seems to be located within a few feet of the surface soil of the marsh. We think we know why this wreck is so close to the surface."

Maggie looked up from her work as Frank spoke. She nodded in agreement as he explained the site condition to Jake.

"As we see it, the ship was in shallow water, maybe low tide. For some reason, she caught on fire and burned almost to the keel. The tide came in and put out the fire leaving the ship a charred hulk. The tidewater probably covered the wreck at high tide. Over the following months and years the cove silted in from runoff as the fields were tilled. There was also an underground stream feeding the cove which is still active and is the cause of the wetness. The stream added to the silt. There might have been some fill carried in by workers, maybe to try to level out the area. We know some pilings were set into the bank at some time. The backwater in here dried out. It became a marsh. So for quite a few years this shipwreck was pretty well buried. Now, with recent climate changes in the Chesapeake, the river has started to rise. There are more storms, more flood tides. The river is washing out the silting more quickly. I think if we had come along a few more years from now, all our work would be done for us. This shipwreck might be showing right on the surface with all its secrets."

"The shorelines are changing all the time along these river systems. You must have known this, being a native," asserted Maggie, looking at Jake. "I expect you or your father must have worried about losing part of the marsh as the bank has been washing away."

Jake became visibly restless. "What difference does all this research make?" he said.

"To tell you the truth, Jake," answered Frank, "It doesn't make any difference if the wreck is not worth the research. However, if the wreck is an important one, everything that happens in this marsh will be studied."

"I'm working here on a test pit that covers where we think the captain's cabin was," said Maggie. "Artifacts buried in the earth from the ruins of his cabin will tell us about the ship and that helps to put the story of the shipwreck together."

"You find a few soggy bags of wheat and we can all cover this thing up," chuckled Jake.

"If it's wheat from a few decades ago like you suggest, yes, we can cover it all up. I agree with you, I don't think the wreck of a wheat schooner of maybe a hundred years age is worth very much in maritime research," smiled Frank.

"There's no way you're going to find a few grains of wheat in all this muck," said Jake, winking at Spyder.

"I wouldn't be so sure, Jake. This is a strange site. We already noticed preservation of materials that should be in much worse shape."

"How far down do you have to go?" asked Jake.

"As I said, it's a shallow site. We don't have to dig very far, just until we find what we call sterile soil, the soil before humans came along, the soil left by the glaciers."

"Sterile soil has to belong to a period before the wreck," said Maggie.

"Right. We double check that strata and make sure there's no evidence of human activity, that it wasn't disturbed and then we stop going down further. That's the soil we call sterile."

"So how far down is that?" persisted Jake.

"Well, judging from the silting, and from the height of the piece of ship's bow we have already found, the keel and the other parts of the wreck that still exist are probably only four to five feet below the surface, maybe less. "

"What I'm getting at is that there's not a lot of dirt to dig into," said Jake. "Way I see it you folks should be able to finish up soon."

"That's right, Jake. That's why I wanted you to see all this. It's possible to get enough done by end of tomorrow. At least we'll know a lot more by then."

"I 'd still like it sooner if you can."

"We'll certainly consider the costs that you are running up with the construction halt. I understand that."

"Hey, leave that alone," yelled Maggie.

Spyder was poking a board at the remains of the conglomerate that fell off the cannon. Frank looked at Jake. Jake smiled.

"Come on, Spyder. You're not wanted around here," said Jake. "What is that stuff anyway, Frank?"

"We call it conglomerate. We value it because there may be other things imbedded in that hard cluster. Sometimes there are all kinds of pieces of the wreck that joined together like glue with the water and pressure. Tools, early eating utensils, pieces of chain, all kinds of interesting things."

Jake let his eyes move over the piece of conglomerate. He stood carefully, his shoes close but not touching the artifact, his patent leather away from stains by the black swamp liquid still dripping from the cluster. Spyder had returned to the station wagon and now honked the horn. Jake turned away and, without another word, walked quickly over to his car.

Spyder held a cellular telephone out the car window, and called "New York wants you." Jake took it beside the car and began listening, his face unsmiling. Then he got into the car, still listening, and Spyder drove out the lane.

"He's a busy man," said the Pastor walking up behind Maggie and Frank.

"Yes, he is. I could tell that yesterday when I met him at the hotel. Seems to be a popular man too, judging from all his friends I saw there."

"Don't be fooled by that, Frank," said the Pastor. "They are not friends. His father, Mister Terment, ran everything in the town. He was royalty, like a king. Now, Jake's hoping his television celebrity status makes up for his father's death and that loss of the family status around here. The celebrity status is weak though. I 'm not sure very many of those so called friends would lift a finger to help him if they weren't getting something out of it."

"Same thing at our university," said Frank. "People come to us and say how much they love the school but they only send in a contribution when they have a real reason."

"I'll bet they pay up when their kid is in the school," said Maggie.

"Exactly."

"There's a lot of folks with interest in this island development, that's for sure," said the Pastor. "It's just about the biggest building project that has come to River Sunday in our lifetime. Jake's right about one thing. There are going to be lots of jobs putting up all those houses."

The Pastor smiled. "Tell you two something about that man though."

"What?"

"He's got to be the most superstitious person you ever want to meet. If he has a weakness it's his superstitions, his worrying about bad luck. The man held up traffic one day in the middle of River Sunday. " The Pastor moved his hands up to imitate Jake stopping traffic. "Terment stopped his car because a black cat crossed in front of him. He squealed the brakes and turned his car around right in the middle of the street. He hates cats."

"I saw Spyder kick a cat out of the way for him at the hotel."

"Jake doesn't change."

The Pastor looked at the dust cloud of the disappearing station wagon. "Maybe part of his problem was the way he was brought up. I mean we all had tough times, but he always seemed to be alone. He was raised by a woman his father lived with but never married, as far as I know. She came from Baltimore. His real mother died when he was born. Some say that Mister Terment wasn't the father. His real daddy was some Thunderbolt pilot stationed up the Chesapeake Bay who came by the local airport doing landings during the war. Lot of folks treated him like he wasn't a Terment, like he was some kind of bastard child. "

"That must have been tough on him," said Frank.

The Pastor nodded. "What made him so deep down mean. Then again, I think he got all the superstition from the woman who brought him up. She was something. Folks liked her better than they did the old man. She wore real bright clothes. I think she had been a dancer, a burlesque queen, up in Baltimore. She started coming around after Jake's real mama died, after the war was over. Jake's father met her and brought her down here with him. One of my friends told me. He was butler up there on the island one evening when she got drunk. She put on her G string for some of the old man's poker friends, dancing for all of them out there at night at the mansion after the little boy was in bed. She danced there in that paneled colonial room with all the old furniture. My friend and the other servants watched this through the partly open kitchen door. There was loud music. Terment was clapping his hands in time to this music, slow beat it was, on the record player. She was swaying around the room, stepping up on all the old antiques, her all naked. She kept throwing her clothes at the poker players, having a good time and laughing that real hooting laugh she had, her hair flying after her.

"Mister Terment went through a lot of servants. He fired any servant who saw too much of her dancing. He did this after he found out they were telling stories that he didn't like down among their families and cousins in River Sunday. Of course it was his own fault. He would get the poor woman drunk and then she would carry on the only way she knew. He was a drinker, too, and that's what killed him, his whiskey. Killed a lot of them old time white people.

He chuckled. "Talk about stupid. They got into this idea that their status was based on having their whiskey branded with their family name. The bottler went along with the damn fools but he said they had to buy a lot of cases to keep his inventory cost down. They weren't alcoholics when they started as I understand it. They had to keep that whiskey coming though so the man would keep their mark in stock. They couldn't pour out the whiskey so they had to drink it. Folks told me they'd see a couple of cases coming in every month. Poor fools drank themselves to death, that's what I think, and just to show off. Kinda came to a halt in the late Fifties. Most of those people were dead by then and their children were too poor to keep up the orders or else they didn't have the livers for all that whiskey."

Frank laughed out loud at the story. So did Maggie.

The Pastor went on, " There was a story that Jake got his name when his mother was carrying him and his father was off in a poker game in Baltimore. Mister Terment had traveled over there to win some money off some rich black businessmen from East Baltimore. Turned out one of his black opponents was holding all the cards that night. He kept on goading Terment, making him careless. Terment wasn't a member of the white hate groups around Maryland but he didn't oppose them neither. Everyone at the game knew Terment didn't have much use for blacks getting any financial power. He didn't like the competition. So his opponent got Terment off balance, made him crawl and in the final big hand, taunted him with a bet, that if he won, he'd get to name Terment's kid. Terment by then was so angry he took the bet. Like the man planned all along, Terment lost big, lost all his money he had brought to Baltimore. Then the black man grinned, laid down his hand of four Jacks and said, "Mister Terment, four red and white Jakes. I'll just say Jake 's a good name for your baby." He had to come home that night and tell his pregnant wife, who most of us around River Sunday knew didn't like black folk any more than she liked him."

"The woman, the dancer, who brought Jake up, wasn't a bad sort. She was just ignorant. She was nice enough to me. Always putting out good food for me and my brother. In those days my father was gardener at Peachblossom. He had survived because he stayed away at night and never saw all the going's on.

"My father's job ended when Jake went to his father and got him to throw out my dad and mom and me and my brother. Jake was angry at us two kids for some reason, some game out in the yard that he had lost. He made up that my mother was stealing some of the silverware. My mother never stole anything in her life but some of the silver was missing. I was pretty young at the time. I didn't understand that Jake had probably hid the silver himself just to get my mother in trouble. I still played with Jake for a few more years. I just didn't live there at Peachblossom anymore. "

"I remember the dancer woman kept a bottle of dye for her bright red hair. Jake told me one time that he poured the dye out on the floor. He got slapped around pretty good for that, maybe by her but I think by the old man."

"Does she still live up there at the mansion house?"

"She never did live up at the big house. The old man kept her down in a little cottage about a quarter mile from the house. It was one of the old slave quarters that he had fixed up. She would just come up to the big house during the day. After the old man died, Jake sent her away. Jake told folks that she wanted to live in Baltimore. She was an old lady by then. Still had that bright red hair. I guess she and Jake didn't get along. I bet he didn't give her a cent out of the old man's money either, probably not even bus fare."

" Jake would do that?"

"It's a side of him that people don't know. The woman liked animals. She was superstitious sure but she never hurt animals. I remember she would take a fly outside. A housefly. Wouldn't let anybody kill a fly. Jake may hate cats just because she liked them, just to spite her memory. "

"I guess you learn to figure out people, being a preacher. You get to know both sides, the good and the bad."

"Yes, you do. Little hard finding the good side of Jake Terment, though. It's been one of the toughest jobs in my ministry, finding something good to think about that man," he said, as he climbed down into his probe pit to continue his work. "Even in all the evil I saw in Vietnam I was able to find some good in the faith of some of the men. Not as easy when I start thinking about Jake Terment."

Frank paused, "I wanted to help children in that war," he said thoughtfully.

"Children?"

"Yes, in those days I thought that the war was to make South Vietnam into a haven for children, a place where these kids would grow not being slaves to the communist government, a place where they would be free."

Frank worked at the soil again, "I went over there to help kids. Then this little boy comes along and nearly kills me and kills all my buddies, guys I had spent months with."

"Viet Cong sapper?"

Frank nodded. "Big explosion. We never knew what hit us."

They worked silently for a few minutes. Then the Pastor changed the subject. "So you and Maggie worked together before."

"Maggie was the best field school student I ever taught."

"You two make a nice couple, both archaeologists. It's good to have the same career. My wife and I were both in the church. We talked about similar things. It was good."

Frank had never thought of Maggie that way, of the two of them as a romantic couple. The last time he had seen her she was a student finishing college and he was a hardened war veteran just getting his feet back on solid ground as a teacher. On this site, they shared their expertise as professional archeologists. It was a form of equality, a mutual outlook on the problems and excitement of this wreck excavation. The equality brought them closer together, made him look forward to her opinions on each new discovery, as the hours went by in the tension and heat. They were not related in the normal sense of the word, not brother and sister, but, the Pastor was right, a special kinship was there between them.

"I hope to meet your wife before I leave," said Frank.

"She passed away several years ago. It's just me. Me and my church."

"I'm sorry. "

"I live with the loss of her. I gather you do a lot of this kind of archaeological work, working on real estate deals, I mean."

"We get a lot of requests at the university for expert opinions on sites. There's always someone who wants to build something and hits into an historic artifact. It always seems to be a situation that requires everything to be done in a hurry. It's easy to understand if you think about it."

"Why?"

"I got this theory. The colonials who settled these areas were not stupid. They picked the same sites that developers today want. The Native Americans, they were smart too. That's why Maggie found all the arrowheads near here. Each new century people want to change what they built. However, they want the same strategic locations on river banks, same vistas, all that kind of thing. Bridges are always built at important spots. So when the rebuilding starts new owners run into the old construction and guys like me come out to see how important the artifacts are."

"That's where the trouble starts," said Maggie from her digging place.

"Sure. The historians and the developers are going to go round and round. "

"Most of the archaeologists feel there is no room for compromise," said Maggie.

Frank sat back on his heels. "Maggie was involved in that Southern Maryland controversy, yet you say you chose her to come down here. Why, Pastor?"

"Don't you think she is qualified?"

"Of course she is qualified. One of the best I know."

"Why should the controversy affect our choice on this site?"

Maggie added, "Frank, you thought that because I was fighting to save Confederate relics that I was a racist and unsuitable for work on a site that might have black history."

"I know you're not a racist but I thought there might be folks who would not understand what you did."

The Pastor interrupted, "I don't understand how I can see Maggie as a racist if she is just being a good historian. Her job is to find the relics and describe them and preserve them. What was it, some kind of site for Confederate spies during the Civil War? Just because it's not likely that I will be interested in the history of men who wanted to keep my family enslaved, doesn't mean I don't want her to do her job as best she can. It also doesn't mean that I can't respect her. I wanted her down here because of her reputation. I know she will do this job correctly and that she will fight to save anything that is significant, no matter what it is."

"You are thinking about my being politically correct, Frank, just like any modern college professor," said Maggie.

Frank smiled, "Pastor, I like the way you talk. I got to admit, I'm jealous of Maggie's freedom to fight for good research. "

"That's why I'm a little worried about what you are going to do down here, Frank," said the Pastor.

"We'll all do the right thing if we find anything. " He looked at the Pastor. "Jake seems to think you are kind of controversial too."

"We're all controversial in one way or another. "

The Pastor stood up and stretched. He had left his coffee on the ground near his pit and he reached for the cup. "Did you see the Terment monument out in the harbor?"

"Jake showed it to me."

"Bet he did. There were all these newly freed black folks living in the town after the Civil War. Instead of giving them jobs building the monument, the jobs went to returned Confederate soldiers. The irony of it was that the Terments bet their plantation on the outcome of the war."

"Bet their plantation? You mean, Peachblossom?"

" They got family members into high level positions in the Yankee government and army. After the Civil War was over, turned out the family members on the Northern side had title to all the land and wealth. They arranged transfers of the land back to the southern members of the family. The Terments never lost anything in that war. "

"The money they had invested in slavery?"

"They sold most all their slaves to cotton farmers down in Mississippi in the last five years before the war broke out. Like people sell out their shares before the stock market goes down, that's all it meant to them folks."

"Jake is the last of one of the oldest families in this part of the United States."

"Yes. That he is. The Terments were here in the early days. Two brothers. One of them had the money and the other one worked for him. The one with the money, his name was Henry Terment, went back to England, got sick and died. The brother that was here, Richard Terment, the ancestor of Jake Terment and his father, was the sole heir and inherited the money. Then Richard started buying up all the land around River Sunday and on the island, all he could get his hands on. He was the colonel of a local militia, kind of a paid private army." The Pastor smiled. "His money could not buy one thing though. Did you notice that the island is called Allingham Island?"

"You'd think that it would be called Terment Island," observed Frank.

"That's right, but the Allingham family settled the island long before the Terments arrived. Then, the Allinghams died and left the island to their infant son. The Terment who inherited all his brother's money, well, he somehow became the trustee for that Allingham infant. The child died and Richard Terment bought the Allingham property at auction. The Maryland colonial legislature investigated, it was so shady, but Terment bought them off. Turns out though that the colonial Maryland governor had more money and friends in England than Terment did. The governor wouldn't let him change the name of the island. Terment got the land but didn't get the name. It remained on the maps as Allingham Island. Terment owned all that land but he had to call the land by someone else's name. Knowing the Terments as I do, that must have aggravated them over the years. Jake has a lot of that family allegiance. I think that's why he named the new town Terment Town. Jake probably hopes that the place will become known under the town name and that will get rid of the island name forever. Then he will have accomplished something his ancestor couldn't do. Hard to believe that today a man like Jake even cares about his heritage, but he does. Probably the only thing he cares about. Yessir, I made a life study of that family, so I know Terments."

"Your name is Allingham, Pastor," said Maggie.

"My great grandfather was freed in the will of a man named Allingham. He also was given a small farm. His name was Jefferson too. When he was a slave that was the only name he had. After he was free, he took the name of his former owner. "

The Pastor smiled. "Of course, I don't recollect any white Allinghams would own to being kin to that branch of their family."

Maggie walked over and looked down at where the Pastor was digging. She stepped down beside him and squatted, her bare feet backed into one corner of the small pit.

"Pastor, I think you've found something." She worked for a few minutes, switching from trowel to paint brush. Bones appeared in the soil.

"Looks like the skeleton of a human adult. Frank, come take a look." Together, they worked swiftly, methodically. The skeleton was on its side, the skull was pressed to the chest, knees up to the skull. There were small patches of faded but still discernible dark blue cloth still attached to the bones and in the soil.

"A man. See the torso bones," said Frank.

"Likely Caucasian," Maggie said. "The nose cavity. It's hard to tell though. He may be a black man. Maybe one of your slave graves, Pastor."

"Yes," said the Pastor, excitement in his voice.

"There's another thing, though, Pastor. If it's a grave, especially African, there ought to be some jewelry, some food dishes even if there is no coffin."

"Yes, slave families buried their relatives that way." Maggie added, " We know from some of the plantation sites that have been researched."

"What about this cloth?" asked Frank.

"It's a strong material, thick, like a woolen."

"Let me look closely here for a minute or so, " said Frank. Maggie moved up to the surface to give him more room. "Unfortunately," he finally said, "the cloth and bones are located well above the strata associated with the ship." Maggie looked where he was pointing. "Yes. I'm afraid, Pastor, this skeleton is from a later time period," she affirmed.

"There looks to be a small bit of metal here." Frank brushed at the small glint in the soil.

"A metal buckle. Belt buckle, I think. See, it's near the torso, the waist area."

"There are letters on it."

"A "U" and an "S." What do you make of it, Maggie?"

"Military. A Federal soldier?" she suggested.

"Strange place to find a Federal soldier. I don't think there were any Civil War battles around River Sunday. The war was all fought to the south of here, across the Chesapeake Bay in Virginia."

The Pastor smiled. "I got an idea who this was," he said.

Chapter 6

Frank wiped the sweat from his face, dirt streaking his skin.
He had climbed out of the pit and sat cross legged on the topsoil
at the edge. The Pastor and Maggie hovered over the fragile
skeleton in the small space.

"I knew he was up here somewhere," said the Pastor. "I didn't
know he was in this marsh. I thought he was somewhere out on
the island."

He paused. "Who was he, Pastor?" asked Maggie.

"We were taught not to talk about him to the white people.
He disappeared in the summer of 1863. "

"You mean we won't find his story in the history books?"
smiled Maggie.

The Pastor brushed at the bones. "In those days this area of
Maryland was occupied by the Union Army. The black folk called
them liberators. The army was here to stop the supplies from up
north from coming down here and going to the Confederate
Army. I never did understand how companies in the north would
sell to the enemy in the south. But the Eastern Shore was a
natural route for smuggling like it had been since colonial days.
This fellow," he pointed to the skeleton, "he was one of the
liberators."

"I assume he was killed by the white locals," said Frank. "
There must have been a lot of Confederate sympathizers around
here."

"Everybody thought the southerners did something to him. The man disappeared right after the news of Gettysburg had come in. People thought it was local people taking revenge for the licking that the Southern Army took. What really happened was that a black man who worked near here killed the soldier."

"How did it happen?" asked Frank. " I mean, that's a little strange a black man killing a Union soldier in the middle of the Civil War."

"Yessir, it was. The black community kept the truth quiet for the same reason. You may be the first white people who have ever heard the real story. You see," he continued, "this soldier was stationed here in River Sunday. Soldiers didn't make much money so some tried to supplement their income. If a man had money he could have a good time. "

" So this fellow liked to have a good time," said Maggie.

The Pastor nodded. "The Yankees shipped south all the people they found that worked for the Confederacy. So this Yankee soldier decided he could use this as a kind of blackmail. He would go around and make the black folks who bred a few chickens give him some or he'd make up that they were aiding the Confederates. Then he'd send his chickens over to Baltimore to be sold in the market there. He'd get produce of all kinds but the one thing that folks around River Sunday were always good at breeding was good fat chickens. "

"How could he get away with that?"

" You had people who didn't have the courage to trust any white. Anyway, come along, he ran into one black farmer who was braver than the rest, that's what happened."

The Pastor continued. "This black farmer jumped him in the dark, jumped him and tied him up, pushed the soldier headfirst into the muck near the bridge and held him there until he suffocated. I thought the soldier was buried out on the island, as I said. I can see he was left right here in the marsh."

"Next day, the Union soldiers came looking for him. Cavalry rode up and down the county roads and searched a lot of the houses. They figured like you did that the southern sympathizers had killed him. There was some talk even that there was an invasion coming from Virginia. "

"You could have kept all this to yourself," said Frank.

" I guess I figured you folks would find out who he was. I'm sure you got ways."

Frank looked at the Pastor, suddenly realizing how the Pastor knew the story.

"The man who killed the soldier was a relative of yours."

"He was my great grandfather."

"We can't disguise this," said Maggie. "The story will come out."

"When the time comes, we need to tell about everything at this site. Everything. It's important," said the Pastor. "Whatever gets found no matter what history gets changed. Besides, my great grandfather was protecting his family. I got pride in that. His story should be told. "

Frank glanced at Maggie, realizing her dedication to accuracy. He sighed, "Well, I'm sorry that this wasn't one of the slave graves that you've been looking for, Pastor."

"Local coroner has to be contacted when we find human remains, " said Maggie.

"The man you want is Doc Bayne. He's up at the Health Department, " said the Pastor.

About an hour later a balding man with wire frame glasses, sweating, his sleeves rolled up, came and inspected the find. "Ain't nothing to bother folks about. Ain't no grave and it's too old to match up with any killing I ever heard of around here. You call me, you find someone a little younger." The fat man laughed at Frank's solemn face as he stood up to leave.

"Is there a report to be filed?" Maggie insisted.

"Oh, I'll report something for you. We ain't exactly fools down here, young lady."

The Pastor shrugged his shoulders as the official drove away.

"I thought he'd do all kinds of tests and hold up our work," said Frank.

"I wouldn't worry about it," said the Pastor. "He's got money in Jake's project just like most everyone else in town. He wouldn't do anything that might hurt the profits. He's got reason enough, though. He hates Jake, I can tell you that."

"Why?"

"His daughter died in childbirth on her sixteenth birthday. Died right in his arms. Most people in town knew Jake was the father. Jake didn't even show up at the hospital or the funeral. There got to be so much bad talk about Jake, Mister Terment invited Doc Bayne to Peachblossom. Way I heard it, Mister Terment asked him to help stop the rumors about Jake and the daughter. The Doc wouldn't sit down. He stood there and said to him, " You pack that boy of yours in a box and put him under six feet of Eastern Shore earth next to my dead girl and her baby and maybe that'll stop the rumors, Mister Terment."

Another car approached the farmhouse. They could see its roof above the hedges of honeysuckle, then flashes bouncing off the metal as it passed behind the boxwoods.

"It's a car like yours, Maggie. A state car."

"That's my boss," said Maggie.   She and Frank stood up from the test pit and started towards the farmhouse.   The car stopped and a well dressed woman got out and waved to Maggie.

"Hi, Cathy."

"Hello, Maggie. I thought it was hot in Baltimore, but, oh my, the humidity here in River Sunday. This is terrible." Cathy was a tall lanky woman, dressed in summer white. As they talked, Cathy changed her heels to a pair of low leather shoes. She opened the car door and put her suit coat on a hook in the back of the car. On the back seat Frank saw boxes of files he guessed were records of other sites.

"You're making the rounds today?" said Maggie.

"Same story, Maggie. Too many projects, not enough money, and I'm supposed to see everyone of them every week. It's been a bad day."

The two women did not look anything alike. Maggie was shorter, tanned with her hair tied up carelessly. Cathy's suit was carefully pressed, her blouse without wrinkles even in the intense heat. Maggie wore a dirty white tee shirt like the Pastor and Frank and her cutoffs were uneven and ragged. Cathy kept her polished shoes carefully out of the wet earth as she walked across the field, following behind a barefoot and unconcerned Maggie.

" You certainly get into your work," said Cathy, noticing Maggie's appearance.

Maggie looked back at Cathy, "You didn't hire me to look good on a site, Cathy."

"No, but you're a state employee. You should remember it. Remember the taxpayer and his or her opinion of the government employee."

"You are really upset about my appearance aren't you?" said Maggie, trying not to smile. "Can we take a look at the site?"

"Yes, of course, Maggie."

"We found a cannon and a skeleton."

"Oh. I'm sure you're handling it well as usual. " Cathy's attention shifted. "I must say hello to Pastor Allingham." She smiled at the Pastor, who stood up from his work to greet her.

"How are you, Mrs. Smith? It's nice to talk to you again," said the Pastor, shaking hands.

Cathy spoke with a wide, very friendly smile, "I hope you are enjoying your volunteer work. The Governor wanted me to send his regards."

"Well, that's very kind of him. Yes, I am enjoying my work here. " Frank was walking behind them. Cathy turned to him.

"You must be Doctor Frank Light." She held out her hand. Frank wiped his hand on his shorts and extended it to her.

"Sorry. A little dirty," he said as they shook hands.

"I got a call from Jake Terment recommending you for this job, Doctor Light."

"Yes, " said Frank.

"Well, what do you think of him?"

"Kind of impressive man," said Frank.

"I should say so. I think this is a good idea, don't you, Doctor Light? An expert like yourself can really help. We are so shorthanded. "

"Sure."

"Of course, Jake Terment will do all that has to be done. After all, his family has lived here for centuries. We're fortunate that the site of the old wreck was on his land. I'd much rather work with a landowner whose family has a record of caring about historic things. Why, that monument in the harbor alone. That monument is a testimony to the Terment family dedication to River Sunday and its history. "

"Jake Terment is all the time pushing to get us finished, Cathy," said Maggie. "I'm not sure he is very interested."

"Maybe if you had as much money at stake," replied Cathy, "You might feel the same way. Anyway, I'm sure he'll do the right thing on this site. I'd like to see your notes."

Maggie handed over her work journals. Cathy looked at them quickly and gave them back. Then Cathy walked slowly around the site, lips pressed together. Frank and the Pastor watched the two women.

"When the sunlight hits her hair a certain way, Maggie reminds me of a girl I knew a long time ago in Australia," said Frank.

"There's not a lot of women like her in this world," said the Pastor.

Cathy stopped and began to talk to Maggie. "Can you finish up, be back at the office tomorrow?"

"Finish up, no. I can be back in the office but then I'll have to return here."

"I don't want to have to send you back again. What do you have left to do, Maggie?"

"We want to try to find some more of the ship. We still don't understand enough about it."

Cathy leaned over to Maggie. Frank and the Pastor could hear what she was saying even though her voice was lowered. "The Pastor, is he happy? Are you taking care of him as I asked you to? For God's sake, don't let him work too hard in this sun. I don't want the office blamed for a black preacher having a heart attack."

"He seems to be enjoying the work," said Maggie.

"These graves he talks about, any sign of them?"

"We found a skeleton, but it's not one of the old slaves. It was a white man."

"Well, let him look all he wants," said Cathy. "Don't get the office involved in the slave graveyard business."

"What if we find the graves?"

"You still don't get it, do you, Maggie?"

"Maybe I don't."

"Well, let me explain it to you," said Cathy, staring at her. "You are a state employee in one of the smallest departments in the bureaucracy. A nice dedicated professional department which doesn't have enough budget, has to fight the other more needy programs in the legislature every year to get the budget to keep you and a few other professionals paid."

"You get paid too, Cathy," Maggie added.

Cathy went on without replying, " We have to keep the department going, Maggie. We have to try to do a reasonable job for the people who care that our work is done correctly and we also have to try to keep the department budget. So, don't get nervous in the service. When I tell you to get a job done and get back to the office, you listen to me and do as I say. Believe me, there's a lot has to be done to keep you working."

She grinned, "Just think how much it would cost to move all the graves in a slave graveyard to some other site. A lot of that cost would come from our budget, and take funds away from other projects. Do you want that?"

"I've always been a professional, " said Maggie, moving from foot to foot.

"Maggie," she said as she lowered her voice even more, "The Governor gives me my orders. On this job he said to please the preacher and to please the businessman. That's all he said but I knew he meant that both these men were very powerful and could cause him a lot of adverse political pressure. He expects to hear no complaints from Jake or the Pastor. As I see it, the best way to please both of them as well as the Governor is to have you both do as little investigating as possible here and to cover this site soon with tons of impermeable concrete."

She gave Maggie an understanding smile. "I've always tried to help the people who work for me. I keep you protected from the politics so you can do your job. This site might become very controversial if you archeologists find anything out of the ordinary. So, in order to please everyone, I find it useful not to care what is here. Frankly, I don't want you to find anything at all."

She winked at Maggie. "I'm sure you'll do the right thing here."

She walked over to where the Pastor was working. He was holding a small bone up in the air, examining it.   She did not ask to look at the bone. Instead she ruffled her papers to let the Pastor know she was standing there. When he turned around, she said, "Thank you for helping us out. I understand you're a pretty good volunteer archaeologist."

The Pastor stood up. "I'm trying to be some help. A little too old for some of this though," he smiled.

"I've told Maggie to keep an eye out for your graves. Of course, we'll have to stop our research when we have decided about the shipwreck. "

"I understand that. I appreciate your concern. The Governor has been very kind."

Cathy then turned to Frank. "I'll bet you're enjoying working for Jake Terment. Isn't he a delightful man? He looks just like he does on television except I think he looks a little shorter in person."

Frank smiled. She continued, "Well, I've got to get back to Baltimore. I'll be back again soon to look in on the project. I'm scheduled to meet with Jake Terment tomorrow." She turned to leave and then noticed the broken conglomerate in the grass.

"What's that?" she said.

"That's the cannon I mentioned to you earlier."

" Well," she said and continued walking, calling back to them, "Maybe what's left of it can be set over at the side of the new bridge as a marker of some kind."

The three of them watched as Cathy got into her car and started the engine. She waved as she drove down the lane.

Frank gave Maggie a friendly nudge. "Why is a bright person like you working for a political appointee like Cathy?"

"Why is a bright person like you working at the university? We got to eat like everyone else. Besides, it's interesting. There's more potential sites in Maryland than many other places. Just like everywhere else, it seems, most of the time the sites get concrete poured over them no matter what we think might be there. We learn a little each time though. I keep hoping that I'll find a site that I can study for a while, spend some time with, study. That's why I became an archaeologist. One good site would make the effort all worthwhile."

"I guess, "said Frank.

"Cathy isn't the slightest bit interested in this site, Frank."

"I overheard a lot of what she said," said the Pastor.

"She sure was interested in you, Pastor."

"The Governor wants the votes of my little congregation next election. It's the real estate lobby versus the minority lobby."

"She wants it finished," said Maggie, looking out at the site.

"Why bring me here if everybody has made up their minds already and no body is interested no matter what we find here?" said Frank.

"They figure that you'll just go along, add authority to their move," said the Pastor.

"Is that what you are, Frank?" asked Maggie. "Jake's insurance policy?"

Frank didn't answer her. They went back to digging. Frank was working at Location Q, Maggie still at T, the Pastor working on the remains of the soldier near H.

"Frank, you remind me of my parents," said Maggie

"How?"

"The way you still think that Jake Terment is somehow OK. My parents would do that, put off a decision about people. Being in Vietnam didn't teach you anything. I think you've agreed to put up with anything that comes along, right or wrong. "

"You think I'm kind of hardened?"

She didn't answer him directly. "My mother and father were flower children. The only reason they stopped living in a shack in the woods was that I was getting older, needed to go to school, needed clothes and shoes. There were other families there. We ran around naked in the summer. It was like a village. I remember the ramshackle house that my father built, like a painting with all the strange colors and the octagonal windows. Then, my father gave up on the lifestyle. He started wearing shoes. He went to work in a hardware store and was so good at it that the day came when he bought out the owner. Even then he managed to give away goods to poor people. He never chased people for bills that they owed. My mother was the same, so wonderfully competent and perfectly willing to spend her energy on anybody who needed her."

Frank smiled. "Maggie, I never even knew my parents' real name. They changed it after they came to the United States. They are both dead so I guess I'll never know. I think they helped to kill a lot of German soldiers during the war. " He brushed intently at a spot of dark soil.

"They took the name of Light when they were allowed to emigrate to this country, " he continued. "The name was in a copy of the music for the Star Spangled Banner. My mother learned the song. She liked where it said the "dawn's early light." My family name was from the song and then my first name was after President Franklin Roosevelt. I don't remember them ever telling me the original European names. They never even talked their old language."

"Why?"

"They hated the place they came from. Whatever home they had was destroyed in the war. They had been fighters, probably underground soldiers. Their bodies were covered with scars. Their wounds caused them serious medical problems when I was growing up. They had a pass to go to the Veterans Hospital. I would ask them but they never told me how they got the scars.

" My father had a big knife that he kept in a box in their bedroom closet. I sneaked a look at it one time and I thought I saw stains on the blade. I grew up thinking that those were bloodstains from when my father killed enemy soldiers.

"One night my mother was drinking wine and talking a lot. She told me about a night during the war when a great number of children were freed from a concentration camp near her village. The camp had been attacked by the underground. After the children ran into the woods, three guards were killed by hand to hand combat by a village man and his wife. The couple then had to flee soldiers who hunted them for months. She began to tell how the man and woman almost starved to death and how the woman's own baby died of hunger. My father told her to stop talking, that he did not want to hear the story. The next day, I went to look at that knife again but it was gone. I never saw it again.

" My father was a cabinetmaker. I have some of his furniture. Beautiful. He was an artist. She was too. She helped him build the furniture. I remember when their customers used to come to the house and sit in the kitchen and talk about the furniture. They had many wealthy clients. I overheard my father asking one of them to write a letter to help me get into college. My father would never tell me about things like that. He did not like to admit that he ever took a favor from anyone.

"My parents were the reason I went into history as a career. They owned every book they could buy about the United States. They taught me about this country, about American history. Every day when I was little they would quiz me about America, about the Presidents, about the American heroes. To them everything the country did was right. Europe was always wrong. "

" Later I got into archaeology. I began to find out that what actually happened here was very different from the history that had been written. Heroes were really scoundrels, and scoundrels were really heroes. Archaeology didn't lie. It laid bare how people actually behaved. There was no argument with an artifact hidden under the soil that no one has tampered with. I did not talk with my parents about my discoveries in archeology. They were happy with their own view of history."

"Then Vietnam came," Maggie said.

"My parents were very patriotic. They thought it was their duty to support me going to the war. My parents insisted it was a just war because they believed simply that the United States was always right. Maybe I thought too much about my mother's story of those children escaping the concentration camp. Anyway I convinced myself I had to go to Vietnam."

"My folks," Maggie said, " could never decide which side was right, which one to cheer for. It was against their nature to choose. In the beginning I worked for the Viet Cong in the student marches at my school. My parents would watch and look sad about it all. Then when the soldiers came home and some of them were so terribly wounded I worked in the Veterans hospital helping out. They were sad about that too."

She smiled. " Maybe my flower children parents are why I like flowers so much. Children too. I like children." She looked at Frank.

"I like roses," said Frank. "I respect them."

"Why?"

"They overcome the thorns."

"You have something to learn about roses," Maggie said

The Pastor called, "Should we try to lift out these soldier bones?"

"No, leave them. Come help me here. We need to work on the shipwreck itself. We can come back to that area if there's time." Frank scratched his neck. "That waterman, Soldado, said he would be here to take us down the river."

"You think looking at those other wrecks might help figure out this one?"

"I'd like to see what those hulls look like. That could help us direct our work to the best spots on this wreck."

They worked silently for a while, the Pastor digging at the opposite corner from Frank. The Pastor spoke first, "Let me tell you about my family. When my father and mother were let go from Peachblossom, we moved back to River Sunday. We lived upstairs at the church where I preach. My father and mother were hired as the custodians. He cleaned the place, repaired it, and she cooked for the itinerant preachers. Then my parents died suddenly. My brother and me were taken care of by the visiting preachers and some of the church members who looked in on us. They did all they could for us but they had their own families to take care of. It was cold in that old church. In those days there was not much insulation just boards on the walls. In the summer there were all kinds of bugs. We got along except that we were always hungry. Most of the time my brother would steal some of the food left out on Sunday morning for the church breakfast. He would sneak it back up stairs and hide it and he would share the food with me during the week. At first I wouldn't eat any of it because I said we shouldn't be stealing. I said that the preachers had told us not to steal. Then I got too hungry at night and I started to eat.

"My brother, Lincoln, had an idea that Jake would give us some food. He thought that because Jake was a little kid and little kids care a lot about other people, that he would be generous. Lincoln figured we could get enough food for a week. So we set off in the morning, walked all the way out to the island and up to the big house and knocked on the door. It was cold, I am telling you. A wet wind was blowing hard off the river, and my feet were just about frozen in some old red rubber boots I had. My brother was cold too but he stood there and rang that front doorbell over and over. He wouldn't give up.

"Finally the big old wood paneled door opened just a crack and we saw Jake peering out at us, his arm reached over his head like this." The Pastor demonstrated with his arm stretched upward. "That arm, you see, was holding the doorknob. Jake, he smiled at us through the crack and said, ' What you want, Lincoln?'

"My brother said, 'Jake, we're hungry and we want some food.'

"So Jake said, 'All right, you wait here,' and he closed the door. Just closed the door. We waited there in that cold for this little fellow to come back. My brother was smiling then like he had won something.

"Byembye Jake comes back to the door. We hear him turning the knob inside and then it opens up a little bit more. Jake's hand comes out in the cold air and in the palm of his hand is a handful of corn flakes. Then he says,' You better not eat too much because I've heard my father say that black folks won't work when they got too much food in their bellies.' Then he drops the food on the snow on the step and slams the door. Well, my brother, he looks at me and we both reach down and pick up every one of those flakes and just gobble them down we were so hungry. Then we set off for home. My brother told me then he said he knew I was cold but that he was warmed up by his hating Jake.

Maggie nodded.

"I lost my brother a year after that. He got caught stealing food by one of the preachers and he was thrown out of the church building. He went off to Baltimore and I heard in a while that he died up there in the children's jail. That was the end of my family till my wife come along. "

The Pastor brushed at the ground with one of the excavating brushes. "I thought about that all my life, that kid and his corn flakes. "

He paused. " I'm hopeful though," he said softly. "Always hopeful. People around here might just surprise me. They may turn on Jake, throw him out of town with all his money. Just tell him they don't want it. One of these days they might."

Frank pointed to a hard curved object coming out of the soil under his scraping. He was working into a new area. "Test pit Q is finally showing something. I'm surprised there hasn't been more. This is right where the main cargo hold should be."

"What did you find?" asked the Pastor, as he leaned closer to Frank, trying to see.

"It's a pipestem, part of an old clay tobacco pipe."

"What does it tell us?"

"Could have belonged to a sailor. Here, we can date the pipe with some precision. " Frank reached in his pocket for a small steel ruler. " OK, " he said as he measured the bore. "You see, Pastor, there was a fellow named Binford who developed a formula for archeologists to date tobacco pipes. Pipe bores got smaller from the Seventeenth to the Eighteenth Centuries. So if I measure this bore, " he calculated some figures on a piece of paper, " Then multiply a formula, Binford tells me the age of the pipe." He paused as he looked at the paper. "Well, this is not very helpful for you, Pastor."

"Why?" said the Pastor.

"This pipe is dated about 1700."

"The slave graveyard," said Maggie.

" I see what you mean, " said the Pastor. "Slaves were not imported into the Eastern Shore until then. For this to be their graveyard it would have to be dated later, 1720, maybe 1750, giving them time to live for a while then die. The strata where we're digging is too old for a graveyard."

"The pipe is not definitive. We'll keep looking. It does tell us about the ship in here. It's an old wreck if I'm reading this pipe correctly."

The tawny cat reappeared and was standing at the edge of Frank's area.

"Cat knows something we don't," said the Pastor.

"That cat understands it's too hot to work," joked Frank.

"Cat might know more than you think," said the Pastor, staring at the animal and leaning down to stroke its light orange fur. The cat purred. Frank stood up." I'll get the camera and take a record shot of the clay pipe in its site." He set the fragment back into the soil strata where it had been. "Say, I just thought of something."

"What?" said Maggie.

"Maybe that tobacco smoke I smelled came from this pipe."

Maggie threw a handful of muck at him and he ducked, laughing. The cat jumped into the pit and sniffed at the pipe, rubbed against Frank's bare leg for a moment and then bounded away into the high grass.

"One thing I learned from my father," said Maggie, watching the cat and Frank. "If an animal likes you, you're probably all right."

Chapter 7

It was the time of day when the heat was so heavy the insects did not move. Maggie, Frank, and the Pastor watched as Soldado drifted his craft into a mooring. Their hands tried to shield their eyes against the brilliant river glare.

"If Soldado said he'd be here, I was pretty sure he'd come."

The Pastor continued, "He'll take us out around the island. You can get an idea of the land here. Then we'll come up on the wrecks from down the river ."

As they prepared to wade out to the boat, Frank asked the Pastor, "Tell me more about Soldado."

"Soldado goes back a long time around here. Most of that time he's hated Jake Terment. Soldado and his mother used to live out on the island. It was a little house, tar paper walls, just a mile or so over the bridge. His mother came from Mexico. The Yucatan. She was a very beautiful woman when she was younger. Very tall. She worked in one of the Terment migrant labor farms. Soldado was born in the camp. Some say his father came from around River Sunday. Some even say it was Mister Terment himself. Jake's father did provide her the little house, helped her with her citizenship. Of course, Mister Terment never really let go of anything he gave. The house had a large mortgage.

"We were all kids together, growing up on the Island. When Soldado was a teenager, he was a lot bigger than the rest of us, me, Jake, Billy, the other kids that we played around with. Soldado knew stories of famous sailing ships . He wanted to go to China, he said. He used to make up games. He'd pretend to be the captain of a clipper ship and we were the crew. Then we'd go into his warm house and his mother would make us molasses sandwiches, nodding her head with a toss of her black hair and smiling at Soldado making up all these ship stories. "

The Pastor smiled. "There were these ship models in his house. Jake wanted to be captain too but in those days we could vote for who we wanted and we always chose Soldado. Of course Jake didn't like anyone being in charge over him so he and Soldado were always fighting. Jake was smaller and Soldado used to just hold him by the shoulder and let him flail his fists at the air. One day Jake sneaked into Soldado's house when no one was home. He broke one of the models. Then he went and showed some of the pieces to Soldado. That model sat inside the front door on a yellow, black and white table and it was Soldado's favorite. You should have seen it, Frank. Anyway I think that was the last time the two of them even tried to get along, playing or anything else. Soldado threw Jake hard against the wall. The nails holding on the tarpaper cut Jake's face. That was how he got that scar over his eye."

"In a few years Soldado went off to the merchant marine. He was on a ship that got sunk during a typhoon. He helped save some of his fellow sailors . The town of River Sunday gave him a parade when he came home. I remember seeing him in the convertible with Miss River Sunday, the high school girl who won the Fire Department beauty contest that year. All the ministers of the white churches and the mayor were there in cars too. Maybe there might have been one or two black preachers too. Not me, you can be sure. In those days, my church was outlawed by both the blacks and the whites. After a while Soldado went back to sea and commanded freighters for a long time. He finally retired and came home. That's when he and Jake went at it again. Jake's company was buying up the land. Jake's father had died and Jake wanted all the island. The development had not been planned yet. Jake was just doing what he always did, trying to control everything. Anyway, Soldado didn't want to sell. For one thing his mother was getting right along. He wanted her to live out her time on the island. Jake's people wouldn't go away. They found a way to get the property anyway by taking over the old mortgage at the bank. They found a way to push for payment, money that Soldado and his mother couldn't handle. Soldado was not alone in getting bought out. Jake's company found mortgages on tractors or buildings that they could foreclose and then forced sales of many farms out there. I heard that folks mysteriously had their dairy cattle get sick and die or their chicken houses catch fire. Soldado didn't have a lot of cash. His retirement was a pension from the steamship company that he had served with. He had been a captain when he retired and he had saved fairly good money, but it wasn't enough to handle paying off his mother's mortgage. Terment's father had made that mortgage on the shack so big there was no way Soldado and his mother could clear it. So the day came when Jake moved him out. Jake even came down to River Sunday that morning to see the job done and stood right on Soldado's porch while Soldado had to pack his stuff, the models, everything, and take it out of the old house. Jake was there with Billy and three or four other police officers. Jake gave the house to the River Sunday fire department to burn down, to use for a practice house fire to train their new volunteer fire fighters.

"A few months later Soldado's mother died. He blames Jake for her death. Says losing that little house, as poor as it was, broke her heart. These days, he lives off his pension and has his water finding business. Like most of the men around here he does a little crabbing and oystering. He has a room he rents in River Sunday but most of the time he lives on his boat. I'm one of the few folks he still talks to. He says that all the people in River Sunday work one way or another for Jake Terment."

They came to the side of the boat. Soldado was on his knees working on the engine, the engine cover on its side to the left of him. He did not look up.

"I was over to your site and made some marks where you might want to dig," he said.

"We noticed," said Frank. "We appreciate your help. We want to thank you for taking us up to see the old ships." Soldado still did not look up.

The salt smell of the river mixed with the odor of rotting seaweed. That stink drifted around them in the heat. Soldado walked over to the side of the boat where the steering lever was located. He pressed a small black button and the engine turned over and began its slow throb. Exhaust smoke puffed from the tall stack into the air above the boat. Then the smoke, as slight as it was, drifted down on Frank and the others, and mixed a new pungency with the river smell.

Maggie sneezed.

"You all right there, little lady?" asked Soldado.

Maggie smiled and nodded.

With his boat entering the channel, Soldado began to steer for the bridge. "We'll run up around the island."

The throbbing engine made tremors in the surface of the coffee in the cups. Maggie took her coffee and climbed up on the top of the small cuddy cabin. She pulled her tee shirt up up under her breasts and tied it so the sun was on her skin. She took the white string off her hair and her long blonde hair fell past her shoulders. Then she leaned back on her elbows on the cuddy roof. The slight breeze from the forward motion of the boat flicked her hair upward so that it served as a burgee for the boat.

The boat moved under the rusty center span of the old bridge. The span arched over them about ten feet above. The motor resounded as the craft went under the span, loud echoes pumping against Frank's ears. There was darkness. The sunlight created a pattern of shade lines from the grillwork above in the road, the lines raining like prison bars over the boat. . Frank could see decades of bird nest history on the ledges of the old concrete bridge supports. A gull, surprised and angry, flew off with a sudden whipping of wings.

"You want to look at these fracture cracks," Soldado said over the throb of the engine. "Terment got himself into a bind. All his talk about building on the island so the town decided to stop fixing up this bridge. Just let it fall apart. The mayor and the rest of them in River Sunday figured they'd get Jake to build a new one. Kind of foxed him. Jake has to replace it whether he wants to or not. It's too worn out to support all that new traffic coming over to his houses. Didn't seem too smart of him if you ask me but he's the big businessman, not me. I just run a crab boat. I expect if he'd been a little smarter, made them keep it repaired, he might not have had to build no new bridge, might not have had to go near that swamp at all. "

"That's what I wondered from the beginning," said Frank. "Why couldn't he have built the bridge, if it was so important, somewhere else along the river?"

"From what I understand," said Maggie, her words drifting back to the others in the middle of the boat, "This bridge was put here because it was always the simplest place to build, the shortest distance. Other places along the river were much wider and deeper with more soft bottoms and currents."

"You're right," said Soldado. "He's got to build it here or not at all. For one thing the other folks along the river won't let him build anywhere else. Second, he owns this area here. His neighbor, she won't let him build on her land." He pointed to the Pond house, back under trees. "She's in there plotting how to muck up old Jake, I bet," chuckled Soldado. "Her old man left her a ton of money. Just the other day I heard another story about her. Years ago, this fellow told me, she'd go into the Chesapeake Hotel during the hunting season, November, December, when all the tourists were in River Sunday, coming in to hunt geese and ducks out on the Nanticoke and on North Creek. In the hotel the hunting guides left their brochures all over the tables so the tourists could get their numbers and call them up to arrange hunting trips. Well, Birdey'd go in there and pick up the brochures, carry them outside and throw them into the trash. Then she got all the bird watchers, peepers, to do the same thing. Got so there had to be a guard in there to keep them from taking the brochures. They started going right up to the tourists and giving them material on not hurting animals. It got so the tourists were canceling their reservations. Finally the guides just stopped contacting their clients in the hotel. She made it a lot harder for them to do business. Most of them guides don't dare tell where they meet their clients, afraid she'll show up. She's got a mind of her own, she does."

A large Coast Guard channel marker was ahead of them to port. Its green mass strutted into the sky with a blinker light and small railing on top. The shoreline on both sides of the Nanticoke River at this point were covered with small pines and bushes. In addition, there was earth of red and brown colors. Roots of decayed trees were caving into the river or already lay buried in the shallow water of the river's edge. Ugly snags struck into the air, bare of leaves. Where Frank could see beyond the masses of honeysuckle and brambles, he had quick glimpses of tassles waving in rich cornfields.

"This swamp probably hasn't changed since the Native Americans were here, before the Europeans came," said Frank.

Soldado corrected him. "Before them, there were the visitors from the south. I know, because my mother descended from those southerners. They were Mayan nobles, warriors," said Soldado. "My mother taught me that the Mayans traveled here two thousand and more years ago. "

He glanced at Frank. "Long before the Europeans came to plant tobacco, the place on the mainland where the bridge to the island begins was where the tribes from the north would meet to trade with the Nanticoke. The Mayans would come there too. These northern people were eventually called the Iroquois and the Susquehannock. In time there was war between them. The Nanticoke fought the Susquehannock and Iroquois for many years. There was a final battle right here at this place in which the Nanticoke were completely vanquished. My mother said that in her magic she could still hear the screams and see the blood of the dying children. In their defeat the Nanticoke were forced to give up their children to the northerners. This place where you dig was where the children were taken prisoner and were carried north as slaves. The slave bands were put on their arms and these captives never came home again. It became a place of misery where no Nanticoke would visit or live. "

"If that's true, that explains all the arrowheads we found, " said Maggie.

Soldado looked at her solemnly, "You dig enough you'll find the Mayan things too. "

The craft chugged further along. After about twenty minutes, the river came to a fork.

"We'll go up to port and head towards the Chesapeake Bay and open water," said Soldado.

Frank could see that the Nanticoke River continued inland and narrowed as it extended away from them into the backcountry of the Eastern Shore. As they turned to port, the craft entered a small deep creek, about two hundred yards across. On both sides, there were the same pine trees and hedges and endless swampland stretching away from the riverbank.

"We're on North Creek. You're in the middle of the wetland we know as Wilderness Swamp. This swamp has always been famous for its black duck and canvasback hunting. Supposed to be the best duck gunning on the whole Eastern Flyway. The birds come in from rafting out on the Chesapeake Bay and feed in here on the wild rice in the shallows. The hunters wait in their duck blinds in the marsh grass and reeds. In the old days, market gunners from Baltimore would hunt in here with great guns that looked like howitzers. They could kill several hundred birds with one shot. "

A breeze picked up. Soldado raised his voice high to be heard. "The creek makes Allingham Island honest, makes it into a true island." They watched to port as the boat moved slowly past the marsh, about twenty yards offshore from the first of the green reeds poking up in the water.

Sodado went on, "This area is the reason Mrs. Pond is so anxious to keep the island from being built up with lots of houses. The sewers from those new houses will kill the wetland and all the birds and animals and insects that live in it."

"I've found that the nature folks care more about the animals and the insects than they do about any people," said the Pastor. "I could never get any support from them for helping people."

"It's beautiful here," said Maggie, dipping her toes into the river and making small ripples. "It's the last of the wet areas along the Eastern Shore of the Chesapeake Bay. The real estate developers have built on every other one. "

The wetland stretched back several hundred yards and stopped at a cliff that was higher by twenty feet over the swamp grass. The breeze blew currents of air which moved over the grass like waves. A dense smell of life came from the grass.

"Smelled the same way ten million years ago when humans started coming out of that kind of muck. You go in there, " Soldado continued, "You'll come across little pot holes and trails where the muskrats and the other animals live. It's like a city in the grass. We go in there and we can't survive like the wildlife can. Boots, bare feet, mosquito juice, it doesn't matter. We get beat halfway across the swamp and we have to come back. Sometimes

I think that's why we destroy these wetlands because we can't live in them and the animals can and we don't like letting the animals have anything on us. "

Two mallard ducks, male green and female brown, got up and skimmed the creek as they lofted together. The wake from the boat barely kissed the marsh grass yet made the fragile water reeds tremble. Soldado's workboat approached the open area of the Chesapeake Bay. The water under the boat was changing from a slightly rippled current to a movement of slow swells, lifting and dropping the narrow hull. After several swells hit the boat, Maggie almost lost her balance and then pulled her feet out of the water. In the distance a harbor tug was heading up the Bay to the right, its exhaust boiling a dense black smoke into the blue sky.

"That's channel water out there," said Soldado. "No seaweed to foul our prop. We'll head south along the island." The shoreline gradually changed to sandy beach, backed up by lonely trees and fencerows. Some of the island farms came into view behind lines of more trees, the barns and farmhouses floating on cornfield seas.

"Lots of corn grown here for the poultry business. Big chicken plants further south. Fortunes have been made in the little creatures. People got to eat. When I was still on an ocean deck I carried lots of them to Africa, breeding stock for the chicken business over there."

A mansion, white columns against red orange brick walls, with a sweeping lawn and ancient trees carefully arranged by some ancient plan stood out from the rest of the houses on the island. At the right of the mansion was a small cove extending into the island abut two hundred feet. On the left of the cove there was a large wharf where the white Terment yacht was moored along with a small Boston whaler runabout.

Soldado pointed at the mansion. "That's Peachblossom, the Terment house, " he said. "To the right are pilings where in colonial days the tobacco ships used to land for cargos of island tobacco. Jake has to keep it dredged out all the time because it silts so much around here. There's something you might be interested in." Soldado pointed to great trees a few hundred feet down the shoreline from the yacht, the size of the green trees showing well the many centuries they had stood and grown big with life.

"Those are the trees where the Monarch butterflies land. You see them flies in the fall when they fly through River Sunday heading south."

"Hard for a butterfly to get a good lawyer," Frank chuckled.

"You got that right." Above them a small red airplane began to circle. Maggie pointed to it just as it began to trail orange smoke.

"That pilot's almost as old as I am. He keeps to himself like he's still fighting out in the Pacific.. I'm one of the few people he'll still talk to. Flies out of his own field. Just a runway through a cornfield with one shed to keep his plane. He made ace flying Hellcat fighters shooting down Japanese Zeroes out in the Pacific. Came home to his farm and hasn't gone much out of the county since."

The plane circled the first letter of its message into the blue sky. A "B" took shape. The mouth of the Nanticoke River appeared, signifying the end of the island. Where the river poured out into the Bay there was a slight chop and the spray began to soak Maggie.

"You getting too wet up there?"

"No, " she said, " I love it." Frank could not help noticing how her tee shirt was soaked, fully outlining her well shaped breasts. Soldado steered his boat near a steel buoy to port, its anchor chain tangled with seaweed, the rusty channel marker rising and falling with the swells. A fish hawk nest was in the top of the buoy. The hawk got up and flew around and threatened to dive on them as they went by.

"Osprey's just trying to tell us to stay the hell away from her children in that nest. Can't blame her," said Soldado. He pointed ahead. "That's Stoke's Point. Some call it Fort Stokes. There's the fortifications for an old War of 1812 outpost there. Then, if we go by Stoke's Point we come around into the harbor of River Sunday. We're not going that far. We'll head back up this side of Stoke's Point."

As they went up the Nanticoke River Frank could see off to the right three hulks of large ships. Soldado began to describe the wrecks. "Here's what folks call the wheat or lumber schooners. These wrecks been here as long as I can remember. I guess this is what Jake is trying to tell you he's got up there by the bridge. Anyway I'll bring her on by and you folks can go in and study them all you want. They stopped using these sailing ships for carrying wheat when the highways got built and the trucks started hauling to the processing plants. The owners just left these hulks in here to die."

"Maybe Jake is right," said Maggie. "It just seems like our shipwreck is older than a hundred years."

"I wouldn't believe anything Jake tells you," said Soldado. "However, I do know this. You come back here in a few years and these wrecks will look just like what you got up there."

Soldado anchored the boat against the current so her bow was pointed toward the channel. The water was very shallow. Maggie and Frank waded from the stern into the muddy shoreline to study the wrecks. Above them, trailing its cloud of orange smoke, the airplane completed its second letter, a " T."

The arching bow of the first wreck was pointed towards the channel as if its hull was still straining to be free. Tension in the old boards was still trying to spring lose from rusty fastenings, from the bending and clamping of its straight fibers to make the curves. Two masts stood proud and there was a stub of a bowsprit. The trailboards and railings were all washed away. Inside this wreck some of the deck remained. Frank and Maggie agreed that they would not try to walk on the old deck. It looked far too rotten. All of the wood below the tide line was covered with the green and brown growths of the thousands of water creatures infesting the hulk. The two of them examined the frame and planking structure of the bow, which was ten feet above them. There was nothing but slippery seaweed growth to climb on..

"One of us has got to get up there to look at the bolts and fastening patterns."

"Here, get up on me," said Frank.

Frank helped Maggie climb up on his shoulders. They lost their footing and fell into the water twice. Soldado and the Pastor laughed at them, giving advice. Finally Maggie climbed up and was holding on the ship framing, her bare feet leaving wet prints on Frank's bare shoulders.

"Anything for archeology," said Frank. After studying the worn timbers for a few minutes, she looked down. "She's built entirely different than our wreck, Frank. There's almost nothing the same. Timber size, planking, fastening methods. This, I would think, is a later type of construction."

They waded over to the second hulk, rusty chains linking it to the third wreck so that the bows of both were side by side. This hull had charred railings as if it had been in a fire.

Maggie climbed up on Frank's shoulders again. "I can see some handmade spikes here, Frank, " Maggie reported.

"That may mean late Eighteenth Century. The lines still seem to be different. We don't have the same apple shaped bow that we have at the site. These boats have sharper bowlines, entry lines more like Nineteenth Century clippers."

They waded back to Soldado's boat. The soft bottom caused them to lose their footing several times.

"He's finished writing," the Pastor pointed to the sky. Frank looked up. A wavy line of mist spelled the word BTRFLY.

"Like I say, he fights wars," said Soldado.

"There's a lot of them to fight," said the Pastor, thoughtfully, as he watched the letters vaporize away to nothing. Soldado got his boat underway and they moved slowly up the river. After a few minutes Frank noticed a fire blackened building on the right bank, hidden behind a row of loblolly pines.

"That's the cannery I was accused of burning down, " said the Pastor.

"It's a large building," said Frank. "Looks like some of it is still useable."

"Not much. By the time the fire department finished there was nothing left of the wiring and improvements we had done. The walls were weakened. The fire destroyed the building as a space for ours or any other business. You can't see it from here but the roof on the other side is completely open.

The Pastor went on, " Back when I came home from the war, the other men from River Sunday who had been in Vietnam, some black, some white, some Hispanic, they came to see me. They had saved their mustering out pay and they were waiting for me to return. I remember it was a hot day like today."

"One of them said, 'Pastor, we have this money and we want to start a company. We been fighting for free enterprise so we want it ourselves. We want to do something with the money, something that will free us from working for the people who have always given us orders. If we start a company of our own we can have that freedom, work for ourselves, and also make enough money to live here in River Sunday. We need to make a living but we don't want to be in the position of losing our jobs whenever some rich white man feels like firing us to save his profits. We need our own company. Will you help us put it together?'"

"The young man talking to me, we all called him Chipmunk. Nervous like. Always tapping his fingers. Played good drums. As for me, I had never done much business before. All of us grew up doing a little trading but most of us did not have much of the finer training in books and accounts, the kind of know how needed to run a first rate business . We all knew, however, that the key to our future success was economic power, green power. We knew that we had to have money to be free. The white people in River Sunday had always been in charge of most of the farms and little assembly factories and the lumberyards. They were the people who had traditionally owned and run those businesses. So we first had to find something to do to make money . We sat around and decided that our best product was going to be ourselves. We all knew how to work hard. We just wanted to get the money out of that hard work into our own pockets. We decided that we were going to sell our services to whoever wanted them. We agreed that the money would come back to the company, not directly to us. I remember we also agreed that we would use the money to help each other, not to become like the same people we wanted to escape."

"You guys banked the profits," said Frank. "Go on. I'm listening."

"We wanted to bank the profits. That's right. So we started out. We ran the business from the church. The congregation helped out. Byemby the business started making money. If someone wanted to have a roof fixed, there was our company and our roofers and there was the competition. If someone wanted a television fixed there was our company and there was the competition. Many of the white owned businesses in River Sunday had black employees and after a while some of those black employees threw in with us. It took a lot of courage on their part to leave other jobs and come with us, but they did. It got so we had a lot of the trained workers and a lot of the jobs to be had

·

around River Sunday and the other close by towns. We had white workers too. This wasn't any black only business. Nossir. It was a business of the people. Like we'd say, it was by the people and for the people. Keep in mind, too, that all our employees were stockholders and, besides their salaries, they started getting dividends. They got part of the profit, some of these people, for the first time in their lives, getting more than a little envelope at the end of the week with some money. They had ownership. It meant a lot."

"What was the name of the business?"

"General Store. After a while we had outgrown the church building. We rented the old cannery building that Mister Terment still owned near River Sunday. The Terments ran that cannery all through World War Two and the Korean War, canning tomatoes for the Army . When the California farmers started growing cheaper tomatoes , the Eastern Shore canneries like the Terment one in River Sunday just went broke. The army contracts moved out there and that was the end of the cannery business. The building had been vacant for years when we went into it. Jake's father wouldn't sell the building to us. He would only rent it on a short term basis. We had the money but he wouldn't take it.

"Why?"

"Control. His type of white man did not want us black people to own anything in what he thought was his town." He went on, "Then the trouble came. I remember it was late one night. I was closing up, standing there in the dim light in my office in a back room of the cannery building. I had sent everyone home. Everyone had been working so hard. I thought I saw a person in the shadows outside my office window. The window looked out over the back of the cannery area, into some brush and then the river, maybe twenty yards to the bank of the Nanticoke. "

" So I went outside to see what it was. We didn't have a watchman. We had grown so fast and we thought we knew everyone in town. We didn't think we had anything to worry about. We were wrong.

"Inside the old cannery we had set apart offices, filled the rooms with accounting machines, file cases, typewriters, all the records. We even had the first IBM computer in River Sunday, one using the paper cards. Since the building had been a cannery, we had to take all the machinery out of it. The parts of those food processing machines were piled up out back of the building. There were also some junk cars there. I think one of them was a Terment truck that had carried the tomatoes from the Puerto Rican and Mexican migrant worker farms. It was there worn out with flat tires, vines growing through the open bracketed out windshield."

"My mother probably rode in that truck few times," said Soldado.

"There was lots of scrap metal and wooden crates stacked up and lots of briars, I remember the briars pulling at me as I climbed back of the building and followed a small footpath in the darkness. Ahead, I saw a man running away from me. He had seen me first. I heard his feet crashing into the trash back there. He was maybe a hundred feet ahead of me down behind the building, his shape showing up on and off as it was lighted by each window he passed.

" I knew right away it was Jake Tement. I knew the way he ran, how he kind of bent sideways when he ran, like he was trying to hide. I called out, 'What you doing back here, Jake?' There was no answer. Then the running figure was gone. There was only the noise of a few insects buzzing. I could smell the river."

"It was then the blast of flame screeched up the wall of that old wooden building, pieces of wood flying off in the air towards the river, landing with steam in the water, the flames accelerating towards the sky with so many sparks like stars, all the new paint we had put on that building peeling off in burning sheets."

"I knew Jake's lurk. I knew him from when I worked up at Peachblossom for his father when I was a little kid. I knew it was Jake because the Terments like to burn things. That's the way they do."

" All this was before Jake became a celebrity businessman?" asked Frank.

"Yes," said the Pastor. "He was just starting out, still working for his father in River Sunday in those days. I knew it was my word against his and it was his father's building. What could my business partners and me do? We had no records. They were all burned up. We had great losses but we could not document them. All the records burned up. The next day all over River Sunday white people, many of them our former customers, talked about how foolish we were to use a black electrician on that building, how we should have got a good firm to come in and make it right, how the old wiring always starts fires, how all the black homes around River Sunday always had bad fires because the black folks wouldn't fix old wires, how they were too ignorant to fix old wiring. We had to listen to all of it."

The Pastor was quiet for a few moments, his face showing the pain of the memories. Then his eyes brightened. "You ought to come down to my church office sometime after this project is settled. I'll show you the picture they took of me with President Lyndon Johnson at a big luncheon in Washington at the White House. Yessir. We got an award from the Office of Economic Opportunity for our work at General Store."

"Nobody ever investigated the fire?"

"Mercy, Frank. In River Sunday in those days, to get any real law, to get anything changed or done, you had to have whatever it was you wanted done be something that everyone around here wanted done. Mister Terment and his son were part of the majority. If they wanted it done, it gets done. If they didn't want it done, it didn't get done. Let me tell you, there wasn't any outcry for justice when the cannery burned down. When the Terments broke the law they just made sure they had the majority on their side."

"Ain't nothing much changed," said Soldado.

"Why would Jake and his father burn you out?"

"The have nots were winning. The haves fought back, protecting their interests. Leasts, that's the way we see it," said the Pastor.

"You didn't really lose," said Maggie. "Your picture was on the bulletin board of my high school for several years, your picture and part of one of your speeches. You looked great in the picture."

"That was the difference. You went to school near Baltimore, a different part of Maryland than River Sunday."

"The line I liked was 'To get the real size of a country, you have to measure the hearts of its leaders.'

"That was what I said in my acceptance at the award July 17, 1968, standing in front of the courthouse in River Sunday. Mr.

Johnson came in by helicopter too. A lot of Washington people attended, not many folks from River Sunday, but that was the way it was in those days."

The top of the crane that was moored at the bridge was in sight over the distant treeline. It was a black speck engineered above the natural randomness of the trees. As the boat moved along the river channel the crane details became more exact, outlining a black beacon against the blue sky. Then in a few more minutes they were nosing into the anchorage. The crane was a huge bludgeon towering over them as they waded ashore.

Maggie was a hundred feet ahead of them and as she climbed to the top of the low bank at the shoreline she yelled back, "The site. It's been wrecked."

Soldado waded back to his boat, reached back over the side and pulled down a sawed off double barreled shotgun. He splashed to catch up with Frank and the Pastor.

The white twine connecting the various grid stakes had been cut and was in disarray. "No human tracks," said the Pastor, looking at the soil. "They were careful to leave no tracks."

"We may have surprised whoever it was."

"Someone wants to delay us. Why else would they cut the markers?"

"Who wants to delay us?"

"Think about it," she said. "It could be your friends, Pastor, who want to slow us down so we will find the graveyard."

The Pastor shook his head. "No, I would know if anyone from the church had done this."

"Frank, it could be Jake and his friends trying to scare us out of here," said Maggie.

"Maybe it's the butterfly people," suggested Frank. "I would think though that they'd be more interested in our staying here as long as possible."

"I'll take Jake," said the Pastor.

Maggie ran to the farmhouse to call the police.

"She's wasting her time," said the Pastor.

In a few minutes she came back. The Pastor and Frank were already restringing the stakes.

"No harm done, just a little delay," said Frank.

"Well, so much for the cops," she said, a dejected tone to her voice.

"What did they say?"

"I talked to the chief."

"That'll be Billy. He and Jake are pretty close," said the Pastor.

"The chief said there's been some reports of dogs tearing up stakes at the construction sites at the bridge. He said he'd keep a car on patrol up our way in the future."

"No animal did this," said the Pastor.

"Jake," said Soldado.

"Look, " said Frank. "We've fixed it. Let's just get back to work."

"Jake, he knows I'm always waitin' for him, watchin'," said Soldado.   He waved his shotgun as he started back towards his boat. "Ain't no way a man like that should be allowed to keep livin.'"

Chapter 8

Soldado had been gone for several hours. It was getting darker and the mosquitoes were incessant. Frank's skin itched with the dirt and sweat. He was tired. His exhausted mind kept thinking that one more scrape with his trowel, one more uncovered micro sphere of earth, one more spoonful of dark soil might provide the next clue to this ship's past.

"Hey, there are more bones here, " said the Pastor working a few feet away. Frank crawled quickly over to the Pastor's grid. Maggie was not far behind.

"Good Lord, you have found more skeletons," he said, surprised. "I had a feeling we'd find something but I didn't expect more bones." He looked closely at the first skull that the Pastor had uncovered. " It's a Caucasian. The nose area is definitely the same as the soldier. Keep in mind, Pastor, you'll be looking for African skulls if there are slaves buried here."

"There're three skulls," said Maggie. "All Caucasian. Over there's a big hand around what looks like the grip of a sword."

"A cutlass. A pirate's weapon. See the jeweled decoration coming through the encrusting. The way the man is gripping the hilt shows he was using it as a hammer, not as a weapon," observed Frank.

"These skulls, they are all adult skulls but the one, it's huge, like a giant. Try to work down to the center of the grid pit. Maybe we can find the legs or arms of one of them, " said Maggie.

"Did you notice how the skulls are in the same direction, like they are looking at something?" asked the Pastor. "That ought to be a clue. You'd think the skulls might be a little bit more in disarray in a fire."

"Yes. What do you think, Maggie?"

"The giant fascinates me. "

"There might be something in the records about a man this size being in the Chesapeake," said Frank.

"Anyway, there are the same burn fractures in the skulls but then see how the skulls are almost tortured in their position," said Maggie.

"Like they were hit by something, a falling beam perhaps," said the Pastor.

"Or restrained. They might have been locked into a compartment in the ship. They might have been trying to escape. They were pushed up against a door. I've seen similar body positions in fires where the bodies were trying to get out a closed exit door," observed Maggie. " That would explain using the sword as a hammer. Maybe these people were trying to escape from the fire and that's why they are looking in the same direction."

"If they were crew, and that's a possibility, they would have had to have been restrained in some way. If they were crew and were not restrained they would have escaped the fire," added Frank.

"Why would anyone burn the crew?" asked the Pastor.

"Witnesses to something?" suggested Maggie.

Frank ran his fingers over the soil strata marks at the edge of the pit. "There's not much evidence of this part of the ship having any more damage than the rest. I mean an explosion, like of the ship's gunpowder stores."

"These skulls might rule out the plague theory," observed Maggie.

"Yes, a restrained crew doesn't fit that theory. Dead and dying sick people perhaps, but not men pushing against restraints. I think we have ruled out plague," said Frank. He continued, "So what do we have? A burned out wreck that was never salvaged. A dead crew and a giant with a jeweled sword. I've worked on many shipwreck sites, some of the best ones in this hemisphere. Usually an archaeologist has a mystery or two to figure out. The mystery might be something like what kind of wine was in the old bottle that was unearthed or what town in Europe manufactured a ceramic shard. Nothing to wake up in the middle of the night worrying about. However, I worry about this."

They decided to stop for the night and sat on the porch of the farmhouse in the dark. Bugs were scratching and crashing against the worn screen of the porch to get to the light that was on inside in the old kitchen.   Frank munched on one of the sandwiches that the Pastor's church group had prepared.

"These are good. Maybe we can contribute something to the church," said Frank.

"You two are doing enough. The people want you to have this food. The church elders committee sent it up here with me special."

It was still very hot and the soil stuck to their skin. They were dirty and tired. It had been a long day. The three of them looked alike, human shapes covered and stinking with the muck. Maggie joked that they had fooled the mosquitoes and the bugs were swarming around them instead of the marsh.

"I wonder," Frank asked," if anyone saw this ship burn. Maggie, your initial research would have turned up any written records so we know there's no documentation. I wonder though if anyone could have seen it burn. It must have been a spectacular fire." He took off his hat. His hair fell over his face and he pushed it back, creating black smears of dirt on his forehead.

"Sure. Native Americans might have seen it," said Maggie. "From what I've read about the Chesapeake Bay and especially this Eastern Shore area, there were not many Europeans here in those days. Not many Native Americans either. The big tobacco farms were managed by overseers who worked for European absentee owners. There are even some legends that report pirates careened and scraped their ship hulls in these rivers."

" The Terments were here," the Pastor reminded them.

Maggie was thoughtful. "There should have been stories about it that came down in the local history books. How could the Terments or anyone else have missed seeing a ship on fire? It must have been visible for many miles, even across the Bay."

"Maybe because it was quick," suggested Frank. "If it happened in daylight and the ship was fairly dry it would have been fast, over in a short time. I think judging from the depth of the remains that the hull was probably in pretty shallow water anyway. I think she burned fast at low tide. When the high tide came back in there would not have been much ship left. The water would have covered up the bits of frame that were not burned. Anyone coming here to investigate a fire would have seen nothing but water."

"I think that the tide came in faster than she burned. I think there was something here to see. That's why more soil was added to fill in the cove so the wreck would not show at low tide," said Maggie." That additional soil intrigues me. I think there was something that happened that someone wanted to cover up."

" There's one thing you two keep forgetting," said the Pastor.

" What?"

"This fire happened on Terment property. "

"What are you talking about?" asked Maggie.

"The Pastor is making the point that the Terments like to burn things, "said Frank.
"The point is the skulls don't seem to indicate an accident. Those imprisoned men suggest that the fire was set, probably to do them harm."

" Tell me though, why would a Terment burn this ship?" asked Maggie.

"I don't know," said Frank. The single light bulb hanging from the kitchen ceiling inside the door behind Frank made his shadow stretch out into the grassy yard till it joined the blackness of the summer night. "We owe it to those people out there in the wreck to find out what happened," he said.

"I feel the same way," said Maggie, emotion tearing her eyes. "Burning to death is an awful way to die."

"I've been thinking about Soldado since this afternoon," said Frank. "His threats against Jake. Shouldn't we warn Jake?"

"How serious is he?" said the Pastor. " He has been saying that about Jake for years. People mostly disregard it. I almost took aim one time at Jake myself."

"I didn't think that preachers could want to kill a person," said Frank.

"Couldn't do it. I had to calm myself a lot though before I got through it."

The Pastor leaned back against the post of the porch. "I was out in my boat fishing. Just a little fourteen footer that I keep down in River Sunday to row out around the river some evenings when the water is quiet."

"I was directly in front of Peachblossom Manor. It was getting late, but there was still some of the sunset left in the west of the Bay, some red, some light. The fish weren't biting or they didn't like the clam snouts that I was using for bait.

"Then a light went on up at the manor house. The glimmer came down over the lawn and out on the water. It was a lamp in the big open room that is on the first floor of the mansion. Jake was illuminated, sitting in a chair, reading some papers. He was a pretty good way off but I knew it was Jake from the way he was sitting, all sprawled over the chair, careless.

"This compulsion came over me, a feeling of intense hatred of Jake, something difficult for me to suppress even though I had spent my life learning to love my fellow man. I remember looking at my rifle on its brackets in the front of the rowboat. I knew at that moment I could get even for what Jake and his father had done to me and my people at the General Store fire. I could probably get away with the murder. My mind worked fast. I knew the police would suspect that the shot came from the water, would trace the rifle. My rifle was not a rare gun but there were only a few like it in River Sunday."

He stopped, watching Frank's face. "That night my whole existence as a minister was in jeopardy, Frank. I knew that my only chance to shoot the man and to get away with it would be an alibi from my congregation. People would have to lie to protect me like they had done for my great grandfather after he killed that Union soldier.

" I'm telling you I reached for that rifle. I pulled it up on my shoulder. I saw his head just at the tip of the rifle sight." He paused. "My father's voice came into my mind teaching me how to hunt when I was a kid. I heard his voice telling me how to aim the weapon, how to breathe, how to squeeze gently the trigger, how to carefully launch the death sentence.

"I held the rifle there for a long time, repeating Jake's name over and over. Then my love of the Lord Jesus took over. I put the gun down. I could not pull that trigger. I stowed the rifle and picked up the anchor and rowed home."

The Pastor looked at Maggie.

"If I had pulled that trigger, if I had killed Jake Terment, he would have beaten me more in death than he ever had in life. You see, I set myself out as an example in my church. I say that I am a better man. My church folks look up to me. If they shoot each other they come to me for forgiveness. How could they do that if I was a murderer too? How could they have any excellence to look up to if I were as weak as they were?

The cat came into the light beaming out from the farmhouse kitchen, stopped on the top step to the porch and looked at them. Her fur seemed more orange in the glare. Maggie took some tuna from her sandwich and put it on the porch near the cat. The animal sniffed the food and then devoured it.

"I'll bring out some cat food tomorrow, " said the Pastor.

The cat tensed, her head bent forward at the darkness. She sniffed the air, made a gruff meow and then bounded into the night towards the river. Their words slipped out into the darkness at the porch and were lost, one by one, in the night.

"The commitment of your congregation, I admire that, " remarked Frank.

"You said you were committed to the children of Vietnam," observed the Pastor.

"Yes, I had this idea that the communists were destroying the minds of the kids. My father talked about when he was a child in Europe, how his friends in school were taught to hate. I listened to him. He convinced me it was the same with these children in South Viet Nam, that they had no chance to choose their future, to learn how to love, to care for others. "

"You could have found a way to stay out of the war."

"Yes, but I didn't try. In those days I wanted to fight back about things which bothered me. "

"What happened?" asked Maggie.

"When I got home, the survival instinct was all I knew any more."

The Pastor smiled. "Tell that to these modern Confederates shooting off that cannon in River Sunday."

Frank looked at the Pastor and then continued. "I'll tell you how I began to lose my enthusiasm for the kids of Vietnam. I remember we had been in country only a few weeks. We were in Saigon on leave one night. The city lights sparkled and there was the smell of fish everywhere, always fish. The five of us soldiers sat there on a terrace at the big French hotel in Saigon.

"There was a little boy there, shorts, tee shirt with the faces of the Beatles printed on it. He wore flip flop sandals, and had a big grin. He was pushing his bicycle. In the front of the bicycle was a wicker basket suspended from the handlebars and in the basket was a large glass jar filled with clear water in which there were multicolored fish swimming around.

"The Pastor remembers. It was like a carnival, Maggie. There were so many children and they were selling everything from Coca Cola to the bodies of their older sisters. We were drinking the Vietnamese "Thirty Three" beer on the terrace, having a good time. That night all our thoughts about the country were the virginal ideas of young men who had not yet seen death up close.

"This little boy wasn't more than twelve years old. He looked so happy. One of us motioned to him to come show us his fish. It may have been me; it may have been my buddy across from me at the table. The kid came over, pushing his bicycle through the crowded terrace. There were Vietnamese and French couples there having drinks. We were the only Americans. When I looked at the kid, I forgot that the child's brother probably sold his mother for sex in the biggest room in his small shack, while the rest of his Vietnamese family huddled in a smaller side room waiting to count the money when the American soldier was finished. I forgot that the shack was covered with American tin pressed from beer and soda cans. I forgot that this kid knew that most Americans and Vietnamese hated each other. I thought in that moment that he was simply a merchant's son helping his father in the family business. I thought he was like an American child. In some fantasy in my mind, he was just like a kid at home in Massachusetts selling lemonade out on a summer evening. I thought he was just like me and I could relate to him. He was like me at that age out with his bike collecting deposit bottles to return them to a general store somewhere so that he could buy bubble gum and baseball cards, his bicycle no different than my shiny Schwinn.

"I leaned back in my wicker chair to reach into my pants pocket to get some Vietnamese money to give to him. At that moment the bicycle blew up. Just blew to bits. I saw the metal table top wheeling off like a flying saucer into the air above the terrace. There were arms and heads and legs moving almost drifting by my eyes in the haze of flame and noise. I found myself with my body and face painfully pressed into the edge of the terrace against a stucco white washed wall. There was warm blood everywhere, but my body was intact. The explosion was absorbed by the unfortunate bodies of my buddies and by the frame of the table. There beside my face almost out of focus it was so close was the hand of the little boy still holding the plastic handlebar grip. The hand was upright, like it was ready to continue guiding the bike, but only a stump of the boy's arm was still attached.

"As I sat up dazed, the dust and smoke settling around me, the tile walls covered with splotches of blood and flesh and clothing, I heard different screams, each coming toward me from a great distance. Around me there were distorted bodies of my friends and the locals. A few feet away a naked Vietnamese woman, her eyeless face a mass of blood, pulled with blind fingers at tiny threads of her shredded dress. Then the sirens began and helpful people pulled at me, making me stand up and stagger out of the flames.

"There were few other survivors of the blast. The little boy died, of course, and all my friends and many of the others on the terrace that night. I found out later from Vietnamese intelligence that the boy was known to them. The boy had been a soldier, a twelve year old soldier, giving his infant life in equal measure to his own brothers and sisters and aunts and uncles and father and mother fighting elsewhere that night in the Viet Cong . He got his American soldier that night.

"That night in my quarters I pulled bits of flesh out of the lacings of my jungle boots, those cloth boots with the long laces. I remember that I thought about whose flesh it was I was looking at, touching, and I couldn't identify it because flesh has no race below the skin line and there was no skin to inspect."

An owl hooted in the black night.

"That must have been pretty rough on you," said the Pastor.

"Yes, and confusing," Frank said, "This job is making me remember these things. It's strange. In a way it's like the war. Most of my jobs have been simple. No emotion. The developer wants the archaeologist to get off his land. The archaeologist wants to finish his research. The two of them sit down and think it out, talk about it, compromise. Here it's not like that. Like the war, there's more to it, more that seems to force me to take a side, to join one side against another side, although I am not even sure what the sides are yet."

The Pastor answered, "I'm telling you, though, you're here and you'll have to choose."

"It's just that I don't think this shipwreck or anything we find here is going to change the world or anything here in River Sunday, " said Frank." It's not going to get the island back for Mrs. Robin Pond and her environmentalists. It's not going to help restart your General Store. It's not going to end Soldado's hatred. It's not going to create a new economy for this town. "

"I'm not sure about any of that, Frank," said the Pastor. "If you let Jake Terment get his way, if we overlook something important, I think it will hurt all of us. It will hurt you too."

Maggie said then from her seat on the steps, "People have the right to understand their history. They have a right to know the truth of this wreck."

"Just do your job, Frank," said the Pastor.

"Truth or not, Frank," said Maggie, " if an expert like you says the site is worthless, believe me, it will be considered worthless no matter what the rest of us might think."

"That puts a lot on my shoulders, doesn't it?" said Frank, looking at the porch floor, scratching his neck.

The Pastor stood. "I have to get back to my church. I'll be back early in the morning. At least we get one more day to try up here."

Frank and Maggie watched him walk to his Cadillac, start its engine and drive out the lane, the headlights flashing off the loblollies as the car bounced on the ruts.

Chapter 9

The noise of car doors, slamming one after another, woke Frank. The sun was a large red ball just above tree line. There was still enough dew in the air to keep the temperature bearable. He sat up on the pallet of canvas he had arranged on the bed of the truck. Before he went to sleep last night the old memories of his fellow soldiers had come back in bursts of emotion. He had seen again the young faces of the men he called Philadelphia, and Texas and Alaska. Always over the years when he was overtired and worried about his work, the thoughts of these men came again. He had known them as closely as one knows brothers. With them he had been in a special fraternity, one formed against the loneliness and fear of the Vietnamese nights. They had been his strength in that tough time and the thought of them came when he needed it to comfort him and to give him energy.

He crawled out by the hoist and climbed down through the open tailgate. His skin still itched from caked earth and several mosquito bites. He stood beside the truck, the mist wet against his skin, his eyes opening more and more. From where he was, he could see without being seen. A convoy of Terment Company station wagons had entered the yard. The green cars were stopped, their hoods pointing in all directions as if in a sudden sweeping attack. Men in green jackets, holding rifles and side arms were searching the small yard, kicking at the tall grass. Spyder was there too, his bent posture even more ignoble compared to the others who held their heads and shoulders erect like trained soldiers. Even so, Spyder was in command. He ordered one man to stand beside the decrepit gate. As the man moved into position, his legs became buried in the honeysuckle, his body twisting to maintain his balance against the vines.

As if waiting until this sweep for danger had been completed, Jake finally appeared. He walked, no longer with his golf club, looking carefully around him. The path he was following to the site would lead him directly by Frank's truck. Frank walked around his truck, reached into the cab , found his work shorts and stepped into them.

Jake called, "Frank, where are you?"

"Over here, Jake. By the truck."

Jake walked through the boxwoods to where the truck was parked. Jake for his part was dressed as usual in stylish white pants and shoes with a silk shirt. In his right hand he carried a cellular telephone.

"Billy, the chief of police, reported to me about the vandalism out here. We can't have that. I brought out a guard to help watch the site. We can't take any chances. There's too much equipment here. There's the safety of you and Maggie."

"The chief told Maggie it was animals."

"I haven't got much time," Jake said. "My directors are meeting in New York. This bridge is behind schedule." He looked intently at Frank. "Still nothing definite?"

"We found some new skeletons, Jake. Come on, I'll show you." The morning sun was filling the excavation pits in the site with various brown shades, and the darkest shadows were disappearing as they walked up to the area. A few small birds had been picking insects from the earth and they flew up with some shrill cries.

"Watch your step in this muck, Jake. You're going to mess up those white shoes."

"I'll be all right. I've been walking in this stuff all my life," he answered. He stepped carefully and his shoes remained clean. Frank walked directly to test pit Q, the surface water rippling slightly under his bare feet.

"Let me start up the pump and we can take a look." Frank worked on the machine. It started on the fourth pull, a cloud of white oil smoke drifting across the site in the still air. The water began to surge from the hose. Frank left the nozzle slightly in the air so that he could monitor the outflow. A titmouse flew up from the brush where the water hit in spurts, shaking the branches.

They spoke in higher voices over the noise of the pump. "There, that's taking out most of the water. I'll keep it running while I show you." Frank stepped down into the pit which was more than four feet on each side and at least four feet deep. He knelt in the wet soil. "Strange," he said. "There are more of them. Look at this, Jake."

Jake stood close to the edge of the pit, standing over Frank, his face intent, "Those look like skulls, Frank."

Frank nodded. "It must be the water that is opening up this pit." Frank pointed out the new skulls. He continued, as though he were thinking out loud, oblivious to Jake's being there. "They seem to be the skulls of adult men, burned to death. They are Caucasian, we think. It's very hard to tell. We try to see the width of nose bones, projection of teeth." Then Frank remembered Jake was there. He looked up at Jake. "The mystery is why they are here, why so many, why the fire. Our best guess is that they were crew members, somehow trapped here. One of them is a big fellow. See his hand on his cutlass?"

Frank stood up and sat on the edge of the pit. "Jake, we think that the ship was an early Eighteenth Century wreck. We know that because of the type of construction we found in the part that the bulldozer pulled up. Yesterday we compared the timbers here with those of several hulks down the river and there is no doubt in our minds that this wreck is much earlier than the hulks."

He saw Jake's smile, and said, "I can see you're not convinced yet, but that's what a lot of archaeology is, piecing little clues together until we have a pattern. We look for something that points to one direction or conclusion and that's what we finally accept as the story of the site."

"Frank," said Jake, glancing for a moment at the giant hand and then almost interrupting Frank's last words, "Here's what I really want to know. Do you think you can finish up with whatever it in that you need to do so we can get started by early tomorrow morning?"

Jake smiled, his drawl heavy, " I've told my bulldozer people to be ready to start."

"Jake, I can't say that for sure," said Frank, holding his eyeglasses, speaking in a serious tone. "You are really pushing me."

"Hello, " called Maggie.

"We've found more bones," answered Frank.

She started across the field, wearing the same shorts and tee shirt as before.

"You are the dirtiest scientists I ever saw," said Jake, grinning. "I've got to leave," he said. "Keep in mind I expect to start my equipment in the morning."

"I was telling you that I'm not sure I can be finished by then, " said Frank.

Jake put his arm on Frank's bare shoulder. "Frank, I want this job finished by tonight."

"Jake you see what we are finding here. These men died. We have to find out why."

"Why? Nobody in River Sunday gives a damn about some old skeletons except the Pastor. Most people in River Sunday who even think about history and the past prefer to think about beautiful colonial manor houses like Peachblossom, beautiful types of things, not some damn graves."

"I'm not so sure about what interests people in River Sunday. To do this job right, Jake, to do my job, we have to analyze these bones, find out what we can."

"Look here, Frank." Jake suddenly became angry. "You are not here to delay a construction site for the next year while you fiddle around with some bones you happened to find near the wreck."

Jake stared at Maggie. "I thought you were a woman with some common sense. If you want to research these bones, you are going to hold up a multimillion dollar project and a lot of local people's jobs. "

Maggie started to speak, then stopped. She turned off the pump. The site was suddenly silent. She ignored Jake and said, "I need this pump, Frank over at my test pit."

Frank started to help her, but Jake restrained him. "You stay here. I haven't finished with you." They watched for a moment as she pulled it towards her area, the pump skids bumping on the few ruts that were dry in the sun, leaving a mark of its runners on the soil.

"Let me give you an example, Frank, " Jake said, his hand still on Frank's shoulder, his voice smoothed again to a pleasant drawl. "A while back I wanted to watch the ducks and geese forming up on the Bay, rafting up. I wanted to see whether they were starting to fly over the North Creek because that's where I have a hunting blind. The old fashioned windows in the mansion house are too hard to see from so I wanted to open up the front side of the house. People in River Sunday heard about my renovation plans. I got telegrams up at my office in New York. They wanted me to keep the house in its original condition and design so the tourists could come and see the historic architecture. Guess what, Frank? I went ahead and changed the windows. People who did not like what I was doing realized the cost of trying to beat me in court. No one wanted to put up the money to take me on. Money wins. That's the way it will be here at the bridge.

"I have faith in you, Frank. You're supposed to be a professional. When I heard about you I said there's a man who is alert to what's happening in the world. Youngest chairman of archeology in the whole country. You don't get that kind of job without being a team player. I said to Spyder, get this man. He will help us to keep the folks in line."

Frank persisted, tried to reason with Jake. As he spoke he watched Jake's face get red with anger. "If we find something in here, it not only belongs to the people of River Sunday but it also belongs to the scholarship of the world. There are many historians who'll be very interested in what we have found here."

"Look, Frank, you are supposed to help me."

"So what happens? Do you fire me? If I don't finish up by tomorrow morning, what happens next?" Frank was trying to joke. Jake just looked angry.

"Frank, I won't have to fire you. There just won't be any place left for you to dig.
You folks can't dig through concrete."

Jake's manner had become dictatorial as though he were ordering entry level employees, not professionals. "This afternoon, I got visitors coming to the site. I want them to see progress, I want them to see you finishing up. These folks got a stake in the building of the bridge." Jake suddenly smiled, a consoling smile. " I'm sure you'll help us, Frank. Your boss as much as guaranteed me that you would do what had to be done."

He walked back towards his car. As he did he pressed buttons on his telephone and began to talk into it. He nodded to Spyder, like a man who thinks he has just solved a big problem. Maggie walked over to where Frank was working and the two of them watched Jake leave.

"You can see what's going on, Frank,"

"It's a set up," he said.

"Working for the State doesn't give me any great choices either."

Frank said slowly, "It's not what I decide to do here. It's what Jake decides to do."

She put her arm around him. "It's tough to face up to reality."

The Pastor arrived at that moment, his black car covered with dust in the sunlight, jouncing as it maneuvered the ruts.

"I'm going to buy the Pastor a new set of shock absorbers. I bet he has the original set on that Cadillac, judging from the way it bounces," grinned Frank.

"Glad you still got your sense of humor, Frank," Maggie said. "Getting depressed won't get you anywhere."

The Pastor walked up to them, holding two large paper bags with food. "Here. Coffee inside. Hot." Frank reached for the bags and put them on the ground. He pulled out the coffee thermos and cups and poured coffee for all of them .

"Jake was just here," said Maggie, "Giving us the word."

" He went by me, the other way, going into River Sunday. Didn't even notice me. He was talking on his cell phone."

"We have until tomorrow morning. Then he's going to start up the bulldozers again."

"That's about what he's been saying all along," said the Pastor. "Jake knew we wouldn't have enough time."

Maggie said, "The project's not hopeless. We can take out of here anything we find. Our records and our photographs can still be studied."

"You're right. Let's find what we can . We've still got a day," said Frank, moving towards his dig. "Besides, I might still be able to reason with Jake."

Maggie and the Pastor smiled at Frank's remark. "I'll work as long as I can," said the Pastor.

"We've found more bones, Pastor," said Frank over his shoulder.

The Pastor hardly looked at the new find. "I don't have to see anymore. These people were murdered."

No one spoke. The mention of the word "murder" gave the project a definition, a stature. The Pastor had labeled these skeletons in a stark and horrible way. If he was right, this was a crime scene, a place with all the proof of a hideous crime. They touched the bones carefully, even more aware of the pain that these humans must have endured.

"Murder might be too strong a term to use," said Frank.

The Pastor ignored him and went on, "I've been telling my church members about these horrors we are finding up here. Trouble is the church has only a few members. Not enough of us to make any difference. Over the years, many of our church families have left River Sunday, gone to Baltimore and Philadelphia to find work. None of those people are aware of all this."

"What about the nature people, the human butterflies? What will they think of these discoveries?" asked Maggie.

" Their only interest in this dig is that it holds up Jake's building that bridge," the Pastor said in a disgusted tone. "Besides, she's not tough enough to beat him."

"Why don't you got to the press?" Maggie suggested to the Pastor. "I've seen the power the press has on public opinion of these excavations."

"The press will back Jake," said the Pastor. "People want jobs."

Then he said, "There might be another way to stop him." The Pastor remained silent after that.

"No skywriters today." a voice boomed behind them. It was Sold ado.

"It's started," he said.

Frank looked at him. "What has started?"

"Jake brought in his soldiers. He's got them green coats posted on all the streets of River Sunday. They got guns too."

"There's no war here."

"You still think it can be all talk," shrugged Soldado as he looked at the array of skulls below him in area Q. "Jake Terment killed these people," he said. Frank and the others looked at him and saw how serious his face was.

"No, Soldado," said Frank. "These skeletons are very old, from long before Jake was born."

"His family, they have a hand in it. It's the same as if it was him that did it. Skulls tell their story. Maybe the skulls, they tell you something. This is proof."

"Jake is the landlord, not the murderer," said Frank. He immediately regretted using the word, "murderer," fearing he might encourage Soldado to start more violence. "It's all part of archaeology, doing a dig, working with the land owners, Soldado."

"That's the problem I got with you, professor," Soldado replied. "You can't decide what to do. When you can't decide, you can't beat the bastard. You're the kind of guy wants to get along with everybody, rather than be on the right side."

Frank stepped into the bone scatter of area Q. He began to brush soil off the bones that were in front of him. Then he said, "I can't do anything about what you think, Soldado."

Frank was silent for a few moments. The others watched him. Then he looked up from his work and said, "I'm going to continue working. Maggie, if you will, you could continue in your test pit. Pastor, perhaps you can help me here for a while. Soldado, if you want to help, there's a lot of sifting to be done over at the soil pile by the bow of the wreck. I'll get you started and show you what to look for."

Soldado smiled. "I just tell you what is true. They is always good guys and bad guys no matter how much a man wish different."

Chapter 10

Soldado left to tend to his crab lines. They listened to his engine fade into the distance. Frank looked at his watch. It was nine AM.

"You're thinking," said the Pastor, "that finding these skeletons is not going to be enough to delay the bridge."

"If they were the bodies of some people who had been killed recently by some serial killer maybe that would stop the bridge construction. I'm sure in fact that it would. But these persons died a long time ago and, like Jake said, most people don't care that much what happened to them. Like that Doc Bayne said, call him if the bones are recent."

"Some people do care."

"Yeah, but do they care enough about some burned sailors, even if they were killed by some colonial criminal, to give up several million dollars of investment money?" said Frank.

"It's a tough job convincing people the loss of the money is worth finding the answers to the history puzzles," said Maggie.

"You learned that at your Southern Maryland excavation."

"It was a lot like it is here." She dumped some soil from her dustpan on to the plastic sheet laid out beside her dig and studied it for a moment then went back to work. "We were called down there when the shopping center, was almost completed, and the contractor was applying blacktop. There was still one section open to insert another drainpipe. The hole was right in the center of the lot."

She stood up and stretched. "Ah, that feels better. Anyway, the men working on the hole for the piping found a part of a brick foundation. Same as here, the project had to immediately stop. We got a call that afternoon and were down in the evening. We worked by lights. Cathy made sure we got everything, portable x ray equipment, magnetometers. I was put in charge of several archeologists."

"We began to enlarge the hole, Frank. Like here, all we had to do was prove it was nothing more than a smokehouse, or an old barn of no importance, and we could go home. I remember there was this large paving machine full of macadam that was sitting right next to the hole. The smell of tar was getting all of us sick.

"At about midnight, we dug into wire, coils of the stuff, all copper. The wire was the type used in telegraphs back in the Nineteenth Century. Then we started new holes ten feet out from the original. The contractor had to move the paving machine back. He also had to come in with jack hammers to cut out the blacktop. He was not happy at doing all this extra work. On top of that, the police there were not able to stop the workmen from making angry remarks to us. There were the usual remarks that the redneck workmen made to our women. One tried to say something about my body and I glared at him so hard, he walked away and left me alone."

"He probably had never run into a woman who had the guts to threaten him," said Frank.

Maggie continued, "Research was being done in the local library. We were told that the land had been farmland and woodland. There had been no railroad within twenty miles and no telegraph lines. Then we made an astounding discovery. Down a few inches below the strata where the wire was located were a variety of Confederate artifacts. In small metal boxes were the remains of cloth ribbons with Secession mottoes, Confederate flags of various sizes and some uniform material and insignia. Then we found rusted guns, mostly revolvers but also rifles."

"The word went out to Washington to the National Archives and to museums that were involved in Civil War history. About seven in the morning an intern in Richmond working at the Museum of the Confederacy turned up an obscure reference to a secret telegraph station in Southern Maryland. It had been used in

1864 for transferring messages from the Confederate intelligence agents located in the District of Columbia.

"We did not report any of this to the media. I was a state employee and it was a State of Maryland project. There was a certain requirement of privacy between the landholder and the government. That did not stop a local reporter from sending the story to the Washington newspapers. The result was that by noon we had visitors standing all around our site. Some of them were unfriendly and all of them had one cause or another.

"Cathy was pretty good about it. I told her I wanted to finish the work; she told me that the Governor's Office wanted the project finished yesterday. She went out on a limb and gave me half a day to find what I could, document it, and cover it up.

"Then I found a skeleton. With the equipment we had at the site we could not determine the race of the skeleton. The time period of the soil strata around the body was all Civil War, no question.

"More research came in from the museums. There was a son of the landowners who had served in the Confederate Army intelligence service. He had disappeared right after visiting his family and on his way into Washington on a mission. It seemed that this might be a Confederate hero. There was suddenly political pressure from black politicians to close the site. Needless to say, relatives of the white landowners called the Governor to request more extensive digging. I told Cathy that she had to give me more time, that this was an important site, that little was understood about the Confederate activities in this part of Maryland. I argued we ought to collect the information. She told me she was getting in her car and coming down to close it herself."

"I was interviewed on national television. The reporters buzzed in with a helicopter and a great noise. In three minutes of live coverage, the fact that I answered only the simplest archeological questions about the site meant that I became the poster girl for every radical group in America. When I said that we were digging to get more accurate historical research on the Confederacy meant only one thing to those creeps. It translated that I was either for or against their agendas. Every reporter twisted what I said to support whatever his news report was covering, every kind of radical idea possible.

"Cathy closed us down that evening at dinner time. I went home before they poured the blacktop. I did not go back to work for a week because I was so disgusted. Then Cathy convinced me to come back to the office. She said I had the strongest credentials of anyone in the office. She said that to replace me, she would have to submit budget requests for two years in the state bureaucracy. I realized that without enough workers, many other Maryland projects would be jeopardized. I came back, out of love of archeology more than anything else. The first thing Cathy told me was that she had learned her lesson, that she would never go out that far again. That's why she's the way she is."

He smiled. "I know the feeling."

"Do you?" Maggie looked at him, a long hard look. Then she went on,

"Cathy did me a favor in a way. She kept me in archeology. I owe her that."

"Maggie, " Frank said earnestly, "If we can find some reason to fight for this marshland, I'll stand in front of Jake's bulldozer myself. I just wish I had a few more workers here today."

Maggie said, " There's no time to train anyone. We should have had them two days ago when we first started.. I wish we could get another worker like you, Pastor. You have a great attention to detail. If you ever want to change professions, we could bring you into the archaeological field."

"Unfortunately my church people work long hours in day jobs. They can't get out here," said the Pastor.

"You must have made some compromises in your life. How does a Pastor of a small church get a Cadillac?" asked Frank.

The Pastor didn't take offense. He carefully scraped some more of the clay away from the leg bone in front of him. " That car got willed to me by a woman in River Sunday. She wasn't even a member of my church. She lived on the far side of the harbor, the other direction from the way you come up here. The folks around here call that area Tulip Neck. This lady had a mansion, not quite as old, but just about as large as Peachblossom.

"Well, one morning in the spring of 1980 I got a call to come over to the center of town to this lawyer's office, her lawyer, a white man who had lived in River Sunday all his life. I can tell you though that this was the first time for me, even though River Sunday was a very little town, that I ever said a word to him. So his secretary let me into his office and I sat in front of him while he finished up some call on the telephone. Then he got up and came around his desk and shook my hand.

"The lawyer said, 'Pastor Allingham, I'm sure glad you could come by here this morning.' then he looked at me with a sort of smile and he said, 'I don't expect you to say yes but did you ever know Mrs. Steers?'"

"I said, 'Nossir, I never had the pleasure. Might be long ago my father knew her.'"

"So he continues, 'Well, she has passed away.'"

"'I'm sorry to hear that. I'm sorry for her family.'"

"'Well,' he said 'that's very nice of you.'"

"Then he sits back down at his desk and lifts up a folder and pulls out an envelope. 'I wanted to tell you as her executor that she has left you an automobile.'"

"'A car?'"

"'A car. Yes. She has authorized me to buy you a new Cadillac coupe and to maintain and insure it for your use from the estate as long as you want the use of the car.' He pulled a set of keys out of an envelope."

"'Here you are. I assumed black would be a good color, you being in the ministry and all.'"

"Well, I can tell you I was mighty surprised. I said, 'Thank you,' when he gave me the keys."

"Reasonable thing to do, say thank you," smiled Frank.

" Yes. Then I sat there while he was rummaging through the file folder . Finally he said to me, 'There's a note in here for you also from her.' He handed me the letter. It was written in large flowing script like nothing I had ever seen before, not like the handwork that we had learned in our River Sunday schooling, but maybe something foreign."

'Dear Pastor Jefferson Allingham,

Before his death, your father was a frequent and welcome visitor at Tulip Neck. He came to preach to me in lieu of my going outside the farm to a church in River Sunday. He also helped me plan and grow my flower gardens. Your father grew the most beautiful peonies. He said that these flowers were the most reliable, that they kept on being beautiful every spring without all the care the other plants required. I grew to depend on those plants just like I depended on your father tending to their physical health and to my spiritual health. The talks with your father were as valuable to me as any other moments in my life.

In my life, being often misled by emotions, I spent my money on poor goals. Your father was one of the few who helped me do penance and find forgiveness, a forgiveness that was like the peonies coming back as beautiful each spring no matter how poorly I had lived my winter. Perhaps in memory of your father I can do some service that will be valuable. It seemed logical to give you something reliable for your own life as a way of remembering your father. I know that you travel to see your parishioners.

Please accept the gift of this Cadillac automobile. My attorney will see that it is properly insured and maintained for you. I have told him that it is my wish that you get every expense on this car covered by my estate.

Sincerely, Mrs. Steers'"

"And that was all there was to it?"

"That was all. The lawyer seemed to be a little upset. He said that the estate would be willing to pay me money instead of the car."

"I said ,'No, that was what she wanted so I would use it for the work of the church.'"

"Strange," observed Frank. "She didn't take the time to find out about you and your brother starving up there at the old church building. "

"I was wondering about that," said Maggie.

"No," said the Pastor. "I understand her. It's like in the old slavery days. Nobody got their freedom while the white slave owners were living. They only got freed in the wills after the white folks died. "

"There's a lot to learn," said Frank.

"I heard later though that she gave out several of these kind of gifts from her will. She was an odd old lady and had kept mostly to herself. There was a story around that German submarines used to come up to her house to get money for Hitler."

"Did they?"

"Nobody ever found out. There are lots of those stories going around on the Eastern Shore."

"You've had that car for a long time."

"Yes I have. I think I was right to keep the car too. I've had it for a while and had it repaired a few times. I can understand why that lawyer just wanted to give me the money. I think he gets tired of me still coming around with repair bills."

"You're going to have a high mileage Cadillac."

"I think, Frank, that I will probably drive that car into my grave."

"We'll put on your gravestone a little poem," grinned Frank:

"Here in God lies Allingham
Never to part his Caddy sedan."

Maggie laughed. "You can do better than that, Frank."

The telephone rang in the farmhouse.   Maggie stood up and splashed through the muck. She called back, "Frank, you've got a call."   Then it was Frank's turn to run across the muck towards the house.   Maggie was standing inside the doorway, holding the telephone.

Frank sat down at the table. He pushed back one of the piles of Maggie's handwritten field reports and pulled a piece of clean paper in front of him.

"Frank Light," he said.

"Just a moment, Frank," a female voice said. Frank recognized the soft sound of the university president's receptionist. In his mind he could see the carpeted office, the mahogany desks, the computer terminals and the portraits of past university officials.

The line clicked.   "Frank, how are you doing down there on our little reconnaissance?" said his boss.

"Yessir. I had not called in because I wasn't sure how much longer this job would take."

"Well, that's all right. I just want you to take care of Jake Terment. Is everything going well?"

"I think so."

"I got a call from New York. From the tone of the call it sounds like something is wrong."

"Who called you?"

"One of our trustees, Frank. "

"Well, Jake Terment is in a hurry for us to get out of here."

"You can understand that. What do you think of him?"

"He's a little pushy," laughed Frank.

The president also laughed. "I didn't expect him to be as interested in history as we are, Frank.. I'm sorry you have to rush this one. Maybe you can wrap it up today and get back here."

"I can't get out of here for a little while yet."

"Well, just don't overstay your welcome. I don't want Jake Terment to get the wrong idea about our university. Frank, it's people like him who support our departments including archaeology here."

"I certainly can't leave today."

"Frank, if I have to ask you, you will leave. Don't you agree, Frank?"

Frank did not respond. There was a long pause. Then the president went on, his tone less friendly, more demanding. " Frank, I guess I'm asking you. You get back up here in less than twenty four hours, a lot less if possible. You leave Jake Terment in a damn happy mood when you do get out of there. I want to see you as soon as you get back on campus. Do we understand one another? "

Frank didn't say anything.

"Well, I guess that's a yes," said the president. "Come on, Frank. This reconnaissance is not the end of the world. There's someone else here, wants to talk to you."

Another click, a new voice. "Frank?" It was Mello.

"Yes," he answered. She seemed far away, a stranger, not the warm flesh, the clever mind, he had loved so fiercely only days ago.

"You sound different," she said. "I was thinking you'd be back already. Then I thought you might get tick fever or some other disease from being done there in that God forsaken place. I've never been to the Eastern Shore of Maryland. What's it like?"

"I feel different," he said, looking at Maggie as she made some notations in her site journal. "The place here is raw, new , different. I feel like I did back when I first got in country in Vietnam, strong like I was in those days. "

As if she had not listened to what he had just said, Mello went on talking with no change of tone, no real worry in her voice, "Working in all the heat and sun probably isn't doing you any good. You'll soon be home, sitting in our air conditioning. When are you coming back?"

"Not until I finish my job." He realized he had never heard her say she was worried about anything or anyone.

"Your BMW needs an oil change. The schedule just came up on our computer. You told me to remind you. You treasure that new car."

"I'm not concerned about the car."

"That's a change. What is going on? You sound very different." Her voice was strained, maybe concerned. "The president says you finished the work down there."

"He's wrong." There was silence. He knew she was sitting down in the President's office, her short dress up on her thigh, her left hand caressing her leg the way she did unconsciously, the way she did that had brought him running from the first day that he saw her.

"I think the insects down there bit you, maybe gave you a fever. Don't do this to yourself, Frank. The President says you are excited about some piece of wood you've found."

"I have to do this right."

"Frank, all you have to do is what the president says," she said, her voice loud. "Your career is here, being a member of the university team. I've told you that. Have you forgotten the most important lesson I've taught you? Where the Hell do you think that car came from? Where the Hell do you think I come from? We like winners, Frank. You want us, you have to do what you are told."

He answered her slowly, "I'm beginning to think I may not be grown up enough for you, Mello."

"Then I guess there's nothing more to say. You know how I feel. Business always comes first."

"I'm keeping that in mind."

"All right, Frank."

"I understand," he said. "It's all or nothing."

She paused. He could see her swinging her leg, puzzled like she got sometimes when things did not go her way, thinking what to say next. Then she made her basic decision. He had watched her do this many times. Whenever she was on the telephone and ran out of words, he'd seen her just hang up. She did that now to him. The dial tone returned. Frank looked at the telephone receiver for a few moments as Maggie watched him.

"Bad news?" asked Maggie.

" You could say that. More proof why I got selected to come down here. I think my boss almost guaranteed Jake Terment that I would do whatever the man wanted on this job. It's nice to know that people you work for have confidence in you."

As Frank walked back across the site to the pit he suddenly felt very tired. He looked down. The cat was walking alongside him. Strange he thought how he was getting more muck on him every step he took while the cat's light orange fur remained clean.

Frank kneeled down in area Q and returned to work without speaking further to the others.   He thought back to the last time he had seen Mello, to the feeling of her in his arms. Then his mind was back to the present, to the site in front of him. The thoughts of Mello did not linger.

 He saw his face in the shallow puddle beside him. He did not like what he saw. There was not much reflection in the dark water, but there was enough to see that he had changed from that young man of a few years ago, far more than he had realized. The professor who had driven into this country was not the man who had gone to Vietnam. Even the returning veteran, as disillusioned as he was in those days, was not the man he saw today. The face was that of a man in the control of others. He worried if he could trust himself to have the integrity that the Pastor and Maggie needed.

He should have realized that his career had come along too quickly, that life had become too easy. He had moved too fast from an academic life to the administrative responsibility that came with being director of his department, from his teaching to his involvement in the business of a university career. Then, with this trip to the Eastern Shore, all of a sudden, the real world had burst into his protected university career.

Frank was disappointed in himself but he was also happy that he was here with these two. He also knew that he had taken off the custom tailored suit, the uniform of his career. Dressed only in the old khaki work shorts he had worn on countless other digs, he was bare enough to feel free of the pull of the university bureaucracy and its money driven hypocrisy. He felt that he could think and see his life more clearly. He saw a movement behind him, something more in the reflection in the puddle. He looked up at the edge of the test pit. There, the cat, its Mayan leopard markings shining in the sunlight, watched Frank to see what he would do next.

Chapter 11

Frank worked as fast as he could, knowing little time was left. Maggie was working in area T. Nothing had been found there yet. This was disappointing to Frank because that was the stern section, the Captain's area which he had expected to be rich in artifacts. As for himself, he still expected the cargo area Q in the center of the wreck to produce something more. He would continue to work methodically as he expanded the pit. He kept the Pastor working at area H where the bones of the giant were found. Soldado's divining rods had been right about area H but they had not been as effective on pinpointing area Q. The Pastor worked hard, stubbornly scraping at the earth. From time to time, Frank looked over in a supervisory manner at the Pastor's work. He knew this wasn't necessary. The older man was too dedicated to make a mistake.

"Frank," the Pastor said, after a while, " I know you don't think there was much to that graveyard story of mine."

"I didn't say that."

"I know there's not much proof. You younger men, you all want touchable proof. I just rely on faith in an old man's words. Maybe I shouldn't have faith. "

Frank kept working. The Pastor was right. He, Frank, had no faith in anything he couldn't see or touch.

The Pastor went on. "I always believed there was something up here. There wasn't a black kid in this town that didn't hear about the old slave burying ground and the magic up here. Our parents used to scare us, say they'd set us up here by ourselves, when we were bad. I had never done anything about researching the story. None of us had. Then the talk started about building the new bridge over this property and covering it up with concrete. There was a feeling among my church members, among many of the River Sunday black community that something should be done. No one knew what to do. Just about that time Mister Henry Johnson came to see me and told me his story. "

" Why did he come to you?" asked Frank.

" His wife was a member of my church. He didn't have much religion . She was in my choir. A fine voice. She was a lot younger than him. They had one baby baptized by me. Let you know something about this old man, that baby was born when the father was in his eighties.

"It was early in the day when she brought him in. He was a short skinny black man with white hair. He could not walk real well. His wife supported him and he had a cane. Came in and sat in my office by the wall. Took off his cap. He had a John Deere cap, like a green baseball cap with a little yellow deer on the front. Told me that hat meant a lot to him.

"'It proves I can still plow straight,' he said to me.

"'Yessir, Pastor,' he said, ' Still driving my own tractor. ' His voice was very low, but he pronounced his words carefully, like a man who wants to be known for good speech habits. His wife smiled at me to tell me to relax and just sit back at my desk and give her husband some time to get his story out at his own speed. So I did just that and waited for him.

"'He's not been too well,' she said. 'Besides that he just mostly contrary. He gives us a little trouble here and there, don't you?' she said to the Pastor but looking at her husband.

"'Yes ma'm , I do,' he replied.

"'Mister Johnson, I sure appreciate you and your wife coming by the church today,' I said to them.

"Mister Johnson stared at the floor of my office for a while. He turned his head once to look at his wife and then he stared at the floor again.

"'Does it bother him to talk about this?' I asked the old man's wife.

"'No,' said his wife. 'He sure talks enough at home.'

"She went on, 'Well, he told me that when he was a little boy this farm was his favorite fishing spot. He used to find old pieces of rusty metal lying around. He said there were no gravestones there just the bits of iron here and there all pitted and rusted. There was little bit of marsh then but the marsh got worse as he got older. Pretty soon it was wet in there a lot of the time, especially under the brambles where the sunlight couldn't get. There was an old white wooden gate to the property. It was closed up and chained most of the time when the farmer wasn't working the fields there. Henry remembers sometimes when he got up there he would find a wreath of flowers on the old white gate and one time he saw one of the traveling preachers that used to come to River Sunday every week. The preacher was putting out some flowers too. They always put the flowers outside the fence. They never went inside on Mister Terment's land. Henry went in though, snuck along the muskrat trails and went down to a hiding place on the riverbank where no one could tell he was there or not. No one couldn't even see his fishing line because he didn't use a bobber. He could feel a fish without using a bobber.'

"Mister Johnson smiled with pride at that comment.

"' Did you ever see any sign of anyone getting buried?' I asked him," said the Pastor.

"The old man looked up at me and shook his head. 'Nossir,' he said. 'The folks,' he said, 'that were buried in there were all old time slave folks.'

"Then he said after a moment,' I was told by my grandfather that the slaves buried there were Africans and that they were some of them great magic men. That's what I was told ' Then he went on to say that back in slavery days the black folks scared the old Indians, they call them Native Americans, away from the graves by telling them that the dead men buried there would make spells on them, would play tricks on them, if their graves were interfered with, if they tried to rob them. He said mostly the Native Americans, the Nanticokes, they were scared of the place anyhow. He said, ' My father told me that if I went in there I might run afoul of them hants and get me a spell too.'"

"Well, he went on to tell me, 'It was a good spot right along that shoreline. The weed wasn't too bad in those days and there weren't no snags to speak of. It was fair water for fishing. '

"'There was this time I was there, this time I came to tell you about, one strange time. The tenant farmer was away somewhere and the farm was deserted, ' Mister Johnson told me.

"'I was sitting there on the riverbank fishing. It had gotten dark. There was almost no light and I was getting ready to pick up my line. I knew my way out of there in the dark. I had been there so many times.'

"'Up by the road, near the white gate to the farm, I heard this noise, sounded like a large truck. It slowed down, backfired like a shot, and stopped right past the gate. I peeked out at it from where I was in the bushes and saw a bus. I could see people standing up and moving out of the bus and then standing along the road. They were black folks, all ages, about fifty of them in all. I could not see the markings on the bus but I thought it might be a church group just because I had been in buses like that with people of different ages when I had traveled with my own church and my parents.'

"'They were talking low and I could not hear the words. They moved along the road and climbed over the gate. Pretty soon all of them were walking single file towards the center of the marsh. Each one had a little candle in their hand, held up in front, and it made a procession of candles in the dark. It was real pretty. I had never seen anything like it. Then the talking stopped and they started to sing the words of the song Amazing Grace:

> "Twas grace that taught my heart to fear
>   And grace my fears relieved;
>   How precious did that grace appear
>   The hour I first believed."

From the light of the candles I could see their faces. They were all smiling and their eyes were very wide open. Their dress was real fancy too like they were going to church. In the front of the line there was a tall black man with a white beard. He was blind. I could tell because there was a little girl right next to him that pulled on his hand to show him which way to walk. That man was the leader though even though he could not see. They went exactly the way he did and when he raised his hands they raised their hands. He would hum the bar of music and them they would sing it right after him the same line just like he did and so I knew he was the leader.'

'"Then the old man stopped just about at the center of the marsh. In the flickering of the candles, I could see the heads of the folks and I could see the whole shape of the man. I had a pretty good view. Where the old man was there was a little stream of water and a kind of small pond about six feet or so across with a lot of soil in it. I got caught in it one time and got filthy trying to get out. The muck just grabs at you in that old marsh up there.'

'" The music flowed over me. I was tapping my toe in the river lap just behind me. After a while they were all standing around this old man. I could have told them a better place to stand but from the looks of it they were so excited that they would not have listened to anyone maybe not even the Lord himself. "'

'"Pretty soon this blind man raised both his hands to the sky. Everyone got real quiet. He started to talk. He had a voice like you wanted to have the music of that voice float all over you like warm water.'

'"Holy mud,' he said. 'Holy mud. This is holy mud.' He went on and on saying words like he was chanting.'

'"When I was a young boy,' the old man chanted, 'I was a slave.'

'"The people repeated ,'I was a slave."

'"Yes, born a slave right here on this farm.'

"The people replied, 'Right here on this farm.'

'"I'm free.'

'"He's free.'

'"Come touch this soil, children.'

'"Come touch this soil.'

"You're free children of God.'

'"Free children of God.'

'"Free I say.'

'"Free he says.'

'"This is sacred ground.'

'"It's sacred ground.'

'"It's where our ancestors are buried, a slave graveyard. Yes, it's the home of Adam and the home of Eve."

'"It's Adam and Eve.'

"'While they were chanting they were twisting and turning all over that mucky patch. Then folks got back into a line and the started coming up one by one, the old folks and the young folks, and they each one kneeled in front of the old man. They would come up and carefully put down their little candle so it would not go out and them they kneeled in the wet earth and bent their head real low. I watched the light flicker off the bramble bushes and reeds all around them.'

"'Then the old man touched the mud at his own feet. He had on these big boots. Then with a little bit of mud on his finger, I watched him draw a cross of mud on the forehead of the kneeling person. He did that to each one of them in turn. After each one the old man said, 'Amen.'

"' Pretty soon they had finished with crossing themselves and they all stood around and started singing again. Then the old man raised his hands and then put them down. The little girl came along and took his right hand and led him through the group of folks. They all started back towards the bus that brought them. '

"'I heard the bus engine start and listened to it idle while they climbed on board. Then I heard the driver shifting, clanking the gears as he missed shifts getting' that old transmission to go. In a while the night was dark again. When the insects started making noise again I figured it was safe to move and I got up and walked real slow towards the spot where they had been standing.'

"' So Mister Johnson looked up at me then, and he say, 'Pastor, the ground there, the muck they were standing on, it was hot to the touch. It wasn't just the sun of the day that had made it hot that way all day and still into the night. No this was more. It was hot on my bare feet and when I touched it, it burned my hand, it did. It was like there was a fire under that ground, right where he was sayin' that the slaves were buried.'

"Mister Johnson got more excited and twisted in his chair and his wife reached over to him. Then she said to me, 'Pastor, he felt he had to tell you about this.'

"'Yessir, ' Mister Johnson said, his eyes getting big, 'That was the fire of Hell, Pastor, the fire of Hell under that ground there.'

"He stopped for a moment to catch his breath, then continued, 'I did not go back into that marsh for a long time. I realized that my father had told me right that it was a graveyard and that there were spirits there and that I best be leaving them alone. Then I started sneaking back in there hoping that the spirits would not see me and the farmer would not see me either. When I went in there everytime I would go first to the place where the ground had been so hot. It was never the same way again. The hot ground was all gone, all cooled down regular. '

" The old man sighed, 'I sure loved to fish in those days. Still do but I can't get around anymore. Mrs. Johnson, she don't go with me no more. She don't like to fish no more.' His wife winked at me on that one.

"So I got even more intrigued with this old marsh after hearing that story," said the Pastor. "First I tried to find out who the people in the bus were. They could have been from one of the churches of the itinerant preachers the old man talked about. One of the ministers might have brought his flock down with him, instead of just leaving a wreath. I asked around among the parishes in Baltimore and Philadelphia, especially about a blind man."

"Like finding a treasure map," said Frank.

"In time I found out about that preacher. He was a man called Blind Tom who worked with poor blacks and migrants in Baltimore. He liked to take them on trips across the Bay to the Eastern Shore to remind them of their heritage. Most of them descended from slave families on the old farms here. He's long dead."

The Pastor stopped digging. "I tried to bring the story of the slave graveyard to the attention of the state people."

"You got nowhere."

"I didn't understand what to do. Of course, in those days I was not aware of Maggie. Evenso, she could not have helped me much. I needed lawyers or professional historians. The forms they gave me to fill out were too difficult. I would have needed years of research to make the application. All I had was a legend and a story by an old man."

"You saw how quick Jake got permission to bring you down here from up North, Frank," said Maggie. "The Pastor needed that kind of power."

"I got nowhere," continued the Pastor. "Everyone was real polite. I still got nowhere. When this shipwreck was uncovered, and I think that was by the grace of God, why, Frank, it was like a second chance. I had some leverage because the State of Maryland had to investigate. The black community, my church, we had some political power since it was in the jurisdiction of the state. Even with Jake's political pull and money working against us, there was still a chance we could get something done for us, something he couldn't stop."

The telephone rang. Maggie said, "Frank, it's probably another call for you. Here, I'll go with you."

"I'm sure it's my boss again." Frank said as they navigated the mire again, this time avoiding some of the larger puddles. As the two of them approached the house, Frank thought about what words he would use, how he would try to convince his boss to allow him to stay, to ask for the university's support if he had to stand up and anger Jake further. He knew that if the voice were that of Mello, he would have nothing to say. She would have to change to his way of thinking, the way he was developing on this trip, and he knew that was impossible for her. Mello was the kind of person who would never change. Since her childhood she had told him often that she always bet on a sure thing.

"Yes." he said, picking up the telephone and glancing at Maggie.

"Frank, it's your editor," a gruff voice answered.

 "Oh, yes," he answered. Frank's voice was excited even in the dulling heat of the old kitchen room. He covered the mouthpiece and said to Maggie, "It's all right. My editor in New York. He wants his galley proofs." He spoke into the telephone.

"I was called out of town unexpectedly for a job."

"What about your galleys? We're holding up a lot of people waiting on you, Frank."

"I'll need a few more days," Frank answered with a smile.

"The best I can do is tomorrow, Frank. If I don't get the work here by close of business tomorrow, we'll have to cancel the schedule and stop our work on the book."

"Stop the work? We've been planning this for two years, all my writing and then the revisions," Frank was no longer smiling.

"It's all money, Frank. Money and marketing."

"Can't you give me some more time? I'm just caught up in a special project."

"That's real fine, Frank. You got to do the jobs that come across your desk. Your boss told me. He says you're working for Jake Terment's company. That's a pretty good client. It will look good on your resume. Might be good on your dust jacket for the book. Nice going, Frank. "

"When did the president talk to you?" asked Frank.

"I called your office and the call was switched to him. He is handling your calls for you. He said he owed you in return for your going to the Eastern Shore on such short notice. He filled me in on the special project you are on. According to him it's just some piece of a boat that Jake Terment dug up on one of his development properties. "

"I expect you'll see an article about it in the future," offered Frank.

"That good? Well, I'm happy for you."

"It's more work than I thought. There might be more here than parts of a ship."

His editor said nothing.

"You still there?" asked Frank.

"Yeah, sure, Frank. Say, can I make a suggestion as your editor and an old friend?"

"Sure."

"Get rid of this one, Frank. Pack up your stuff and get back to the university."

"Why?" asked Frank. He couldn't believe what he was hearing.

"It sounds like you are in over your head. "

"Why are you saying this?" asked Frank.

"First of all it's a project financed by Jake Terment and if you don't do it well it's going to reflect on you in a big way. From talking to your boss, I get the feeling that your university is not too interested in this project if it goes against what Jake Terment wants."

"What are you telling me?" said Frank, knowing the answer.

"Frank, we're a small publisher. We have financing from our bank same as everyone else. We sell our books through distributors and book shows, same as everyone else."

"Go on."

"We're just a textbook publisher. We don't carry any banners for anybody's causes. We just train the kids."

"The question is," said Frank, "How do you train the kids, if you don't carry any banners?"

"I don't want to get into this, Frank. I'm just a businessman who has to see his banker once in a while to get money to publish. I don't want trouble."

"You think you'll have trouble if one of your authors is not on the good side of Jake Terment?" said Frank.

"Let's say I don't want to be that publisher. Do you want me to go on, Frank?"

Frank finished the call politely and then walked out of the farmhouse. Maggie came and stood beside him on the porch.

"Trouble with the book?" asked Maggie.

"There's a lot of fear of Jake Terment. I just got a deadline of tomorrow or no book. Something to do with the financing."

"I'll just bet he gets his loans from one of Terment's banks," she said. "You could publish your work yourself. I'll help you."

"This was supposed to be the best press for my kind of book. "

She pulled him around to face her and then put her hands on her strong hips.

"No, Frank, you think about it. The whole world of publishing, thank God, is not made up of little companies who are afraid of where their next bank loan is coming from. If you publish yourself, you can write what you want. We could publish your work and send it out ourselves. There's independent bookstores. There's the Internet."

"I wouldn't sell very many copies without this publisher."

"You'd sell some, though," she said. "Look, if the editor can be that scared, then what is the value of the publisher anyway?"

"Why would you do this for me?" asked Frank, seeing a different Maggie than he had seen before.

"Jake and his banker friends must be going to a lot of trouble to get you out of here. I don't like anybody being pushed around. I think you're a good archeologist. I'm betting on you. I think if you really get pushed toward poor scholarship, you'll stand up and push back."

"Why do you say that?"

She looked at him with a smile. "I can't stop believing in you. You can't cheat."

"You think that about me?" said Frank.

"You have more emotion inside that head and heart of yours than you want to let on. I get a big message when I hear you talking about Vietnam. It's like Vietnam was a great disappointment for a man like you and you don't want to ever risk that disappointment again."

She continued, "Guys like Terment, it's easier for them to take risks, because they don't deal with the same kind of truth. Most times their truths are just lies and if they lose they just change the rules of the game. You can't play that way. You go for truth and if you lose, you always remember that you lost. There is one thing though, Frank."

"What's that."

"Like the other women in the class, though, I did have a little crush on you."

He smiled. " I never realized."

"Some of the girls would try all kinds of things to get your attention. You remember the blonde girl whose breast fell out of her shirt on the practice site?"

"No," he smiled.

"She cut the threads on her bra so she could get your attention. She didn't have much of a figure but the boys did notice her after that. You just went right on telling us about measuring strata. You were so interested in the archaeology."

They heard car horns on the road, beyond the honeysuckle.

"The Pastor is waving at us. " She squeezed his hand. "Remember, you don't need that editor."

He squeezed her hand. He felt the warmth. "OK."

Chapter 12

"We better see. It may be more trouble," said Frank. He walked quickly with Maggie and the Pastor towards the fencerow. As they got closer they could hear angry voices churning at each other from beyond the honeysuckle.

Frank pointed through a break in the foliage. "There's the reason for all the commotion," he said .

Several farm trucks and some cars coming from opposite ends had met face to face at the center of the single lane bridge. The drivers were walking around the roadway, agitated in the heat and shaking their fists. More vehicles coming up to the bridge were expanding the traffic confusion. From the gate area, the Terment Company guard, sweating in his green coat, was trying to wave cars away. One car had tried to turn around and was hopelessly snarled against oncoming traffic in the narrow road..

"Stoplights were changed," said the Pastor. "There's a switch box up there. Someone's prank."

They stood behind the high mass of honeysuckle, unseen by the motorists. More drivers got out of their cars and milled around. The screaming and cursing was increasing in the summer heat. Frank watched this for a few more minutes, then turned to Maggie and said, " I think these folks are going to be here all afternoon, the way they're going."

Maggie pointed across the road where, gathering on the lawn in the shade under the ancient trees, were a few persons dressed in the orange and black butterfly costumes. More were coming from behind the old white house and lining up. As they did , they adjusted their wings and stood side by side across the yard, parallel with the road. Then together the human butterflies slowly moved their eight foot wings. The color of the costumes was a startling contrast to the deep dark green of the yard. The clutter of automobile and motorist noise continued to increase. Seeing the butterflies, the drivers who were still sitting in their cars honked their car horns again and again. Others began to shout at the orange and black costumes which, in turn, continued their waving motion..

Behind the line of human butterflies, the door to the white house opened and Mrs. Pond walked out and looked at the cars on the road, her arms folded. She turned and spoke to someone standing behind her in the dark interior, someone Frank couldn't see. Frank watched her call to one of the butterflies who walked back to the porch. Frank could see the costume from behind, the human underneath who was dressed in a black shirt and trousers with straps holding the wings. The person stood in front of Mrs. Pond, then nodded his head and proceeded back to his fellow human insects.   They gathered in a simple huddle and were given what appeared to be instructions. In a few minutes some of the butterflies began to cross the road through the crowd of angry drivers. They lined up directly in front of the hedgerow which hid Frank and his companions.

The owners of the jammed vehicles, becoming more angry, milled around, kicking at the stones in the gravel road, little clods of dust lifting at each kick and drifting down like small parachutes. Judging from the smile on her face, Frank assumed Mrs. Pond was pleased with all the confusion. He watched her walk down the steps of her porch and stride imperiously towards the human butterflies and the drivers. With her was her companion, a tall black man, dressed in African robes.

One of the drivers who was also black, pointed at the African saying, "Who is he? I ain't never seen him around River Sunday."

Frank heard a driver near him muttering almost whispering, "What does she want? Everybody knows she's crazy. Just a crazy old rich lady."

Mrs. Pond walked into the center of the road and stared at the drivers. The human butterflies gathered around her. Then she proceeded alone towards the bridge. The drivers, quieter, nervously made a path for her. She moved up under the stoplight, looked up at it and then at the switchbox on a metal post at the side of the bridge. Then she turned toward the drivers and spoke, her voice shrill like a bird.

"This bridge work must stop at once. Yours are not the only lives that matter."

One of the drivers spoke up, a young black farm worker. "You don't have no right, Mrs. Pond. No M'am. We don't care nothing about no animals. I'll hunt them all down for you and put them out of their misery. You are crazy, you old lady." The driver moved towards her, his arm raised as if to strike. Another man restrained him, wrestling with him, saying, " You don't know what you are saying, man. You're going to get into a lot of trouble." The man was held on the ground, kicking, by several of the men.

The butterflies began moving towards Mrs. Pond, their wings raised. Her face showed no alarm although the crowd was becoming more violent. Frank thought that the butterfly people and the drivers would start fighting momentarily.

Then he heard the police siren. At that moment a River Sunday police sedan arrived along the wrong side of the road, moving deftly by the stopped cars and trucks, its stern faced occupant motioning to different drivers he passed. The car stopped beside the group of butterflies, separating them from the drivers. The policeman whom Frank had seen at the meeting during Jake's speech, stepped out. In the sunlight, he was a large tough looking man carefully dressed in his uniform, his holster and belt leather glinting.

"Hello, Mrs. Pond, " the office said, in a friendly manner.

She did not answer him and instead called to the African, who had remained several yards from the road, waiting up on the lawn in the shade. "Doctor," she said haughtily, " as you can see we have no support from our police."

The African grinned and held up two small books from a pocket in his robe. From the distance Frank could see what looked like a butterfly on the cover of one. The African nodded vigorously to Mrs. Pond. Yet after a few moments of this movement of his head, Frank realized the man was dazed, his mind elsewhere, unable to do anything more than stand there and bob his head up and down. About once a minute, he methodically thumbed the books, ready, it seemed to Frank, to look up the specifications of a butterfly as if that was the best answer to his friend's moment of distress.

With the coming of the officer, the crowd had calmed. Mrs. Pond had returned safely to the side of the African. She touched his arm almost in apology for disturbing him and turned finally to speak to the policeman, who stood patiently, as if he had been through this type of experience several times before.

"Billy, the Doctor teaches in London," she said. " He's one of the world's greatest lepidopterists, his specialty being migration of butterflies. He graciously agreed to stop in River Sunday on his tour around the United States. He could tell you how important it is for all of us to leave these insects in their habitat. He could tell you what will happen to all of us if we do not respect nature's ways, its rules. He could tell you so much."

Billy, the officer, sweating in the sun, looked at her and the African, then around at the people in costume. "Mrs. Pond, we've been through this before. I'm sure your guest doesn't want any trouble."

The African, quickly nodding his head, selected a page to read, the picture of the butterfly on that page particularly colorful as the limp paper hung over his large hand. He read softly to himself in careful English. The tall woman looked down at the officer who was easily a foot shorter.

"You have no idea how much trouble there will be in the future if you do not act," she said, her voice like that of a shrill bird.

"Mrs. Pond, I don't know what happened here. I expect one of your people got a little carried away again. You know better than to do this sort of thing. We got to let these cars go or I'll have to start arresting your people."

Her look was one of pity mixed with authority as though she were the policeman and were letting him go. She slowly turned away, then motioned to the butterflies and walked back towards her house. The human butterflies fell back into their original solid line away from the road and on the lawn by the house. By then Mrs. Pond had reached her porch. She turned and watched, her hands on the porch railing as the butterflies began to move

147

their wings and sway from side to side. Frank could hear them chanting.

"Say the word and the bridge will be stopped,"
"Say the word and the bridge will be stopped."

Billy began backing the cars off the bridge.

"It's all over. Let's get back to work," said Frank. He led the others back to the site.

"With all her concerned heart, " the Pastor said, "That lady doesn't have any idea about the poor folks here.. So maybe that's why I don't care too much about her animals, her butterflies."

Then his face turned into a broad smile.

"What?" asked Maggie.

"You two look like slaves," said the Pastor.

Frank and Maggie looked at each other.

"I guess he's got a point," said Maggie.

"The old folks worked just like the two of you in this heat," said the Pastor. "They were always filthy from the working conditions and the dirt floor huts they lived in. Their clothes were not any different, Maggie, than the ragged shorts and shirts that you two are dressed in. Look at yourselves. Bare feet, rags, covered with dirt. Yessir, you could pass for a couple of field slaves working up here before the Civil War."

Chapter 13

Over beyond the honeysuckle hedge, the traffic on the bridge was running freely. The butterfly costumes had been neatly stacked on Mrs. Robin Pond's porch and the actors had disappeared inside the house. Frank and the others had been at work in the pits for more than an hour when they saw Jake's station wagon stop on the road outside the gate.

Frank watched Jake talk to the company guard for a few minutes, the two standing at the far side of the highway, an occasional car or truck rumbling by and hiding them for a moment. Jake's face was animated. The guard in his green jacket held his head in a slight bow as he listened to Jake, sometimes talking but mostly listening. Then Jake walked away towards the site.

Jake slammed the old gate open and walked through, two birds flaring in the honeysuckle hedge as he did so. There was a mud smear on the bottom of his left trouser leg. It was the first dirt Frank had seen on the man's immaculate white suit. Jake carried his white jacket in his left hand. His right hand was clenched in a fist which he held in front of him as he approached.

"We didn't expect you until later, Jake, " said Frank, as he raised himself to a kneeling position, his back straight, his arms stretching upward.

"That stoplight was broken on purpose," he said. "Pond thinks she can stop the bridge. She doesn't realize who she's up against. "

"I guess your company guard must have called you," said Frank.

The Pastor said, "I bet Billy, our chief of police, called you right away with a report. Tell Frank how you know all the cops, Jake," said the Pastor.

He turned to Frank. "What he's not telling you is that this is a small town and we all grew up together, cops, preachers, and Terments. The same group of tough white boys that hung around together when Jake was a kid, they got to be the policemen we have here today."

"She can't do this to me," Jake said, as he turned to look over the road. Jake's expression was one of rage. "I went out of my way to get along with her. She's still pissed off after all this time."

"What did you do to her?" asked Frank.

Jake calmed down and began to smile again, the television smile. He glanced at the Pastor who was staring at him. "You'll never get the true story from Jefferson."

"Come on," Jake said to Frank. They walked to the station wagon out on the road. Spyder stepped out of the driver's seat and opened the back door for Frank, smiling as always.

The air conditioner was running inside the car and the air was cold to Frank's bare arms and legs. Jake handed him a small silver flask.

"Drink it. Good whiskey."

Frank declined. "I drink that, I'll start tripping over Maggie's grid lines, " he laughed.

Jake grinned. "That's not such a bad idea." He laughed to himself. Then he said, "My father gave me that flask when I was sixteen years old, the beginning of the fall dove shoot right here at this farm. "

He pointed at the cornfield. "That's where we used to shoot them. Corn left standing and the doves would roost in there. The tenant farmer would scare them up for us and we'd sometimes get shots for the whole afternoon. My father said he gave me that flask to keep me busy until the birds decided to fly by again."

He looked at Frank again, his eyes pleading, as if looking for a friend to confide in. "Let me tell you about Birdey." He took a pull on the flask. "My father was buried from the church behind the Court House in the middle of River Sunday. My family built that church. The first church in River Sunday. One of the oldest in the whole country. We gave him a beautiful funeral until she ruined it. I spoke at my father's funeral and so did several friends of my family. Birdey had asked to speak and we let her, never expecting what she would say.

"She's a tall woman and she towered over the pulpit. After looking at me for a minute or two, she started talking about how my father had been so aware of the environment, how he was a tribute to his family, how he was like the Terments of old, farming men who had, of necessity, a great respect for the land and the animals.

"Then she started in about her last visit to my father at Peachblossom. On this visit she said that he told her how he had stopped hunting, how he had started taking photographs of the wildlife out on the island. He took her into a small room off his study where he had hung these framed photographs of ducks and butterflies, that kind of thing. He said she was the only person who had seen them, the only person he wanted to show them to. She told the assembly at the church that she thought the photography was very good, almost that of a genius and that if he had pursued this creative work early in his life he could have been one of the great nature photographers.

"Then she said that he told her to announce after his death that Peachblossom Manor and its adjoining acreage on Allingham Island had been willed to her with the condition that she create a nature preserve from the land.

"Frank, with that bit of news you could have heard a mouse squeak in that old church. Can you imagine that? Bringing up a man's last will and testament at a holy gathering. She didn't even wait for the poor man to be buried. Of course, it was all a filthy lie. In her lack of respect she even lied at his funeral. Frank, I can tell you that tore me up. She started a legal claim on the estate which, while we handled it, cost us a little bit of money to take care of, not to mention the aggravation and the public scrutiny of my father's memory and his mental state. "

He looked outside the car for a moment. "I had to witness this desecration of my father's funeral. I had to do this alone. I'll never forget it. When we came out of the church, Birdey was standing there shaking hands with most of my family and friends. I went up to her and she smiled at me, pretending she had not done this terrible thing. I think she expected me to congratulate her on the kind words she had said about my father.

"'I'm so sorry about your father, Jake,' she said.

"'I'm so sorry about you,' I said back to her, watching for only a moment as her face angered. Then I got into my limousine for the ride to the grave.

"Well, at the grave site I stood on one side and she stood on the other. She glared at me the whole service. The minister, seeing us, was very embarrassed and made his talk very short. He said that my father had lived his life trying to make the Eastern Shore a better place for people and animals to live. When he said 'animals' he looked over at Birdey but she was too angry for that little bit of compromise. He looked at me and I wouldn't even look at her or him. Far as I was concerned the minister was guilty of letting her up on that pulpit. Believe me, he knew right then he was fast losing his big yearly Terment church contributions. The preacher quickly added that my father's work in real estate would be remembered by all of us, poor and rich alike. Then the man ended the ceremony and that was it.

"The next day Birdey and her lawyer came to Peachblossom to speak to me.

" She started in, 'I never meant to embarrass you, Jake. I thought you would see this gift as a tribute to how great a man you father was, ' she said. We talked by her car in front of the house. I had no desire to have her inside. My father's car was still there where he had left it the day he died, still parked with its front wheels a little bit into the grass like he always did. "

He looked at Frank. "If she and my father hadn't been so old, I might have thought she had seduced him, slept with him at the house."

He went on, "' Birdey, ' I said, ' I don't care what you meant to do or did not mean to do. I just want you to leave this place and never come back here again.'

"'I can't do that, Jake. Your father gave me this place to use as a home for wildlife.'

"By then, Frank, I was getting upset. You've seen me in a lot of situations here in the last few days and that I have had to worry about more than my share of problems in trying to build a few houses here on the Island. I'm sure you'll agree that I am a pretty calm fellow. This lady had overstepped. I mean, what would you do if someone came around the day after one of your parents died and told you an absolute lie about what that parent had done?"

Frank said nothing.

Jake continued. "So I said to her, ' Birdey, you're a liar.' "

"That's when the lawyer spoke up. I knew the man. He had brought his practice to River Sunday from Baltimore a few years before. He had taken many of the early civil rights cases when the old segregation rules were changing. He wasn't a native, didn't have much money and he sure did not understand anything about Peachblossom or Allingham Island, much less the Terments. I didn't have anything against him. On the other hand, I didn't have anything for him either.

"He stood there in the sunlight and tried to console me. 'Jake,' he said.

Jake grinned. "You tell me, Frank, don't you hate it when they use your name and they don't even know you?"

Frank nodded.

"This fellow went on. He said, 'Jake, my client says that there was a will written by your father and that she saw it written and put away in the safe up here at Peachblossom.'

"So I said, 'There's no will like that here. There's my father's only will that he had prepared when I was a child that gives me everything. The will is in the hands of my father's attorney in River Sunday. I 'm sure that you'll find it in order. Another thing. I want you to get you client here to admit she lied about my father photographing all those animals. There is not a one of those photographs here in this old house and anyone wants to see, why they can just come and look.'

"The lawyer and Birdey traded glances. Then he said to her in his outsider's twang, "Come on, let's get out of here. " She didn't say anything, just turned and walked away.

"Later that day I got a telephone call from my father's attorney to come into his office. I drove into River Sunday. His office was in a large white building behind the Court House. I went in there and talked to him and he asked me if there was any other will that I had heard about. I said , 'No, my father had only told me about one will, the one he had.' I said that my father had explained to me that I was going to inherit Peachblossom Manor and the Terment Company stock that he held.

"So my lawyer said, 'Well, Birdey sees it different. However, what you say, Jake, that's good enough for me.' " Jake smiled at this point in his story. He took another swallow from the flask.

"A few days later Birdey drove out to the house again. This time she came alone. I was there working at my desk in the living room. I used to take work out to the island to finish it."

He sighed. "Anyway, I looked up from a report I was working on, and there she was standing, looking at me, from the patio in back of the house. It's a fine brick terrace where there are white iron chairs and tables. My father and I used to like to sit in the evening. We sat out there many a time and talked about Terment Company. I think that's where he and I first talked about building houses on the island.

" So she stood there, her hands on her hips like she stands sometimes. I went out on the terrace to talk to her.

"She said, 'Jake, what did you do with your father's will?'

"I said, 'Birdey, you ought to forget this lie. I don't know where you got all this story. My father would never have let Peachblossom go out of the family. He loved this farm.'

" 'Jake,' she said, ' I was here when your father drafted the plan. We sat in his study one summer evening and worked on it together. He was going to finish it himself just the way he wanted it and then give it to his lawyer. That was a few months before he died. He was still in pretty good health. He asked me about what I thought would be the future of the Island. I said that if Jake did not develop it then a child of Jake's in the future would. I told him that sooner or later someone would come along who wanted to make money off the sale of the island. He was very upset about all of this. Your father was a changed man from the way I had known him even a few years earlier. I guess he had learned that he was going to die. His liver was gone from the drinking. His lungs too from the smoking. He laughed about his lungs, said they were payback for the original family fortune made in growing tobacco.'

"She told me that they went for a walk about the property. The brick walk through the garden and down to the river was pretty at that time of evening. There was a small breeze blowing in from the Bay and so the mosquitoes were not bad. They walked all the way down to the water.

" The brick walk became a wide path. He told me that it was an old road that the Terments used in the colonial days. The slaves would roll the great tobacco hogsheads on this road down to the riverbank to load into the cargo ships for the convoys to England. By the river, she and his father looked at the old foundations where the warehouses had stood.

"'Your father,' she said, 'told me that the Terments had to change the loading place for their tobacco. They had to build this great landing right on the Bay even though the waters were not as sheltered. I asked him why and he did not reply, just kept walking.'

'" Then we walked down near the butterfly trees. They were large, old. The butterflies loved them. The Monarchs came to those trees every year. I told your father about the insects, how they live and fight and love and die, in a smaller version of our world. He was very interested in all this. I told him while the two of us stood there looking up at those trees, that the butterflies had been coming to this spot for hundreds of years on their flight south and that we had no real idea why they did this. He was very subdued, I remember, thinking, he said, about the effect that we humans had on this tiny creature's existence. I think your father was impressed that he had the power to change the future for the better for that animal.'

" 'A butterfly flew up when we were there. Your father watched it until it flew away. Then he said that when you were a kid, you used to bring him bags full of mashed butterflies. It was a game you played every fall when they flew over the farm. He looked at me then and he said he knew that you had no interest, that you hated the creatures. I remember him saying that the colors of the Monarch were orange and black, the Maryland colors he told me, same as in the state flag.

Jake sipped from the flask. "What she didn't say, Frank, was that my daddy paid me for cleaning up the bugs. He didn't like them dying all over the lawn."

"Then she went on with the lies, 'We walked back toward the manor house in the twilight. 'Birdey,' your father said, 'I'm going to do something different this time, this generation.'

"'What do you mean, Richard?' she asked him.

"'Jake,' he said, 'Jake only wants to develop this place for the money in it. He's talked to me for hours about his plans. He wants to dig up the land, change it, build houses.'

"Well, Frank," said Jake, " I told her right then and there. I said, 'Birdey, that is not true, my father didn't say all that to you. Why did he even talk to you? I find it all ridiculous. You're not family, you're not a Terment.'

"Frank, she looked at me and tried to claim, in her high pitched voice, 'Well, Jake, he tried to talk to you about it but you just went on and on about your business plans, so he talked to me.'

"I said to her, 'Birdey, I mean he used to try to figure out ways to aggravate you, to get you to leave him alone, all your talk about the animals and your criticizing him for the duck hunting he did up at Wilderness Swamp. He hated you.'

"Well, Frank, she goes on then, 'He talked to me because he knew that I care about the land and the creatures and that I had always been this way, that I was honest and he knew he could rely on me.'

"So I said, 'My father didn't think you were honest, Birdey. He used to call you every name in the book and none of them were honest.'

"So then she went on, 'He said that he would give you the Terment Company, his shares and that you would make a lot of money. He told me that you could "torment gold" Those were his exact words. He said that he didn't want you to have Peachblossom because the land should go back to the animals. He said the Terments had taken it by force from the animals and from the Nanticokes. Peachblossom belonged to the animals above all.'"

" Frank, she was right about one thing. That was a favorite expression of my father. He always talked among family members about 'tormenting gold.' I don't know where she heard him say that phrase. Probably heard it in the gossip from one of our servants."

Jake smiled. "My father always respected me for making money."

"'Your father wanted to free you,' Birdey continued telling me there on the terrace. 'He told me that he never wanted a son, a new generation of Terments. When you came along he had tried to help you. He said that you would die young if you stayed on the land, if you owned Peachblossom. He said you didn't have the strength that he did, that you didn't have the ability to scare people away like he did. He said that returning the island to its original state where only animals lived there would mean a fresh start for you, for the whole family.'

Jake looked at Frank, "Why would he say a thing like that, abut scaring people? He had respect for me. I tell you she was lying."

"'Birdey, ' I said to her, 'This whole thing is a lie. I want you off the island.'"

"'Jake,' she said to me, ' your father said that this place would kill you. He said it made him drink hard all his life but surviving was different during his lifetime. He knew life would be harder for you.'

"Then she left. I heard from her lawyer for a while but the case went nowhere. They didn't have a will to disprove my ownership. From that day, however, she has tried to hurt me here in River Sunday. This butterfly costume gimmick of hers is a nasty way to try to hurt my project and my friends and me."

"I heard you had a step mother," asked Frank. "What was she doing while Birdey was coming up on her visits. What happened to her?"

"I see Jefferson has been telling his lies. That woman never meant much to me or my father. She lived in one of the old cottages. She was a housekeeper, that's all she was. She certainly wasn't my mother in any way. My mother was a very beautiful woman."

"I shouldn't have asked."

"That's all right, Frank." Jake smiled. "You and I, we have to get this cleaned up. I've got some of my business associates coming out here pretty soon. I told you about that."

"We haven't finished with the research yet, Jake. I don't want to mislead you," said Frank, opening the car door and climbing out into the heat. Jake followed him outside and they stood together beside the car.

Jake was suddenly impatient. "I guess you don't understand anything I've told you." He motioned towards the site. "Maybe these bones could have been planted here by someone who wants to hold up the construction."

"That's not likely, Jake. They are very old. We will excavate what we can and make our recommendations about the site. That's all," said Frank.

"This is not a very attractive display for my friends," he said.

"Well, I can't disregard all these, Jake. This is a very unusual find. Especially the giant man.."

"I don't really care about what may or may not have happened in ancient history. I just want to get this place cleaned up. "

Jake motioned to Spyder who was standing by the gate. The two men followed Frank as he returned to the site. When they reached the excavations, Jake jumped down into the pit where the Pastor was working on the new skeletons. Before anyone could stop him, he had picked one of the skulls out of the soil and placed it up on the edge of the pit. As he reached for another, Frank jumped down into the pit beside the Pastor and put his hand on Jake's arm.

Jake stopped and turned to Frank, smiling again. "What are you doing, Frank?"

"You can't do that, Jake," said the Pastor.

"What do you say, Frank?" Jake stood straight in the pit, looking directly at Frank. Spyder was towering over Frank at the edge of the pit, his highly polished shoes outstanding on the edge of the pit, while below him Frank's feet were muck covered and bare.

"He's cleaning up his place for the afternoon reception," said Spyder, his words like bullets.

"You heard my friend, "said Jake.

Frank stared at him, dropping his hand from Jake's arm.

"This is my land, my place, to do with as I wish, " said Jake.

"We should handle our disagreement professionally, Jake. " said Frank, motioning to the Pastor to stand back. Maggie had come over to the pit and was standing near Jake and Spyder.

"I think that's a great idea, " said Jake. "I knew I could reason with you, Frank. You just continue to be an archaeologist."

"I am being an archaeologist."

The cat reappeared and perched on the edge of the pit near the Pastor, The Pastor picked him up and held him in his arms as he watched Jake bend over and pry at another of the bones in the floor of the pit.

"Past catching up to you, Jake? Worried about what we are finding?" the Pastor said.   Then the Pastor let the cat drop. The cat landed near Jake with a snarl.

"God damn you," shouted Jake as he jumped back from the cat which then hissed, leaped up on the edge of the pit and then ran away from the site into the hedge.

Jake tottered then lost his balance and dropped into a sitting position, ungracefully on his backside, his feet in front of him. He raised himself, his face furious. He brushed at the wet soil on his trouser seat.

 Frank said, "We all have to be careful around the pits. The walls are so soft. Anyone can have a pretty bad fall, maybe hurt themselves."

Jake ignored him. "What are you going to do next, Jefferson? You going to pull a razor on me?"   Then, composing himself, Jake smiled at Frank and Maggie and said," I hate cats."

"He just jumped out of my arms," said the Pastor.

"No, Jefferson, no, I'm not worried about what you folks find up here. I just want you out of here."

"Then we see this as equals, Jake," said the Pastor.

"What do you mean?"

"We both just want the truth," said the Pastor.

"I want a bridge and I want to put a lot of your friends and mine to work building it,"
said Jake.

"Those friends, are they all white?" asked the Pastor.

"There are many black people involved with the project," said Jake.

"Who?"

Jake did not answer him. At this moment, three green station wagons, one after the other entered the small lane going to the farmhouse and moved up the road, bouncing with much noise as they did so.

"Caterers are here," said Spyder.

"Frank, can I talk to you privately for a minute?" Maggie said, pulling at his arm. When they were a few feet away from Jake and Spyder, she looked at him. "You're not going to compromise with him? This field is important. You can't allow this to be wrecked. You are going to have a tough time explaining this to other archaeologists. You and I know people who would give anything to work on a field like this."

"Maybe there is a solution," said Frank, scratching the back of his neck.

"Jake," Frank turned and walked toward him. Jake was handing some more of the bones to Spyder.

"What is it, Frank?"

"I have an idea."

"Hurry up. I haven't much time."

"I think it will be a liability for your company to have folks walking around these open pits, with the possibility that they could trip on the surveyors twine. Maybe some of them might have a little too much to drink, you know what I mean."

" What do you suggest, Frank?"

"Well, when we've had this before at other sites I have worked on, we just roped off the area. You don't want people out seeing the bones anyway so that will solve your problem without your having to pick up all the skeletons. Besides, it would take a long time to find all of the bones especially the small ones. We'll just cordon off the area. I'll personally stand by the rope and tell the folks what they want to know about the archaeology. You can say something about what we are doing too, how we hope to be finished soon. Your investors don't have to see any of it."

Jake looked at the rest of the bones at his feet. He looked at the soil on his hands and trousers. "All right. I want this pit covered up though. It looks like a massacre up here. That's not good for business."

Maggie turned to Frank as Jake walked off with Spyder to see the caterers.

He said, looking at her, "You think that I didn't stand up to Jake, that I'm quitting on you and the Pastor. I'm not. I'm just trying to figure all this out, figure out what is best to do with the time we have left."

"You should understand what is best to do. There's a lot to be found and we have to find it. Our purpose here is being lost in all your figuring. That's your problem. You think too much." said Maggie, turning away from him and walking back to her dig, her bare feet leaving small puddles in the muck.

"You got to have it in your heart to do the right thing without thinking. There's just not enough time to do it any other way, " she called back over her shoulder.

Chapter 14

The grid stakes cast shadows, daubing the field with black smears. Frank and Maggie rigged a barrier rope. The rope was suspended from pine posts quickly struck into the soft ground. At the center of each rope span Frank hung a small sign on which he printed, with Jake's approval, the words "Restricted Area. State of Maryland Archaeology Site." Jake had made him add the additional words "Do Not Enter."

Frank had managed to keep most of the discoveries out of sight in deference to Jake. A large piece of canvas taken from the cover of one of the farm implements was stretched over the Q location to hide the crew skeletons. However, he could not disguise the large cannon which was still off to the side of the excavated area. Also, the sword parts were still embedded in the spot where they had been found, waiting on additional careful and patient work to fully uncover them.

Meanwhile, Jake and Spyder were busy supervising the catering staff near the farmhouse where the tables were being set up. Two young women in white dresses were occupied arranging flowers and food trays on white tablecloths. A small folding table had been set up with rows of name tags arranged alphabetically for the attendees. Two refrigerated trucks from the Chesapeake Hotel arrived and disgorged great quantities of liquor and cooked food.

The Pastor had gone home and returned, attired in the dark clothes of his ministry. Frank kidded him that this was the first time he had seen him dressed up; he did not recognize him standing on the porch in his black suit. Frank and Maggie remained in their work clothes, such as they were. They planned to stay behind the rope barrier, away from most of the guests, and to return to archeological work the instant the visitors left. Maggie did brush out her long blonde hair.

Several waiters and serving persons were bustling also with the setup work. Men dressed in white coats were assembling the beer kegs. Along the back of one table were neatly arranged bottles of various whiskeys, gins, and mixers. One of the black waiters waved to the Pastor.

"Terment pays pretty good, doesn't he?" observed the Pastor.

"Yes, Pastor," the man said, almost in a whisper. "It's not like the General Store days though, is it?"

"No," said the Pastor.

"We all got to eat."

"Yes."

"You find them graves yet, Pastor?" the man asked.

"No, but I'm going to keep myself at it."

"We're all praying for you," the man said as he arranged the liquor bottles.

Out in the yard, a young waitress put down her tray on a table and pointed at the river.

"My God, look at that," she said.

"Jake, something's wrong, " someone else said.

Over the tops of the tall trees at the edge of the riverbank they could see the great arm of the crane, its black pulley wheel stark, the spokes outlined. The boom was wavering, moving slowly then more quickly, back and forth. A turkey buzzard, looking for dead animal carcasses, circled above the moving crane, while steel cables began to slap at the pile driver hammer resting on the barge deck.

"Looks like that bird has found something. That bird bothering your crane, Jake?" said one of the early guests, laughing. He was a big man in a white tennis shirt, pencils and pens stuck in the tiny pocket on his huge chest.

"Seems like it, doesn't it? " said Jake, trying to grin. He started towards the shoreline, first walking, his eyes following the moving sprocket tip of the crane, then running as the crane began to wobble even more. The buzzard suddenly flared straight up and flew off. The crane moved faster, slipping back and forth in a wide arc.

"It's as if a giant is shaking it from below," said Frank.

The crane arm steadied to a vertical position, then began to head downward towards the water surface. It creaked, an ugly noise, as it went, its wire cables reeling forward into the water, the barge itself showing a decided list. The hammer mechanism tipped forward starting to collapse.

Jake and Spyder had reached the shoreline. The cabin and caterpillar tracks of the great crane were at such an angle that the whole rig began to slip and slide slowly across the deck of the canted barge, the great arm and tip closer to the water. Then with a lurch and creak, the long arm stopped not more than fifty feet above the water and stretching well towards the middle of the channel, cables looped into the water like tangled fishing lines. At this moment, with the strained pile driver braces bending , the hammer restraint broke and, metal screeching, the huge hammer crashed into the river causing a massive geyser of brown water.

Jake's face was taut, his mouth halfway between his usual smile and a new look that Frank had not seen. It was a look of cunning laced with intense hatred, like that of a cornered beast. Jake was at the same time trying to determine who did this to him and how he could punish that person. He must have been thinking that the culprit would be hard to find and that was making him all the more angry.

"I guess that barge musta sprung a leak," said the man with the ball point pens in his shirt pocket. "Happens to the old barges all the time. All that weight of the crane and the pile driving equipment."

He continued, " Over in Baltimore the crews always try to put off the worn out equipment for jobs down here in the country." As the man spoke two large oil drums toppled off the raised side of the barge and rolled from the high point to the low corner, splashing their complement of diesel fuel all over the deck as they tumbled, finally jumping the small restraining barrier at the edge and falling into the Nanticoke River with a splash of dark water. The drums quickly righted and floated next to the half sunk barge in the weak current, diesel fuel and hydraulic oil colliding in a rainbow of water hues, the color patterns drifting out from the large letters spelling Terment across the rusty barge steel siding.

The cable that had been hanging from the tip of the crane let go and roared out on the sprocket wheel, the tail of the steel cable whipping through the air towards the shoreline where Jake and the others were watching. The oncoming missile caused screams and several people put their arms up in defense as the cable hit the water surface, fortunately far short of the beach. Like a stone that a child skips at the seashore, the cable crashed against the water surface and sent a great spray of river water into the group drenching two or three persons closest to the river. After the cable had left the crane, the sprocket on the crane arm spun furiously for a few moments, then slowly creaked to a stop. Finally the noise was over and the afternoon river quiet returned. In a few minutes the buzzard came back and returned to its incessant circling.

Frank scratched the back of his neck and pulled his hat forward.

"Well, that was a real nice show, nice welcome, Jake," said one of the guests.   "How long you figure that's going to hold things up?"

"I don't know," he said, as he trudged back up to the party from the shoreline. " We'll have to pump out the barge, steady up the crane. Not long I guess."

Spyder immediately went to the station wagon and made a call, the imperturbable grin still on his face as he talked. More guests were arriving. The lane from the road to the farmhouse was filled on one side with station wagons and pickup trucks. Cars, tilted crazily with the high round crown of the road, were left on the highway outside the gate, wheels perilously close to the ditches.

From the road, Frank heard a new sound. The human butterflies had started chanting at the side of the road. The song interspersed with the murmur of the cocktail party. He could not see the butterflies but knew they were there, wings moving in rhythm, lined up along the road, the old woman cheering them on again from her perch behind the yard full of birdfeeders.

The Pastor had mentioned to Frank that the African visitor was leaving River Sunday, was going back to London. His visit to

River Sunday had been short and was spent only with Mrs. Pond. The Pastor said that his church elders had invited the butterfly expert to dinner thinking that because he was African he might be interested in some of the black issues of the town. The man declined the invitation saying to the elders only a quick 'no' and nothing else.

As soon as Jake heard the human butterflies, he became very agitated and went to the station wagon to talk with Spyder. From what Frank could observe, Jake talked excitedly with the guards. Spyder shrugged his shoulders several times. Then, as Jake grabbed his arm and shook it, Spyder finally nodded. Right afterward Spyder and the guards, there were three of them at the gate checking in the visitors, walked off to their left and out of Frank's sight.

Jake stood at the gate, ignoring the incoming guests as he watched Spyder walk away. Then, rubbing his hands, Jake seemed to calm himself. Frank saw a change come over Jake, his smiling personality returned, as he began to talk and joke with his investor guests.

A small cloud covered the sun for a moment and a whisper of cold swept across the site. Frank shivered and for a moment held his arms around his body. He was almost naked in his work shorts. He had not shaved and his face itched.

More than a hundred came to the party. The guests followed a routine. They arrived, were served a drink, and walked over to look at the wrecked barge and pile driver. Some walked quickly by the excavation, most not even looking at it. Frank was sure they had been prompted by Jake's staff to show no interest. Many simply stood in small groups, talking, drinking and partaking of the many refreshments which the Terment Company employees carried around on small shiny silver trays..

Frank, standing at his barrier rope with Maggie, had seen many of these persons at the hotel the day he arrived. Some were white, some black. The talk that he overheard was generally about the new houses to be built. The black bartenders in their white coats moved among the groups, with small trays, serving drinks and food. The guests talked excitedly about the Terment Town project, the jobs it would create, and especially about who was going to win bids for the work of building houses. When someone did come over to the dig site, however, Frank tried to portray the facts of the wreck as he and Maggie had surmised them. One woman wanted to know if he had found any dinosaur bones. Others noticed the cannon and asked whether the wreck was a treasure ship. He told them that there had been a small gold pouch and he was keeping his eyes open. One offered to help look for treasure but he declined the person's offer saying that the site was going to be closed up very soon and that there was no reason to think that any treasure was on board. Maggie said to him between answers that she would never have been able to be so patient.

She said, "I don't like the talking part anyway. I got in trouble the only time I tried it. I'll just let my work talk for itself."

Jake Terment, from time to time would stand near, eavesdropping, eyes on the ground as he listened. Frank knew Jake was listening to what he was saying about the shipwreck. Frank was courteous. He knew he had to continue trying to maintain a professional standing with Jake. He still wasn't completely convinced he couldn't pull this off and satisfy both his boss and Jake as well as his new friends, Maggie and the Pastor. Somehow as a professional he still felt that Jake would be reasonable. It was a matter of convincing Jake with the right words, words he had not found yet. Frank was good at listening and keeping his mouth shut. The same tactics he used on the president of his university to get and hold his job, he thought he could use here. If he was courteous to these businessmen and then careful in his discussion of the wreck, he could work with Jake to get the job done right. That was the way he had always managed, survived. In turn, if he were successful with Jake, his job at the university would be secure.

A black businessman wearing one of the ubiquitous light blue cotton suits that most of the men wore raised his hand and pointed at Frank. "You can tell me something."

"What's that?" Frank answered him.

"I hear that there was a graveyard up here, for black folks. What can you tell me about that?"

"Well, we haven't found anything yet that would show that for sure. We know there was a legend about a graveyard."

"Tell me what you have found."

Frank looked at Maggie and continued, "The ship was burned. Some men died on board, probably sailors. We don't know why they died. " Frank scratched his neck, wondering if he had already said too much.

Jake intervened, putting his arm around the man. "I hope you are getting the information you want about the site."

"Yes, I am," said the visitor. "I understand this might be a slave graveyard here. That'd be quite an important find, wouldn't it?"

The Pastor came over. Jake continued, glaring at the Pastor. "We are going to do everything we can to analyze all this before we go further with the project. Let me assure you, we will leave nothing undiscovered that might help in local history. By the way, while you're here I want to introduce you to one of the main contractors. Did you get a drink?" Jake steered him back into the crowd.

The Pastor's eyes followed as they moved away from the wreck site, his face showing disappointment. In his shame at the black businessman's relationship with Jake, the Pastor did not return Frank's glance.

A half hour went by. Frank could hear most of the conversations at the party from his vantage point at the edge of the site. He listened as the Pastor talked with a small group of guests.

"Things have changed since the garbage war, haven't they, Pastor?" asked a man, about thirty, his shirt printed with the outline of a faucet, the symbol of a local plumbing company.

"I don't know. Maybe it's different around River Sunday. Maybe it's not."

"What's this about a garbage war?" asked a woman, her hair pulled up against the heat, teetering on her stiletto heels, streaks on her pantsuit where she had already slipped on the tufts of grass.

"It all happened maybe twenty years ago," the speaker smiled, his arm on the Pastor's suit covered shoulder.

"We were younger in body, " said the Pastor, smiling.

Maggie walked up. "What happened, Pastor? " she asked.

The faucet man continued, "I was just a kid at the time. We kids thought it was funny. See, " he leaned forward, "What was going on was that in those days the town of River Sunday burned its garbage once a week. There wasn't any clean recycling like there is today. In those days there was just a dump and it was pretty raw. We'd go out there to shoot the rats feeding on the rotten food. All the garbage from the whole town was collected into a great pile and then burned. The smoke smelled to high heaven."

He went on. "The problem was that the land where the dump was located was owned by Old Man Terment, Jake's father. The town government , all white folks, managed the place, and Terment gave the orders. To get rid of it, the trash had to be burned. The garbage was burned when the wind suited the town government. Since they all lived in the big white houses down along the harbor side, the wind suited them when it wasn't blowing out over their houses and wasn't blowing out over Terment's mansion on the island either.   Unfortunately the only other way the wind ever blew in River Sunday was directly over what we used to call the colored section where all the black folks lived in those days.

"It went on this way for years, " the man said, looking around at the faces to make sure he still had their attention.

" All my childhood I just remember my parents saying that Jake's father done said this or done said that. His way was the way things were going to be done. Whenever there was a new road or a new building or a new fire department or a chief of police, why, Terment was consulted. When the Governor came to visit River Sunday it was Terment had the State Police send some men on motorcycles to give an escort. Just about the only thing here he didn't have much control over was when the Washington people came and give you that award, Pastor."

The Pastor smiled. "The Washington people got voted out of office pretty quick too, didn't they?"

The faucet man nodded and went on, "What some of us refer to as the garbage war took a while to come about. The first skirmish started one night when the wind was blowing over the white section of town. People were out sitting on their porches in the evening the way folks used to do in River Sunday. Garbage smoke started coming over them, making everyone very uncomfortable. People called up the fire department saying that there must be an uncontrolled fire at the garbage lot. It was like somebody had thrown a skunk into the middle of Strand Street.

"Well, the fire department went to the dump, sent out all five trucks they had in those days, even the old pumper. All the guys were sitting around the fire station so they ran out all the trucks just for something to do. The trucks put the fire out and the chief of the fire department had to drive out to Peachblossom and tell Jake's father what had happened. The old man was having guests. The whole party was ruined by the smell of the garbage. The fire chief had some explaining to do. He told Jake's father that it was an accident even though apparently there was some suspicion about the fire's origin. There was talk that the fire had been set but there was no indication as to who had done it.

"So then the next week when the wind was blowing the same way again, the fire started up mysteriously again. The same people called the fire department and complained. We kids watched all the trucks go roaring out to the garbage lot again.

"By this time the fire chief knew something was going on. He knew that these garbage lot fires were not no accident. He had been lambasted by Jake's father. There were a lot of upset folks in town. Just believe it when I say the fire chief was suddenly not a very popular person.

"He was told by Jake's daddy, 'All the money we pay you and you can't keep that fire from breaking out.'

"Of course nobody cared about the fire breaking out. They just cared that it broke out when the wind was wrong. You got to remember too in those days that the fire department members was white men, all ages, but all white.

"In the next few weeks it got so whenever the wind was blowing over the town folks knew that the garbage was likely to start burning. Finally Jake's daddy and some of the other businessmen had a bigger fence constructed. They put barbed wire on the top of the fence too. The idea was to keep out whoever was sneaking in there and setting off the fires.

"After they got that new fence the fires stopped burning when the wind blew over the town. The fires were lit when the wind was blowing over the black folks just as before. Everything seemed back to normal.

"The final garbage war battle took place a few weeks later. Folks black and white have always suspected that our friend, the Pastor here, organized the drivers. No one ever talked. You don't want to admit to it, do you, Pastor?

"I don't know what you are talking about," the Pastor grinned.

"Well, you do too." The man flicked the lime rind out of his drink. "All the garbage truck drivers were black in those days. So what happened was that they came in late on purpose from their pickup routes. The dump was locked up already according to Terment's orders. They left their trucks outside the fence with the rotten garbage still aboard. Then about midnight all of the men went back and got their trucks. They drove the trucks to Strand Street, stopped in front of the courthouse and dumped the loads right there. The trash covered everything. The boxwoods, the Confederate statue, the Revolutionary War statue, not the Vietnam monument because it wasn't built yet. Trash was half up the doorway of the old courthouse building. Come the morning the people who worked in the courthouse could only get into their offices by entering the big side windows or the back entrance. No one dared open the front door for fear the garbage would spill inside. Most of the courthouse employees, the judges and the clerks, did not stay in their offices for long, the smell of all that garbage was so bad.

"Terment came down there and the fire chief and the mayor and they walked around for about an hour discussing the situation, their eyes on the ground." The faucet man bent over, demonstrating the position of the town leaders as they deliberated on the crisis. His audience laughed. "Might have done them more good if they had looked up to Heaven rather than down for an answer," he said. "The citizens, meanwhile, white and black alike, were standing back and watching them to see what they were going to do. The smell got worse and worse as the sun come up.

"Jake's daddy never said anything himself. He let other folks do the talking. So bymby, the mayor went over to the crowd that had gathered. That mayor always had a talent for knowing how to solve situations, mainly by pleasing Terment. That's why he was in office so long. He puffed up the way he did and he said to them people, "We're burning the same day each week from now on, regardless of the way the wind blows." That was the end of the excitement. Pretty soon the trash was cleaned up and some new paint was put on the front door of the courthouse.

"In the end the town had to pay the garbage men overtime. No one else would do the cleanup. You see, the white people in town in those days thought that garbage collecting work was work only for the black folks. So the guys that made the mess also got paid for cleaning it up. Old man Terment was a smart man and he got the point that he wasn't going to win against these odds. The garbage war got settled the way things were done in those days. Just a little push from the opposition." The man winked at the Pastor.

At that moment the sound of barking motorcycle exhausts interrupted the murmur of the party. A River Sunday policeman led a limousine among the parked cars. The guests turned their heads towards the noise. They cleared a path as the limousine pulled into the party area. The name of a famous film company was brightly printed across its side doors.

Frank watched as guests began to crowd around the car and to scream at each other in excitement. The women looked at their men while the men in turn looked at their male friends with grins and victory signs of anticipation. They yelled, "It's Jake's wife, it's Jake's wife, the movie star. Did you see her poses in Playboy? Showed everything, man. Firm tits. She shaves off all the hair on her pussy. We're getting visited by a movie star. Oh myyyy God, can you believe it."

Serena stepped out of the car, effortlessly , smoothly, like fluid. The men crowded around the movie star. She had two bodyguards who restrained the most aggressive men trying to push against the woman, to touch her, to be part of her body. Serena was dressed as though she had no clothes on at all. The color of her tanned flesh could be seen through every seam in the transparent fabric she wore. Her sexual perfume drifted out on the hot afternoon air. Even Frank, his mind rarely drifting these hours from concern for the project, was caught off guard by the fantasy she portrayed so expertly. A song came into Frank's mind, a song from long ago that would not stop, its melody hammering in his brain.

"We gotta get outta this place."

We gotta get outta this place"

He saw again a dimly lit bar. His buddies were there, still young. There was Texas the jeep mechanic who was a poet, always taking out his latest poem and set it in front of him while he drank. There was the helicopter pilot they called Alaska, formerly a bush pilot, who talked about sawdust on honky tonk floors, and sitting beside him, the black soldier everyone called Philadelphia who loved jazz music. In those days he, Frank, was just called Boston, the student. They were all good killers and they had survived together.

The bar was full that night with a couple of hundred American and South Vietnamese soldiers, their guns checked at the doorway. Suddenly up on the small stage a young white American woman jumped out from the flimsy side curtain, her blonde hair rounded up like she was at a beach party. She was dressed like a high school girl complete with sports letter on her sweater, mini skirt, and brown loafers. "Seattle," said a soldier, "This one's fresh in from Seattle. She ain't been fucked out in the boonies yet. " She undid her clothing in front of them, the men cheering her on with more and louder yells and whistles each time she removed another bit of costume. She threw the colorful clothes out into the waving drunk crowd until she was completely naked. Then as the music boomed louder, she laughed and jumped spread eagled on her belly out into the mass of arms, like she was sliding on the sweat in that room. The soldiers passed her on, one grabbing a bare arm, another a bare foot, she cheering as her young body rode around the room on their up thrust palms, her energetic legs thrusting into the cigarette smoke. Finally, she clambered forth out of the multitude of arms and skipped back up on the stage.

"we gotta get outta this place
we gotta get outta this place"

His mind was back at the site again. He was standing at the barrier rope watching Jake look at his wife. Jake had an expression of total pride. Frank's ears hurt from the screech of her microphone. Jake's wife expertly held the mike back from her face and the noises ceased. She smiled and began to speak in the soft voice Frank recognized from her movies. By her carefully chosen words she gave the impression of being just one of the crowd herself, anxious to find out all about the project. She talked about Jake in warm family tones and about her desire to come here to see River Sunday. She wanted, she said, to visit the old family mansion to see where Jake had been a child. Frank could see the movie magic working in the faces of the crowd as the men and even the women fell in love with this actress one after another .

"I feel so sorry about the little bugs," she soothed. "We all know they have to be managed though, managed that's for sure, because I 'm like you, I like butterflies but I wouldn't want to live with them." The crowd laughed loud and long and began to surge toward her again.

Serena, her talk finished, began her silky movement among her admirers, her eye contact radiating heat and driving them to an orgasm of excitement.

Frank heard a boat horn out on the river. Jake 's big white yacht appeared through the tree line , cruising gracefully up the river. The craft could not come all the way up to the site however because of the half sunk barge and the teetered crane and pile driver hammer apparatus. It anchored against the far shore, fairly distant, and with the sun behind it as the afternoon grew, it became a white shape against the blackening trees.

The crane itself was still at the same abrupt angle. Several more of the large diesel fuel drums had rolled into the river and were bobbing near the sunken end of the barge. There was a large swell of oil on the surface and some fish, white belly up, floated in the slick.

The party was going too long. Frank wanted it to end so he could begin work again. With Jake's threat to close operations in the morning, the late work tonight would be important and critical to finding any more of the mystery of the wreck. Jake had made his opinion clear that all he wanted was for Frank to pick up his equipment and leave. He did not expect Jake to encourage this night work so he knew asking Jake to end the party and send the people home would be futile. Maggie was staring at him. Her stare meant only one thing. Get this party out of here so we can work.

Outside the gate, the human butterfly chant continued to grow in volume. Suddenly Frank thought the chant stopped for a moment then started up again even louder. The noise of the party was too great for him to be sure. He could hear guests making comments about the butterflies though. As visitors came in they remarked to Jake, mostly in fun, that they were surprised at all the insects demonstrating on the highway, that he should be careful because the bugs were coming in for their share of his party food pretty soon.

Jake in turn, responded with his remarks about "outsiders and agitators." Occasionally one or two of the guests would agree and bemoan the future of the Eastern Shore or River Sunday. They would talk about the good old days when townspeople knew how to behave and there were no "liberals." They would proclaim, "This kind of behavior by Birdey Pond would have been scared off quick if your father were still alive."

Then Birdey Pond arrived. Frank was actually looking the other way when she came in through the crowd. There was a murmur, then a silence, and as Frank turned around to see what was going on, Birdey had reached the center of the group. Her white hair and strong face contrasted bitterly with the softness of Serena standing only a few feet away. Birdey stood there, her eyes scanning the groups, her feet apart, her right hand holding a piece of orange cardboard. The cardboard, which was a part of one of the butterfly wing costumes, was torn at the bottom. Where the tear was located, it was smeared with blood..

Jake turned to watch her. He was smiling but with his head bent forward as if to withstand a fist aimed at his face. "What do you want, Birdey?" he asked.

"One of the children who was demonstrating outside your farm. Your man came outside and beat the child, hurt him. "

"What man is that, Birdey?"

"Your Spyder."

"Spyder, come over here."   Spyder walked out from behind the farmhouse into the silent group.

"Spyder, do you know what this woman is talking about?"

"They started it, " said Spyder, his voice almost childlike, like a boy who has been caught by a parent doing wrong and seeks sympathy.

"We were having a peaceful demonstration. Spyder provoked this."

"How?" asked Jake.

"He just walked up and started hitting the marchers with his fists. One boy fell and seriously cut his arm."

"Knowing you, Birdey, I'm sure you provoked the fight. Anyone else see this?"

Jake stared at the crowd, almost as if he was daring anyone to come forward, to verify Birdey's claim.

"All my friends saw this monster," Birdey shouted at Jake.

"Birdey, we need witnesses who don't work for your causes. Is there anyone here who saw this who is not dressed in a butterfly costume?" There were titters of laughter. Jake went on, encouraged. "For all we know, you might have hurt the boy yourself just to prove your point. We can't reason with people who would do such a thing. Why don't you go home?"

"Jake, you always did like the short cut, the nasty trick. You've graduated to the big time. You hurt children. You've become a true menace, and I expect you're capable of anything. "

"You have a bad old mouth, Birdey."

"You should have stayed away from River Sunday, Jake. You should have stayed in Baltimore or New York where you look good on television and folks don't have to know you well. Your money counts for more there. Now that you came home people can see you for what you are. We know you around here, Jake. You can't scare us."

"Nobody is trying to scare you, Birdey, " Jake said in a calming way.   He looked around and smiled. "Why don't you just go on home and let everyone have a little fun at the party."

" I heard about you fathering a child by that poor young girl and then running off. I heard what you did cheating those farmers on the island. I heard about what you did to that preacher's business with your fire. All taking and not giving back. Your father knew better. He tried to change, to give back, to end the ravishing of this land. "

She stepped up on the porch step. She was a tall woman and this made her even taller and more imperious. The crowd had become very quiet. Everyone, even Serena, watched her.

"Blood tells, Jake. Maybe why you never understood your father was because you weren't really a Terment."

Jake's eyes narrowed.

"Those of you who can still think for yourself," she said. "Those of you who do not live in this man's pocket. I'm talking to you. Listen to me. The Terment development is not the kind of investment we want here in River Sunday. This man Terment is the worst kind of pollution. "

She held up the piece of butterfly wing. " I ask you to help us get rid of a man who can order this done. Jake Terment lies and cheats. Help us to stop this bridge he wants to build so he will be forced to leave. If we can delay him long enough we can stop him."

She looked at him, defiant. "You hear me good, Terment. You're through taking. The time has come to give back."

She waved the wing above her head. "People, the butterflies can be our future or our past. You must decide."

She stepped down from the porch and walked slowly toward the lane. The crowd parted as she walked through. No one said a word.

Jake calmed down as he watched her leave. He immediately ordered the waitresses to pass out refills for everyone's drinks. The cocktail conversations returned to their former tempo. Frank was becoming resigned to the party lasting well into the night. Then a loud scream made everyone turn their heads back toward the far end of the excavation. Frank turned and ran towards the spot. There, Jake's wife was lying on the ground, her flimsy dress ripped almost off and blood flowing from deep scratches on her thighs. Jake arrived and pushed aside the bodyguards who were kneeling beside her trying to stop the blood.

"Is there a doctor here?" Jake yelled. A heavy set man, red faced from drinking Jake's gin and tonics, stumbled toward Jake, his hand up, saying again and again, "Here, here, I'm the doctor, I can help her."

In a few moments, Jake, the doctor and the security men had her moving towards the beach, one of the men calling on his cellular for the boat to come in from the yacht. "Forget the limo ," he yelled into the phone," The boss wants her taken on the boat. Yes, she'll be all right. Just shaken up."

"What happened?" Frank asked one of the security men as Jake and the others went ahead towards the beach.

"I saw it all," the man said. Then his head turned from Frank as there were three loud shots echoing from behind the old farmhouse. Some of the guests began running towards their cars. Three more shots went off. Frank looked at the man. "What in hell is going on?"

"She was standing there," the guard said, "Just looking at the site, couple of us guarding her while that old lady was talking. Then this spotted cat come along, just purring rubbing her leg. Suddenly the cat snarled, caught its claws in her dress, then jumped right on to her chest, his claws ripping downward on her skin. She didn't have a chance. We think she sprained her arm when she fell back. Should have been dressed up more, jeans or something back up here in the country. Tried to warn her about animals, but Jake wanted her to wear that skimpy stuff for the crowd. Anyway we got the animal off, wasn't a sick animal or nothing. Just jumped at her like it was angry at her. Afterward, it sat there looking at us and then scampered back over to the woods again. Jake said to shoot it so there's someone back there trying to get it. "

A guard came out of the woods, putting his revolver back in its holster.

"Get him?"

"Think I had a shot at him. Damn cat had a mind of its own."

In another half hour, the crowd was gone. The caterers had packed up quickly and left as soon as Jake went out to his yacht with his wife. The movie limousine left quietly too.

Frank signaled to Maggie and the Pastor. They crossed the barrier and began work, the Pastor taking off his suit coat and kneeling down in his good trousers. The only sound was the scratching of the archaeologists' trowels.

Then there was one more interruption of the peace of the marsh. For a few moments there was a tremendous resounding noise. This was the booming sound that Frank had heard when he first came to town. The rumbling came up the river in the late sunlight. One time and then a second time a few minutes later . This time Frank did not tense. He continued to work as fast as he could.

"The Cannon Club rehearsing ," said the Pastor.

Frank sat back on his dirt streaked bare feet and looked at his work. "Maggie," he called, his mind back on archeology. "This Q area is not developing very well. I'm down more than three feet. Except for the remnant of that clay pipe, I've seen nothing here."

He lifted out the soil carefully. He placed it on the plastic sheeting along the edge of the pit. "Before I quit tonight, I'll run this soil through the sifter."

"You've done a good job on that one," said Maggie. "If there had been anything there you would have found it. "

He scraped again. The trowel had become heavy to his exhausted arm and shoulder. Suddenly he felt the change in the friction of the soil.

"Wait a minute," he said. He bent his head down to look more closely. There was a change of color in the strata. Even in the poor light he noticed the brown spot. It was a piece of bone that had appeared in front of him, a pale fleck against the black. The bone was like a drug, a tonic, a revitalizing medicine. At once he was alert, exhaustion gone, every muscle tensing, fingers grasping his trowel with new strength as he skillfully teased the soil away from the bone, to make it come out of hiding.

"What is it?" Maggie said, standing above him in the darkness. Frank worked quickly, not answering her. As he excavated, the bones appeared. In a few moments, there were two skulls, side by side as if they had come to rest in a hug or an embrace. He sat back on his heels, holding his eyeglasses, breathing slowly to calm himself.

"We've got something."

Maggie and the Pastor brought over the lights. After they were plugged in and turned on, the light burned away the shadows in the pit. The insects swarmed at the bulbs.

"The light makes a big difference. These are definitely old bones. This is at an earlier strata, earlier than the soldier, about the same as the giant, the sailors," said Frank. " The soil is different. It's got the charcoal that I found earlier, from the burned shipwreck. The skulls are burned too. See the effect on the bones, the burn fractures."

"But why two skulls this close together?"

"One of the skulls is definitely larger than the other, probably an adult."

"Maybe the larger person was shielding a child."

"The large skull definitely has some African characteristics."

"Yes, it's probably a black man. "

"Maybe the smaller skull is African also."

"This bone," he pointed with his trowel. "It looks like part of the forearm of the larger person. See how it is in the fighter position."

"Pugilist," corrected Maggie.

"What does that mean?" asked the Pastor.

"It means the skeleton was probably burned. When a body is burned the muscles contract and make the arms and legs tighten up like a person is crouching for a fight, like a fighter's stance. That's why they call it pugilist, " said Maggie.

"Could this be a grave?" asked the Pastor.

"It may be. It dates to the period of the ship though. That means it would have been a burial at the time the ship burned, " said Frank. "We already know the ship was likely here before slaves were buried in this area of Maryland."

"Yes," agreed the Pastor.

"Or it's two Africans who were caught in the ship fire somehow," suggested Maggie.

"I just don't know," said Frank. "This is, however the most intriguing discovery yet. The sailors belonged on the ship. These people do not. This is quite a find."

The water was filling in around the skeleton as they talked. "We'll need the pump here," said Frank.   After they had placed the pump beside the pit, Frank pulled the starter and after two pulls the engine popped to action. Frank moved the water outlet hose so that it discharged into the marsh grass ten feet from the side of the site.

"Well, Maggie, shall we? " said Frank as he held his arms toward her with a grin.

She looked at him, unsure what he meant. Then remembrance came across her face. "Sure," she smiled back. "Got to have the discovery dance."

They stood in the darkness outside the spot of the lights. The light flickered off their bodies, first in shadow then in light. They locked their arms in a square dance twirl and turned themselves around and around until they fell on their sides in the muck, laughing.

"What was that all about?" asked the Pastor.

"An old tradition. Something Frank's field students always did when we made big discoveries on our sites. You'll have to let this go by, Pastor. "

"Like winning a skirmish in a battle," he said.

"Yes, just like that," said Frank.

Chapter 15

Maggie had dug to a depth of almost three feet below the topsoil. Above this was the mass of unrelated soil that Frank agreed had been brought in from another area of the farm. The cannon and the clay pipe had been found in soil contemporary to the one Maggie was searching.

She looked up from her work and winked at Frank. He smiled back.

"Nothing?" he asked.

"Nothing yet."

"There's got to be more than this man and child," Frank said.

The Pastor agreed. "We have to find it."

"I just don't want to find more children," said Frank.

"I know what you mean," said the Pastor.

They heard the engine of Soldado's boat.

"He's letting us know, making sure we don't stop working," said Maggie.

""This project starts up and we see a lot of him, "said the Pastor. "For years, since his mother died he's barely talked to anyone."

"Soldado!" Frank greeted the solitary man walking up from the river. Soldado looked up and smiled at hearing his name, as if the saying of it were a welcome he had not expected, or more, a human kindness that he had not received for a long time.

As Frank scraped at the soil, he thought about this old man and his influence on the whole project. From the beginning Soldado had been one of them, gently directing their hands towards the promising spots, divined by old fashioned water finding gear. There was the trace of Mayan magic in Soldado's history that gave him a kind of power, an authority, that Frank heard and considered, even though Frank's scientific skepticism taunted him. Maybe, he found himself thinking, the old man really did descend from Mayan magicians. Maybe those ancient priests did have special insight into the world of the dead. Frank dropped his trowel and as he reached for it he realized his fingers were suddenly shaking. He picked up the trowel and the shaking disappeared.

Soldado stood in the shadows by the site.

"They kill the animal?" There was sadness in Soldado's voice as if the cat were an old companion.

Frank explained what had happened.

"Well," said Soldado, " I guess I should feel sorry for the poor lady but she ought to have known better, getting hooked up with somebody like Jake Terment." He looked behind him at the barge and pile driver. "Jake get mad and wreck his toys?"

"The barge just started sinking," said Frank. "Jake was angry long before that crane fell over. He made sure to tell us that he's coming here tomorrow morning with his bulldozer crew. We have a few hours of light left and I guess that's going to be it for us."

"You don't have to quit," said Soldado, his body tense as if he were ready to fight.

"I'm not sure we can hold back a bulldozer."

"You can do anything you have a mind to do," said Soldado.

"It's not that simple," said Frank.

"Well maybe it is and maybe it isn't," said Maggie.

There was a metallic sound. "Hey, guys, I think there's something here," said Maggie, working faster with her digging tools.

"Let's take a look," said Frank standing up.

Frank climbed into Maggie's dig and squatted next to where she was kneeling, her face close to the soil, picking at the small sliver of color in front of her.

"What do you think it is?" asked Frank.

"It's metal. I'm sure of it. Good metal too. Corroded but no rust. Maybe it's brass or bronze."

"Pastor, what do you think of this?"

The slender preacher climbed down and squatted next to Frank. "Looks like a piece of round metal, curved metal."

"Maybe a tankard or a pot of some kind," suggested Maggie.

"Something like that would not be this big, would it?" said Soldado.

"No, you're right, "said Maggie. "Here. I've got the side done. It starts to curve back in the other direction. "

"That looks like a diameter of about fifteen inches."

"It curves the other way too, look, see?" said Frank.

Soldado stood at the edge of the pit and watched them.

"I know that shape," he grinned. "You folks have found yourselves a bell, a ship's bell."

"Soldado may be right," said Frank.

"I know I'm right. I've seen enough of them in my day." Soldado bent down and pointed at the object. "She's an old one too. Lookee, there's a tiny spot of clear metal. Fancy work, too. Lot nicer than the equipment we had on my last ship."

"They found a bell like this in the Whydah shipwreck up at Cape Cod," said Frank. "Had the name of the ship right on it. It was the only sure way they could identify the shipwreck. There was almost nothing of the original ship's hull left, just small pieces of wood and metal like we have here. "

"Whydah. Sounds like a spider, " said the Pastor.

Maggie said, " Whydah was the name of one of the early slave ports near Nigeria."

"Can we get this bell out of the ground tonight?" asked the Pastor.

"We can try," said Soldado.

They gathered on all sides of the bell and worked. It went quickly. In an hour the bell was completely exposed.

"Let's clean this up for some photos." Frank said as he went for the black and white scale and the camera.

Soldado called after him. "Doctor White, you better get that truck back down here on this thing. Having that hoist will make the lifting a lot easier."

"Good idea." Frank climbed into the canvas bench seat of the old war truck. He looked behind him at the heavy bomb hoist. He set the carburetor choke and pressed the starter button. The old truck started up with a roar. He adjusted the choke and throttle and the engine settled into a steady idle. Frank shifted into low range for the four wheel drive and put the truck into reverse. The machine crept toward the site.

The Pastor guided him back. In a few minutes the hoist was above the old bell. They ran out the cable and attached it to boards stuck beneath the object.

"Just a starter pull and she will be free," said Soldado.

Frank revved the truck and eased in the hoist gears. The bell lifted easily from the soil. hey gathered around it as it hung suspended from the bomb hoist, slightly swinging in the air.

"Keep it there," said Frank. "We'll walk it right up to the house. Maggie, you come here and drive the truck."

Frank lifted the bell against the cable. "It's heavy."

When they reached the porch, Maggie stopped the truck and they lowered the bell to the ground. Soldado and Frank steadied it as the Pastor disconnected the cable. The soft earth and clay fell off . The curves were still obscured by the encrustation. There were even some pieces of rotten wood and rusty iron sticking from the remaining muck.

"Let's get it into the farmhouse, " said Frank.

Frank and Soldado lifted the object again and carefully walked it toward the farmhouse.

"We can work on it later tonight if we have time," said Maggie.

They carried it inside and let it down on the floor in the kitchen. It fell the last inch with a thud, the moist surface hard to hold in their hands.

Maggie looked at the object closely with her flashlight.

"It's too corroded to see any letters on the metal," she said. "We'll have to do some work at the lab."

" One thing for sure, " said Frank.

"What's that?"

"A bell is the best clue we've found yet on this site. That bell may tell us what this ship was, what she was doing here, why the giant was here, maybe even why the fire."

"That's a lot," said the Pastor.

"Every wreck I've worked on where there was a bell found," said Frank, "We were able to establish the history of the wreck. The bell is like a tombstone over a grave. It gives you the name of what is buried there. With that name we can go to the records in England. There's going to be something somewhere that will help us. I've seen all kinds of helpful records develop from family histories, newspapers, port records."

"It has to be cleaned very slowly," said Maggie.

"If we can find any identification on it," said Frank, "we can check it with my friend in Massachusetts. He has a listing of these old ships that were lost at sea. I could call him and see what he can tell us."

"Could he tell us anything over the telephone?" asked the Pastor.

"Sure. The data 's all on his computer."

Soldado disappeared again, saying that he had business to take care of. They worked harder. The evening shadows were deep and time was running out. Frank looked at the river for a moment as he worked on the skeletons in his grid. Beside him the Pastor dug with fury, as if the lives of his congregation were at stake. To the stern of the wreck, Maggie was digging again below where the bell had been, bits of soil still scattering, the look on her face dogged, determined.

Frank smiled, thinking how he must look and what his students would say. They had seen him in these last minute finishes when grant money was running out, when the project was in danger of being shut down and just before the carefully excavated soil was tumbled back again into the holes, all so the landowner would not be angry and would allow them to come back another day.

The landowner would allow them. That was a strange idea here, he thought. That presupposed a friendly property owner and Jake Terment was certainly not that. As he scraped past the strata he trembled for a moment in the heat. He knew it was his responsibility and his fault if his small team, Maggie, the Pastor and himself, were the only ones, the last ones, to study what was becoming quickly a very rich and important archeological find.

Frank's mind wandered with exhaustion. He knew, perhaps he always known but had not accepted, that he was promoted not because he was a great archeologist, but because he followed the president's directives better than any other person in the archaeology department. It had taken many years, many defeats of his own convictions to convince him that it was better, easier, less naïve, to follow some other person's conviction over his own. An occasional reward was better than no reward at all. However, he had become a man that Jake Terment referred to as "one of them." Here in these hurried hours with Maggie and the Pastor and the stink, he was realizing that "one of them" was far from what he wanted to be.

Perhaps this surrender of convictions in his own life was what drew him to admire Maggie, the Pastor too, but especially Maggie. It was her refreshing spirit, unwillingness to give way to others, that he liked. He thought that he must like her because he felt strengthened by her, like he was gaining a will, a power he had not had for a long time. Even with his self searching, he had some respect for himself because she respected him.

He thought about his job, about his not following the president's order to close the site. He was in trouble and he knew it. Causing any displeasure on the part of Jake was a mistake. He might be fired or significantly demoted. He knew his textbook was already in trouble. Yet at this moment he did not feel lost or despondent. He felt strong because he was here with Maggie and the Pastor doing a good job on this site.

He thought about his life since Vietnam, how little love there had been. Of course, recently there had been Mello. He sensed that her love came to him based on his success at the school and that if he was not chairman of his department, he would not have Mello. He remembered the war. There had been a woman during the war, an Australian, an intense love, powerful, at that time all he thought he would ever desire. He was on Rest and Recreation, the R and R trip to Australia. He thought about her, the thoughts easing the exhaustion in his body as he worked.

He remembered the mobs of people standing alongside the buses taking the American soldiers from the airport. These

Australian crowds were waving United States flags and cheering for them. It was different from the reception he knew he was facing when he returned to the States.   He and his lover met simply. There was a restaurant. He was with other American soldiers. There was a glance and then conversation that led further. They slept together that first night and every night afterwards for the whole ten days of his leave. At the airport, when he flew out of Sydney to return to Vietnam, they cried in each others arms and swore to meet again when he was free of the war, discharged.   They wrote letters, full of memories and plans for the future. He made arrangements to be discharged in country so he could go immediately to Australia to hold her once again.

He remembered the heat of the Vietnamese sunlight that day when he got her letter. She wrote she was pregnant with his child. He wrote back with love that same afternoon, scratching a note and putting it in the simple Army envelopes that were there for GI letters home. He was happy that something was purposeful at last in his life.

Like everything else in Vietnam, his happiness was not permanent. On another day her letter came that she had aborted their unborn child.   There were many things left unsaid in their letters after that. In Australia, they had read each other's thoughts with a glance. He did not understand the words in her letters. In time their love affair was over. When he left Vietnam he went directly home to the United States.   It was the final dishonor in his war. He went to war to help children, he was almost killed by a child and in the end he felt he had somehow helped to kill a child himself.

Here, today, at this moment, he suddenly wanted to tell Maggie about this. He looked at her. She noticed him and smiled back, then returned her eyes to her dig. He felt close enough to her to share these memories, to get her advice, to get her aid as a strong person helps a weakling to stand until he is strong enough on his own.

Chapter 16

"With all this tension and the heat, it reminds me of the waiting when we knew Charlie was going to hit us," said Frank, wanting to hear his words against the silence of the night, the desperation he felt.

No one replied and they continued to dig, working in the last light of the summer evening. For a moment Frank looked out at the river. He was reminded by the glimmering from Jake's yacht of how the pathways of the Vietnamese village would blink with the little flames of the ceremonial altars along the streets, how those lights would sometimes foreshadow the explosions to come in the deep night.

A half hour ago a small runabout had come by and taken Jake's wife away, probably to the River Sunday hospital, leaving only Jake and a few friends and staff aboard. The speedboat's waves had long ago washed against the riverbank and the river surface was glass smooth again. The noises of dinner being served to Jake's guests inside the main cabin of the yacht, the tinkling of glasses and of music, and the reflections of the boat running lights stretching across the river water, accentuated the stillness of the darkness.

The heat was overpowering. Along the river the trees were black near the water on the far shore and the limbs of the trees on this side were etched against what still remained of the red western evening sky. Frank slapped at another mosquito on his bare leg.

"People say the mosquitoes here in River Sunday double their size in the evening, then shrink back to fit into their hideouts during the day," said the Pastor. Frank could see that the old man too was fighting his exhaustion.

On the yacht Spyder was leaning over the stern. He was hauling in the Boston Whaler runabout. Frank smiled. "It looks like someone is getting ready to come ashore from the Terment yacht," he said. "Probably Jake with his final orders for the morning."

At that moment, a terrific noise, a thunder boom like a jet fighter breaking the sound barrier, crashed across the river and actually shook the ground under Frank's feet. Out on the river a tower of bubbling water rose up from the surface a few feet in front of the bow of the yacht. All eighty feet of the yacht rose up on the water surge, the bow pointing almost forty five degrees into the air. Then the hull pushed down in a huge wash of waves like a magnificent belly flop. The immediate surge died, ebbing with three and four foot waves gradually getting smaller. There was no second explosion. Mist and bits of river mud and seaweed returned downward pelting the river surface. In the water at the stern, Spyder hung like a great round insect on a tiny thread, being raised and lowered on the bowline of the Whaler. He kept being dunked by the movement of the yacht, as if he were being baptized again and again. Frank watched, powerless to help because he was so far away. Then, as the water surface quieted, Spyder, after several tries, managed to climb back on the yacht.

The water in front of the yacht continued to bubble furiously as though a volcano were astir beneath the surface. Bits of torn seaweed from the river bottom washed up in the froth. A thin cloud of white smoke drifted across the river surface.

"Mercy! " said the Pastor.

The yacht itself had been fully bathed with the plume of river water which had reached a hundred feet into the air then descended like torrential rain over the river and the yacht. Water was still running heavily from the yacht deck. In the confused water around the hull chairs and seat cushions and other furniture that had gone overboard, floated in a tumbled array.

Frank and the Pastor looked at each other and at Maggie.

"Soldado," said Maggie.

"He'd have to know explosives," said Frank.

"I know boys can get any bombs you want. Down here on the Eastern Shore anything can be done you want," said the Pastor.

Frank stood up and went to the shoreline. "We should try to help them."

"Not much we can do," said the Pastor. "They're over there and we're over here. Besides, I'll bet Jake's captain has already called every marine police in the Chesapeake."

A few more minutes went by. Spyder, an oversize towel draped around his neck, had maneuvered the Boston Whaler around to the ladder hanging down the side of the yacht. The small craft was pulled snugly to the side of the larger boat. Then a door opened from the cabin and light came out in jagged patterns on the river surface. In a few moments Cathy, Maggie's supervisor, stuck her head out of the doorway and looked around slowly as if she were expecting another sudden surprise from the dark. Then she stepped out slowly and turned around and climbed down the ladder, her back to the river. Halfway down the ladder she stopped and looked again, then resumed her descent, finally jumping the last few feet into the small boat. She moved to the center and held on to the seat, rigidly facing forward. Then it was Jake's turn. He descended the same way, looking nervously from side to side. He got into the boat and went to the stern to start the outboard engine mounted there. As he pulled on the recoil starter Spyder came down the ladder and jumped into the bow. The small boat rocked and then was steady. Frank heard the outboard start up, heard the bark of the exhaust and then watched as the boat sped towards where he stood.

Frank called out, "Are you all right? "

"We're all fine, " Jake called back.

"What happened?" shouted Frank.

"We don't know, " asnwered Maggie's boss, her voice frantic.

"The Viet Cong sapper teams did that to freighters anchored in Cam Ranh Bay during the War, " Frank said to the Pastor, as they waited for Jake to land.

"I heard about that, " said the Pastor. "The enemy swam up beside the freighter hulls and attached explosives to the steel sides just below the water line. Then the bombs went off and put holes in the ship."

Frank nodded. " Men sat on those ships waiting for their turn to unload cargo, listening down below for tapping sounds that might mean the Cong were at work. "

"Soldado carried a lot of that wartime freight into Cam Ranh," said the Pastor.

Jake was in the back of the Whaler, operating the throttle and steering lever with his right hand, his face intent. Spyder stood in the bow, his grin more forced, his hands holding the bow line. When the boat reached the mud of the shoreline, Spyder jumped to the shore with the line and pulled the boat up. Cathy stepped out, then Jake.

"That old lady is trying to scare us. I didn't really think that she would go this far. She might of killed somebody." He smiled viciously, staring at Spyder, "She wants trouble she'll get plenty."

"You should call the police," said Cathy.

"Someone is going to get killed if this kind of thing keeps up," said Frank.

"We'll take care of it," answered Jake.

"You better have something besides bones, professor," said Jake, anger in his voice.

"We did find something interesting," said Frank. Jake and Cathy followed Frank to the farmhouse. Maggie walked a few feet behind. The group entered the house, their weight causing the boards of the porch and the kitchen floor to creak. The kitchen light hanging from its black wire made the people's shadows race against the stained walls, while moths flopped insanely against the glass of the bulb.

"You found a ship's bell" said Cathy, pushing at the muddy edge of the artifact with the tip of her well shined but obviously soaked shoe.

"Cathy, it's a very important find," said Maggie.. "We think it will tell us what the name of the ship was."

"The ship's name. How can you do that?" said Jake, squatting beside the object, his eyes suddenly showing intense interest.

"It can be done," said Frank. "Jake, we can be sure of the importance of the site. It's strange though. With a bell on board, this must have been a sizeable shipwreck. I just don't understand why your family didn't know about all this."

Jake looked at Frank. "Don't you get started on my family. That's a little bit out of your line."

"Sorry. " Frank pointed to a small patch of metalwork. "Here, look at this. On the surface of the bronze bell we think we'll find some etched letters or numerals that will help us identify the ship. We have to clean and conserve this carefully though so that the remnants of any lettering aren't lost when we clean it."

Jake, acting the southern gentleman again, smiled. "I was telling your boss that it's a real hard job to get anything out of the wreck that you can use."

"We don't have any capability to help you in our little office," said Cathy.

"Well, I just wanted to show this to you," said Frank.

"I wish I could help more," said Cathy." Maggie explains these things to me and tells me what she needs. I'm of course not an archaeologist by training but I try to understand."

"We'll try to clean it up some more tomorrow."

"I hate to break up this party but as long as I was forced to come ashore with my guests," said Jake, "I wanted to remind you all of my plans for the morning. Tomorrow morning, Frank," asserted Jake. " I want you guys out of here. My bulldozer will start early."

Cathy smiled. "I guess that's it. We all know, shipwreck or no shipwreck, the bridge has got to be constructed. Maybe this bell could be a nice exhibit for a local museum in River Sunday."

"Cathy, " said Maggie, "This wreck is old. It's very important."

"Maggie," said Cathy, "The time has come to close the site. I can't do any more for you. I'm sure Doctor Light will write an appropriate report. That's my job. Maggie."

"Looking over the construction work to be done, Spyder?" Frank asked. Spyder grinned without answering.

Frank decided to make one last appeal to Jake. "Can't you see, Jake? This is something important. This is not a site like most of the ones I have worked on where there was no value, where it was easy to argue that it could be closed. Finding an old ship like this one is important to the history of this whole community. There was a true catastrophe here, a mystery. The puzzle should be solved. You've got to give us a few more days."

Jake stopped and looked at Frank. The Pastor and Maggie went ahead with Cathy.

" What I don't expect, don't want to deal with, is people who change on me. You should have known though, Frank, that you can't change your mind halfway through the job. Remember the army, Frank. How they taught you to follow orders. You were brought here to work on my team. You best remember that."

Frank answered, feeling he was being forced. He did not like the feeling. "What if I don't chose to remember?"

Jake went on," I haven't got time for this. My wife's hurt. I got a lot of money riding on a bridge construction. Frank you are bought and paid for. Bought and paid for. You are here to do what I say when I say it. I don't care what you call it. " He stared at Frank. " I had some doubts about you in the beginning when I read your resume."

"You told me you found something you didn't like."

"More something I didn't understand. I couldn't understand how a smart man like you could have ended up as a soldier in Vietnam. Then, I thought, this guy must have gone over there to make some money, maybe as a civilian contractor after his hitch was up. I know there was a lot of money to be made."

" Your first impression was right," said Frank. "I was not smart going over there. On the other hand, I served with some of the best men I'll ever know and many of them gave their lives stopping bullets meant for me."

Jake smiled, "I guess I should have looked more closely, followed my hunch. I sure picked the wrong man. No matter. Let me tell you what your report to the Maryland people is going to say, Frank. As the wise archaeology scholar from the world famous university, you have thoroughly reviewed the site. You have decided after two days of reconnaissance probes at the site that this old wreck is likely not of historical significance. While it might be old, you believe the age is too difficult to determine at this time. You also make note in this report that some bones have been found but it is almost impossible from their condition to determine whether they are human or animal. So based on two days of intensive work by yourself and another archaeologist, you feel comfortable with the bridge project proceeding as planned and will recommend that the site be filled. "

"I can't write that, Jake," said Frank.

"I expect to get a report like that from you before you leave tomorrow morning. I suggest you write it. If you don't write it, I'll have someone write it for you. If you don't sign it, I'll find another archaeologist who will sign it. I'm sure that will not be a problem. I'll just have to make sure he's a little better at taking orders than you were. As for you, cross me any more and I think you will find that your job back at that university of yours doesn't get funding in future years. You may find also that no one is very interested in what you have to say or write in the future. "

Jake smiled and turned to walk toward the boat. He said over his shoulder, "Frank, without my friends helping you, you don't exist. If you were the big scholar you're pretending to be, I never would have hired you. I wanted someone who could compromise, who knew how to make a bargain. "

"I never though we had a bargain, Jake."

"I knew we had a deal the moment you got in that fancy BMW of yours to drive down here."

Jake reached the side of the runabout, and Cathy reached out a steadying hand. The engine roared, cavitated the river water in a huge swirl of mud and seaweed. Bits of the weed landed at Frank's feet. The boat then shot forward into the dark river night, towards the twinkle of the yacht lights a few hundred yards distant.

The Pastor, who had returned and had the last of Jake's tirade, spoke. "Jake Terment never intended to let us study this site. His political pull has convinced your boss too, Maggie."

"You heard my boss," said Maggie. "She's so wrapped up in preserving the department, she can't hear anything else. "

"Her job too." Frank scratched the back of his neck.

"She wants me in the office tomorrow," said Maggie.

"It's pretty discouraging," said Frank. He continued. "I guess I came down here for all the wrong reasons."

"Your university sent you. You didn't have any choice."

"I had a choice but wasn't thinking about choices at the time."

"You had no way of knowing it would be like this. How could you have known that he would not keep the project open if you actually found something? Everyone thought there was nothing here. No one considered what to do if we actually found something."

Frank shook his head. "With other jobs it was always assumed that the property owner and everyone else would be so excited that they would grant extensions, go out of their way to get more information, help us out. The projects are usually so weak in historic value that no one complains when we close up the sites. Your Confederate site excited people. The media made weak historical value into a political problem. We have a location far more important but we can't get any excitement."

"Jake thought that you were like him."

Frank looked out into the darkness. "He even told me I was like him. I guess I used to think that was a compliment. He says that if I was a real scholar he would never have brought me down here. What bothers me is that he had that original impression of me."

"What are we going to do?" asked Maggie.

"How do you stop a bulldozer?" asked the Pastor.

"You could make this work, Frank. When I was your student I thought you could accomplish anything. I haven't lost that faith in you."

He looked at Maggie. "Since I've been down here, I've thought a lot about those early teaching days, about who I was."

"What are you going to do?"

"Like in the war, there's a time to lock and load."

The Pastor and Maggie looked at him.

"We've got to become winners," said Frank.

Maggie turned on the floodlights and for a while , the Pastor and Frank worked beside each other at Q. The skeletons were more exposed. Frank was working on the thigh area of the adult figure. The Pastor was scraping soil from the lower part of the leg of the child's skeleton.

"Strange there's nothing about them that shows why they were here. Usually there's jewelry or some kind of possessions. These people had no possessions buried with them."

"There's the fact of the fire that burned the bones. Maybe that took away any of the possessions. Burned them up, " said the Pastor. "Hey, here's something," he said as he worked at the ankle. Frank moved over to where the Pastor was. He scraped at the bone while the Pastor watched.

"What is it?"

"Looks like rust," said Frank, his face close to the soil.

The object took form among the bits of the mud and clay of its home. As Frank worked he followed trails of the artifact which led out from the initial point. The rust led in a brown path towards the leg of other skeleton. "It seems to be attached to the ankle area."

Then Frank looked at the Pastor. "I know why there were no possessions."

"What?" said Maggie.

"This is part of a leg iron. See, Pastor, this is where the hasp was attached. I think this is one of the old type padlocks. See the bag shape. That kind of lock shape means they are very old. They used these locks long before the padlocks that we have today. "

Frank stood and motioned to Maggie to come over. He looked at the Pastor. "Chains on a child. These poor people were slaves."

"Children were very valuable in the slave trade," said Maggie. " They had less disease than the adults so they were a better investment for the traders."

Frank continued, "These chains indicate that the child here was burned to death with no chance of escaping. " Frank shifted his position squatting and ran his hands with care over the earth in front of him.

"If these two skeletons were slaves, I expect that there are a lot of slave skeletons in here, probably a lot more children too. "

The Pastor touched the aggregate also with a tender touch, softly with his fingers, carefully wiping back the trickle of ground water. "So this was a slave graveyard. The legend is true. "

"Yes," said Maggie.

"I wish I hadn't found this," said the Pastor.

Maggie stood up. "This graveyard legend, Pastor. It could have been a story made up by the surviving local slaves, maybe the ones who were forced to bury the wreckage. The legend was a way to keep the story alive, a way that the white overseers could not suppress."

"The murderers would not want to let anyone live who witnessed anything. Any witness would have to be very careful the rest of his or her life, " said the Pastor.

"It could have been an accident," said Frank, as usual speaking as a scientist, trying to consider all sides of the issue. " We still have no reason to believe it was murder."

Maggie said, her emotion showing in her tone, " An accident maybe but it was an accident where no one was saved. In those days if there was a shipboard catastrophe, lots of times they saved the Europeans, put them on the lifeboats and left the slaves on the ship. There are lots of stories of that kind of thing happening."

"That giant and his associates in the other end of the ship were burned to death too," mused Frank.

"More likely the slaves were killed because the others were killed, " said the Pastor. "Keep in mind they were considered the same as livestock. There may have been no thought about whether the slaves would die. "

"The slaves had great value," said Frank.

"That just means the murder of the others was significant, something that had to be hidden or covered up by fire even with the great loss of the slave value," continued the Pastor.

"This explains old Mr. Johnson's story about Adam and Eve," said Maggie, who was sitting on the ground. Her hands were around her knees. She stared at the leg iron.

"How's that?" said the Pastor.

"Adam and Eve were old slave names. When the traders loaded the ships over in Africa they would name the first male and the first female brought on board as Adam and as Eve," said Maggie.

"Maggie, you must have been interested in black history to know all this," said the Pastor.

"No," said Maggie. "I was actually studying European history. My mother told me of her heritage, of her family's generations in very early England. In college I was doing research to write a paper on the English tribes. "

"How did you get into slavery?" said Frank.

"In the early days the Romans took the English tribal captives back to Rome as slaves. The story of slavery began to fascinate me. I changed the paper and I read about all the civilizations that practiced slavery. I read the diaries of the captains in the African slave trade, some of them dating to the Seventeenth Century. That's how I found out about the Adam and Eve names. I just didn't think of it when the Pastor told that story. That old preacher must have heard some earlier story about this place," said Maggie.

"This wretched child here," said the Pastor. He looked at the fragile yellowed bones and tenderly tried to wipe them clean of the muck. "Young, too young to know anything, maybe eight or nine years old. Terrified."

"Let me tell you what I remember from the diary descriptions, how it must have been for them," said Maggie. "Of course I can only guess at the ending, when the ship got up here in this creek." Her eyes were closed as she slowly spoke.

"The children had to surrender with their families to some other African, perhaps a debt collector or a conquering warrior from an enemy tribe. Then they were separated from parents and marched with others in tropical woodlands for miles and miles. Their little legs would be exhausted when they would reach a gathering point, a riverbank, maybe something like this river here, fairly narrow, muddy, with long dugout canoes drawn up on the shoreline. Iron rings were put on the children's ankles and they were loaded into these boats, pushed down into the bowels of the canoes until there were many packed inside. The canoes were guided out into the river by expert boatmen, and they were taken down river to another place. The children would cry and cry but there were no parents to hear them and after a while they would stop crying and begin to think about survival. One of the children would become a leader, the strongest child, and would whisper in the village language about plans of escape. The thought of escape would keep the children warm for a while in the chill.

"The iron bites into the flesh of their ankles and the pain becomes intense. They scream or moan, bodies shaking with cold and shock in the night. Their skin has no cover. They are stripped of even the simple loincloth they had worn, and all their body hair shaved so no one can tell their ages and so each can bring a higher price. The iron pulls constantly against their skin with each touch causing more pain.

"Another move and they reach the trading factory at the port on the Guinea coast and are put inside a large room that houses many other Africans of many different tribes. The darkness is overpowering except there is one small window where they take turns looking out. There they can see the beautiful white beach and the ocean and the low black ship with the white men working on its deck setting up a great canvas cover for when they will be loaded and set out on the deck of the ship in the hot sun. Again there are those who would escape this wretchedness and they listen to the various ideas and they hope and pray to probably Allah because many were Muslim or maybe a woodland god that they had been taught from their tribe. Each hopes that some of these new leaders will have the power to fight the white men who are called English.

"Then the time comes and each is led in chains outside to stand in the sun and be prepared for the sale. Each body is rubbed all over with palm oil so it will shine. Perhaps each is given brandy so he or she will smile with a drugged smile and indicate that he or she has a good temperament. The slave trader king who is offering the slaves to the English walks around with his own Africans and with the English themselves. These people probe each body for illness and weakness, with a total disregard for dignity, studying penises, vaginas and rectums for disease, mouths and gums for rot and strength. They haggle over a price for each slave, the price denoted in cowrie shells, these shells brought here from far way because the African slave traders prefer them for trade. These shells are carefully counted out and then a child becomes the property of the English. The same selling sequence happens with each of the others, the other boys and girls, the young men and women, the older men and women, each manacled into their human destiny. They know that those who are not sold are discarded in this process. There is no place, no food for them here on the coast, no one will return them to their village, and they are them taken away sometimes to be killed for sacrifice to the African slave trader's gods.

" Then they are taken together to a spot on the beach near a great fire and there strong men hold each child while the shoulder is branded with the first letter of the ship's name, a mark which the children do not understand but which they think means that they will be eaten sooner than the others. They fear that they will soon be eaten by the white men on the ship.

"They see and hear the great waves that crash on the beach. They watch as the African king's men try to launch their small canoes through the breakers, watch as the cargoes of humans going out to the ship scream their way through the terrifying water and they see some slaves fall into the water and drown carried down by their chains. They are packed again into a small boat and they pray to that god they had not seen, they hope and they cling to each other, the grasp futile as all are slippery with the palm oil.

"They go through the waves and then are being propelled towards the great black ship. They see the fins circling the small canoes, the sharks who have feasted on others who capsized, and they shrink back into the small boat, knowing their naked black skin can be no protection against the sharp teeth of that shark.

"They are prodded by the men in the canoe to grasp the wooden steps on the side of the great black ship, the barnacles on the hull rising and sinking in the water beside the small canoe, their sharp edges threatening to tear skin to pieces, the children trying to climb with the edges slicing their bare feet. Then they are on the deck of the great ship, down behind the great walls of wood that hide the water, the great guns on both sides of them, the canvas stretched overhead protecting from the sun and the sailors standing around watching. They want your parents. They hear the word Maryland. The word strikes fear and they cannot control themselves and urinate on the deck. They are whipped by a sailor but in such a way that it hurts but does not leave a mark. They soon learn Maryland is where they are going, where, the children think, they will be eaten at some great sacrifice or feast.

"Some slaves began breaking free and jumping overboard. A teenage girl quickly and soundlessly cuts her foot off below her ankle on a sharp piece of deck hardware, so she can remove the chains and drag the remains of her bleeding body up the black wall of wood of the slave ship and with her last strength throw herself over the side into the water and into the mouths of the waiting sharks below."

"They live on the ship for a few days as the other slaves were brought aboard. Then one morning the sailors climb into the great masts and huge white pieces of cloth are dropped down and soon fill with wind. The ship is underway, they see the clouds move above them but they do not see the vision of their homeland falling behind because they can not see over the great walls of the ship. Then they are forced down wooden steps into the inside of the ship where they are placed in a small spot with others massed on all sides of them. Some are very sick and on all sides are other boys who were crying. There is only a smell of vomit and excrement , the stench of fear and disease, and the room is so dark that none can see. The movement of the ship makes them sick too.

"In time they are permitted on deck in groups to eat. The food is what like home but at first they are too sick and afraid to eat. After a few days they begin to eat. They are given a wooden spoon to eat with. While the children are eating the sailors try to clean the hovel below decks but they never get all the filth and it reeks of death. Each day more dead persons are thrown to the always waiting sharks off the stern of the ship, the sharks literally following the ship across the ocean from Africa. "

"At night each listens as the young girls are taken up to the sailors' berths in the front of the ship and to the captain's quarters in the stern of the ship. There are the cries and laughter as they try to please the men for a few more minutes of warmth in the cold night air. The smell is so bad that no one can sleep. A mist is now always present in the hold. A cloud of filth. Each sits in a pool of his own fluid, a pool of fluid that you can no longer control, that mixes with the filth from the others.

"After many days of this routine, and after the deaths of a great number of the children in the hold, the ship stops moving. There is a clanking noise of metal against wood coming from the front of the ship.

"They are locked in the darkness but have more hope. The ship has arrived in Maryland. Perhaps before the feast where they will be sacrificed there would be an opportunity for escape. Perhaps the children can slip under someone large. Some are faster than these men. In the village they had won the races against the other children. They feel the strength that arrives with hope coming back into their bodies.

"Above on the deck there are voices. There is some shouting. Footsteps and then silence.

"There is a faint glimmer at the edge of the ceiling. A tiny light that flickers. Then there is a smell like the great fire in the village, the burning wood, the pungent smell and the children smile thinking of the food that will soon be roasting on that fire. Some are also afraid that it may be the fire where they are going to be cooked. They hope for a chance to escape. Soon there is more smoke and their eyes begin to sting. They rub them but the irritation does not stop. There are lines of flickering light along several of the ceiling planks and some along the side of the room. There is the noise of screaming and pounding of fists. They hear more and more cracking of wood and a huge noise like a tree falling right above. When that happens there are sparks flying in the air but still there is nothing but the smoke and the tiny flickering lines. Then a plank falls from the ceiling and several of the chained people die screaming and there is a great amount of light. For a moment the children can see the timber work of the ceiling and brief patches of blue Maryland sky. Some had probably had been good at building things in the village. They had liked to watch the men who could do carpentry. It was their chosen trade. They liked to see woodwork. As the light plays with the carefully fitted boards above them, they are intrigued by how the English have fastened the boards together. They reach towards the timber above them but the chain on their ankles restrain them. The man and the children in front and beside fight to get away. Most of the children still do not understand why this is happening. Suddenly none can not get enough air into their lungs. They are coughing. They all try to tear at the chains. The blood pumps out from the rips they force deeper and deeper into their skin. They begin their last naked screams' as the fire touches their flesh." Maggie stopped. She opened her eyes.

"Amen." The Pastor looked out at the river. After a few moments, he shook his head in disgust. He walked toward his Cadillac, saying, "It's time for a miracle."

"The bell," said Maggie.

"Lot of good that will do," called back the Pastor. "No matter what we learn from the bell , after tomorrow, these children will be buried under tons of fresh concrete."

The Pastor left them then. Frank and Maggie walked back up to the porch and sat there on the top step in the dark, looking toward the dark site, the light from inside the kitchen sparkling on the tiny leaves of the boxwoods, showing the underside of the leaves of the trees above them, the sky black but pinpointed with the tiny lights of stars. Out on the river Jake's yacht began a slow trip back to River Sunday, its lights growing dim as it moved farther away.

He saw Maggie, her back up to the old porch post, her shorts and tee shirt filthy with mud, her hair tangled, and her earth covered feet pulled up. For a moment he thought how Mello would have looked sitting there. She would have had a soft blanket under her neat silk dress, her feet in carefully selected shoes that were as clean as the day she purchased them. Mello would not be as concerned about all this death they had discovered. Mello would be thinking where to sell an article about the find, about how to compute her billing for consulting hours, about how to find other work with the great Jake Terment's huge real estate projects.

"Frank, " she would be saying here in this heat filled evening, "Frank, you have to be realistic. This is your chance to make some real money. You've met a player, Frank. Cash it in. Do him a favor and he'll give you something in return. A few archeology jobs on Jake Terments other projects. They money you make would be nothing to a wealthy man like him. You could make enough to be set for life. "

The image of Mello vanished. Looking at Maggie made Frank feel wanted and warm, as if he could be loved. She turned her head and saw him looking at her. Her face was soft and she smiled at him. "You're tired."

"I guess we all are. " She touched the end of his fingers. "I've got some cream for the sore skin."

They were in the kitchen when the telephone rang. Its abrupt metallic clatter was without harmony, strangely out of place among the steady insect buzz. On the phone was one of the Pastor's council of elders.

"He wanted you to know, Dr. Light. It's Pastor Allingham. He's been hurt."

"How, where?" Frank's hand shook as he held the telephone.

"His car. Someone ran him off the road. He's going to be all right. That big old Cadillac saved his life when he went into the ditch. The car was all tore up but he's pretty much together."

"How bad is he hurt?"

"He'll be sore for a while."

"Who did it?"

"He say they come up behind him. Happened too fast. He's got a pretty good idea who done it but he ain't got no proof for Mister Billy, the chief."

"Where is the Pastor?"

"We've got him in a secure room at River Sunday Hospital." When Frank hung up, he looked at Maggie sitting across from him in the dimly lighted room. She was staring at him, fear in her eyes for an instant, the first fear he could remember seeing in her face since he had met her so many years ago.

"Someone just tried to kill the Pastor," Frank said, taking her hand.

Chapter 17

The modern part of the River Sunday hospital was a multistory building of red brick. The oldest part of the hospital was, however, in the back and of mostly wood construction, and had been constructed in 1889 as a Confederate Soldiers Home. Over the years the facility had grown and had an emergency helicopter link with a larger facility in Baltimore. The hospital was situated in an area of River Sunday that had been developed around the local spur of the Pennsylvania Railroad. Rusty unused track sections of the once busy right of way still existed in the weeds at the back edge of the hospital land while along the front street were neat Victorian style houses, built by the businessmen who profited in the railroad days. These houses were owned by lawyers and doctors from Washington and Baltimore who for the most part kept expensive sailing yachts in the River Sunday harbor and used the houses as second homes and investments. Many had been painted in bright colors and surrounded the hospital like an invading army, one that owed no allegiance to memories of Yankees and Rebels.

Inside the hospital Frank noticed that several of Billy's black police officers were sitting in the lobby along with their white counterparts.

"There's a lot of attention on the Pastor's safety," he said to Maggie.

"Yeah, sure," she said. "More likely for Jake's movie star."

Frank nodded. "I forgot about her."

He asked at the desk for the Pastor. A woman with a warm smile directed him to a corridor on the right. As he and Maggie walked through the hospital, they saw that many of the sections and wards were worn with use and some had old plaster walls which might have dated to the construction of the original building. The Pastor's room was in one of the older wards. Several black women in nurse uniforms stood guard by the door.

"We're from the shipwreck site. The Pastor sent word," Frank said to first of the women. She turned and went inside. She spoke to one of the men standing around the Pastor's bed.

Frank and Maggie were given permission to enter the room. The Pastor had been assigned to a double room but the Pastor's church elders had quickly made the room into a private area for their minister. The other resident, a farmer with a broken leg, had been moved out quickly without the hospital's permission and was being treated several rooms away. On the other bed table there were still the magazines and open can of soda that the other occupant had been using.

The room was crowded with black men and women Frank had not seen before. Frank pulled on Maggie's arm and edged the two of them to the foot of the Pastor's bed. The Pastor was sitting up, piles of faded computer papers and printouts surrounding him on the covers, his left arm in a sling and a bandage on his forehead over his right eye.

The Pastor managed a weak smile when he saw them. "They gave me a lot of medicine. Makes it hard to speak." He motioned weakly to the others around the bed. "Frank, these are the members of the council of elders from my church. " Frank nodded and introduced Maggie. The others returned the greeting with murmured hellos.

"Thank God you're all right," Maggie burst out.

"Jake didn't get me yet," the Pastor said, shifting his weight and grimacing in pain. "I'll be all right in the morning. Don't worry. I'll be up to help you stop that bulldozer."

"What did the police say?"

"There's nothing they could do about it. Chief Billy told us his men couldn't find any witnesses. There were no paint chips because the other car did not actually hit mine. Chief Billy did about what he was expected to do. Everybody in this room knows who did it, don't we?" The Pastor winked at a large round faced man with silver hair.

"He won't get away with this," said the man, his words slow and forceful. The other men murmured assent to this statement. The women in the door said quietly, "Amen," among themselves, reassuring each other with nodding heads as they spoke.

"Remember, Frank, at the site when I told you I had an idea," said the Pastor.

Frank nodded.

The Pastor held up the printouts. "This is what's left of our General Store. All our employees and friends, their addresses, hundreds of them all over the United States. " He smiled and leaned forward with some pain, "We're calling them, asking them to come here, to demonstrate, to march with signs, just like we did back in the Sixties, to make him keep the site open."

"When will they come?"

"Some have already called back and told us they were on the way. Others maybe will arrive tomorrow, more perhaps the next day. Only a few will come at first, but this time Jake will know we are here to stay, that he can't force us out again."

"What will you do?"

He smiled. "That's the simplest part. We'll just sit up there on his land. With us in the way he can't pour his concrete."

Frank woke up. He looked at his watch. It was past midnight. He had been asleep only a short time lying on the bench seat of the old truck. Something had woken him up, some noise. It was not one of Jake's guards. Jake had taken them off the duty for some reason. He had thought it strange when no one had been at the gate as he and Maggie returned from the hospital.

He thought of Soldado. Maybe the old man was moving around at the site again with his dousing wires. He looked over the back of the truck seat. In this part of the farm yard the overhanging trees made it very dark, very black. He moved his head, trying to see around the cable rigging of the hoist on the back of the truck. In the distance he could see shadows of overgrown leaf filled trees and hanging vines. He could see no movement. He knew he would have to get out of the truck and walk over to the site.

Then he heard a noise again. This time he recognized the sound. It was not Soldado. It was a car horn, coming from the bridge. He shook his head. He looked at his watch. It was after midnight, late for someone to be blowing a car horn way out here in the country. Sometimes a farmer hit the railing at the bridge. Jake had said that. A drunken farmer returning from a night in town. Then he thought, maybe the person was hurt. Maybe he had better go see what it was all about.

He knew the next sound all too well. It was a rifle shot. He recognized the familiar sharp sound of an M16 rifle. In his mind he felt the recoil against his shoulder and smelled the pungent round going off. He sat up quickly and rubbed his eyes. In a moment he was standing at the back of the truck, looking towards the site, dressed only in his thin boxer shorts, his bare feet on the dew covered grass.

He looked back at the house, a dim shadow, the kitchen light off. Maggie was asleep there. The old bell had given the kitchen a certain marsh stink, from the odor coming out of the dirt on its surface. Maggie said that she was so tired she did not even care and had stumbled upstairs to where she had her sleeping bag. "My home with the squirrels," she called it. It was still hot out in the night air. An insect of some kind flew by Frank's right ear. He could hear its wings whirring as it swerved to miss his head. His skin was sticky in the heat.

He started towards the site. Not wanting to use a light, he walked the path from memory, toes feeling the way. As he came through the box bushes and walked into the area of the shipwreck, he could feel the air currents in the open space of the field. There was still not much light even from the stars and there was no moon. His eyes were becoming aware of shapes around him, lighted somewhat by the dim starlight. He decided to move slowly towards the riverbank. He knew from memory where the gridlines were located and passed beside them.

He saw a glint of the starlight off the pump engine on his right. He smiled. They'd start it first thing, try to get a little more water out. There might be time for a few more minutes of digging before the bulldozer started up. He reached the small riverbank. The tall reeds brushed against his bare skin, sharp against his feet. His foot snapped a small branch.

"Be quiet," someone whispered to him from a few feet to his right.

Maggie. Frank knew the slight perfume she wore. Charlie Cong always said that his Viet Cong soldiers could smell out the Americans. They followed the trail of the deodorant, the stuff the GI's bought at the Post Exchange by the gallon to keep their body odor down in the intense heat, the stuff they bought to impress the Red Cross nurses, because they did not bother to wear it for their Vietnamese girlfriends.

"What are you doing here, Maggie?" he whispered back.

"I walked down for a quick swim it was so hot. There's something going on up at the bridge."

"I heard a shot."

"There were two."

He moved toward her. The starlight trinketed her body.

"I'm sorry. You don't have any clothes on," Frank whispered, moving back a step.

"I thought I was the only one out here, " Maggie replied. "Quiet. There's something going on out there."

Another shot was fired. The muzzle blast came from the island end of the bridge. The glare flashed over the bridge railings and through pinpoints of light into the river surface.   Frank instinctively ducked down to a squatting position. He pulled Maggie's left arm and she dropped down beside him in the cattails. He could sense the heat of her body next to his.

"Come on, let's get closer to the bridge," she said. She broke free from his grip and waded out into the river.

"Keep low, Maggie," he whispered as he followed her, his heart beating. He was anxious to see what was going on but apprehensive, his legs wobbling slightly with his own fear and his increasing concern for Maggie's safety. Maggie moved ahead of him, inquisitive, not showing yet any concern. Racing through Frank's mind were bits of Vietnam memories like echoes of incoming explosives and screams of pain.

They waded slowly along the riverbank towards the bridge. They crouched as they moved, trying to hide, the dark water up to their waists. Halfway to the bridge they had to go out into the river to bypass several large fallen trees whose limbs had crashed together forming a convulsed mass of branches. Maggie threaded her way through the limbs first stepping up on a branch then moving to another closer one and then dropping quietly back into the sometimes shoulder high water. Frank did the same, his feet feeling for support among the wet wood, his eyes almost useless in the pitch black, his ears listening for the direction of Maggie's tiny noises ahead. Too much noise and he knew they could be noticed by the person with the rifle on the looming bridge, noticed and fired upon.

Suddenly Frank missed a step and found himself underwater, his right hand searching in vain for a limb to grasp. His mouth filled with water. He resisted the urge to cough, to make noise, to draw attention to Maggie and himself there in that darkness. Then his hand found a rough branch and he pulled his head to the surface. Briars tore against his bare skin, ripping his shorts into fragments as he came up to the air. His feet moved against water trying to find any grip. Finally he was free of the last of the entwined jungle of old wood.

Maggie's hand was there waiting for him. They moved ahead side by side, their bare bodies glistening with the wet of the river, like a modern Adam and Eve. The bottom changed to deep muck and it was hard for them to make quick progress. They were in waist high water several feet from shore. Frank had a new worry that the person on the bridge would see them, hear them, shine a light down and perhaps put them into the sights of the rifle. Frank could hear Maggie's fast breathing, fear beginning to replace her impetuous curiosity. They held hands and, through the touch of each other, the trembling, Frank realized that they were foolish to be here, naked to the terror above.

The bottom of the river became their guide in the blackness, the muck interspersed with hard sand and oyster shells guiding their bare feet into the high reeds where they could rest and hide like the animals Frank knew were around them. Frank motioned Maggie to squat and they moved down into the reeds, wetness up to their chests, heads hidden in the tangle of the reeds and branches of overhanging trees. They waited in the darkness, in the silence.

Across from them the dim starlight reflected from the huge crane of the dredge barge, silent, hulking, strained out into the air at the middle of the channel, its cables still awry from the afternoon collapse. The massive pulley wheel of the top of the crane arm was directly opposite Frank and Maggie, its great sprocket silent, still, powerless.

Frank was aware of the closeness of her body. He sensed her complete trust in him, a total trust they had by chance achieved with each other, a complete reliance on each other in a moment of peril, a trust not unlike that of lovers. Their nakedness in this isolated place far enough away from danger yet close enough to be suddenly inescapably drawn into the conflict, gave them even more vulnerability, more than soldiers who went to war in armor. Yet, this was still the same absolute reliance soldiers had in each other. The memories came back of mortars coming in, waiting with his fellow soldiers in places of safety that were not safe, trusting them.

Frank smiled as he silently pushed away another mosquito. Maggie grinned back, the white of her teeth all he could really see in the black. .

"Mosquito lover," she whispered. "You've been around Birdey Pond too much."

Maggie motioned to Frank to duck his bare skin into the river water every few minutes to keep the bugs away. She did the same.

The bridge was dark but they began to make out some shapes. The stoplight had apparently been turned off again. Its regular changing from green to red was not working and there was no light. Up on the bridge, about a hundred yards to the right of where Frank and Maggie were hidden in the reeds, were the shapes of four silent and halted automobiles and a pickup truck, looming as dark hulks pointed across towards the island and with the first car stopped at the middle of the bridge. There was a smell of burning rubber and a few sparks tumbling on to the roadway.

"There's an electrical fire up there ," whispered Frank. He could feel Maggie nodding agreement in the darkness beside him.

Another car arrived above them on the road before the bridge. Its headlights punched over the riverwater outlining the bridge with the beams of light. A thin wisp of smoke, reflected in the glare, could be seen drifting up from the engine compartment of the first stalled car at the middle of the bridge.

The lights played on the treeline across the river, reflecting off the tall evergreens and the leaves of the full oaks that grew untamed a few feet from the river. A willow drooped its fronds into the river lap. Light also glinted from the wrecked leaning steel of the crane, its dead square metal contrasting with the live curved trees, a scrimmage line of opposites, the unnatural and the natural.

There was a flicker of red. Across the river they saw a small American flag draped from one of the Gothic window openings of the old church. In addition, at the end of the bridge on the island side the lights picked up a pile of small logs barricaded the road.

A voice roared out. "You got the River Sunday police patrol up here. You all stop before somebody gets themselves hurt. You put down them guns. We won't hurt you none." The voice droned out over the water.

A rifle shot answered. Automobile glass shattered and sprayed against the hard road surface. The light on the river surface dimmed. Another shot took out the other light with a second shattering of glass. The night was black again.

"Whoever he is, he took out those headlights," whispered Maggie.

They could hear the angry voices. "What in hell happened here?" said one voice. Another voice answered, "Old Clemens there, he works for Jake Terment on the island. He was just going home to his house out there and somebody shot out his engine right up there in the center of the bridge. He stopped the car. There was a bullet right in the engine. It's still smoking. Then the other cars got held up by him being stopped. He came back to talk to them and then there was another shot into his engine, and more sparks. Folks shut down their cars and ran back over here. Maybe we better call the fire department. "

" I 'spect we can fix this car ourselves if we can just get this boy to set down his rifle. You think there might be more than one of them? We got the call from another car that turned around and came back into River Sunday. Tell you the honest truth I didn't push it too much coming out here after all the trouble at the bridge already today. On top of that, did you hear that black preacher wrecked that old car of his?"

"Probably drinking wine, but ain't nobody going to ask him for no breath test. All his church people would start complaining about discrimination."

"You got that right. Goddamn shame, that car was a classic and worth something. I'll just be glad when they got that old marsh all covered over."

Another voice, "Nobody wants to walk out there and get shot at. Anybody tries to talk they just going to get shot at. Clemens he say he called out to the guy and that's why he got the second shot into his car engine.. He say he don't want to try no more."

"Nossir," said an old black man in a white shirt and blue overalls and a rattled straw hat.

"What do you think we ought to do?" said one man, scared.

"I called for some backup," replied the officer.

"How many do you think we are up against?" the scared voice said.

"Yeah, is it just one guy out there with a grudge against Clemens or is it something worse? Maybe some of those human butterflies," said the officer. Frank had heard this voice before at the party. He was the fat deputy named Cheeks.

A man chuckled. "You mean the 'butterfly butts.' That's what my wife calls them. No, they just walk around. They ain't got no guts. You know what I think we got over there? Bunch of guys with some rifles, fooling, just rowdy. It's a hot night that's all."

" I'm not planning on taking any chances. I radioed the Chief to ask for some help from the State Police."

Two more cars drove up, their headlights whisking across the bridge , then there was darkness and the car doors slammed.

"Going to hell around here," said the voice of Billy, the chief.

He said to Cheeks, "The boys over to Baltimore are sending me over a helicopter to scare these folks out of here."

"Terment going to be mighty pissed, Billy."

"Yes, he probably will be," said the chief.

"These folks over there with that flag, they want trouble, they can have it," said the scared man, becoming braver.." I got a rifle too, right behind the seat in my truck. It'll shoot a man just as good as it'll shoot a deer."

"You stay out of it. One angry civilian with a rifle is enough for one night."

"You boys better ask some of us pretty soon because I for one am getting pretty damn sick of these damn liberals," said the man.

"OK. You just sit over there with the rest of the folks until we get some more information about all this," said Billy.

A radio squawked. "Billy, that you boys down there, over?"

"You come on back, helicopter."

"We're gonna light up the bridge, over"

"That's a 10 4."

"Approaching the bridge," squawked the radio.

"You do your thing, over," said Billy.

Frank heard the chop chop of the machine rushing up the Nanticoke River, its lights flashing first far distant then closer in the night. The water in from of the bridge began to ripple from the air currents. The wavelets began to splash against the reeds in front of him. He reached out his hand and took Maggie's hand in his. She was trembling.

The machine rose up in the night right above the crane with a tremendous roar. The wind from the revolving blades smashed the water into large waves which crashed against the bridge supports. The water washed against Frank and Maggie. Still the machine was invisible except for its lights.

"He better watch out for that crane," said Cheeks.

The radio crackled. "Billy, you didn't tell us about that crane boom out in the water."

"You watch yourselves, over, " replied Billy.

"Proceeding." There was a popping noise and a white parachute flare opened and began its dainty descent into the stillness at the bridge. The water surface was dazzled. The piers of the bridge became huge forceful barriers with many shadows. The small flag flapped taut in the helicopter wind. On the far shore light ricocheted off the leaves and limbs of the large trees in an insane dance.

Frank remembered a night long ago at the start of Tet. His small team was outnumbered by masses of Viet Cong. He remembered shots and the padding noise of Vietnamese running in their sandals. He recalled the shadows where they hid inside a small chamber of the old once beautiful Buddhist temple. His team had fled with the loyal villagers into the temple to try to protect themselves from the onslaught of the Viet Cong attack. The enemy was everywhere, in the outer buildings, in the courtyard areas, in the other rooms of the building..

Then the American gunships began a counterattack. The rockets came into the temple. The American gunners did not realize Frank and his buddies were inside. They did not know that the villagers were there. The building began to collapse around them. The villagers died and his buddies cried out as the timbers crushed them. He heard Texas die, screaming, "Boston man, get me out of here." There was another explosion, knocking Frank unconscious. Then he woke up, the crushed building all around. He was untouched, but once again all his friends were dead. In the blackness a shape was coming towards him, a furtive shape. He could see a glint of a rifle barrel held level. He assumed the person was the enemy.

Frank moved first, swiftly, stomping the rifle back into the man's face. There was a grunt and the shape was still. Frank picked up the rifle. He saw a bloody face, that of a boy. He didn't wait to see if the boy was dead. Then Frank escaped outside into the night air of the temple courtyard. Texas, Alaska, Philadelphia were all dead behind him. He was the only one to get out. Frank heard the familiar chorus again

> "we gotta get outta this place
> we gotta get outta this place"

"You're shivering, Frank." Maggie put her left arm around his bare shoulder. He could feel her breast against his skin.

"It's like Tet."

"Yeah, they caught us with our pants down," she tried to giggle, her teeth chattering instead.

The helicopter circled around behind the trees on the Island and then began another run at the bridge. Water splashed again on the piers of the bridge. Frank and Maggie were spattered with water and seaweed particles whipped from the river surface. They crouched lower, hoping to remain out of sight of the machine.

The helicopter pilot turned on his searchlight and the beam sprayed over the small flag and the simple pile of logs. Frank could see it was a small barricade, high enough to hide several men, but lightly built. None of the barricade logs were heavier than those that could be carried or dragged by one or two men at most. There was no sign of movement behind the barricade.

The helicopter moved along the island shoreline for a few minutes its light searching up the riverbank for any sign of the source of the rifle shots. Then it began the trip back toward the bridge.

Frank noticed the person in the scuba suit first and pulled on Maggie's hand. Then he pointed to the person. They could see him under the bridge but he was out of sight of the police on top of the bridge and the officers up in the helicopter.

"Maybe we should warn them, " said Maggie.

"Keep low. If we stand up, we might get shot. They're all trigger happy up there."

They crouched lower and continued to watch as the person climbed up under the pier of the bridge until he reached a perch on one of the concrete slabs. The person brought out a rifle from a pack on his back . Before Frank or Maggie could decide what to do, the person fired. Frank recognized the crack of an M16.

The searchlight of the helicopter shattered, bits of the glass dropping, glittering in the waning light of the parachute flare. The helicopter roared its engine and lifted away. In another moment the flare reached the water's surface and it too went out with a hissing sound. The river was again dark except for the blinking lights of the helicopter which was very high off the river in the distance.

"Damn," Frank heard the chief yell.

The radio crackled, "Billy, you boys got too much action down there."

"We got trouble all right, over."

"Glass all over this Goddamned cockpit and one of us got a little nick from it."

The helicopter throbbed off into the darkness, its blinking lights competing with the stars in the blackness. Then all was quiet.   Frank could hear Maggie breathing next to him in the darkness. He squeezed her hand and she squeezed back.

"I'm all right," she whispered.

"Hell of a way to cool off," whispered Frank.

"The great Nanticoke bridge attack," she said.

"By the police or by the mosquitoes?" Frank tried to joke.

A motor boat rumbled in the black river to their left. "Marine police. He's coming up the river by his radar," Cheeks said up on the bridge.

"Smart. He's keeping his lights off," said Billy.

The radio spoke, " You on the bridge. We heard you have a problem."

"You got that right. Get the church."

"Stand by, Billy, " said the radio.

The night was illuminated by the tracers and the flame that came out of the motor boat as a crewman raked the far side of the bridge and the church ruin with a large deck machine gun. Frank pulled Maggie lower into the water, his arm around her shoulders, trying to protect her. Bits of concrete popped into the water around them as the bullets ripped into the old bridge sending color filled sparks spinning high into the air. The bullets hit into the stone, skittered off the surface of the bridge roadway, and impacted on the window glass of one of the cars with a shattering of glass dancing in the air. The machine gun was then silent, the tracer light died and the noise stopped echoing against the treelines up and down the river. Frank smelled the sickening odor of exploded ammunition. A small fire had been started at the barricade and the flag pole on the church had a race of fire climbing toward the flag.

Frank turned to Maggie, his face contorted. "I can't believe that they did that. This isn't a war." The voices above them on the bridge began again.

"That 'll end this quick, I betcha," said Cheeks.

"They sure put some lead in there," said Billy.

The motor boat engine rumbled out in the blackness of the river.

The radio spoke. "We're getting ready to rush them."

218

Just then a huge explosion from under the river surface on the opposite side of the bridge sent a geyser of water fifty feet into the air. Frank and Maggie felt the pressure of the blast. The splash and rain from the explosion came down all over the bridge and the persons up above. Maggie covered her face and lay down on her side in the water, her face barely above the surface. Frank bent over her, pushed her legs forward and made her sit up, to get her head and neck above the water.

"I'm sorry, Maggie, " he whispered.

She looked at him, the river water streaking across her cheek. "I didn't think it would be like this."

"You're going to get out of this," whispered Frank.

He sat down in the water beside her. She sobbed a couple of times and then was silent again. The radio spoke again. "Getting a little violent in there."

"Yeah. You boys better do your thing," said Billy.

Maggie looked at Frank. He could just make out her features a few inches from his own face. "The water put out the fire on the flag." she whispered, her body shaking.

The machine gun began again. Frank held Maggie close, cradling her head with his arms, keeping both their heads close to the water, with their faces just high enough to breathe. Chips of concrete dropped around them again. The sparks flew up from the bridge as the machine gun fired tracer after tracer into the barricade.

Then the helicopter reappeared, a new searchlight blazing at the far shore. Frank could see a group of five figures with rifles moving slowly up the far shore towards the barricade. He saw a muzzle flash from under the bridge. The helicopter light went out, glass falling again.

The radio spoke. "They got us again. That's all for us. We're out of here."

Maggie pulled Frank's arm. He looked at the shoreline where she was pointing. The five figures there were moving up the side of the bridge, and in a few moments had reached the barricade. Flashlights moved their beams of light all over the old church walls and the structure of the bridge. One of the figures jumped on top of the logs and waved.

"That's got them," said Billy from the bridge darkness above.

The figures moved forward, their guns pointed ahead of them as they stepped around the stopped cars.

"Good to see you boys," said the chief's voice in the darkness.

"Billy, whoever it was they got away."

The marine police officer added," I don't think there was too many of them. Might just have been one guy. "

"Why do you think that?" asked Billy.

"Well, there wasn't time for more than one of them to get out of there. A guy in a scuba suit could have done the whole thing. It hurts you people's pride, but that's the way I see it," said the marine policeman.

"Jake Terment ain't going to stand for this. He'll want us to do something about it," said Cheeks.

The logs were being moved away. The chief called to the drivers to come get their cars. Frank heard him call a wrecker from River Sunday to haul away the automobile that had burned.

Porch lights blinked on at the Pond house.

"One of you better get up there and tell Mrs. Pond that it's all over." Out on the river there were several flashlights. Dark figures were paddling small rubber rafts back towards the motor boat. On the forward deck a crewman was lashing the cover back on the machine gun.

Frank and Maggie kept low in the water. None of the police bothered to search Frank's side of the river. After about a half hour, the police left. Finally the motor boat turned away in a slow curve and headed out the river. When Frank no longer heard its churning, he motioned to Maggie. They looked at each other, their faces green, then yellow, then red from the glare of the innocent stoplight from the bridge above.

"Are you all right?" asked Frank.

"Yes," said Maggie, forcing a grin." I think it's time we got the hell out of here ourselves."

They were on the far side of the fallen trees when Maggie grabbed Frank's arm.

"Look, " she said.

There was a flickering light in the blackness ahead of them.

"Your flashlight. You must have left it on where you were swimming."

"I didn't have a flashlight," she answered, slowly. "My God, Frank, that's the farmhouse. It's on fire. One of those flares the helicopter dropped must have drifted into that old dried out roof.."

Chapter 18

"We've got to get our research materials," Frank said as he scrambled up the embankment. Maggie was close behind. When they got to the edge of the site field they could see the house better. Great flames roared behind several of the upstairs windows. In back of the building was a smaller fire.

"Your car is burning too," said Frank.

Maggie was crying and screaming at the same time. "The notes. The equipment. All our work. "

He stopped her from running into the house. "It's not safe. Keep back."

Frank saw someone running around the house toward him. He was too far away for Frank to see his face or to do more than guess that it was a man by his heavy build.

"Hey you, mister. What are you doing there?" he called. The man stopped, turned and ran back around the house and out of sight. He resembled Spyder in his bent over running position.

Sparks were dropping from edges of the roof and were carrying into the trees. Burning leaves were floating in the air around Frank and Maggie. A fire siren began to wail in the distance.

"River Sunday," said Frank. "Somebody saw the fire."

He reached the truck and pulled open the small steel door.

"Get in," he yelled to Maggie. She jumped past Frank into the cockpit and fell across the canvas seat. She pulled herself to the other side of the cab.   Frank followed her on to the seat. He turned the key and pressed the starter. The truck churned to life and Frank put the vehicle into reverse. He looked out the side as the truck lurched backward.

"Are you all right, Maggie?" he said over his bare shoulder.

"I'm all right."

They were still naked from the river. "We need clothes," said Frank. "There's some of my stuff on the floor in front of you."

She reached down and absently pulled on Frank's jean shorts and tee shirt Her eyes full of fear, gazed at the flames, the reflection of the fire fierce on the windshield in front of her. He stopped the truck.   "I'm going to leave it here down at the end of the site near the river. It'll be out of the way of any fire trucks."

They watched as Maggie's government sedan exploded, roaring up in flames and then as quickly subsiding as the gasoline was used up. She was shaking as she watched it.

 "My car had everything in it, all my records from other jobs, my tools."

Frank pulled on a pair of work shorts. Then he reached over and hugged her tightly. She was trembling.   "I could have been sleeping in that house, Frank."

"You're safe. It's all right."

"Who was that man, Frank? Why did he do this?"

"It looked like Spyder. He could have killed you."

"Why the house? They had us out of here in the morning. It would all be over."

"No, it wouldn't ," said Frank.

Realization came across her face. "That's right. The records. The bell."

He looked at her, her face lit up by the flames in the distance. She held his hand. "We're targets too. "

"Yes," he said.

"Promise me you won't let this site be lost, you won't let Jake win."

 "I promise," he said.

Just then a fire truck pulled off the highway and into the lane, its siren adding to the anxiety. It was followed by a long tanker truck and then by a small rescue vehicle. As the firemen began to lay out their hose, one of the men noticed Frank and Maggie walking toward them, a portable radio in his hand.

"You over there," the fireman called. "Anybody in the house.?"

"No," said Frank. "We're all out."

"You folks hurt?"

"We're OK," said Frank.

"There's a car burning out back," the radio crackled. The fireman motioned to a team who then went over to the car with one of the hoses.

The fireman continued. "You folks got any idea how it started?"

" I saw a man running away when I came up here."

"You weren't in the house, Mister?"

"No, we were at the beach. There was trouble at the bridge."

"Yeah. I heard. So you guys came up here and found it burning and some guy running away."

"Yessir," said Frank. The fireman looked at him, smiled, and walked away.

"What did they say?" asked another fireman standing by the pumper truck.

"They don't know. It's probably electrical. These old houses have a lot of bad wires. They weren't in the house so maybe they left something electrical turned on inside, something that shorted out."

"That's the shipwreck site over there, isn't it?"

"Yeah. Jake Terment's problem child."

The firemen turned back to their work. Cars filled with teenagers, families, various local people, were beginning to arrive on the road outside the farm. They parked on both sides of the road. People were walking in the middle of the road toward the burning farmhouse. Frank watched the arrivals for a few minutes and then said,

"It's like a carnival for these people," said Frank "They don't belong here."

"Happens at all these fires, Mister, " said the fireman as he pulled at the folded hose on the back of the truck. "Sometimes we try to stop them if it is a big fire. Most of them are our cousins and families anyway just coming to see us work."

Frank and Maggie stood watching as the spectators began to gather.

"I bet this will be seen for miles," said an excited teenage girl standing next to Maggie.

"It's my home," said Maggie.

The teenager looked at her, her face almost angry that Maggie had challenged her.

"I wonder if anything will be saved," Maggie said to Frank..

"You people are lucky to get out of there alive," said the fireman. "This place was a real firetrap. I'm surprised it hasn't gone up before, old as it is and nobody living here much anymore, " said one of the firemen. "Jake Terment offered us this place a few years ago to use in our practice. We were going to burn it down for training."

Another fireman said," One of the guys said it was burning in two places when he walked out in back. Both of them up in the roof. A car burning too."

"Two places. That don't sound like an electrical fire to me," said the fireman. "Maybe somebody don't like you folks."

The building was engulfed in flames.   There were two hoses playing water on the fire but the water was useless against the high flames.

"We just want to stop it from spreading, grassfires, the outbuildings, that's about all you can do with a building like this," said the fireman.

"You two must be exhausted," said a voice from behind Frank and Maggie.   Birdey Pond stood there. She reached out to comfort Maggie. Maggie moved toward her. The older woman put her arms around Maggie.

"I know. I know," said Birdey, comforting Maggie. "We saw the shooting out at the bridge. Jake Terment telephoned me as furious as I've ever heard him. Threatening. He claimed it was one of my friends who was shooting at his tenant farmer."

She paused, " No, I didn't do it but I wish I'd thought of it."

She looked at Frank.   "Come over to my house at least for the rest of the night. You two need some rest."

"I'm staying here," Maggie said, sudden strength in her voice.

"This fire more of Jake's work?" Birdey asked.

"We think it was set," said Frank.

"Sorry," Maggie sobbed. " I just see myself inside that house."

A crash of the falling roof sent sparks high into the night air, red specks twisting and turning against the blackness, against the gray wisps of acrid smoke. A sigh of excitement rose from the spectators. They spotted the cat. The animal had been trapped in the farmhouse. It came out on a window ledge on the second floor. The flames were behind it, making the animal a blur of black against the rapid light and the red glare of the flames. The cat had only moments to escape. It sat calmly on the ledge, looking from side to side in a trance like manner as if looking for a mouse to chase rather than trying to keep its own self alive.

"Look, he's going to jump," screamed a woman in the crowd. Then, as the crowd let out another sigh, more like a communal scream, the cat, its black spots almost glowing against its orange fur, jumped directly towards the ground, the full two stories, legs spread apart as if to help it fly through the air. Then hitting the grassy ground, it bounced upward, mouth open in a hiss which had no sound. Finally the cat tore through the crowd toward the far hedge of honeysuckle and disappeared in the night.

Frank and Maggie turned toward the dig area, the flames behind them casting their shadows far ahead, the shadows dancing with the flames, the smell in the air sharp with smoke. The site had become a spectator bleacher. Its closeness to the road, its relative openness and the pits of the dig allowed the spectators to sit on the edges of the pits with their legs dangling over the sides. All this had made the scholarly dig site into an outdoor party peopled with laughing and carousing guests of all ages.

In the darkness there were many pinpoints of light where the spectators had flashlights. The beams randomly shot rays into the night or against the gray shroud of smoke rising over the house fire, the wall of smoke drifting away but still solid enough to bounce the light back.

There were dozens of men, women, children of all ages, all of them white. Frank looked for any blacks but saw none. Some of the people had brought along folding chairs. The spectators could be heard complaining as their chairs sank sideways and spilled them into the wet soil. Others had brought beer and portable radios. There was the sound of rock songs mixed with country ballads all producing a heavy beat, not a melody just a beat like a huge drum. Children tied each other in the surveyors twine or played swords with the dig stakes. Several men and women had established contests comparing their performances at urinating on the skeletons.

Occasionally the farmhouse would flare up and the intense light would reflect from the upturned faces of the crowd. The faces were hundreds of small white ovals, dull orbs in the black, punctuated by the tiny lights from their flashlights.

"All gone. All we've worked for," said Maggie.

Frank held her close as they walked across the site, not speaking to the people. One very old man, barechested, his white chest hair glistening with sweat, complained that Frank was blocking the man's view of the fire. Frank and Maggie said nothing and kept moving on. The fire was dying, the dry wood almost used up and the flames tearing at a few remnants not yet incinerated. The excitement ebbing, some of the people were starting to move back to their cars.

A cardboard box of empty beer cans was perched on top of the pump which had been overturned. Maggie removed the box. Frank helped her turn the pump upright. In the dark, they could not see the probe pits. Frank felt some of the skeleton bones in the earth under his bare feet. He knew then that the skeletons had been tossed around in a ghoulish game by some of the spectators.

When they reached the gate to the property they could see the extent of the madness. There were cars parked in skewed attitudes along the road, some with headlights still turned on. Even as many of the persons were leaving, along the road there were more spectators approaching the farm. Mothers and fathers with their children looked anxiously for a place along the side of the road to park. Among those walking towards the fire, there was disappointment in their eyes that they were late. Children pulled at their parents' hands, urging them forward.

Jake was standing in the middle of the road with two of the policemen. As Frank got closer to them, he recognized the chief of police.

"What happened here, Frank?" asked Jake, his southern smile broad on his face.

"We don't know, Jake. There was some guy running away when the fire started."

"You two must have left some light on, ". said Jake. " The wire in the house was all frayed, worn out. This place really wasn't livable. I'm glad you folks were not hurt. I tried to get you to stay in at the Chesapeake Hotel. You can't blame me."

"That's where I slept, Jake," said Maggie, staring at him. "Aren't you at all concerned that we might have been killed? I was lucky. I was out of the house when it started."

Jake moved his eyes from her stare.

"Look at what these people have done to our work," said Frank.

"I 'm afraid our local people don't have much regard for holes in the ground, not when there's a fire to see, " Jake grinned at the police chief who smiled.

"Our work is ruined," said Maggie.

"I can't worry about that, Maggie. I just lost a house. Seems to me someone could think about that. I just lost my tenant farmer house. Besides, this digging here wasn't supposed to be permanent. I've already given the two of you fair warning that my men will begin bulldozing tomorrow morning. "

"We planned to work until your machines start."

"Well, " said Jake, his voice dictatorial, "I guess your work is really finished."

"How can you just let all this happen?" said Frank. " You told me the other day you didn't want a lot of strangers hanging around. How can you let all these people in here?"

"Look here, I'm not letting anything happen," said Jake. "This is my house that just burned down. Somebody tried to blow up my boat. This is my land that you are digging up. Folks know I 'm getting all kinds of trouble. They came here to help. That's the way we are down here in the country. They found my house was on fire and they came to help. Down here in River Sunday this is the way we do things. I'm not about to tell my friends to leave when they have come to help me. You two get yourselves together, get your stuff packed up, because in a few more hours you two are going to be trespassing on my land. If you are not gone by then, I will have to remove you."

Jake looked at the chief. "Billy, you see them around here in the morning, you get them off my land. You get something on that old woman too for what she did to my boat."

228

"We'll take care of it, Jake," said Billy. "Come on, boys," he waved at the other officers near him. "Let's get these cars moved so other people can get by."

Frank stood with Maggie at the edge of the honeysuckle hedge for a long time. They watched as the rest of the farmhouse collapsed inward, sparks twisting upward into the sky in the white smoke of the dying fire. They saw the fire engine blinker lights switched off one by one as the firemen packed up their equipment and left, the drivers gunning the engines with roars of unmuffled exhausts.

Chapter 19

Frank awoke just after dawn. Maggie was still asleep, her body against his on the seat of the truck, her breasts flecked with cinders and exposed in his ill fitting shirt. They had climbed into the truck, exhausted after the last fireman left almost two hours ago. He smiled at her, sensing a closeness with her, as though they were two comrades who had fought an enemy side by side and survived. He moved his fingers softly against the side of her face. Maggie slowly opened her eyes and smiled at him. She turned and moved closer to him, her eyes closing again.

He kissed her lips. He wiped a smudge of the soot from the fire that had landed on her nose. Her eyes opened. "Do that again." This time their lips touched with a passion that surprised them both. When they drew apart, he said, "We'll have to explore that when this is all over."

She smiled. "Yes."

"I've changed my mind about a lot of things, " he said. It wasn't just the kiss. He knew that Mello was out of his life forever.

She touched his lips with her finger. "I know." Then she said, "You have a little mole on your forehead, right with the freckles."

"My Mom used to say it gave me wisdom."

"She was right, your Mom. I wish I could have known her." She smiled as she pulled up the neck of the tee shirt and then looked inside. "There's room for both of us in here." She looked around, holding her head just above the steel dashboard. The truck still had its military panel of switches and dials, the stark faces and numbers contrasting with the softness of her hair and face.

Frank sat up."We need to get out on the site and see what we can preserve." He looked through the windshield at the desolation of the burned house.

"My God, "he said. "Just like Tet was. Everything busted up."
 She touched his arm.

"There's no doubt in my mind that Jake did not care whether he killed us last night," Frank said slowly. "He wanted to get rid of the artifacts and he didn't care who got hurt."

She looked at him, her eyes asking him what to do.

"The Pastor's got the right idea. Only trouble is he's not here yet. I've tried not to take sides but Jake's forced me. I'll stand in front of the bulldozer myself. Jake'll have to run that yellow bulldozer right over me," said Frank.   He climbed down from the truck, his skin and cutoffs coated with sticky bits of black ash.

Maggie climbed out of the truck. "I'm going to stand there with you," she said. He took her hand and they walked toward the house. The sky was clear blue, with a hot orange red sun rising big above the treeline and cornfields. Insects buzzed in the morning dew. There was, however, the unpleasant smell of smoke and steam from the wet charred stud wood. Scorched tarpaper hung in long sheets from the exposed frame members of the house. Windows had fallen out on the ground and timbers, bricks and pipes hung without order and with no resemblance to the once weathertight construction.

Frank's skin itched from the embedded soil and cinders. His left foot still ached from slipping off the underwater limb last night on the way to the bridge and his side felt bruised where the briars had shredded his underwear. His toes felt the damp soil and the grass that was smashed down from the heavy tires of the fire trucks.   Some of the boxwoods had been broken in half by the trucks. The fire engines had left great tracks in the grass where only a few hours ago people had stood with cocktails at Jake's party.

He looked toward the site, beyond the remains of the boxwoods. He could see the top of the bulldozer. The crowd had pulled the canopy from the machine. It was upright on the ground, its mounting poles up thrust like a great dead beetle.

231

As they got closer to the house, Frank noted the muck that was splattered on what little grass was left, the soil that the heavy tires had brought from the lane with its new ruts and deep potholes full of black water and broken charred timbers. The house itself had fallen inward for the most part, the remains of the roof collapsing with the layers of asphalt shingles spilling into the first floor. Large sections of sodden plaster bent forward from sections of walls, the plaster still held together by fragile electrical wiring and water pipes.

Maggie's car was a blackened ruin. Its cloth upholstery still steamed. Broken glass was sprinkled on the ground, tires were flat, and a pair of her shorts and various of her digging tools were scattered on the ground outside the wreck. The grass under the car's gasoline tank was blackened in a large circle.

They circled back to the front of the house and started toward the site. Much of the honeysuckle had been torn out of the hedges by catching against the fenders of the fire trucks. The broken vines were dying quickly in the morning sunlight but even with the dank odor of the wet burned wood of the house, there was still a faint smell of the sugar of the honeysuckle.

Suddenly Frank smelled burning tobacco and looked behind him expecting to see someone standing there with a pipe or cigar. There was no one. Maggie stopped and looked at him. The smell was overpowering. He felt like he was choking on the fumes. He reached for his throat. He began to cough. Then the odor disappeared. He looked around again, remembering what the Pastor had said about the tobacco legend.

"What's the matter?" she said.

"That tobacco smell."

"You better watch out," she smiled.

"There's not much more can happen to us," he answered. "I'm going over to the site."

"I'll want to look around the house," she replied.

As he approached the site he noticed the sifting pile, the heap of soil that they had run carefully through Maggie's screen as they excavated it from the various pits. This hill was several feet high and surprisingly untouched by the vandalism. The screen itself had also been left alone.

A few feet beyond the pile he saw what remained of the excavation. He noticed first that the carefully established marked sections were all destroyed, the twine torn down and the markers pulled out in the rampage of the previous night. The several pits had become one large hole, the carefully measured and staked walls or balks between pit areas, all tumbled in the frenzy of the crowd.

Then he saw the horror, a sight that made his stomach heave with disgust. He stopped and kneeled in weakness. His eyes moved to the center of the area where the white datum stake had been. There was a great pile of bones and skulls with the skulls stacked on top in grinning frenzy. Sadly, most of the skulls were small in size. He knew that his worst fear, and Maggie's and the Pastor's too, that there had been many slave children burned here, was indeed true. The pile stretched from the middle of the wreck area to the edge of the site on the farmhouse side. Towards the road a few boxes were still upturned where the merry makers had apparently sat and tossed the skulls and bones at the pile.

The site was changed in another way. Much of the frame of the shipwreck was visible. Wood frames strutted above the soil, exposing sections of the ship's ancient flooring. Rising from the boards were rusty iron rings, coupled to long chains which were entangled with dozens of skeletons, almost all of them children..

"Maggie," he called back to her. "It's beyond belief. The spectators cleared out the loose earth when they were walking on the site. We were proceeding so carefully, so slowly. Their feet hurried up the whole process. In trying to destroy our work, they actually helped bring the wreck out of the ground. "

He heard her rushing through the bushes from the house. He climbed down quickly into what had become a large rectangular trench. The sides of the trench waved and sloped with the soft earth. In the center of the great pit, the pile of jumbled bones stuck above the ship wreckage like a fat white mast.

"There must be hundreds of small skulls here," Maggie said from behind him. She kicked at the soil, trying to punish it.

He reached back for her hand.She walked forward and squatted beside him.

"Let me just look at this for a moment," he said.

He jumped up and moved toward the bow of the wreck where some boards were showing. He knelt and looked closely at the boards, talking quickly. "We've got to study this, and this has to be done right. Help me." His voice shook as he fought to control himself, the nausea at seeing the remains of the murdered children.

He spoke carefully, the technical terms helping him to control himself. "First of all I see some ochre colored boards. Below them are a section with boards with tar in between. That tar system we know was a Seventeenth Century way of protecting the hull from worms. The outside board was eaten and the tar stopped the predators from getting at the inner board. The ochre was the color they painted most of these old ships. Made the hull look like strong new oak so pirates would not think the ship was easy to destroy with cannon fire."

His knowledgeable fingers traced the board edges. " It's definitely the British and American style, the bulging beam near the bow like a fish, the stern real narrow. "

He looked up at her.

"New York," she said. "The old merchant ship wreck they found there."

"That's what I was thinking. "

Frank walked to the stern area and stopped at a board protruding vertically from the earth. "Look at this."

Maggie moved to his side.

"See the little curves to the top of the rudder," he said. "That means she's Chesapeake built. I can spot the rudder trim anywhere. Same as the wreck in New York. Let's look at the bow again."

Walking forward again, they kept spotting fragments and showing them with excitement to each other. At the bow there were pieces of wood with carving and what remained of two shapes that might have been some type of figurehead. One shape looked like a hand holding a ball.

"Those figures. They remind me of something. I'll think of it, "Maggie said.

"The carving is all early," said Frank. "Definitely Seventeenth Century. Nobody could afford this work in the later ships. "

234

"Come see what I found at the house," Maggie said, new energy in her eyes.

They moved back up toward the wreck of the house, she holding his hand and pulling him along gently, the two of them walking through the remains of the high grass, the insects noisy around them, coming out from hiding after the inferno of the previous night. Maggie lead Frank, turning anxiously from time to time, hurrying him along. They reached the remains of the porch and stepped through the ruined black wood into the space where the kitchen floor had been.

"Careful. Your bare feet. The nails," said Frank.

"Seeing those children has made me tough," she said.

He followed her into the jungle of broken wood. Her excitement, her impish figure like a wraith, a spectral and physical presence amidst the awful holocaust wreckage, was cheering to Frank.

"Look at this," she said.

"The ship's bell. I thought it was lost in all that heat," said Frank

" Look at it closely," she said.

The ship's bell lay in the midst of the wreckage, several pieces of plaster resting on top of it. He scratched his neck.

"I see what you mean. The aggregate has been burned off. There's raw metal left," he said.

They bent over the object, no longer survivors, but scientists and scholars again.

"It's got some letters on it," he said.

"Yes," she said, excitement in her eyes.

"Let me move some of this wood." He pulled at one of the fallen studs that was resting on the bell. As he shifted it, a piece of plaster fell backward, crashing into the rubble with a huge cloud of black soot. Maggie and Frank were both showered with some of the gray and black fire dust.

"Are you all right?" she said.

"Yes," he answered, impatiently brushing off the clinging flotsam. They moved closer to the bell. The metal was clear on all sides of the object.

"It's beautiful," said Frank.

"Look at the scrollwork up at the top where the bell hanger is."

"This was very expensive to cast," said Frank. He tipped the bell upward. "Still pretty heavy."

Maggie leaned over and pulled on the object with Frank. They tipped it further and Maggie got her hand around the bottom lip of the bell.

"There's conglomerate inside. Can you get your hand around it to help me lift it?" Maggie said. She was bent well over, her feet close to the lip of the object.

"Watch out for your toes," said Frank.

"You too," she said.

Frank stepped ahead, his right foot along the opposite side of the object, his left hand bracing himself against the ruined timbers of the old kitchen wall.

" OK. I've got it, " he said.

They lifted the bell and moved it, walking backward out of the broken timbers. Then they stood on a patch of scorched grass, the bell on the ground between them.

"Let's get it over to the truck in case this building collapses any more," said Frank.

Frank placed a remnant of porch flooring under the bell and they skidded the object along the ground to the truck. He opened the tailgate and cleared a small space near the hoist.

"Do you think we can lift it up or do we need the hoist?" asked Maggie.

"Let's try it. One, two, three," Frank counted off and they hefted the object up on the truck.

"It must be a couple hundred pounds at least."

"It's heavy all right," agreed Frank. "Let's see if we can make out any of the letters."

"They are very fancy letters. I think that one is a "A" and this one is a small "d."

"We'll try a little water on it." Frank took his shirt and dipped it in a puddle. He looked at Maggie. "We're supposed to use a clean special conservator's cloth."

"I'm sure the association of antique metal conservators will not mind this one infraction," Maggie smiled.

As he wiped the surface the letters started to come out more clearly. "Adam is the first word. Another is Eve. Underneath there is another word, the port I think. London. I'm sure it's London."

"I think you're right. Adam and Eve, London. No date. We can guess at that. Probably early Eighteenth Century or late Seventeenth judging for the design of the bell."

She stopped talking. Her face lit up. "That's it. Those figures on the ship bow. The one holding a ball. It was Adam and Eve with the woman holding the apple."

Frank looked at her, his eyes wide.

"What?" she said.

"The old blind preacher, remember that Mr. Johnson described. Maybe it was the ship that he was referring to."

She realized what he was saying. "All those years of living in fear," she said. "Some of the Terment slaves must have seen the fire. Their code for the horror, for the dead children, was Adam and Eve."

There was a sound of a tool hitting a sheet of steel. "What was that noise?" he said. The metallic sound clanked again behind the boxwoods.

"Let's take a look."

A small yellow truck had arrived quietly and was parked near the large bulldozer. The broken canopy from the tractor was already loaded in the back of the truck.

"Somebody is repairing the bulldozer," said Maggie.

"We haven't got much time left," he said. "Come on."

"What are we going to do?"

"We've got some fortifications to build."

He looked at Maggie. Her eyes said yes.

Frank explained as they ran back toward the shipwreck. "The best defense is a structured site. That will be our fortifications. There's got to be something for him to destroy. It will take him more time. If Jake runs it down, he has to run down all our measurements, and not just a field of bare earth."

She nodded. "Anything to slow him down.Let me start with restoring the dig area. You try to remeasure what you can of the survey lines and grids. There are a few posts that were not destroyed. The datum stake is gone but the crowd did not move Soldado's markers. "

The two white stakes stood vertically from the site marking the spots that Soldado had discovered in his wild dance. There was evidence that someone had tried to pull one of the stakes out. The top of the stake was broken off but the base had remained secure as if it were locked into the marsh.

"We can work from his locations," said Frank.

Moving as fast as she could, Maggie pounded in each new stake and restretched the white twine. Frank helped on some of the longer sights, holding a post while she sighted it by eye and guided him back and forth until they had a fix. Meanwhile Frank tried to rebuild the excavation. He started with the Q dig area. Most of the bones in the great pile had come from this original pit. Frank noticed the remnants of blue cloth in the side of the pile. The bones of the Federal soldier had been thrown into the pile with the slave and sailor skeletons.

During this time the two of them also kept glancing at the workman at the bulldozer. The operator in turn looked at them occasionally as he continued to service the tractor, adding grease to its grease points and its tracks . He also ran a hose from the large fuel drum on the back of his truck to the bulldozer fuel tank and pumped fuel over to the tractor.

After stretching the surveyors twine over the new stakes, Maggie and Frank started the difficult task of restoring the bottom of the pit. Although the ship was more exposed and beams and planks of the wreck were in evidence, much of the wreck was in disarray, changed by the crowd into a mass of twisted bones and wood rather than the orderly pile that nature had preserved in its original form. They worked as quickly as they could, placing the parts of the wreck back in places where they were sure the parts had originated. They used water marks and shapes in the soil strata to place the parts. The walls of the enlarged pit showed more definitely the strata and indicated more fully the large amount of fill that had been brought into the site sometime in the past to cover the shipwreck.

"Someone sure did a lot of work to cover up this old wreck," said Frank.

As much as they could, they tried to remove the trash that had fallen or been thrown into the pit, the beer cans and the human vomit and excrement. Minutes, then an hour, went by as they worked. The sun inched higher. The mechanic tapped his way to his conclusion , the start of the tractor engine. As Frank had wanted, the marsh changed gradually into a restored site, what Frank referred to as his fortification.

The scholars and the mechanic gradually faced each other across a dead area, land heavy with tire ruts and debris from the fire, on one side of the area the sharp bulldozer blade, on the other, a battle line of white twine and wooden stakes.

Chapter 20

Then, the morning silence was broken with the grinding clatter of the large yellow bulldozer as its diesel engine started up and signaled the beginning of the challenge. Frank watched as choking puffs of black diesel smoke infiltrated the green leaves of the trees around the tractor. Then the operator straddled the driver's seat and the big machine made the soil tremble, sending ripples into even the small pools of water in the pit.

The tractor did not come towards the site. Instead the driver turned the machine and began smashing the small trees and bushes, twisting and tearing from where it had rested. He drove across the lawn towards the blackened farmhouse ruin.

The operator, his face intent, directed this noisy rampage, a precise, non feeling, non emotional, non caring charge. With a few twists of his fingers on the steering arms, he shifted and adjusted the tractor's direction until the machine crawled steadily toward the house, some of its beams already shaking from the tremors in the land. Mice and other small animals appeared standing up from the grass, looking quickly and fleeing before those great metal tracks and the acrid smoke.

"He's going to start out by pushing the rest of the house down," said Frank.

"He's smart. He'll use the wreckage of the house to fill in our ship excavation," said Maggie.

Like many of the rural structures around the River Sunday area, the farmhouse had been constructed without a basement or cellar of any kind. Instead it stood on piers of brick which in turn supported the massive corner posts and joists of the house. Under this platform there was a space a few feet high running back under the house. This filthy place had been filled with dust and dirt and probably decades of noisy play by happy children.

The stories were still there but were hidden in rubble. Beneath blackened timbers were shreds of generations of children searching out their fantasies, the tracks of their bare feet once imprinted in this haven from the sun, in this shelter from the afternoon thunderstorms. In the dust were countless tales of games of hide and seek, of cowboys and Indians, of Confederates and Yankees. Other footprints told of chickens or pigs let loose in the yard to forage endlessly and to hide under the house until their true dinner was cast outside for them. Still other shreds told the saga of the foxes and raccoons smelling the chicken tracks and searching for their own food, the eggs. This old space was a simple library of the history of the creatures that used its space. All this repository was converted to black ash, the brick piers barely extending above the collapse, weak from the intense flames of last night's instant. These weak piles and the strength of the history could offer no resistance to the steel blade of the bulldozer.

The bulldozer operator, guiding the machine along the side of the farmhouse, had reached the opposite side. He turned the machine again, shifted the great tractor transmission and inched his machine backwards away from the house, the huge tracks crushing a small shed overgrown with vines that had been a hundred feet or so behind the farmhouse. A small section of chicken wire fence attached itself to the steel track of the machine and refused to fall off, entwining its tiny wires tighter and tighter on the track sections. The operator lowered the big blade until it was a few inches above the surface of the yard. Then, with an impassive face, he shifted and inched the machine forward, its crushing tracks moving directly at the house.

Frank watched the man's face and saw that even with all the power at his disposal, the operator was being careful as he approached the structure. His maneuvering was calculated because the structure was very weak and could collapse at any moment. He directed the machine forward until the bottom of the steel blade just touched the closest corner post. Even touching it made the remains of the house sway slightly with a rain of black ash falling towards the ground and causing a mushroom of dead smoke to rise. If the bulldozer operator miscalculated the blade might break the corner post and travel under the second floor. Then the remains of the second floor and roof might topple directly down on the tractor, burying the operator in broken wood and plaster.

The operator backed away and then slowly approached the corner post again. This time he brought his blade in at a lower angle. The wreck of the house swayed menacingly towards the tractor. He backed off again and after moving a few more feet from the back of the house, shut down the machine's engine and climbed down.

Another car had joined the operator's truck parked in the field.

"Buddy," an older man dressed in blue overalls yelled at the operator and he climbed out of his car. This man walked up to the bulldozer while the operator was shutting off its engine. The new arrival moved his arms wildly as he talked to the first man. Then the operator, Buddy, with a nervous face, slowly climbed back into the bulldozer. He started up the engine and allowed the machine to travel forward again towards the post. The blade, traveling a few feet off the ground hit the corner post and this time the operator did not slow the machine down. The corner post cracked and broke in half, the top part moving inward and the floor above leaning toward the bulldozer with a shrieking sound. Buddy, his face frigid with fear reached for the lever that raised the blade and the blade began to move up slowly, counteracting the downward shift of the house. At that moment the structure reversed its slide at the bulldozer and shifted quickly and harshly in the other direction, snapping the remaining corner posts and throwing pieces of plumbing pipe and sections of plaster through the air as the building let loose a final spring of energy and collapsed.

Frank could barely see the operator. Only his head showed over the trash even though Buddy was forced to stand up on his small driver's seat in order to see ahead. The diesel speeded and the bulldozer moved quickly into the remnants of the house, its tracks crushing the few studs that were still erect As the bulldozer reached the other side of the wrecked house the timbers and electrical wiring and plaster had combined into a large roll of trash, the roll almost as high as the roof gutter of the original house and the circumference a good sixty to seventy feet. The roll moved ahead with a crunching tearing sound.

"Oh, my God," said Maggie.

She had been right. Buddy would fill the site with the wreckage of the house. The roll was coming directly towards Frank and Maggie. Suddenly though, Buddy stopped the machine's tracks, its engine still idling. He climbed down and walked towards Frank and Maggie, his eyes on the ground. The man walked in front of the roll of broken timbers that towered over him by at least ten feet. He held up his arm to shield himself, as from its top small bits of soil and shingles tumbled from time to time like drops after a terrific rainstorm, bouncing from broken boards to pipes on their way down to the mud.

He did not look at the two archeologists several hundred feet in front of him. In a moment Buddy had reached one of the few remaining patched of green grass. He stooped to pick a tiny blue blossom that had survived the crushing of the heavy fire truck tires the night before. Frank could barely hear his voice against the purring of the diesel.

"My wife's favorite color," he yelled back to the other man, holding the flower up. "Thought I'd save it for her."

Immediately behind where Frank and Maggie were standing was the remains of the test pit H. This was the bow spot where the Pastor had found the skeletons that they thought were the crew. A few feet in front of that spot was the frame section that the bulldozer had originally uncovered which had been the start of the whole project. The crowd the previous night had not walked near this up thrust piece of timber. It was untouched by the beer cans and the other trash. Even the ground near it was not marked with footprints.

Frank moved towards the bulldozer, the sifting pile in front of him. Maggie was beside him. The bulldozer noise was deafening. Maggie climbed upon the small sifting pile hill.

"Is this what soldiers do, Frank?"

He nodded and joined her. "Except that in the war we'd have killed that driver right away. Funny how you think you've forgotten how to kill but then you realize you can't forget. You see something crude, hateful and dangerous like that bulldozer and you remember."

For a moment Frank gaped at the big machine, his eyes open but dull. He rubbed his neck. Maggie stood there on the small mud hill, her stance daring the opposition to attack. Frank was less jaunty. He was like a reenlisted soldier, still adjusting his posture, slowly remembering how to march, but knowing from experience what danger they were in.

The two of them from time to time glanced behind them at the entrance road. They still had hope that the Pastor could bring his demonstrators, whatever few persons he could convince to come to this isolated spot, to be voices to hold Jake and the bulldozer back with their pleas.

Frank's mind searched for some answer, some way to make the peace. He and Maggie both knew that they were in a hopeless position, one which they would have to leave momentarily, whether bravely or cowardly, unless they wanted to be killed, crushed by the great roll of steel and wood in front of them.

Police cars wailed from the road. These cars were closely followed by a green stationwagon. The cars bounced on the ruts at they entered the yard at high speed, then braked suddenly and parked near the vehicles of the bulldozer operator and his boss..

Both black and white officers hurried out of each car. They assembled in a small group, ten in all, and their leader, Billy, ordered them to stand near where the bulldozer was idling. Then from the green car Jake stepped out with Spyder behind him. Jake placed his feet carefully, looking at the ground as he walked toward the bulldozer. He was dressed in another white silk suit and walked deftly so that the suit and his well shined shoes would not be covered with the mud and black ash that was everywhere. He stopped for a moment and stared at the excavation, then continued on. He ignored Frank and Maggie, passing beside them by fifty feet, his face directed forward as in a trance.

When he reached the tractor he talked for a moment with the chief and then with the bulldozer workmen. He had the same smile he showed Frank that first day. He waved at the tractor operator who waved back. The operator held up the small blue flower and Jake nodded.

244

The operator eased the clutch and increased the throttle. The tractor engine speeded up and began again to push the great roll of debris forward. Jake turned his face toward Frank. He stared at him and Maggie, then shook his head and put his arm on the shoulder of the chief. The police did not move toward Frank and Maggie but appeared ready to do so at Jake's command.

The mass of wreckage rolled closer. Frank glanced at Buddy's face a tiny orb above the heavy roll of broken wood and plaster that was tumbling toward the two of them. The face of the driver was impassive, the only emotion it had shown so far was this procurement of a flower.

Maggie was shaking but she was resolute in her stance. Frank watched her, the way he would have watched his fellow soldiers in Nam, the way they had watched him, each to see if the other would run. Her face showed non belief, as if she could not grasp that she had become a soldier. Like Frank, who understood her feelings and pressed her hand to let her know he was with her, the two of them desired most at this moment to be left to be archeologists again. Yet both knew they would not run, they were here, they knew they had to be here, and they knew they had to stop Jake somehow.

Frank watched the puzzlement with Maggie on Jake's face, knowing that he was not seeing a woman, just an impediment, a low level civil servant. Seeing her ready to fight him confused him. When he met Frank's eyes, his face changed as if Frank was more his equal, as if he were more experienced in fighting against other men. With Frank, however, his face showed another kind of puzzlement, perhaps one of not understanding why Frank wasn't beside him, as if Frank should be working on the final report, encouraging the bulldozer's progress, continuing his upward bound professional growth as a young professor. Jake had brought Frank into the project and could not understand why his carefully selected appointee had rebelled and was standing on a little hill about to be totally destroyed.

The police shifted their feet, some of the officers seemingly restless with their assignment. Frank and Maggie continued to cheer each other to appear brave. Jake smiled and motioned to Buddy to speed up the machine. The juggernaut moved more quickly, the crackling rolling thing of twisted sharp metal and

245

wreckage, tumbling, lurching, smashing toward the two archeologists and their bare skin.

About a hundred feet from the hill, a can of bright red paint appeared at the top of the roll, once probably stored in some remote cupboard in the old house, and strangely unexploded from the intense heat of the night before. It tumbled in the wire and branches and suddenly burst open with a popping sound just at the top of the roll. Frank watched as the roll turned forward and the paint dribbled from the bent container. It ran down over the various pieces of blackened wood like blood and dripped on the tiny bits of green grass still left on the old lawn.

Then the operator stopped the engine, quiet returning to the marsh again. Jake rushed over, his arm waving in surprise. Buddy climbed down, his boots clumping on the steel of the bulldozer frame. He inspected the engine and shook his head. Then he pulled some tools from a metal box on the running board of the great tractor and began to disassemble a part of the engine. Jake stamped back and forth, his hands on his hips.

Frank listened to the clanking of the wrenches, dreading the end of that noise. He reached for Maggie's hand and together they waited for the inevitable.

Chapter 21

Out on the river, a small breeze had come up. In the quiet without the diesel engine roar, Frank could hear a loose cable slamming against the side of the barge, the steel resounding, still sounding to Frank like the cry of a child. Hanging across the river, the great crane still struck eerily towards the site, moving slightly up and down with the tidelap and the wind.

This was the first time he had been able to inspect the damage to the bridge from last night's firefight. Frank could see the terrible scars ripped into the ancient concrete of the bridge by the machine gun bullets. Here, the iron central draw mechanism of the bridge was bent in some places where shells had ricocheted from them. In an absurd tribute to the workmanship of the previous century's Maryland ironworkers, none of the rounds from the police boat had been strong enough to pierce or destroy the old iron. The church too was more tumbled. The walls were scorched black from the tracers.

The breeze brought a new sound that contrasted with the clank of the crane. This was the swishing and squeaking sound of oars in oarlocks. Along the brush and tree trunks at the river's edge, there was movement, flashes of orange and black against the bright glare. Then, from under the bridge arches, small wooden rowboats moved single file toward the site shoreline.

Frank showed Maggie the rowboats. Frank could see the orange and black of human butterflies, several in the front part of each boat, wings folded to their sides. Behind the butterflies, two others, their wings folded beside them, sitting side by side, rowed the craft. The rhythm of the oars resembled drumbeats as they touched the water, dipped, pulled and then spat the river water behind.

At this time, Birdey Pond appeared in the stern of another craft, her hands on a large pole that pushed her boat onward against the current. Like a tall Viking chieftess from some distant mythological century, she was directing the boats towards the beach at the site. Frank watched her poling around the same trees he had been trapped against in the night.

After the first boats had landed and human butterflies were striding up the beach, Birdey, with a few strokes, beached her craft. She in turn stepped ashore and began to organize her people, using hand signals and making very little noise.

"Jake hasn't seen her yet, " Frank whispered to Maggie.

"We may have some hope yet," she replied.

The butterflies assembled on the small riverbank, forming a wall against the quiet river behind them. Human hands came out of the insect fabric and brought up binoculars to eyes that were still hidden in the costumes Birdey walked back and forth, less dreamlike and more like a sergeant drilling her troops.

Then the butterflies were discovered. One of Jake's guards ran down to the riverbank and began to yell at Birdey to no avail. The guard was surrounded by three of the butterflies and forced to return to where Jake was standing with his police escort.

Jake began a tirade, walking back and forth also, waving his arms at the assembled policemen, trying to get Billy to order his men to force the intruders off the site area.. The policemen milled about the bulldozer waiting for orders from Billy. Billy in turn watched Birdey Pond's group growing in size. Meanwhile, the operator, Buddy, continued to repair his bulldozer.

From the highway came a new sound, the roaring of powerful engines and squealing of brakes. Entering the farm and moving against the cornfield and the trees, Frank saw the flickering glare of multicolored buses. Some had the names of churches and of cities like Baltimore and Washington printed on their sides.

One, a purple vehicle, gave the name, in giant letters, of a Baptist church in Philadelphia. This blustering machine drove through the small gate, its side breaking off one of the posts. In front of it, two guards in the green Terment jackets tried to stop the bus but jumped back out of the way as the truck ran into the marsh brush at the right of the lane, disappeared in the tall cattails and then reappeared at the far side of the excavation where it stopped against the honeysuckle hedge. More than thirty persons got out, some of them elderly men and women, some with canes and walkers.

The buses were in various stages of repair. Some trailed the smoke of burning engine oil. The other arriving buses were prevented from entering the property because the guards had formed a solid human line. However, one at a time the machines discharged their passengers on the highway. Then with revving engines and straining bus transmissions, each truck pulled ahead and turned away to park back along the road. The passengers pushed their way into the lane and circled around the guards until the green coated men gave up and stood back out of the way.

"General Store," Frank shouted, squeezing Maggie's hand.

She stood on tiptoes, straining to see more.

The people, black and white families from these churches, women, men, children, gathered in small groups in the site area and stood restlessly against the honeysuckle mass. In a few minutes there were several hundred people assembled there, the yellows and whites of their clothes bright against the green honeysuckle vines. They moved among the patches of high green marsh grass and sat on the piles of construction materials stored in that section of the site. Some of them were close to the furthest edge of the surveyor twine outlining the edge of the shipwreck itself. From time to time one of the adults would point to the pile of skeletons and whisper a few words to children nearby who would look quickly and then retreat behind their parents.

Finally a small car reached its turn at the gate. The Pastor climbed out, arm in a sling. He was dressed in a black suit with a bright tie. The bandage was gone from his forehead. As he approached Frank and Maggie he stopped and looked back at the assembling lines of church people. He removed the sling and raised his hands in salute, then turned and yelled to Frank.

"We're here, Frank!"

Then the Pastor saw the skeletons of the child slaves in the excavation. He stopped and knelt on one knee beside the great pit. Then he looked up at Frank. Frank nodded.

"There's not much joy I can have in seeing this horror," he said approaching Frank and Maggie.

As he climbed up on the small hill to stand beside them, he said, his voice subdued, "When Jake set that old farmhouse on fire, tried to burn you folks, he lit a fuse under these people. The word went out on the telephones and the computers all night."

He turned and glanced at Jake standing beside the bulldozer. Jake stared back.

"Jake has made a big mistake," said the Pastor. " He gave us what we needed. Jake himself provided the push. Those skeletons push even more."

The Pastor pointed at the police. "I know every one of them police. The station dispatcher is a black woman goes to our church. She tells me what is going on. Billy is here today because he and Jake have been together since kids. He always does what Jake wants. "

He caught his breath. "These folks come with me today, this is an army. They will fight with their bodies. They will stand right here on this hill with you and they will stop that bulldozer with their bodies."

"Some of them are very old. Some are children," said Frank.

"It's what they want to do. Frank, there's a line of them buses stretches away down the road. In town the traffic is all blocked up. There's a lot of unhappy local businesses, too, especially down around the harbor. Tourist customers can't get through."

A black man with a beard and large protruding teeth came up to them.

"Chipmonk, these folks are the archaeologists," said the Pastor.

Chipmonk shook hands solemnly with Maggie and Frank. "It was time," he said. "It was time to start this. If it had not been here at this marsh it would have been something else. Jake has been in charge too long."

The man swept his arm towards the others. " We intend to stay here this time. "

A fragile looking white woman holding a baby in her arms came up. "You know, " she said," there is a heritage day celebration this weekend, starts the day after tomorrow. I just want this one, this little baby, to have some part of that. So I got to be here today. It's like this old marsh here means something for all of us. "

"Amen," said the Pastor. Then he climbed down off the hill and walked out among the bus people.

From the end of the marsh, Birdey Pond began walking toward the Pastor. She reached out her hands to him. The Pastor clasped her hands in return.

The Pastor's crowd had grown considerably against the honeysuckle hedges. With a movement of his hands, the Pastor directed them to close ranks with the human butterfly group that was spread along the riverbank. As the murmurs poured out and smiles were shared, an alliance became fact.

The united movement began to express itself in a chant or perhaps it was a war cry, that was repeated over and over. As the chant reverberated with different human accents, it increased in power and force until it became high pitched, like a scream or yell. This was a human fellowship. Here, Frank could see all the causes, the requests for justice, all blending into one cry. There were the two leaders hand in hand, the tall white aristocratic Robin "Birdey" Pond standing with the warm black preacher, the man of God, Pastor Jefferson Allingham.

The crowd began to move forward. The people from the riverbank moved up, and the people from the buses came across the field. The wall of people were fused together as they moved, their emotions bursting out ahead of them.

Then a large orange banner, the size of a dozen bedsheets sewn together , was unfurled above the crowd. Hands grasped its edges so that it was a square with fingers of many colors around its borders. It was held, stretched and flat, across the heads of the demonstrators. Frank could see from his vantage point on the hill several feet above the crowd that there were large black letters painted on the fabric, the letters spelling out, "BUTTERFLY."

Frank heard that word repeated over and over in the chant. He looked around the site. Toward the river, the site was lined with the human butterflies. In front of the massive honeysuckle hedges by the highway were the arrivals from the buses, the former members of General Store who joined and mingled with the butterflies. The area along the entrance lane was still open. Then, between Frank and the ruined house were Jake Terment and the policemen, as well as the two bulldozer employees.

Jake stood watching the new situation in front of him, his face impassive. From time to time he spoke to the chief, pointing to one person or another as though he were taking names, suggesting people to be arrested or prosecuted. The operator had parts of the bulldozer engine spread out on the great tread of the machine. He kept dropping them as he nervously tried to finish his repair.

Other men and women began coming through the gate. They moved tentatively into the open space along the lane. Many of these people had been at the cocktail party. Frank recognized the black businessman who had asked about the slave graveyard legend. None of them walked forward to speak to Jake. Instead they stood by themselves.

"They are not sure whether to support Jake or to support the people on the site. The buses coming through town must have alerted them that something was happening up here," said Frank.

Maggie nodded. "Maybe Jake sent for them thinking they would support him out here."

"Doesn't look like they are going to," observed Frank. One of these men stood with his eyes fixed on Jake, his hands at his side, a grim smile on his face. It was the mayor, who had introduced Jake at the hotel speech. Frank knew any mayor of a small town was a powerful figure, a cheerleader for economic development like the Terment Town project. This man was the caretaker of the townspeople's hopes for the future. Yet, as Frank watched, this man made no attempt to walk up to Jake. Instead he stood with the new arrivals, hesitant, nervous, shifting his weight from one foot to the other and looking around at the crowd in front of him.

Jake waved to different people but received no greetings in return. It was as though he were suddenly an outsider, no longer part of the inner circle of local power. Jake turned back to stand again beside the bulldozer.

"Pushing out these scientists, the mayor ain't for it, Jake," said Billy.

Jake ignored him, looking at the bulldozer.

The chief turned to the line of the other officers and said, "Each of you boys do what you think is right. " Then he left Jake's side and walked over to the group at the cornfield where he stood by the mayor and waited. Billy looked at the ground, not returning Jake's stare. Several other policemen followed including all the black officers. Three officers remained with Jake, one of them, Cheeks, moving the leather restraint off his holstered service pistol with his thumb.

"Hey, Jake. They're choosing up sides," called the Pastor from out in the field. "It's back like it was when we were kids. You're ending up on the worst team again."

The sunlight had become very hot. Frank felt the burn of the sun on his bare skin. Maggie wiped the sweat from her forehead, streaking her face with black soil from her dirt covered hands. The people around the site inched closer, some of them in the back standing on tiptoe to see. The murmurs of conversation slowed. There were no air currents to move the leaves in the trees. Frank could hear some animal noises, the creatures venturing out to peek, but even the animals and insects in their subdued racket sensed the danger of the moment.

Buddy finally finished attaching the last part and looked up with satisfaction at Jake. "That'll do it, boss." He dropped one of his wrenches and the bang of the metal sounded like a gunshot.

Jake nodded, impatiently. Buddy climbed up on the tractor. Frank could again see the tip of the operator's head behind the great roll of trash. The engine began, first faintly as the starter motor whirred, then building up revolutions and rolling its terrible thunder out over the site. Buddy held back on the forward clutch, restraining this power. The machine shook with pent up destructive force, the tracks slipping inch by inch forward.

Jake looked up, almost reverently, at the huge roll of trash, the pieces of sharp steel and fire blackened wood hanging out precariously in the air, then turned and, after straightening his silk tie and tucking it back into his summer suit, walked toward Frank and Maggie, a confident smile on his face.

Chapter 22

They faced each other, Jake, spotlessly clean, Frank, barefoot, dressed only in his muddy work shorts. Jake spoke first, quietly, only to Frank. "I told you to write me a report, Doctor."

"I can't do that," Frank answered.

"Don't you for one minute think I'm going to forget this. Your career is finished."

Frank didn't say anything. He returned Jake's stare.

"Doctor, you know why you came down here?"

"I made a mistake."

" You didn't make a mistake coming here. You just forgot why you came. "

Frank then raised his voice so the crowd could hear. "When I first came here, Jake, you told me I was like you."

"I was sure as hell wrong about that."

"No, you weren't wrong. I was like you, all business, the wrong kind of business. It took working up here for a couple of days in all this heat and finding these horrors in the wreck to realize that I was also different from you."

"None of what you are saying means anything to me."

"Jake, there's skeletons of dead children in here. There was a crime committed."

Jake continued to stare.

"I don't expect you to understand what I am telling you, Jake, but I'm going to say it anyway. You have to start to care about this. There was a murderer who burned all these innocent people to death in the old ship."

"Go on, " called the Pastor, "You're doing fine."

Frank continued, "I don't understand you , Jake. I think business and profit has become more important than the people you hurt, the people who die, because of what you do."

Jake started ahead again, saying nothing.

"These children who died here, their deaths can not be disregarded. Your bulldozer can't be allowed to torture their remains any more. This is like a graveyard. We have to bury them properly at least. "

Jake ignored Frank's words. "You up there on the tractor. You come on ahead as soon as I signal. Come on ahead, hear me."

Frank tried a different approach. "Jake, is all this some kind of family secret, something that has been passed down to you, something for you to hide? Is that why your family changed the place where they loaded their tobacco, because they wanted to hid this place?" Frank could see Jake's lips begin to tremble, the first clue that Jake did indeed hear what he was saying.

"By God, " Frank goaded, "I see, Jake. This is your turn to protect some rotten bastard who lived three hundred years ago. "

The Pastor called from behind Frank. "He won't tell you, Frank."

Jake, suddenly confident, a softness to his voice, said with a smile. "Frank, you're holding up a lot of people's paychecks."

Frank persisted. "Part of hiding the secret had to be getting rid of evidence. You knew that even if you concreted this site into the ground there would still be the records of what we found. You started the fire to get rid of all the records, didn't you, Jake? You knew that all our discoveries were in that house and in Maggie's car."

"I don't know what you are talking about."

"I'm talking about the bell, Jake. The bell was not destroyed. If anything, it's in better shape." Frank turned to Spyder. "Was it you I surprised setting the fire, Spyder?"

"You're lying," squealed Spyder, traces of a grin still on his face.

"If they tried, the local police might have a hard time accounting for your time last night."

Jake's stare had turned to a look of intense hatred. "Get off my land."

"The ship's name was the Adam and Eve." Frank saw Jake move his head back, a sudden jerk, a glimmer of recognition of the ancient ship name. Jake reached down and grabbed two beer cans from the mud. He was back in control of himself once again, smiling, still slightly trembling.

"These will make good fill for my Goddamned marsh," he said as he continued walking toward Frank. "Here, I'll throw these right in the hole, Doctor." The crowd was silent. Jake's eyes hardened.

"You, Billy, come on, " he called. The chief started to move towards Jake and the mayor stopped him, putting a hand on his shoulder. Jake called out, "Cheeks, you and the boys come help me." Cheeks was a fat man, his police blouse darkened with sweat, his belly overhanging his pistol and gun belt. Cheeks shoved forward the other two police beside him and with a smirk, walked quickly to assist Jake.

Frank knew, the crowd knew, that nothing could or would stop Jake's dedication. Jake's face gradually lost all semblance of rationality. A look of madness, insanity, came over the once photogenic face. Frank, in turn, had become a soldier again. He was calm, ready to kill if necessary. The two men were like warriors facing off, maneuvering to strike first.

"Don't make him mad, kill him," the voice of his sergeant from long ago at Fort Jackson Army basic training hammered back into Frank's consciousness. "Don't make him mad, kill him. "

Then Jake made his move as his right hand reached out to pull Maggie off the hill. She stepped back. He muttered, "Damn you, woman," and leaned forward to grab again at her arm. As he did, Frank instinctively hit Jake hard, his right fist smashing against the surprised man's jaw. Jake fell back, collapsing on his back in the mud. He looked up, his hand touching his jaw, his face showing pain but only for an instant. Jake scrambled to his feet, his hands and body alert.

.   Frank waited for the next onslaught, nursing his fist with his left hand.

"Maybe it's over, Frank," said Maggie.

"No," said Frank. Cheeks, the other two officers and Spider were rushing to Jake's aid. There was a flash of metal as Spyder pulled out a small revolver and pointed it at Frank, his silent grin still there. Maggie instantly threw her digging trowel at Spyder's arm knocking the gun out of his hand. Spyder grunted as blood spurted from his wrist. Cheeks unfastened the hasp on his service pistol. Billy, from his place with the businessmen, raised his hand and called out, "You hold up, Cheeks. I don't want no guns."

The crowd murmured but did not move forward. The guards stayed back waiting for orders. Spyder, glaring at Maggie, stood still, his revolver still on the ground, blood dripping from his wrist onto the mud and spattering his well shined leather shoes.

Jake wiped his face leaving a streak of mud across his forehead, swore, and rushed again at Frank, knocking him off balance. Both of them crashed off the hill and into the mud, pummeling, scratching at eyes, seeking advantage. They rolled in the muck. Frank was hit hard in the stomach and crawled to his knees, his face still against the ground. Jake stood up over him and grabbed a shovel from the nearby sifting table. He raised the rusty tool over Frank. Just before he could bring it down on Frank's head, Maggie yelled, "Look out. He's trying to kill you. Somebody stop this."

Billy took a few steps towards the hill. He was too late. Jake moved forward, all his body weight behind the blunt weapon. Just before the shovel reached his head, Frank was able to roll to his side. The shovel continued and hit the mud, its impact throwing dirt and water through the air, the handle snapping with a loud crack. Jake gave a surprised look at the broken tool, then flailed at Frank again and again with the piece of handle. Frank on his part tried to fend off the furious blows with his arms.

Suddenly there was a new sound, a new cry. Jake stopped, his concentration broken. He looked over his shoulder, still holding the shovel handle above his shoulder. The line of human butterflies opened in its center. There, Soldado came forward from the beach, the cat preceding him.

Soldado was startling, tall, angry, with yellow, white and black paint on his bare skin, a red cape across his shoulder. The metal jaguar head hanging from his waist reflected in the sun from its golden metal jaws. Soldado held aloft a torch, its flames flying out into the sunlight as he moved it back and forth. He repeated over and over one word, loud and distinct, and fully understood by the crowd. It was the word "fire," and it was like a trumpet to the crowd.

The shuffling steps of the people speeded their advance on Jake, their hands stretching in front as if to grab him and tear him to pieces. "Fire" was chanted over and over, sound rumbling over the site, easily matching the roar of the bulldozer. One by one, Frank saw other torches raised among the crowd, flames licking at the air, bits of fire falling off. The people had become a furious army, torches their weapon, and their intent seeming to scorch or to burn Jake, to burn Jake with his own kind of weapon.

Moments passed. The crowd became even more vicious, prodded by the angry shouts of encouragement by the Pastor, Soldado and Birdey Pond. There was also the ever present sight of the skeletons. Even if the police had wanted to stop the mob, they would not have been able to accomplish this easily with the few men they had. Jake, still holding the splintered wooden handle, saw Soldado and the crowd, then looked back at Frank, fear and confusion in his eyes. He stood at the edge of the large pit, his back to the great pile of skeletons and bones. Then he raised the handle preparatory to crashing the wood against the prone Frank.

"Look out, Frank," screamed Maggie.

Jake hesitated, allowing Frank to suddenly twist his own body and kick hard at Jake's belly with his bare feet, leaving blobs of filth on the remaining whiteness of Jake's suit. The surprise of the blow made Jake drop the shovel. Picking it up, he swore at Frank. At that moment the ledge of soft earth on the side of the excavation collapsed under his weight. Jake lost his balance and fell, lurching backward, one hand still in a tight fist, the other waving the handle.

As Jake realized what was happening to him, he tried to move his arms behind his body to shield himself from the sharp up thrust bones of the resurrected skeletons. Those arms, failing to

258

protect him, moved upward almost like supplication, but more like vaudeville.

Frank, meanwhile, scrambled to his feet, fists ready to take advantage, as Jake fell, out of control, backwards into the grid pit. As Jake's body came down heavily into the excavation, the bones that were torn out by the wild crowd the night before, the bones of the slave children who had been so hideously burned to death, cracked like pistol shots against Jake's body weight. Some broke from the impact but others tore into the back of Jake's careful white suit with spurts of blood as they thrust out through his stomach and chest. As he was impaled on the skeletons, small grinning skulls flew into the air from the impact, turning slowly above Jake's prone and crooked body, then dropping back around him, partially burying him in bleached bone and blood.

One by one, the bones came to rest, each one making small ripples in the water of the pit. Jake stirred and moved upward, first leaning on his right elbow then raising himself, his face contorted with pain, his back bleeding from multiple cuts from the sharp bones. Frank saw the killing wound. A large thigh bone, likely a part of the strange ancient giant, was protruding from Jake's chest, blood gurgling at its browned base. Jake attempted to grasp it, to pull it out of his back where it had entered. He managed to stand and stagger forward. He stepped up to the edge of the pit and then fell forward into the muck, motionless and silent, the bone upright like an arrow above his body, his knees still down in the pit. In a few more moments of convulsions, he had slipped back into the excavation, lying on his stomach.

The only noise was that of the diesel engine. A sense of surprise pervaded the crowd. Frank, his desire to hurt Jake gone, kneeled beside the horribly wounded man. Billy, Maggie and the Pastor rushed forward. Frank attempted to turn Jake's mouth upward from the puddle of water.

Soldado stopped several yards away, the cat motionless at his side. Soldado crushed his torch into the wet mud where its flames sparked and died. The forward shuffle of hundreds of warrior feet stopped, the chant hushed to ripples of noise. Other torches were lowered and extinguished. Then there was no sound except the rumble of the bulldozer engine. The cat hissed and jumped up on Jake's back, sniffing at the bloody bone. The old man approached Jake's writhing form. Standing over him and looking towards the sky, Soldado raised both arms, then put them down and walked back through the crowd, toward the riverside. The cat jumped off Jake's back and went with Soldado.

Jake's hand slowly pulled at his back, its motion slowing then finally halting as his blood flowed out on the muddy ground. His face turned sidewise in the mud, looking up at Frank . His body was twisted with pain from the multiple wounds but he made no sound. Two police officers brought up a blanket from which was handed to the chief.

Billy tenderly placed it over Jake. "The ambulance is coming. " he said.

Spyder stood in the background, still holding his wounded hand. He did not speak. His grin was gone. Jake turned his head to the other side and saw his old friend, Billy, his gray police uniform splashed with mud. Jake whispered, with a slight smile, aware of what had happened to him and how seriously he was hurt,

"Goddamn it, Billy, I think I'm cleaned out."

"Sorry, I couldn't help you this time, Jake."

"Looking out for yourself," Jake gasped, his smile jerking across his face with the waves of pain. " I would have done the same thing."

"You ain't done yet, old friend. You just had an accident, that's all. You fell. You'll be all right."

Jake was having trouble getting his breath. Then he tried to raise his head once more. His eyes turned towards the island. A steady flow of blood came from the corner of his mouth and ran over his tanned cheek. His lips moved, trying to form words, but his voice, once strong and familiar to all of them standing and kneeling around him, was silent. His face had lost its look of pride. Frank thought he noticed a tear moving down Jake's face.

Jake tried once more to say something. Frank bent closer to hear. Jake gasped from the pain and his eyes dulled, staring without life. Frank knew he was dead.

The Pastor stood up. "It's a sad time when any man dies," he said, moving away.

Billy was still on his knees next to his childhood friend. He said, "Jake was a better man than people gave him credit." He slowly pulled the blanket over Jake's head.

Soldado turned and walked back towards the riverbank, the crowd parting to let him through. The people, as if they were still fearful of Jake, even in his death moved closer to the body. A line formed and one after another, white, black, young and old, filed by the corpse. They stood around in clusters. Frank saw in those faces not only fear but an astonishment, as though the people expected the very still and dead body to raise up off the ground, stand up and become Jake Terment again.

Spyder walked quickly toward the highway. Spyder climbed into one of the Terment Company cars and kicked up dust as he raced out the lane, narrowly missing the white gateposts. It was the last time that Frank or anyone else in River Sunday saw Spyder.

"I ain't going to hold you, Doc. You was just defending yourself. There won't be any charges," said the chief almost in a whisper, looking around at the hundreds of people. He motioned to the operator to shut off the bulldozer engine.

The shriek of the River Sunday ambulance came through the trees at the edge of the site. The ambulance team quickly removed Jake's body from the pit. He was carried to a patch of matted grass. The Terment Company guards clustered around the corpse and stopped the line of viewers.

"Who's going to tell his wife?" Billy asked the mayor. The mayor didn't answer him.

Then out on the site, the banner was pulled taut. Carefully, men and women at each section of the great orange flag pulled it out over the shipwreck and laid it down in the sun, placing it as a shroud over the ancient dead. A faint breeze sent tremors across the cloth.

Jake's body was finally put into the white truck. The siren was turned on and the ambulance slowly moved out the gate.

"I'm going to make sure that's the last Terment ever walks on the land of this farm," said the Pastor.

Chapter 23

Charlie and his yellow bulldozer were gone, the machine loaded on a flatbed truck and removed. The great roll of debris from the destroyed farmhouse was still perched beside the site, the red paint dry, a small puddle of the red blotched on the soil. A stylish television reporter from a Baltimore station was standing near the bulldozer roll, her cameraman recording her report.

"Jake Terment, a true American hero, was killed in a strange accident yesterday in this muddy field near his ancestral home here on the Eastern Shore of Maryland. In the words of the town mayor, one local man who had known Jake Terment since childhood, ' Jake Terment was the best thing ever happened to River Sunday. We don't know what we are going to do down here without him.'

"As we reported earlier in the financial news, the Terment Company offices in New York are closed today partly in mourning for Jake Terment and partly because the company has declared bankruptcy. Acting President Spyder, of the Terment Company, who was formerly a close aide to Jake Terment, stated that the company is highly leveraged and failure to finish this Maryland project has caused several large loans to come immediately due. The Acting President insists that every effort will be made to repay joint investors on projects throughout the United States and to maintain Terment Company stock values."

"That's a laugh. I bet those suckers will get nothing," said the Pastor.

"That reporter's national. I was interviewed this morning, Frank. You were still sleeping, "said Maggie.

"What did she ask?"

"She couldn't understand what prompted anyone to have a fist fight with Jake Terment. She was amazed at the demonstrators. You're going to get a call, Pastor. I told her about your General Store and the fire and she wants to do a follow up story. She also spent some time out on the road talking with the butterfly people who are out there handing out materials."

Maggie smiled, " Oh yes. She wants to meet the jaguar man."

"Good luck to her," grinned Frank.

"I showed her around the site. She had many questions about our discoveries. Her main point was, however, that the television public was very shocked by Jake's accidental death. He was such a popular and well known businessman. "

"I got no problem after a man is dead if people see him as better than he was, " said the Pastor.

"I think Solado and that cat just scared the hell out of Jake, but I wasn't going to tell her," said Maggie.

" I felt sorry for Jake. As bad as he seemed to be, I don't think he deserved to die."

"You 're getting to be the old Frank again," said Maggie.

"You're a better man than I am," said the Pastor.

"Where is Soldado anyway?" asked Frank.

"Nobody will see him again for a while," said the Pastor. "He'll take his boat and go hide down on some creek in the southern Eastern Shore or out in the Wilderness Swamp."

Maggie handed Frank a cellular telephone. " I 'd like to know about that bell."

"Let's do it," said Frank. They sat in the grass on the edge of the site.

In front of them there was great activity in the dig area. Several teams of Maryland archaeologists and specialized personnel had been brought in from other projects around the state. A variety of sophisticated electronic instruments were being set up to penetrate the soil.

"Cathy was put under special orders by the Governor yesterday afternoon to get this project straightened out, " said

Maggie. " The new orders are that the site and especially the skeletons are to be excavated and studied with great care."

There was dirt on Maggie's forehead. Frank reached over and rubbed it away. She smiled. He dialed the call.

"You and the Pastor would enjoy this place I'm calling," said Frank. As he waited he described it to them. " It's a large room lined with books. In between there are large multipaned windows which look out on the city of Boston. Small iron staircases climb among the bookshelves. Alcoves display ship models and marine items like compasses and sextants marked with the names of famous ships. In the center of the room are long massive wooden tables with researchers working among piles of papers and research reports and computer terminals. There are great glass exhibition cabinets with ancient logbooks displayed and in spaces among the bookcases there are antique paintings. When you stand at the door you feel like a ship, ready to knife through the room, your mind filling with knowledge the way a ship's sail fills with wind, ideas tumbling around you like waves, tidbits of exciting data winging by like strange sea birds. The lights hang from the ceiling and illuminate all this in strange shadowy ways that reflect differently each way you turn. It's like being able to see the history in that room from different perspectives, almost different centuries, each time you move your eyes."

He paused, listening. "Research room please."

After another wait, "Is Antonius there?"

He looked at Maggie. "The secretary is trying to find him. He's a tall guy with long grey hair. He towers over the other researchers."

He smiled as he heard the boisterous voice on the other end. "Antonius, it's Frank Light."

"Frank Light, " said Thomas. "It's good to hear from you. Where are you? At that university?"

"Still there. How are you?"

"Putting books back in the right places."

"You and your systems," said Frank. "The reason you have to work so hard is that no body can understand your filing systems. I tried and failed. I don't know any of us who ever really figured it out up there."

"So what's happening?" asked Antonius.

"I need a favor."

"Sure," said Antonius.

"We've got an old ship's bell down here."

"Where's here?"

"A marsh near a little town called River Sunday, Maryland."

Antonius sighed, "The Maryland town where the big name real estate guy got himself killed."

"Yes."

"Wait a minute. You're working on that same project?"

"The same."

"Tell me more," said Antonius. Frank nodded at Maggie and the Pastor. He knew Antonius was hooked.

"We need to know about the name lettered on the ship's bell we found."

"Sure. What's the name?" asked Antonius.

"The "Adam and Eve," said Frank. " Also it says "London." There's no date on the bell but we think the wreck was about 1690 1710."

"Hold on. Let me get to my files."

Frank put down the telephone. "He checking his computer." He returned the telephone back to his ear. They waited in the hot sunlight.

In the space which had been Grid Q where they had found all the slave skeletons there were now five workers.

"They have found more layers of those skeletons," the Pastor said.

Maggie said, "We think that some of the slaves were on half decks built up over the main deck of the hold. When the fire occurred the half decks and their occupants tumbled down upon the slaves chained below. That would explain the jumbled bones that they are finding. They have found more than fifty sets of remains so far, some chained directly to the large ring bolts in the flooring."

"This morning we heard that there is interest in forming a local group to operate this site as a monument," said the Pastor. "People like Birdey Pond want to serve as board members."

"That would be wonderful, " said Maggie.

"There will be a need for some good archaeologists to be on the staff."

The telephone crackled. "I've found her," said Thomas. "It's a strange story. Got a few minutes?"

"Go ahead," said Frank.

"The citation on this story is from a probate case argued in London in 1693. The lawyers for the litigant were arguing that a Richard Terment, a colonist in Maryland, had the complete rights to the fortune of his brother Henry Terment, who had been lost at sea on a voyage to West Africa and Maryland. The case was not contested. Apparently these brothers were the only family who had any right to the estate. It was a very large estate for that time. According to the summary of the case, this Henry Terment had been a merchant, mostly in Africa, and had made a fortune in the slave trade to the Caribbean. He had a mansion located on the Thames River and a country estate in Kent as well as his own ship, the Adam and Eve.

"Richard Terment was in Maryland at the time of the case. He had a plantation in Maryland, a small plantation apparently. His brother Henry had a substantially larger land holding next to Richard. Henry owned a sizable number of slaves and indentured servants who worked for the brother Richard. All this land was on the Eastern Shore of Maryland near a port called Sunday. The records call it a parish or church town. I assume this must be one of the early names for River Sunday.

"Henry had an agent in Whydah which was a slave port in West Africa. That agent's records state that he purchased a substantial quantity of cowrie shells from London, specially imported from India, to engage in trading in Africa.

"One thing I noticed immediately, Frank, that was odd about this Terment. He owned the ship completely in his own name. Usually these trader merchants would own the ships in shares, several merchants to a ship. Then if the ship was lost their mutual ownership acted like a kind of insurance to share the risk and the loss. In his case he owned the ship all by himself. I expect he was so sure of his success he wanted to keep all the profits for himself.

"Here's some details about the ship itself. The Adam and Eve was a merchantman, a little under a hundred feet between perpendiculars, sternpost to bow stem. It had a figurehead of two naked figures embracing each other. It had galleries on its stern, apparently quite fancy because Henry traveled with the ship as its captain. It was ship rigged which meant that it had three masts.

"In the agent's records there is a lot of inventory information. In a case like this there are always debts and even though he owned the ship some of the cargo was financed. So the court demanded to know how much was lost so the creditors could be satisfied. For example there were ten guns on the ship, iron guns, twelve pounder semi culverins which Henry had purchased with some of the cost being paid on the return of the ship to London. In case you are wondering, Frank, these traders carried a lot of guns because of the pirates who used to raid the shipping lanes down through the Atlantic passage into Africa and then in the Caribbean and Chesapeake areas."

"Captain Terment sailed to Africa, purchased slaves from his agent and was then bound for Maryland. The agent's records show what he bought and when he left the Slave Coast. The court also had a document from Richard's lawyer in Maryland stating that Henry never made it to Maryland. On the basis of this, the court determined that Captain Henry Terment and the Adam and Eve went down in a storm with all hands and the slave cargo being lost.

"In the court case Richard Terment of Maryland claimed all of Henry's estate as the surviving heir. There was no will. Since there was no other family, the estate was totaled and Richard got himself a very large estate. "

Frank said, "We have the wreck of the Adam and Eve here in Maryland at a spot where part of Richard Terment's Maryland plantation was located at the time of the death of his brother. The Adam and Eve did not sink in the ocean. It sank here in Maryland."

"Seems that way. Oldest motive there is, money," chuckled Thomas.

"Ask your friend about the giant?" interrupted Maggie.

"Here's another mystery, Thomas. One of the skeletons in the wreck was a huge man. Could you run a search on persons in the records who might have been of great size?"

"There's a few newspapers on the computer. The early journals rarely mention names."

"Do me a favor. Try a key words like giant and Terment and tie it to the time of the ship."

"Hang on." After a few minutes, Thomas came back on.

"You won't believe this," he said. "Your giant is Captain Henry Terment."

"He says the giant is the Terment who was lost," said Frank to Maggie and the Pastor.

"It's an obituary in the London newspaper. The kind of thing they write after a major hanging. Only this is for a man they call the "Tormentor." I'll read you the excerpt.

"Today word reached London that the "Tormentor" is lost at sea. This man, also known as Henry Terment, was notably the largest man in civilization, a brute of a person in physical size and mind, surrounded always with his portable army of strong, vicious men. None can forget his long braided hair. None can forget the sharp jeweled cutlass he wore with such impertinence. None of us who had the misfortune to be in his presence can fail to remember the terror, the fear of a disagreement with him which had already cost the lives of twenty good and brave men in duels and other private misfortunes. Here was the terror of a man the King himself could not keep arrested because Terment's power of force and money was so great. This was the man who claimed he could 'torment gold.' The Good Lord Himself has intervened and proved this man dead at sea in his last pursuit of more wealth."

Frank repeated the story sentence by sentence as Thomas read it to him. After Frank hung up he looked at Maggie and the Pastor.

"Jake's father used that phrase, "torment gold," said Frank. "Jake told me that."

"Brother kills brother. One of the oldest crimes in the Bible." The Pastor looked thoughtful. "Back up here on the Nanticoke, Richard could have come down to the ship by himself. He could have got them all drinking and drugged them somehow. It would have been easy then to lock them in the ship and to set it afire. There would have been no witnesses. Later on slaves and indentured servants could have been brought in to cover the wreckage with soil. Any kind of explanation could have been used and in those days, people kept their mouths shut for fear of being killed."

"It's damn close to the perfect murder," said Frank. "If it had not been for the digging up of this so called graveyard, old Richard would never have been found out."

"So what do we do with a three hundred year old murder case?"

"We can be pretty sure from that health examiner that no one in this town will have any interest."

The three of them laughed.

"We can document it, that's about all, " said Maggie.

"So that leaves the question," said Frank. "How much did Jake actually know about what was out there in that marsh?"

"He knew," said the Pastor. "You mentioned they both knew about "tormenting gold.."

"We'll never be sure, " said Frank. "If he did know, Jake thought the secret was safe. He probably didn't worry about the river rising, the soil erosion exposing the wreck. He knew he could quietly fill in the marsh and plant a cornfield. He could get rid of any artifacts, " continued the Pastor. "What he did not count on was that he had let the bridge fall apart over the years and had to fix it. That got him in a bind about this little marsh property. There was no other land on which to build the bridge supports."

The Pastor smiled. "The tide water had washed out more soil than Jake realized. That's how come the wreck got found by that bulldozer, 'cause it was so close to the surface."

Maggie added, "Then, you found the clues and, because you were more honest than Jake had calculated, you couldn't quit, Frank. All this put Jake in a position where he became desperate."

The Pastor smiled. "Even more desperate because Jake couldn't let that mansion be lost. Peachblossom was his family heritage. That manor house was probably the only thing Jake cared about all his life. That's where you got to understand people like the Terments. "

"I got this feeling he looked on this as a duty," said Frank.

"Yes, " said Maggie. "Maybe even more so because of the rumors about him that his real father was not a Terment. Maybe that led him to assert himself as the savior of the family."

The Pastor said, " Some of the demonstrators stretched that orange banner on the monument out in the harbor. The word 'Butterfly ' in big black letters can be seen from shore."

Frank looked at Maggie.

"You could write this," she smiled.   "The dead slaves get new life. Jake, who in an ironic way, was also a slave, a slave to his family, gets death."

"Yeah, but what would we have done if Jake hadn't had the accident?" Frank said.

The Pastor looked at them. "Sad to say, if he had not had that unfortunate accident, if he had not died, all those people out there would only have been able to slow him and his company for a few hours. Even if you had succeeded in beating him up and chasing him away to stop the bulldozer, all would have been only for a short time. In a few hours Jake would have been back with plenty of lawyers and a lot more green coated guards. Maggie's boss was on Jake's side. She wanted to close the site. Without State of Maryland support, all of us would have been forced out of there."

"What made the change? His death?"

"His death allowed the Governor and his people to cater to those demonstrators. There were a lot of votes out there, white and black," said the Pastor.

Frank pulled on the brim of his hat. "What about the Union soldier?"

"Let the story be known," said the Pastor.

"Adam and Eve," Maggie said to herself. "That's why it's so hard for most of us to be sorry for Jake."

"What?" said Frank.

"Go back to the Bible," she smiled. " After Adam and Eve blew the deal in the garden, we all became slaves, each in our own way, and we're not likely to love whoever we think are our slave masters."

Chapter 24

It was the morning of Heritage Day.

Hundreds of people were at the funeral. Their cars formed one of the longest lines River Sunday had ever seen for a burial. Old timers said with authority that the only time more people had shown up on the streets was when General Eisenhower came through looking for votes. The Pastor told Frank that Lulu , one of his friends from the old civil rights days who was now the owner of a twenty four hour strip club on the main highway south outside River Sunday, said she and her girls had made more money since yesterday that they had during the peak of last year's peak summer vacation season. Friends of Jake and his wife were transported from the small River Sunday airport in black limousines. The cars stopped at the small Episcopal church. It was the same church from which Jake's father had been buried. Many of the friends were celebrities themselves. They were richly dressed and their faces showed a common and well practiced expression of grief.

Maggie observed that she would have believed their sorrow was truly felt if only there had been some difference among their expressions.

"You expected an occasional tear," said Frank.

"Yes, " she said, "Or a sob or two."

Those not invited to the ceremony at the church, especially the hundreds of tourists visiting the harbor for Heritage Day, stood on the sidewalk outside. One visitor from Texas remarked casually that he was delighted he could see, if not a wedding of a celebrity, at least a funeral. Frank and Maggie watched from her replacement State of Maryland sedan. Some of the crowd on the street near them, especially the teenagers, they recognized as members of the crowd at the fire. Many of the local onlookers were crying as if a close relative had died.

"They thought of Jake as their royalty," said Maggie.

Clouds had come up and the day had a strange chill, even in the summer humidity. The procession came out of the church. The line of cars moved slowly under the Heritage Day banners stretched across Strand Street. Maggie pulled her car into the end of the line. State government officials ordered by the Governor to attend at the gravesite were in the line in chauffered black state cars, much larger than Maggie's sedan. The Governor had stated that he was unavoidably detained. The mayor had urged a short church ceremony so that the Baltimore television crew would have more time to film the outside procession going through the tourist area of the town. Out in the harbor an offshore breeze chased large swells out to the Chesapeake Bay where a distant roll of black sky foretold storms. Jake's white yacht, its bow showing scar marks from the explosion, pitched with the waves, rising and falling without purpose or direction.

The television cameras, set up in front of the ruined church just over the old bridge, were broadcasting live as the cars rumbled onto the island. People throughout Maryland and across the United States saw the slow limousines filled with mourners pass by, headlights proclaiming the night of death. The television commentators spoke repetitively the keynotes of Jake's audiovisual obituary, his great real estate wealth, his glittering marriage to Serena, his antique house on Allingham Island. They reported nothing about the tall concrete piers thrusting up in the background behind the limousines. Nor did they mention the collapsed crane in the river, oil still leaking. The cameras were set high and did not photograph the strips of bullet cracked concrete and the scorches from machine gun tracers on the walls of the ruined church. No one mentioned the blackened trees in the distance where the fire at the farm house had burned leaves and treetops.

Other expertly placed cameras captured the cars moving slowly into the ancient graveyard. They panned over the gravestones, televising the names of generations of Terments who lay buried under the ivy and lingered at the Admiral's grave tracing the deep carved Confederate flag, its stone lines filled with the everpresent cemetery moss, the cannonballs at its foot. They caught the dim light of the cloudy sky as it bounced off leaves of the heavy bending trees. If the moisture of the rich vegetation and ancient burying place could be transferred to film, the photographers accomplished this.

Frank and Maggie stood behind the other attendees, barely able to see the grave as the minister said last words. The white preacher had been told moments before to shorten his speech still further because the television coverage requested more linkup time for the interview with Jake's wife.

Billy led the other pallbearers as the coffin was rolled to the gravesite. Now the television cameras turned to the minister.

"He lost his life," quickly intoned this black suited man, trying to accomplish what perhaps was the greatest speech of his church career as he continued speaking, "doing what he cared about most, serving his people, his family, his land. He lost his life but he won our hearts as only a man of principle can do. Jake Terment will be remembered by all who knew him. He will not be forgotten. Here was a man who cared about homes for the people and devoted his life to sheltering his neighbors. Only the truly big man can give so graciously to the small man."

Frank stepped out of the way as the television reporters began interviewing the guests. He watched as a very old woman with red dyed hair came unnoticed up to the gravesite as the others were moving away. She stood looking at the grave for a few moments, tears coming from her wrinkled eyes. Then, as she slowly stepped away, a trumpet began playing "Maryland My Maryland," the song Frank recognized from his first day in River Sunday.

As the words traveled over the other graves, Frank and Maggie turned to leave. He wanted to get some more work done at the site. There was an interview with Jake's wife at the entry to the graveyard, near a pair of concrete and stone posts and a broken iron gate that was pulled back to the side in the uncut grass. Frank stopped nearby with Maggie and listened.

"I knew this was a mistake," Serena sobbed to the television interviewer. She was the same reporter who had interviewed Maggie. Serena was dressed in a loose fitting pantsuit and her right arm was in a sling.

"It's all right, Mrs. Terment," the reporter sympathized.

She looked up from her handkerchief. "Please use the name Serena. Jake would have wanted it that way. He said it was better for my pictures."

"Serena, is it true that you had a premonition of harm coming to your husband? Did you try to warn him?"

"Jake never listened to me. I did tell him not to come to this place. I told him he belongs to the world, not to this island where he was born. I tried to keep him away."

"What did he say when you tried to stop him?"

Then Serena stared at the interviewer for several moments. The reporter moved the microphone in an attempt to get her to talk. "We're on the air. There's no time. Can you tell us?"

"He said we had to make this trip. He wanted to announce here in his home town that we are expecting our first child."

"You're pregnant." The reporter smiled broadly.

"She's got a scoop and she knows it. She smells pay bonuses," whispered Frank to Maggie.

"It's all wrong now," Serena said, wiping her eyes. "Now he's dead. I don't know what he wants me to do."

"You can name the baby after him. He was a great man."

She held her sore arm. "We know it will be a boy. Jake wanted the name to be Henry. Now I must go."

"Just one more question. People here say that he was loved. What do you think?"

"Do you expect them to say anything else? Do you expect them to say that he died because he was hated?" She sobbed as she looked at the reporter, a look that begged the reporter to let her go.

The reporter persisted, "We've heard from reliable sources in Hollywood that your centerfold modeling and your movie career are finished, that the accident you had here with a wild animal has scarred your body so you will never be able to model again."

Serena did not answer.

The reporter continued, "What do you think about the bankruptcy of the Terment Company? Now that your movie career is finished and your husband's money is gone, what will you and the child live on?"

Serena sobbed, then stared through her tears with what appeared to Frank as sudden hatred at the reporter. She said nothing more and the reporter finally walked away leaving Serena crying, standing alone as other visitors to the grave passed by her without stopping.

As Frank left the graveyard with Maggie, the clouds went away and the sun blazed light among the old trees. Outside the shade of the trees, his body felt the brunt of the steaming sunlight.

Later at the site, Cathy reviewed with Frank and Maggie how the technicians brought in from other sites were transforming the dig. She was dressed more simply now in blue jeans and a brown work shirt. She had come out to the site to inspect the installation of a new security fence, a tall chain link affair that would protect the excavation site from any future vandalism. Most of the honeysuckle hedge along the road had been taken down for the fencing.

"There will be a twenty four hour human and electronic security system, paid for by the State of Maryland, " she said.

"Tell me," said Frank, "What's the State going to do here now?"

"The Governor is making this place into a park. There's also some chance that it will be picked up by the National Park Service as a Federal park. We are going to make a maximum effort to get this site established in the best way we can. I'm sure that you will be pleased about that. "

"Certainly am."

"Poor Jake Terment. He was such a gentleman to have come to such a horrible accident. His death will be a loss for the whole State." She looked at Frank. "You mustn't feel responsible."

"I don't," said Frank.

For a moment she was taken back by Frank's earnestness. Then she went on, "The Governor is going to dedicate all of this to the African children who died here in the shipwreck. There's a lot of hope in Baltimore that there will be tourist interest in the site, maybe the same as there is for the old slave monument out in the harbor at River Sunday."

They walked toward the site where a long steel building was being bolted together. "This is temporary," Cathy said." It will protect the site from rain. We will have it there until the site is completely studied. Maybe two or three years. Maggie will supervise the reassembly, study, and proper burial of every skeleton. We are hoping to trace every child as far as we can to his or her original village in Africa."

One of the archeologists, a woman in jeans, waved to Frank. She had a small plastic bag in her left hand.

"It's a sample of what we found this morning, " she said.

"Where?" asked Frank.

"The area where the Captain's cabin should have been," the woman replied.

"Find any more possessions of Captain Henry?" he said as he opened the plastic sample bag.

"Not yet."

Small seashells fell on the ground.

" These are trading shells," said Frank. " Cowries."

The woman continued, " One of the new workers was moving his trowel along the strata line, right below the charcoal and the point of the blade opened what was like a fissure in the side of the hole. The shells just started to pour into the hole, like children's gumballs out of a candy machine. There was quite a pile of them in the floor of the pit. "

Frank bent over to pick up the tiny shells. "Must be left over from the trading journey."

"Yes," Maggie said. "It's horrible to think of, isn't it? I wonder how many of these shells would buy a human child?"

"Antonius could tell us, but I'd rather not know," said Frank.

He looked up at the Army truck parked near the boxwood. "That truck did its job for us. I thought I'd try to locate the real owner. I'd like to buy it from him."

"If you take it back to the university, you'll certainly surprise your friends."

"I'm not going back."

"What will you do?"

"I'm staying here to work with you on this project," said Frank, looking into her eyes.

Maggie looked away, "The Pastor is going to speak in a few minutes. I thought we could listen together."

"There's a radio in the truck," said Frank.

They walked toward the truck, silent for a moment.

Then she said, "You'll really stay here?"

"This is a pretty place. I've always wanted to work in a pretty place."

"What about your department at the university?"

He looked at her. "I'm going to resign. There's nothing more for me there." He paused. "Sometime, I'd like to tell you about Vietnam."

"I'd like to hear," she said. She moved her toe in the mud.

He said, "Would you mind if I worked with you?"

"If you were still the same guy who came down here a few days ago, my answer would be a lot different."

He smiled. "I wouldn't want to work with that guy either."

She looked at her watch. "The Pastor's speech."

He opened the door to the truck. " Here, sit up here." He looked at her across the large sea. " It's a little different than last time."

She smiled. "Last time wasn't all bad. You and I were here together." He reached under the steel dashboard to where a small radio was strapped to the dash supports. He turned the radio on.

"I know how to get the station." Maggie reached over and tuned the set.

A voice welcomed them to the Daily Church Hour with Pastor Jefferson Allingham.

"Birdey said she was taking the Pastor out to see the butterflies," said Maggie. "She's also going to try to raise some money to get General Store started up again."

"I think they could do a lot together if they wanted to."

The radio blurted again. "Here is Pastor Jefferson Allingham."

The familiar voice began.

"Mercy."

"Amen," responded his congregation.

"I say again, Mercy You hear me now."

"Yeah."

"The children were down below shouting for mercy," said the Pastor.

"Yeah."

"Adam and Eve had a son, didn't they?"

"Yes, yes, they did," chanted the congregation.

"The son Cain was up above murdering his brother Abel."

"Yes, yes, he was doing that."

"Then the innocent children were set afire, burned to death," said the Pastor.

"Amen."

"Murdered to hide that crime of brother against brother."

"Amen."

"Do we hear the children now?" asked the Pastor.

"Yes, Dear Jesus, yes."

"Do we hear the cries for mercy?"

"Yes, Lord, yes, Amen."

"I say to you those cries we hear are not for mercy," asserted the Pastor.

"That's right, you're saying it."

"They are for justice."

"Yeah."

"We will make that justice come over the land." said the Pastor.

"Yes, we will," agreed the congregation.

"I say that every one of those souls will have a grave on land."

"A true grave now."

"Every one will have the prayers of the Lord said over them," the Pastor said.

"Yeah, that's right."

"We pray that their own gods will accept the prayer to our God."

"Amen."

"That land were they have lain so many centuries, that land will be made pure again."

"Amen."

"That land will be testament to the Lord," charged the Pastor.

"To the truth," agreed the congregation.

"Let me say again there will be butterflies in this land now."

278

"Amen."

"There will be no bridge and profiteers to destroy the land."

"Yes."

"There will be always butterflies for these children."

"There will be butterflies for all children," agreed the congregation.

"As we walk among these new graves we will shout that Jesus is great."

"Amen."

"Let me hear you now," shouted the Pastor.

"Amen."

"These will not be the graves of slavery," said the Pastor, his tone lower.

"No."

"These will not be the graves of the oppressed."

"No."

"These will be the monuments to the future."

"Like soldiers of Jesus," said the congregation.

"Like the survivors that they are," said the Pastor.

"Amen."

"Like the children that they will always be."

"Amen."

"Let me hear you sing, my brothers and sisters."

Frank switched off the radio. Above the truck a helicopter was circling. It was a television news unit, big silver letters on its fuselage, photographing the site for the evening television news in Baltimore. The noise of the rotors resounded over the area. At the site many of the workers looked up for a moment, then resumed their toil.

Frank and Maggie climbed out of the truck. He scratched his neck and adjusted his hat. Together, they looked out at the shimmering Nanticoke River. A large red white and blue harbor tug was moored next to the half sunken barge. A diver was over the side from the tug working on the leak in the steel hull. They could see the air hoses going down into the oil stained water and small bubbles coming to the surface.

"They'll pump her out. Then they'll tow that equipment out of here," said Maggie. The name on the barge was half under the water. The great white letters spelling "Torment" appeared to melt as they reflected under the surface of the water.   Some other men from the tug were busy attaching restraining cables to the crane and the piled river.

"After they pump it out and get it level that crane won't look so bad," said Frank.

At that moment, the cat appeared from the nearby brush and nuzzled at Frank's bare right foot. He looked down at the cat's orange fur and black stripes.

"A cat that swims. Hard to believe."

"You saved the butterflies, cat," said Maggie.

"Cats don't like butterflies."

Maggie looked at Frank. "Why don't cats like butterflies?"

"The Monarchs," Frank grinned, "They're poisonous to eat. Makes cats sick."

Maggie stooped down and patted the cat.   "You don't eat butterflies, do you, cat?"

"Jake said cats brought him bad luck. "

"He sure didn't like cats," she said.

"Maybe it just comes down to luck," said Frank.

 Maggie looked at him, "Good beats evil."

"The ghosts of all those dead people in the wreck rose up to get him?" Frank smiled. "No, I think maybe Jake just slipped. He had bad luck."

In the distance from far down the river there came the sound of deep booming thuds, each boom separated by several minutes.

"Those people firing that cannon have their own reasons," said Frank. "That old cannon has to insult, has to be heard to be alive."

"There's no way any of it can be compromised either," said Maggie. She recited a poem. slowly, her lips moving around the words,

> "War is slavery,
> Slavery is war,
> Slaves become warriors,
> Warriors become slaves,
> Until we learn to do better ,
> It will always be so."

Frank said, "That's not bad."

"Sold ado taught it to me," she said.

"He knows a lot, that old man."   He pulled her close to him.

"I was thinking about those Mayan relics Soldado said might be found at the site."

She grinned. There's just one thing you should know."

"What?"

"Roses can never overcome thorns. They just learn to live together. So, you'll have to get used to briars when you dig," she said.

He tightened his arm around her waist as she held his hand. They watched an orange and black butterfly fly out from the brush on the shoreline. It flew near the old war truck and landed on the olive drab windshield frame . The insect fluttered quietly for a moment and then took off, circling out over the site where the workers were digging in the boiling sun, flying tentatively to a small mound of wet earth that had just been excavated. Then as it lifted again into the sunlight, the butterfly seemed to tip its wing to Frank and Maggie before it disappeared among the honeysuckle.

The End
Slave Graves

About the Author:

Thomas Hollyday was born on the Eastern Shore of Maryland in 1942. He attended Johns Hopkins University where he studied with Elliott Coleman at The Writing Seminars. After publishing several short stories, poems and drawings, he volunteered for a stint in the Army Counterintelligence Corps which included a year on Vietnam duty. Afterward he entered a business career, but kept writing and doing illustrations. A lifelong member of the Graphic Artists Guild of New York, his illustration work has appeared in such magazines as <u>Saturday Evening Post</u> and <u>Good Housekeeping,</u> where he published the "Christmas Cat." Besides editorial assignments in small newsletters, he has conducted original research in Maryland history which includes "The China Clipper John Gilpin" published in The <u>Neptune</u> of the Peabody Institute and "Readbourne Revisited" published in the <u>Maryland Historical Magazine</u>. In recent years he has concentrated on completing his novels about an imaginary town in Maryland called River Sunday.

·

in the United States
0001B

9 780974 128702